BEEBE AND BOSTELMANN

BEEBE AND BOSTELMANN

KENT POLITSCH

Beebe and Bostelmann. Copyright © 2021 by Kent E. Politsch

ISBN 978-0-9858352-8-6

Library of Congress Control Number: 2021919461

Cover and interior design by Danna Mathias

Other novels by the author:

Global Anger, a thriller: When a career federal bureaucrat is contacted by an old college friend – a Baltimore cop – he steps into more than he expected, including vigilante heroics by 16-year-old basketball players whose fearless involvement to stop a known street criminal sets off a series of bizarre connections to an international drug cartel.

Followed by…

Blood Anger, a thriller sequel: The President's teenage daughter is in danger. Abductors have foiled Secret Service security and kidnapped Bibi O'Neil, making her an innocent victim in a twisted revenge plot. Only her brief and flirtatious encounter with high school basketball superstar Dante Brown offers the First Family a glimmer of hope.

TABLE OF CONTENTS

PART II -- SPHERE OF DISCOVERY

PART III - THE DARK TRUTH

This story is dedicated to family,
mine and yours.
Because the future of life – fauna and flora –
rests with them

PROLOGUE

Atlantic Ocean
August 1934

Fear seemed not to be an issue. Not, at least, for Will. Others, perhaps.

But the snap of a cable, screams from crew members, and Gloria's cries reverberating through his headset sent a bolt of terror through Will's body.

He looked at Otis still studying his gauges and checking for leaks in their submerged craft.

"Gloria, what's happening?"

More shouts, then silence. "Glo! Talk to me!" Will demanded. "Is there a problem?"

The silence chilled him. Things had been going so well. The day perfect for diving.

Otis now looked concerned.

Will turned to his small window to see the light-speckled ocean. *Is the craft sinking?*

The darkness created a dozen mental flashes, torturous memories of fright. Dominant was seeing Blair more than twenty years earlier sitting with tribesmen in an Amazon jungle, her hands tied. No one spoke while the tribal chief contemplated punishment for their trespassing.

Will had failed to appease him. But the chief became over-taken by Blair's beauty, her silky white skin and soft hair. She sat calmly while the sun-wrinkled native touched her face. Gently. The caress of a father.

Will was hurt and angered by his lost power. Her beauty controlled their fate better than his negotiations and boasted knowledge of the Amazon.

Will Beebe, the adventurous naturalist, a man on a mission, confident and courageous, had allowed Blair, travel companion, wife, to rescue them. It was she who kept them alive. Bravely.

That was my responsibility, he mumbled to the bioluminescent fish on the other side.

"Did you hear that, Will?" Gloria finally asked.

"Of course. What's happening, Glo?"

"A guy rope broke. The captain's shouting to his crew. It doesn't look like you're in danger though. You're approaching another distance record, Will."

PART I

CELEBRITY

CHAPTER 1

Oyster Bay Wedding
22 September 1927

Will Beebe gave his bride a gentlemanly touch of lips as the minister bowed to the famous couple and stepped aside. Will turned to face well-wishers with his familiar gapped-tooth smile, proud to introduce as his wife Elswyth Thane, an aspiring author.

Former First Lady Edith Roosevelt, who helped Dr. Beebe with his wedding plans, applauded first. Host Harrison Williams and wife Mona followed. Soon all distinguished guests showered the newlyweds with their approval.

Charles William (Will) Beebe, 50, had wedded Helen Elswyth Thane Ricker, 27, aboard the *Warrior,* the largest yacht of its kind. Owned by the wealthiest man in America, richer than the Rockefellers, Carnegies, and Astors, Harrison Williams could afford the biggest and best of anything.

Generous as well, Williams enjoyed sharing the *Warrior* with the most popular, multi-talented, and charming scientist, ornithologist, and naturalist in America, William Beebe.

Williams financed Beebe's 1920s expeditions to the Galápagos Islands and the Sargasso Sea. New York Zoological Society fellow board members Vincent Astor and Marshall Field joined him in bankrolling the explorer whose published accounts put the zoological society on the front page of hundreds of newspapers.

Williams arranged for Will and Elswyth to take the *Warrior* to Bermuda as a honeymoon gift. He and Mona had used the yacht a year earlier to cruise the world following their nuptials.

The two men watched their friends in conversation and listened to the soothing sounds of a string quartet while sipping from flutes of French champagne. Prohibition be damned.

"Let me tell you why I'm excited about Bermuda," Will began. "Mostly because Elswyth loves socializing with the British and can tolerate Bermuda's climate better than the Caribbean. But also, fewer than ten miles south of Bermuda the Atlantic is two miles deep. I've priced the equipment, Harrison. We can trawl a limited area and capture specimens to support my deep-sea theories. Bermuda provides a base that makes day trips affordable."

"Are you still thinking about a submersible?" Harrison asked.

"Yes, of course; a deep-sea vessel in which I can explore. I just need a workable design. The Colonel thought a motorized cylinder might work."

"You have a Midas touch, Will Beebe, so I'm going to support whatever you decide."

Will downed his champagne and watched his young bride carry on an animated conversation with Mrs. Roosevelt. A caterer quickly refilled Will's flute as Edith Roosevelt glanced his way and lifted her champagne with a smile, a symbolic endorsement.

Twenty years earlier, Teddy and Edith Roosevelt invited Will and a different bride to Sagamore Hill on Long Island. Their conversations cemented Theodore as Beebe's naturalist mentor. The former president's frequent public praise elevated the explorer's status within the science community where he also found plenty of critics.

Younger with enormous energy, Will's unorthodox methods and gregarious personality gave journalists great fodder when writing about his travels. However, skeptics bashed him for having too much imagination. They said the populist writer was more storyteller than scientist. They poked at his accuracy and criticized his nonconformist style.

Roosevelt often came to Beebe's defense.

After Will's divorce in 1913, Edith Roosevelt's friendship comforted an extremely depressed man. Teddy's regular invitations for Will to meet other young naturalists and wildlife enthusiasts became welcomed distractions. Until Roosevelt died unexpectedly in 1919.

It took years for the pain of divorce and death to heal. Five years later, his dutiful mother—Nettie—also passed. His emotions rode up and down life's roller coaster.

By 1927 his young staff at the Department of Tropical Research had revived his enthusiasm. Meeting Elswyth also invigorated the adventure-seeking joys of his early years.

"You're a hell of a lucky man, Will Beebe," said Dr. Henry Fairfield Osborn. He joined the two men wrapping his arm around Will. "Your bride is beautiful. Your friends rich and famous. And now you're taking this *poor* man's floating home away from him bound for where?"

"…Bermuda," Harrison inserted.

"Bermuda! We've all spoiled you."

Harrison Williams laughed and shook Osborn's hand.

Henry Fairfield Osborn launched Will Beebe's career with the New York Zoological Society and its newly formed zoological park in the Bronx. Their friendship and mutual respect had lasted more than 30 years.

Beebe began as Osborn's student at Columbia University in 1896. Before Will could complete his bachelor's degree, Osborn encouraged his star student, barely twenty-one at the time, to go to work at the zoo as assistant curator of birds.

Will Beebe knew more about birds than his professors. He'd been spying on them, shooting them, dissecting them, and stuffing them from the time his father, Charles, put a shotgun in his hands at an early age.

"Henry, I read critical reviews of Madison Grant's and your Eugenic Society. Don't pay attention," Williams told Osborn. "You can't let them distract you from what you believe."

"You're kind to say that, Harrison."

Osborn paused, studied Beebe, and then chided his protégé. "Where's your tongue, Will Beebe? Are you speechless for the first time in your life because you can't believe a beautiful young woman would marry a skinny, bald, 50-year-old like you?"

Williams and Osborn laughed so loudly all other conversations stopped.

"I am, indeed, dazzled by my bride's beauty. No question," Will said. "However, I'm not the only elder statesman who decorates his arm with youthful glamour."

"I should say not!" Osborn exclaimed. "Mona looks stunning, Harrison. How did you ever attract such a lovely bride?"

"My money makes me quite handsome, gentlemen."

Williams' retort brought on another round of masculine guffaws and a sprint from Elswyth. Edith Roosevelt encouraged her to investigate.

"I fear your pleasure is at my expense, gentlemen. Daresay, what are you finding humorous?"

"No need for paranoia, my lovely wife."

William Beebe, known among his loyal readers as *Dr. Beebe*, had authored thirteen books with others on the way. *Doctor*, meaning Ph.D. recipient, was an honorarium he had not yet earned through academic rigor, but his books dealt with such passion for zoological science the title was assumed.

Beebe wrote with colorful everyday phrases, not academic jargon. He hated the way scientists used undefined terms that frightened away children who otherwise would have enjoyed biology and zoology.

No, Will Beebe wrote for people like himself born in Brooklyn, raised in East Orange, New Jersey—industrious like his father and devoted like his mother.

Helen Elswyth Thane Ricker wrote fiction, romantic novels. Using the penname Elswyth Thane, her first novel about an older adventurous man who marries a much younger woman, called *Riders of the Wind*, was selling well and had been put into its second printing. The fact she dedicated the book to William Beebe might have influenced its ascending interest.

At the time of their wedding, Elswyth was releasing her second and third novels while Will awaited the release of *Beneath Tropic Seas*, a recount of his adventure in Haiti. Unfortunately, early reviews were tepid. Critics assumed Elswyth affected his focus.

Will spied Edith Roosevelt alone and hastened to thank her for managing such an elegant wedding.

"Once more, you have proven to be a saintly friend."

"I'm so happy for you, Will. Elswyth seems like such a warm and kind person. Beautiful too."

Will put his arm under hers, gently pulling her aside. "You know, I miss the Colonel's encouragement more today than I ever have. He meant that much to me."

"I have a hard time believing he has been gone eight years now, Will. I'm happy to have our children around me visiting Sagamore Hills. And the Williams are nice people to have nearby. But I think I will see less of Harrison now that he has married so young a bride."

"You don't need to worry about me," Will told her. "Elswyth and I will always be available to you."

"Perhaps now is the perfect time to ask," Mrs. Roosevelt told him. "When you return from your honeymoon, I need you to speak to our club. I want you to tell everyone about your discoveries in Haiti. You know it was one of Teddy's favorite islands–Haiti and the Dominican Republic."

"I will tell your club all about Haiti, Mrs. Roosevelt. But the better story is going to be what I'm looking to do in Bermuda.

CHAPTER 2

New York City
May 1928

A sparsely furnished apartment echoed with a knock at the door. A teenage girl rose from her reading desk and went to answer.

"It's probably the delivery boy," came a woman's voice from the drawing-room.

"I've got it, Mother."

"Thank you, Hada. I'm almost ready."

Hada Bostelmann pulled the door open. A young man, tall, thin, about twenty and neatly attired in his delivery uniform, tipped his hat to the svelte teenager.

"I'm here for a pickup from Mrs. Bostelmann. She has something for J. Walter Thompson."

"Come in. Mrs. Bostelmann is my mother."

Hada held out her hand to the young man. "My name is Gertraude Hadumodt. Most people call me Hada."

"My name's Bobby. Robert, but you can call me Bobby."

"Hello, Bobby."

Hada turned to check on her mother. She was standing in an archway slipping her artwork into an envelope.

"Sorry to keep you," she said.

"Mother, this is Bobby. Bobby, this is my mother, Else."

"How do you do, Mrs. Bostelmann. I met you before. The first time I came to pick up your artwork for the advertising agency. It's okay if you don't remember."

"I remember your face, Bobby. It's a good face."

"Thank you, ma'am. I best get this back to the agency."

The young man turned then quickly turned back. "Almost forgot. The agency has another assignment for you, Mrs. Bostelmann."

He handed Else another envelope from his leather courier purse and tipped his hat again. "Nice meeting you, Hada."

Hada noticed his color turning pink. She smiled. "Thank you, Bobby. Maybe we'll see you again."

He scurried out and Hada closed the door.

"Were you flirting with him?" Else asked her daughter.

"Maybe. He's handsome, don't you think, Mother?"

"There are many handsome boys in the world, Hada. Be careful about choosing the right one to flirt with."

Else opened the envelope Bobby left her. The advertising agency provided instructions for another finished drawing of a woman sitting at a dressing table applying makeup.

"Is it another job, Mother?"

"A drawing, yes. The same as all the others. Women painting their faces."

"I know you tire of producing the same pictures over and over, Mother, but the agency is paying you well. I'm thankful you're getting good jobs. They must like your work."

"I'm also thankful, Hada. I don't mean to sound ungrateful." Else looked at her clock. "It's time for the Christian Science lecture on the radio. Do you mind dialing it in?"

Hada returned to her study table and fiddled with the radio. Else could sense from Hada's pace and slumped shoulders that her daughter had more on her mind. "Do you not want to hear the program today?" Else asked.

"What would you be doing now if father were still with us?"

Surprised by the question, Else thought about her husband and the circumstances that ended Monroe Bostelmann's life. "He became so unhappy, so alone and discouraged..."

"Would we still be in Texas?"

"I don't know. He missed his family."

Hada fought the noisy radio, twisting the dial to find the signal. Else continued...

"...I think he missed his music, but he wouldn't admit it. His pride... it was his pride that kept us in Texas. It would not allow him to return to New York."

"I worry for you, Mother. You do work you don't enjoy."

"My happiness comes from me not my work. I walk outside, see and smell nature and I am joyful. Opportunities to paint in nature will soon come our way and I will seem happier to you. Until then we eat, we sleep through the night, and one day you will choose your own life. Sometimes it's just that simple."

"Mother, we know you want to choose my life for me."

"Only until I can see you're ready to make good decisions for yourself."

"Oh, Mother, I've been ready for a long while."

"You're seventeen. You think you're ready. I did when I was seventeen. I remember."

Good morning. Thank you for tuning into the Christian Science Radio Hour. Today's lesson is from chapter eight of Science and Health in which Mary Baker Eddy talks about the Footsteps of Truth...

"Are you listening, Hada? When you have questions, God within us answers."

"I want to know about my father's death. Where? Where in me do I look?"

Immigrating from Germany in 1909, Else Winkler von Röder came at the request of Monroe Bostelmann, a talented musician whom she had met in Berlin. They married soon after Else arrived in New York City.

Monroe spent nearly twelve years studying and playing throughout Europe. It surprised no one that he became a prodigy on the violoncello. His father, mother, and his five siblings were all accomplished musicians. Monroe was destined.

Else, likewise, had achieved modest success in Germany as an artist. Her 1908 gallery showings of pen and ink drawings and oil paintings received critical acclaim.

A year after their marriage, Hada was born. But money problems and Monroe's aggressive drive for success outside of music caused the family's move to Texas. Waco first then to Mexia, a rural town nearby.

Being the eldest made Monroe the one upon which all hopes of musical greatness rested. But it didn't happen. Other passions got in his way. One of which was his loyalty to Germany, his ancestral homeland, and where he had achieved notoriety.

As tensions mounted in central Europe and the United States was being summoned to join Britain and France in opposition to the Kaiser's threats of war, it was not a good time to be siding with Germany.

Monroe's political enthusiasm put a target on his back. On top of financial failures and struggles to hold a job, his outspoken support for Kaiser Wilhelm's Germany and a wife with a thick German accent brought to his Texas doorstep an agent from the newly formed Federal Bureau of Investigation. The community pressured the FBI, which twice interrogated Monroe. Both times the agency confirmed Bostelmann's allegiance to the United States of America.

"I remember when they came to our house," Hada said. "I remember how gruff they were to father."

Another knock on the door startled Else and Hada. Hada jumped from her seat glad for the distraction and hoping Bobby had forgotten to leave her mother a second assignment. She pulled the door open.

"Hello, Hada."

A well-dressed woman in hat and gloves with an expressive, confident glow stood to wait for an invitation in.

"Aunt Ida!"

"Hello, Ida," came Else's voice from the drawing-room where she had darted to freshen her face.

Ida Bostelmann glided into Else and Hada's modest home. The youngest of Monroe's siblings, she and other family members assisted their sister-in-law with the transition to New York.

"You look beautiful, Aunt Ida. Are you going to a party? May I come with you if you are? Is Louis playing somewhere? Or is Aunt Adda singing? Is it your music?"

"Too many questions, child. And the answer to all is *no*."

Else re-entered the living room and hugged her sister-in-law. She took Ida by her shoulders and admired the dress that accentuated her mid-30s curves.

"You are a lovely woman, Ida," Else said.

"I stopped just for the compliments, Else. Thank you. I can leave now." Ida feigned an effort to depart. "Oh, I had something to ask you... rather, to tell you about your plans for Saturday evening. Both of you."

"I'm already excited," Hada said.

"You are to meet my friends and me at Carnegie Hall for the Symphony Orchestra at seven o'clock. Maestro Walter Damrosch is conducting. He's asked father to sit in the orchestra and play a short solo."

"How wonderful," Else said.

"Father will be playing one of his violins."

"One he made, Aunt Ida?"

"Yes, I think he now has 140, most of them for other musicians, but he still has several in his library."

"How does he have time?" Else asked.

"He is slowing, especially since his responsibilities as a judge seem to be increasing."

Else moved toward her drawing-room. "I need to check our social calendar before I tell you we can be there," Else said.

"Oh, Mother."

"You can joke if you like, Else, but you better attend. And don't have that artist's smock on. Nor those pants. Were those Monroe's?"

"No, Ida, these are women's pants. Working women wear them."

"Well, wear a dress, for heaven's sake. I have another job in mind for you. There will be people sitting with us who I want you to meet."

CHAPTER 3

Coincidence

Else and Hada Bostelmann rode the subway to Columbus Circle. Excited and nervous, they wanted to be early to watch others arriving.

Else took money from her emergency fund to buy Hada a new dress for the evening. It was not fancy, not expensive, but she made Hada feel proud to be included on a special night where they would meet Ida's society friends.

They stopped at Liggett's Drug Store for a sandwich and soda before walking along Broadway to 57th Street, then Seventh Avenue.

Concertgoers already lined the street. The sun peeked over the tops of buildings and tall trees in Central Park. Its late-spring warmth added to the pleasantness.

A lively crowd in front of Carnegie Hall excited Hada. She looped her arm through her mother's as they searched for Ida. A few taxicabs pulled up in front of Seventh Avenue, but Else saw no one she knew exiting the motor vehicles.

"Are you looking for me, ladies?" Ida Bostelmann asked.

Else and Hada turned to see Ida. Her spring hat encircled her pretty round face shading her eyes but not enough to hide the welcoming glisten. Hada embraced her aunt.

"You must not startle us that way," Else insisted. "Where were you hiding?"

"Oh, Else, I wasn't hiding. I was standing over there watching you two move about like church mice nervously searching the sanctuary."

"I love your hat, Aunt Ida."

"Thank you, Hada. Is that a new dress?"

"It is. Mother bought it just for tonight. Do you like it?"

"Quite charming."

Ida turned toward the Carnegie Hall doors and tugged at Else and Hada. "Come. Let's get into our seats before the crowd blocks our way." She waved to a group nearby.

"Are those the people you want Mother to meet?" Hada asked.

"Yes. Let me introduce her before we go in."

Else, Hada, and Ida Bostelmann approached the well-dressed group of five young adults. Else placed them in age between Ida's mid-30s and Hada's teenage years. The business connection about which Ida boasted was not apparent.

"My dear friends, I want you to meet my sister-in-law, Else, and her daughter, Hada Bostelmann."

A chorus of 'good evenings' peppered the curious mother and daughter. Hada dipped her head slightly and grinned a few how-do-you-dos.

"Else and Hada, I want you to meet Edward Cobb…"

Cobb tipped his hat. Else felt her daughter's excitement.

"…and this is filmmaker Ernest Schoedsack…"

Else could not imagine someone so tall. He was a full head taller than anyone around.

"…and Ernest's wife, Ruth Rose, an actress and writer…"

Rose put her pointer finger on her chin and curtsied in mock character. *Of course, an actress.*

"...and this is John Tee-Van, an adventurer, and his wife, Helen Damrosch."

Else and Hada were awestruck by how handsome the men were. Cobb was young but emitted enormous self-confidence. Schoedsack, the giant, also exhibited intellectual intensity—a serious man. And Tee-Van, more mild-mannered, handsome too with his round eyeglasses that gave him a gentler aura.

"Damrosch? Isn't that the symphony conductor's name?" Else asked Helen.

"Yes, he's my uncle. Uncle Walter, my father's younger brother."

"Helen's being modest, Else. Frank–Helen's father–is an accomplished musician too. They recently made him dean of the Juilliard School of Music. The men's father–Helen's grandfather–helped establish the New York Symphony Society and conducted the Metropolitan Opera before his death."

"I never got to meet my grandfather. He died before I was born," Helen added.

"Yes, the news of his death reached Germany. I was a child. It quite upset my parents to hear Leopold Damrosch had died in the United States," Else said.

"You remember that, Else?" Ida asked her sister-in-law.

"I remember my mother's stories about Leopold and Helene. Your grandmother was a popular opera singer in Germany and a beautiful woman. She co-founded a chorus in Leipzig when my parents were young and sang under Franz Liszt in Weimar. We're talking about the same Damrosch family?"

"I am extremely fond of this lady already, Ida," Helen said of Else.

Helen Damrosch took Else's arm and escorted her toward Carnegie Hall's doors. Ida grabbed Hada's arm and followed. "I thought this would work," she whispered to Hada.

Ruth, Ernest, John, and Edward trailed, chuckling that Ida's relative knew about Helen's grandparents in Germany.

Helen and Else continued to chat as they guided the ensemble to Uncle Walter's balcony box to the conductor's right. Box one. Helen motioned for Else, Hada, and Ida to take the forward seats in the box. She sat behind Else to continue their conversation. Ruth Rose sat next to Helen. Edward Cobb moved to the empty seat next to Ida in the front row while Tee-Van and Schoedsack stood at the back, conversing and waiting for the house lights to dim.

"I can read the notes on the sheet music from here, Aunt Ida!"

"Yes, we are close, although Helen has told me the orchestra may not sound as good from this vantage point. The experience is worth the sacrifice; don't you think?"

"We are artists, not musical critics. I don't think Hada and I will notice if there's a difference," Else said.

"I'm glad you brought up your skills," Ida responded. "Helen, would you tell Else what you and John have been doing?"

Helen explained she and her husband worked for the New York Zoological Society's Department of Tropical Research. John was salaried and she freelanced as an artist, photographer, and researcher.

"We work for Dr. Beebe. William. Will to us," Helen said.

"I recognize his name, Mother," Hada said excitedly. "He writes essays and books about his adventures."

"I know who he is too, Hada. I saw him at the zoo and listened to one of his lectures."

"When did you do that?" Hada probed.

"You were in school. I went to the Botanical Gardens for ideas to paint. I stopped at the zoo. The huge outdoor bird shelters attracted me. The birds made wonderful subjects to sketch."

"Are you a trained artist, Mrs. Tee-Van?" Hada asked.

"Trained, yes, but I have many interests, Miss Bostelmann."

"My wife is a talented artist. Important to our team," John said.

He explained their role with the New York Zoological Society. He told Else and Hada that William Beebe was among the first employees at the zoo. An ornithologist. And a naturalist. "Will Beebe wants people to understand all animals so they'll do a better job of preserving them for the future," Tee-Van said.

"I share his interests," Else added. "I spent many days as a little girl at the zoo in Leipzig. The animals amazed me. The zoo was colorful with flowers and plants too. A haven for artists like I wanted to be."

The lights dimmed. Tee-Van and Schoedsack sat. Else, Hada, and Ida turned to face the stage as the orchestra marched in from the four corners. John Bostelmann was second in line among all the string players. He sat next to the symphony's first-chair violinist.

After placing music on his stand, Bostelmann searched the area for his daughter. Ida waved and caught his attention. He remained expressionless, but Else thought she saw a tiny smile.

Hada Bostelmann knew little about her grandfather. They didn't see each other often and he was always working. Still, she and her mother were excited to see him in such a magnificent setting.

Walter Damrosch stepped from the theater wing downstage left with a vigorous stride. The audience applauded as Damrosch leaped to the platform where his music stand held his evening's work. He turned and greeted everyone with a bow. He pivoted back to his symphony orchestra, lifted his wand, and with a gentle downswing the evening began.

Chills ran down Hada's spine. She looked at her aunt sitting next to her, whose eyes were closed as if in ecstasy. Hada turned to see Helen's face as the orchestral sounds brightened. Helen returned the eye contact with a smile.

The evening concluded much too fast for Hada. Dazzled by the spectacle, no princess could have enjoyed the event more, nor been flattered by the attention of handsome young men and lovely women. Further, a legendary conductor had entertained Hada, and she heard her grandfather play a violin solo on an instrument he had handcrafted. A dream. A perfect night.

The music calmed Else. But Ida's invitation still puzzled her. She thanked Ida for the introductions. She told her she enjoyed her young friends. She treasured the common backgrounds she and Helen shared, their coincidental German connections, and their similar Prussian heritage.

The role Helen played in Dr. Beebe's department made Else envious. *It would be a dream job to paint nature for pay.*

"There is a club around the corner if you would like to join us," Schoedsack said.

"Let's have dessert next door first," Ida replied. "I know my sister-in-law; she will want to get her teenage daughter home after that."

"That's not fair," Hada whimpered.

"It's a club known to serve alcohol," Ida told Else. "We assume someone pays the right people. Nothing ever happens."

Else turned to her daughter with a mother-knows look.

Already crowded from the concert, Ida's group stood outside the restaurant for a few minutes waiting for a table.

Ernest Schoedsack pulled a pack of Chesterfields from his evening jacket and offered a cigarette to the others. Ruth, Helen, and Edward each took one. John abstained.

Ida used the break to pull Else aside while John asked Hada about her school.

"I know you're wondering what this evening's concert has to do with a job," Ida began.

"It's fine if things didn't work out the way you planned, Ida…"

"No, no. Things are going along as I hoped."

Else took another step away from Hada and John Tee-Van.

"I can tell Helen considers her drawing for Dr. Beebe to be a minor role," she whispered to Ida, "but I will not ask her to step aside so I can have that job."

"Else, Helen is a fine artist, but according to her husband, Dr. Beebe wants more than someone who can draw and paint. He needs someone with your talents to bring the nature he's uncovering to life."

"If I can make people buy dresses with a few sketches, I'm sure I can do what they ask, but I'm still not going to take another person's job to better my circumstances."

"Now listen, Else, John Tee-Van is Dr. Beebe's closest confidant; he has a thousand responsibilities, including headhunting. He needs you. However, he tells me it won't happen overnight."

"How does he know I'm the right artist?"

"Because I've told him."

"Helen, come this way!"

The voice came from the restaurant doorway. The entire group turned to see Maestro Walter Damrosch and his brother Frank. Walter signaled to them to enter the restaurant. He re-entered assuming they would follow.

"It appears he has a table for us," Helen told the others. "Good ole Walter."

The smokers stamped out their cigarettes. Thirty people in line waited to see whom the men instructed to enter.

Helen beamed. She led the others through the throngs, listening to *who's that? How do they know Maestro Damrosch?*

Else walked behind Ida but could not disguise her embarrassment with so many people staring. Hada carried herself with importance just like the women in front of her.

CHAPTER 4

Bermuda
24 October 1928

The St. George's Harbor had cooled with the onset of autumn, but conditions for helmet diving were better because there was less threat of a hurricane. This particular morning glassy calm hugged the shoreline.

William Beebe had risen with the sun. Already in the water, he had swum a lap around Ordnance Island. He climbed from the water, picked up a hotel towel he had hooked to a scrub bush, and wrapped it around his neck.

Chiriqui, Beebe's pet capuchin monkey, sat on a large rock, picking raw crabmeat from the crushed shell he shattered with a stone.

"What are you eating, Chiri?" Beebe asked.

The monkey lifted the crab's dangling claws in response. He squawked an unpleasant sound and rolled his cheeks back to show a monkey smile.

"Let's get back to the hotel before Elswyth awakens, Chiri. We need to take her breakfast."

Beebe and monkey scampered farther up the hill into King's Square. The sun cast long palm-tree shadows across Bermuda's original seventeenth-century government building and the town. of St. George, the center of St. George's Parish.

Once the epicenter of the archipelago, St. George remained a lively wharf and fishing center a century later. It attracted tourists for its quaintness. The luxurious St. George's Hotel occupied a tall peak on the island. The hotel's top-floor suites oversaw Fort St. Catherine and Tobacco Bay to the north and St. David's Island and Castle Harbor to the south. A strategic location.

Will entered his hotel room quietly. Elswyth slept soundly.

Chiriqui rode on Will's shoulder still nibbling on crabmeat. He jumped off when Will began to remove his wet swimsuit. Will pulled on his comfortable khaki shorts and blue cotton button-up shirt.

He held his finger to his lips to warn Chiriqui to stay silent. The monkey jumped from the dresser where he had finished his meal, leaving behind a few pieces of shell. He leaped into Will's arms and the pair slipped through the door.

Will and Chiriqui walked to the hotel restaurant. The sun scattered rays through the opened windows, causing high contrast between the white tablecloths and dark restaurant corners. There were several patrons in the dining hall. One was a young woman sitting tall in her chair, reading the morning *Royal Gazette*. Her blond hair captured the sunlight, creating an angelic halo. Will and Chiriqui approached.

"Good morning, Miss Hollister."

Gloria Hollister placed her newspaper on the table and pushed her chair back to stand.

"No, please stay seated. May we join you?"

"Of course…"

A waiter took Beebe's breakfast order of Grape Nuts and milk. Will told the waiter he needed to take his wife a breakfast when he finished his cereal.

"Are you ready to go helmet diving this morning?"

"I'm a bit nervous but ready." Gloria took a sip of coffee. "Thank you again for this opportunity. I saw you took public criticism in the science journal for hiring me."

"The science community is not fond of me, Miss Hollister, so ignore those comments. Your credentials speak for themselves."

Gloria Hollister had graduated with honors from Connecticut College. She used her high marks and zoology degree to enter Columbia University's graduate program. Professor William Gregory introduced Gloria to Dr. Beebe when she was still a student. She made a pitch then to work for Dr. Beebe, but he had no position to offer her. However, he encouraged her to stay in touch.

At 5-feet-11, Gloria stood taller than most men. She excelled in several sports, playing basketball and running track in college. Will Beebe heard she beat most men at tennis. He was eager to test her skills.

Gloria was born in New York City, but her physician father took the family upstate and into the wilderness every summer. He taught her to shoot guns and hunt big game in western states.

As a researcher, he also kept an active laboratory. She wanted to be just like her father, a doctor. But his conservative thinking stopped Gloria from entering medical school. He insisted women should not be physicians. So, she became a scientist. Her first assignment after graduating from Columbia was to work with a doctor on cancer research at Rockefeller Institute.

Laboratory work was not Gloria's calling, although she stayed at it for three years and perfected break-through techniques. When Professor Gregory alerted her that William Beebe was planning an expedition to Bermuda to study ocean fauna, Gloria contacted the Department of Tropical Research and requested consideration.

"I'm glad to know you like pets," Gloria said.

The waiter sat Will's Grape Nuts and milk in front of him. Chiriqui pulled the end of a bowknot on the waiter's apron. It fell forward.

"I'm so sorry, Dr. Beebe," the waiter said.

"It's Chiri who needs to apologize. He's full of mischief," Will said. "Miss Hollister, can you assist our waiter with his apron?"

Gloria handed him his apron strings. He pulled them in front and re-tied the bow, still fumbling as Chiriqui let out a piercing laugh.

"I have a dog," she said. "Trumps." She expected Will Beebe to be surprised or disappointed.

"I presume that was Trumps I saw you with at Tobacco Bay last evening."

"Yes. Oh, I'm sorry. Were you there? I would have said hello."

"You wouldn't have seen me. I was on my balcony with my telescope. The stars were coming out. I was testing the scope before Elswyth and I did our evening star gazing."

"The islands are beautiful. Did you choose Bermuda for its surroundings?"

"No, I chose it because its geography should provide us with excellent research opportunities."

"Your critics think only men do good research."

"I've said to ignore my critics. I will handle them. You can help by doing what I expect you're capable of doing. Shut them up by proving your abilities."

"I have many things to prove as a woman, Dr. Beebe. I won't let you down."

Will Beebe ordered a pastry, tea, and a bowl of fresh fruit to take to Elswyth. The waiter said he could have the order delivered to the room if he and his associate were ready to leave.

Will thanked the young man and gave him a few British coins from his pocket.

"Thank you, Dr. Beebe."

Will told Gloria he needed to gather his diving helmet and change back into his swimwear. He said he would meet her at the lobby in fifteen minutes.

Will rode an elevator to the penthouse floor. He shushed Chiriqui, turned his key, and entered quietly.

Elswyth sat up in bed and stretched, greeting Will with a thrown kiss.

"I have your breakfast coming, El."

"Good. I'm in desperate need of tea. You ordered tea, didn't you?"

"Of course."

Will began changing again into his swimsuit. He pulled his shorts back on and slipped his arms into his shirt but didn't button the front. He grabbed the copper helmet he had designed to be much lighter than the sixty-pound helmet he wore the first time he dove. This helmet weighed closer to sixteen pounds. Much easier to maneuver with the air hose under water.

Elswyth walked a few steps to a washbasin. She poured water into the basin and splashed her face. After drying, she walked toward Will and patted his back.

"Are you going out diving this early?"

"I'm going to take Miss Hollister for her first dive. We won't go far, just along the shoreline in St. George's Harbor."

"Will there be much to see?"

"I'm sure we'll find something. I want her to bring up small life she can examine under her microscope. She should look at something she found, not handed to her."

"Good idea, Will. Please be back by noon. I promised Mother we would join her for lunch."

Will, Gloria, and Trumps walked down the hill from the hotel to the dock near King's Square. Chiriqui rode Will's shoulder.

A native Bermudian and his son waited. Father stood in the sixteen-foot rowboat while son kneeled by a rope wrapped around a twelve-inch-diameter post. The boat was equipped with air hoses and a wood-handle pump.

"Good morning, Jefferson."

"Good morning, William Beebe."

Will was used to the unique native accent that included British influence, a touch of Portuguese, and Western African sounds mixed in. Gloria liked the sound. She was eager to hear more.

"I'm Gloria. Who are you?" she asked the young man.

"People call me Jefferson Two."

"Too, like also?"

"No, ma'am. Two like the number. I am his son."

Jefferson Two pointed to his father who was placing Will's diving helmet in a safe place on the boat.

Gloria followed Will onto the craft.

Will sat in the rower's seat. He gestured for Gloria to sit at the bow. Trumps, a wire-haired fox terrier, leaped into her lap when she sat.

"Are you going to row this morning, William Beebe?" Jefferson asked.

"You are the captain of this vessel, Jefferson. I expect you to steer us. I will provide the engine."

"Aye, mate. I shall guide us if you have a destination in mind."

"Yonder, Captain. Toward the west. Only one knot westward and 200 feet offshore.

"Cast off, boy," Jefferson said to his son.

Jefferson Two unraveled the ropes, handing them to Gloria who rolled them into an organized pile at her feet.

The son pushed the boat away from the dock while stepping aboard.

Three make-shift sailors and their captain cruised near the shoreline once Will had rowed the boat past St. George's commercial docks.

Captain Jefferson steered the boat to a light green spot in the water sixty feet from the shoreline. Will lifted the oars and picked up a box about ten inches square and eighteen inches tall with a glass window at the bottom. He put the box into the water and pushed down about six inches. He then stuck his head on top and peered into the water.

When he sat up, he barked, "Two fathoms and sand, Captain. A good starting point."

Jefferson Two stepped around Gloria and grabbed a small anchor and dropped it straight down from the bow. The boat's captain threw a second anchor from the stern and then attached a hose to Will Beebe's helmet and wiped around the pads that covered the diver's shoulders.

"Ready when you are, William Beebe," Jefferson said.

Will peeled his shirt and shorts but kept his canvas shoes on his feet.

"I'll go down first. Take the window and stick it in the water and watch me," he told Gloria. "I'll walk around in the sand a few minutes, then it'll be your turn."

Will jumped into the water. He kicked his way to the boat's stern and grabbed the anchor rope.

Jefferson dropped the helmet over Will's shoulders and handed Will a weight belt to help him descend. Meantime, Jefferson

Two began pumping air into Will's helmet as the naturalist sank hand-over-hand down the anchor rope.

Gloria and Trumps looked over the side. Chiriqui jumped on Gloria's shoulders for a peek. He startled Gloria, which caused Trumps to bark. Captain Jefferson laughed.

"He scared me!"

"He scares me too, young lady. Thinks he's one of us, a human, only smaller. Sometimes I wonder," Jefferson said.

Gloria peered through the window box. Will had landed on the sand. He twisted his head upward a few degrees with his hands holding the helmet at both sides so it would stay in place. Once Will saw the box in the water, he straightened out and walked across the sandy bottom.

Watching from above, Gloria observed Will Beebe lumbering through the water.

"Have you walked through water before, young lady?" Jefferson asked.

"When swimming in the ocean. Sure. I know it can be difficult."

"The helmet makes it hard too," said Jefferson Two.

A few minutes later, Will ascended. Jefferson pulled the helmet and set it in the boat's center out of Will's way so he could climb on board.

"It helps if you're relaxed when you're down there," Will said, huffing slightly. "Get used to how it feels before we move to more interesting scenery."

Gloria removed her blouse and shorts covering her bathing suit. She rolled into the water from a sitting position on the boat's stern. She swam away from the boat a few yards to get comfortable in the water. When she swam back, she grabbed the stern and Will lifted the helmet over her head.

"Don't hold your breath. Breathe at once," he told her.

Jefferson Two began his steady pumping motion with the diaphragm stick. Will handed Gloria the weight belt, and she began to descend.

Will found the window box and watched his new employee touch sand a dozen feet below the boat.

"She's got it, Jefferson," Will said.

Will allowed Gloria to row the boat back to St. George's dock after three separate dives. The final dive gave Gloria a feel for walking while the boat followed her path. It gave her more freedom to explore the surroundings and see the various fish in their natural habitat.

From the road above the landing dock, Elswyth waved to Will, who looked serene lounging at the bow while Jefferson steered the boat under Gloria's power.

"I can see you've been training Miss Hollister well," she shouted.

"Yes, she's getting the hang of it," Will replied. "She found interesting crustaceans she intends to put under her scope. No coral where we were."

"Hurry, Will. I have reservations in half an hour. Oh, and here's an invitation you'll enjoy. It's for tomorrow afternoon. Governor Bols has asked us to a reception for Prince George."

CHAPTER 5

Working for Beebe

John Tee-Van completed his outdoor rounds at the zoological park. He inspected birdcages, checked on reptiles and amphibians from Haiti and Galápagos, and then moved inside to oversee lab work. Volunteer technicians sat over microscopes and categorized species.

Regarded as William Beebe's shadow, Tee-Van had one more task for the day. After that, he looked forward to an evening with friends, Schoedsack and Rose, who once worked for the Department of Tropical Research. He hoped to tempt them with Bermuda. But first, he scheduled a meeting with Else Bostelmann.

He unlocked the door to his small office next to Will's. Tee-Van had access to the famous suite lined floor-to-ceiling with books, journals, and stuffed animals. He intended to use Will's table to conduct his interview. He needed space to look at Else's portfolio of work.

A knock on the door quickened his movement.

"I'll be there in one moment," Tee-Van responded. He took the last stack of papers from Will's table and crammed them onto a crowded bookshelf.

"Sorry for making you wait at the door, Mrs. Bostelmann. Please come into Dr. Beebe's office."

"Is he here?" she asked.

"No, he's traveling."

Tee-Van guided Else to the table. She leaned her large, well-worn leather portfolio against a table leg and pulled out a chair facing Will's book collection. "Dr. Beebe must read," she said.

"He does. And he expects all of us to keep up with our science materials. He says knowledge leads to discovery."

John Tee-Van had learned another important Beebe maxim: get to the point.

"Your sister-in-law says you amaze her with your ability to sketch quickly and precisely."

"Ida is a very good promoter. I hope you agree that my quality is good also, and if you want me to show how fast, I've brought pencils."

"No demonstration is necessary, but I'm eager to see any drawings or paintings of nature."

Else Bostelmann opened her leather folder and removed a stack of pen and ink drawings. She admitted some she did several years earlier when in Germany where she studied art.

Else told Tee-Van she set up an easel in Central Park as often as time allowed. But her current income was from commercial work for ad agencies, local newspapers, and magazines. It limited her opportunities to be outdoors and creative.

"Well, I don't want to mislead you, Mrs. Bostelmann. The artwork we need you to do might be more mundane than you're thinking."

"I'm not worried, Mr. Tee-Van. Can you get me into nature? Can you show me something alive you want me to put on canvas? That's what I'm eager to do."

Tee-Van leafed through Else's samples. She produced several *Plein Air* sketches and watercolors of flowers, ponds in Central Park, ducks, geese, and other wildlife found in the park. There were scenes of farmland.

"Where is this?" he asked.

"Texas. I lived in Texas, but I did not paint often during those years."

"Where did you say you learned your art?"

"Germany. Leipzig at first where I grew up. Berlin. Weimar, Munich. I did some training in Salzburg as well. I studied with Herr Professor Ludwig von Hofmann in Europe. And Sasha Schneider. In the United States, with Howard Giles and Bernard Klonis."

Tee-Van set her paintings aside and opened a large manila folder. "I told you my wife is a successful artist as well. She and other artists have done artwork for Dr. Beebe. They draw and paint portraits of the things we collect for the zoo."

"I remember. You said Mrs. Tee-Van is a good artist."

"Yes. This is her work. Her details of fish, squid, and other aquatic life are excellent portraitures..."

"I agree, Mr. Tee-Van. I do not want to take work from your wife..."

"You're not. She will still work with the team. But Dr. Beebe needs the artwork to have more life. He feels Helen's work is not exciting. It's precise, but not good enough to make patrons, the zoo's board of directors, and others who pay our bills enthused with our efforts."

"I understand. I have been drawing and painting nature – animals, plants, trees, even insects that make nature beautiful – I've been doing it for more than 30 years. I can do what you need."

After seeing Else's work, John Tee-Van agreed. He told Else he wanted her to meet Dr. Beebe, who could discuss his need if she chose to work for the Department of Tropical Research. He added it would be a seasonal position.

"I don't want to talk you out of accepting the job, but there are things you need to understand about Dr. Beebe. He works long hours and expects all of us to do the same. That goes no matter where we are or what project we're working on. He's been described by some as a taskmaster."

"I'm very disciplined, Mr. Tee-Van…"

"When we're on an expedition there are no weekends, no days off. Very few comforts; lots of tent sleeping. And if you're healthy, you work sun-up to well past sun-down."

"I am used to hard work."

"Good. Can you sing?"

Else looked at Mr. Tee-Van puzzled. After hesitating and with a smile, "In German, yes."

Outside Dr. Beebe's office, muffled voices grew louder and moved closer. John Tee-Van pulled a watch from his vest pocket to check the time.

The door opened.

"We're early, John. They were cleaning the gorilla cages and told us to leave."

"Mrs. Bostelmann, do you remember Miss Rose? And Mr. Schoedsack?"

She nodded. It was easy to remember them. Miss Rose was an actress. Very pretty and gregarious. And he was a giant. A very handsome giant whose head appeared to touch the doorframe.

"The gorillas?" Tee-Van asked.

"We can tell you later," Ernest Schoedsack said.

"Mrs. Bostelmann… Ida's sister-in-law, correct?" Rose asked.

"Yes. How are you, Miss Rose?"

"I'm very well, thank you. But it seems you're in a business conversation. Do you need us to wait in your pillbox, John?"

"Funny, but no. I was just explaining to Mrs. Bostelmann what it's like to work for Dr. Beebe."

"Exhilarating," Rose said.

"Never two days the same," Schoedsack added.

"But keep your toothbrush in your pocket along with clean panties. You never know when you'll have time to freshen your breath or put on clean clothes."

"Ruth, I'm trying to encourage Mrs. Bostelmann not to frighten her off."

"Sorry. You'll never enjoy work as much, nor feel more alive than when you're working for Will Beebe," Rose said.

"He loves to party too," said Schoedsack. "The skinny old cuss has more energy than six men his age."

"I'm glad to hear you say those things," Tee-Van told his two friends. "Do you want to go on our next expedition?"

"Can't, John," Rose said.

"We have a project," said Schoedsack.

Else observed Mr. Tee-Van's instant disappointment.

"Well, I'm curious what would keep you from a few months in paradise. Will won't be happy. I told him I could talk you into it, because it's Bermuda," Tee-Van confessed.

"Is that where I would be working—in Bermuda?" Else asked.

"Yes."

"When are you going, John?" Rose asked.

"It will depend on fundraising this winter. Will has a full schedule of lectures and speaking engagements. The zoo's board told him to go as soon as he raised the money."

"I know you want to spend time with your friends, Mr. Tee-Van," Else said. "I'm interested in the position. I would do a good job. I'm not afraid."

"Mrs. Bostelmann, I believe you."

"Me too," Ruth Rose inserted.

"Dr. Beebe has mounds of paperwork when he returns in a few weeks," Tee-Van continued. "I would expect his first opportunity to discuss the project will be around the holidays."

"I will be here," Else told him.

She picked up her folder and loaded her artwork.

"It was wonderful to see you again, Mrs. Bostelmann," Rose said. "I'm sorry we interrupted your meeting."

"It was no interruption. I learned you worked for Dr. Beebe and had a good experience."

"It was great, yes, and valuable for both of us. It's how we met," Schoedsack said.

"Okay, why the interest in gorillas, Ernie?" Tee-Van asked.

"For a film. With a friend. We've done movies together. He asked Ruth to help with the script. I'm going to co-direct."

"Our jungle work with Will helps," Rose said. "The film's about a giant gorilla that gets loose in New York City."

"We know *both* jungles," Schoedsack added. He drew laughter from the other Beebe associates.

Confused, Else smiled. "I hope it's not based on a real event."

"No, just our friend's crazy imagination," Rose replied.

Schoedsack said he, Ruth, and others were returning to Los Angeles soon. They had done scene scouting in New York.

"Tell Mrs. Bostelmann the gorilla's name, Ernie," Rose said.

"Kong."

"I think it's weak. Too ordinary. What do you think, Mrs. Bostelmann?" she asked.

Surprised by the question, Else stammered, "I, uh, I have no opinion."

"Anyway, I feel like we're holding you up," Schoedsack said. "If you haven't decided to work for Dr. Beebe, Mrs. Bostelmann, I would recommend you accept the offer."

"No disrespect, Mrs. B, but you'll have to play mother to a bunch of college kids if you take the job. Will loves young blood. Claims it keeps him young too," Rose said.

Else began walking toward the door. "You met my daughter." She stopped and turned. "I love young people. My daughter and I are friends as well as mother and daughter. She and her school companions have a very different life than mine when I was her age. I do not envy the young of today with so many temptations and so much happening."

CHAPTER 6

His Royal Highness
26 October 1928

Will anxiously anticipated another evening of socializing with Bermuda's aristocracy. He was also eager to get better acquainted with England's famed young Prince George, the youngest son of King George V.

He spent the morning helmet diving with Gloria Hollister who was proving to be an even better athlete than he expected. Comfortable under water, well-conditioned, Will learned she delivered a powerful tennis serve too.

Gloria also quickly became an asset for winning over local Bermudian officials and potential financial supporters. Attractive, well-spoken, and a knowledgeable scientist, she complimented Will's involved storytelling. The feedback Will gained convinced him they made a perfect pitch team.

When Gloria aced a serve to win match and game three, Will gave in. "I need to end this embarrassment," he confessed.

"The club pro told me you play until you win."

"I do and I would if it were not for Elswyth and my invitation to a ballroom dance tonight. It's in honor of Prince George."

"Yes, I'm envious. Did you enjoy meeting him yesterday?" Gloria asked.

"He seemed a little shy at first but warmed up. I thought him earnest when he said he was eager to talk more about our work."

Gloria wrapped a towel around her neck and whistled for Trumps. The wire terrier lifted his chin and twisted his head as though questioning her instruction. The canine showed disbelief the tennis challenge was over.

"Should I expect to sleep in?" she asked.

"Tomorrow is Saturday, correct?" Will asked.

"I believe so."

"Then I won't swim until seven o'clock. Meet for breakfast at 7:45. The weather should be good for another set of helmet dives. I want to explore the shallow waters between Cooper's and Nonsuch islands."

"Are you sure you wouldn't like a day of rest after an evening out?"

"You will learn, Miss Hollister, we rest only when exhausted from work, not play."

"Then I will refer to our tennis match as part of my job, because Trumps and I will be in our room relaxing."

Will laughed and put his tennis racket on his shoulder and headed to his hotel suite. He was expecting Elswyth to be primping for the evening out. Instead, he found her sitting in a chair staring at the late afternoon sun.

Elswyth turned at the sound of a closing door. "How was your tennis game?" she asked.

"I'm afraid to tell you. She humiliated me, Elswyth. I beat most men. I could not beat her."

"Oh, what am I to tell my mother, Will?" Elswyth asked weakly and sarcastically.

"Are you feeling all right, Dear?" Will asked in a different tone.

"No. My head is throbbing. My intestines are in knots," Elswyth replied. "Do you mind if I don't go tonight?"

"Well, I was looking forward to a chat with the young prince."

"Please go, Will. Ask Miss Hollister if she'd like to join you. She's earned a reward for whipping you in tennis."

Will Beebe sulked while moving about their hotel suite quietly, trying to decide if he should press Elswyth with an offer to delay their departure. He wanted Elswyth to make new connections with British nobility. He hoped they might help her with research when writing historic legends about the royal family.

"I need to lie down, Will. I'm sorry to spoil your evening plans, but I'm not well."

"Should I worry? Do you need a doctor?" he asked.

"No, please do not. I'll be fine. It's a woman's thing. But please ask Miss Hollister. She may enjoy dancing as much as I'm sure she enjoyed beating you on the court."

"You're emasculating my pride, Elswyth. It's a *man's* thing."

Elswyth smiled as she laid her head on her pillow. She waved for Will to move on.

Will waited timidly at Gloria Hollister's hotel room door after knocking. He hoped an invitation late in the afternoon to an important event wouldn't insult his new employee.

The door opened. Gloria stood in a terrycloth robe with her blond hair wrapped in a towel high on her head. Will stepped back from the door remembering an imposing sheik he had met during one of his expeditions through the Middle East.

"You surprised me, Dr. Beebe," Gloria said pulling her robe to close it better.

"I'm sorry. I have a favor to ask."

"Is something wrong?"

"Elswyth is not feeling well. I know it's an imposition. I was looking forward to the evening's dance and another chance to meet some important people. She said I should ask if you would accompany me."

"Oh…"

"I have to bathe and put on a tuxedo," Will said, "so I would need some time to be ready…"

"Yes. I would be happy to attend. I can be ready in an hour. Is that fast enough?" Gloria asked.

"Yes, perfect, Miss Hollister. Splendid."

Will returned to Gloria's hotel room by six o'clock with a freshly pressed shirt and a white rose pinned to his lapel. He knocked, took a step back, and waited.

"I'm ready, Dr. Beebe," Gloria announced as she opened the door.

Trumps sat on his haunches a few feet behind her. His forlorn expression showed he knew his master was ditching him for the evening.

Will leaned around Gloria and looked at her dog. "Is he okay? He doesn't look happy."

"Trumps knows the routine, Dr. Beebe. He's fine."

Will turned his attention to the elegant lady standing in front of him. Miss Hollister, dressed in an evening gown, looked stunningly beautiful. A different impression than he had of her when she trounced him in tennis just hours before.

"You look lovely, Miss Hollister."

"Thank you, Dr. Beebe. Is your wife feeling better?"

"She's trying to sleep, but her headache is making it impossible," Will said. "I told her I would stay with her, but she insisted we go with apologies to Governor and Mrs. Bols.

"I'm very sorry she's not well and missing the opportunity. I hope you don't mind my excitement, though, Dr. Beebe. My father has given me many opportunities in life, but I have never met a prince."

Will chuckled at Miss Hollister's admitted excitement. He took her hand and guided her down the hallway.

They arrived at Government House in Hamilton a few minutes after eight o'clock. Heads turned when they entered the ballroom and waited for their formal introductions. A uniformed member of His Excellency's staff announced, "Dr. William Beebe and Miss Gloria Hollister."

Will greeted Governor and Mrs. Bols with an apology from Mrs. Beebe. She has taken ill, he

explained.

"Oh, my. I hope she hasn't acquired some misbegotten island bug, Dr. Beebe," Mrs. Bols said with sincere concern.

"No fear, Mrs. Bols," Will said. "I'm sure she will be fine with a little rest. Our schedule has been a faster pace than she's used to."

"I understand fully," Mrs. Bols replied.

Governor Bols again introduced Will and his guest to Prince George. The Governor's aide assisted with Gloria's name.

"I'm quite pleased to see you again, Professor Beebe," Prince George said. "You seem to have good fortune with the ladies. How are you so lucky?"

"This is my new science assistant, Gloria Hollister. Gloria, I would like to introduce His Royal Highness, Prince George."

Gloria knew the formal curtsy. "It is an honor, Your Highness."

"Gloria Hollister…" The prince repeated her name searching his memory. "I remember you."

The prince's surprising assertion caught both Will and Gloria off guard.

"You remember me, Your Highness?" Gloria asked, somewhat alarmed.

Could this be one of Prince George's famous seduction techniques? Will smiled as though he were witnessing firsthand what was rumored of Prince George's womanizing mastery.

"I was sixteen and playing hooky with some school chums," the prince went on. "We loved watching girls play hockey. A bit of an arousal, if you don't mind my boldness."

"It's coming back to me," Gloria admitted.

Will Beebe remained quite puzzled but eager to hear more.

"You were the tall forward on the American team. Am I right?" Prince George asked. "The lads had their eyes on you. Crude they were in their admiration."

"Should I excuse myself?" Will asked.

"Sorry, Professor Beebe," Prince George said. "Miss Hollister played hockey with the American team against the British, around 1920 I would say."

"I was starting college," Gloria said. "I was on an all-star hockey team. We were daring enough to challenge the Brits in their homeland."

"You took a whipping, I recall," Prince George said.

"Twice, in fact. Your tiny women ran circles around us. It was a humbling moment I shall never forget. I've tried, but now you've spoiled what little success I had."

Governor Bols interrupted the reminiscence with a request Dr. Beebe meet some of Bermuda's lawmakers. He said they suggested a few locations Dr. Beebe might consider for his staff headquarters.

"Would you excuse me, Your Highness?" Will asked.

"I shall look after Miss Hollister for you, Professor Beebe."

Will followed Governor Bols and looked over his shoulder at Gloria and the prince, coveting their youthful banter and amorous energy.

Governor Bols introduced Will to several House of Assembly members. He made sure they were willing to help Professor Beebe before he made the introductions. They asked about Dr. Beebe's plans to examine underwater life near the Bermudian islands.

Two Assemblymen from Devonshire Parish, Dill and Watlington, inquired specifically about Beebe's research needs.

"Space to set up a laboratory," Will explained. "We hope to bring up several species, some perhaps never before identified."

"What are the lab's requirements, Dr. Beebe?" Watlington asked.

"I will need several large rooms, electricity, refrigeration, and accommodations for a staff of about twenty scientists and student interns who will help during the summer months."

"Have you found such a location yet, Dr. Beebe?" Assemblyman J.D.B. Talbot asked.

"Miss Hollister–with His Royal Highness–and I have been scouting the islands while doing our helmet dives. There are many wonderful places, but nothing is what I would call ideal or accessible," Will admitted.

"Good luck with your search, Dr. Beebe," Talbot said. "If you would like me to show Miss Hollister the islands, I would be happy to oblige."

The men laughed. Will grinned.

———◦◦◦◦———

"May I offer you Champagne, Miss Hollister?" Prince George asked.

"That would be nice, Your Highness."

The prince motioned to a servant with a tray of Champagne flutes. The server stopped and allowed Prince George to remove two. He then bowed and backed two steps before pivoting and continuing.

"Here's to America's future athletes. May one day they compete against Great Britain and my fellow countrymen with greater success than you experienced, Miss Hollister."

Gloria acknowledged his sarcasm with a smile and tap of his flute. The Champagne went down easily.

"Are you enjoying Bermuda?"

"Do you mean because I can have alcohol?" she asked tongue in cheek.

"Prohibition isn't causing you any problems, is it?"

"Not really; not for people with money or connections, but if you have neither, then you'd better like cow's milk or ginger ale."

"And what about other substances to relax human inhibitions? Are they substituting for alcohol in the States?"

"I don't know," she answered. "I've been sheltered the last few years because of the work I've been doing."

"And what have you been working on?" the prince asked.

"Cancer. Until just recently I was working with a scientist to understand the illness. Depressing at times. But I learned, and now I hope to do what excites me more."

"And what is that?"

"Nature. Conservation of our natural resources."

"Bully. I share your interests, Miss Hollister."

Their conversation paused while they sipped Champagne. Gloria could sense they were being watched. She felt anxious knowing she dominated His Royal Highness's time when others waited for a brief conversation with him.

"If you don't mind, I would really enjoy a cigarette," Prince George said. "You wouldn't happen to have an American smoke with you?"

"I have Camels in my hand purse," Gloria offered.

A British soldier approached Prince George and passed along a request from the governor.

"Miss Hollister, I'm enjoying your company and would appreciate that cigarette, but I need to make a fast round with Governor Bols. Can you bring Professor Beebe to the terrace? I'll let my staff know," he said. "Let's say in fifteen."

Gloria located Will among several attendees. She waited for his storytelling to end, but then spoke up. "I'm sorry to interrupt your conversation, Dr. Beebe. Prince George has asked that you have a private conversation on the terrace."

She slipped her arm through Will's and guided him toward the entrance where British soldiers stood guard. Will looked at Gloria as she pulled him forward enjoying his new employee's gumption.

"Thank you for freeing Professor Beebe, Miss Hollister," Prince George said. "I hope you don't mind being pulled away from your attentive audience."

"No, but I know many guests will probably resent me for consuming your time."

"I recognize I'm a novelty, Professor Beebe. Besides Miss Hollister, there's no one my age to talk about things I enjoy, such as helmet diving. I'm eager for you to take me. Do you have your Camels with you, Miss Hollister?" the prince asked.

Gloria fumbled with her clutch, unsnapped it, and retrieved a pack of cigarettes. She was thankful she had already opened the wrapping. She tapped the pack and Prince George pulled the cigarette that popped out farthest.

"Will you join me, Professor Beebe?"

Gloria held out the pack so Will could pull a cigarette after she took one for herself. Prince George turned to look at a soldier standing nearby. The soldier removed a book of matches from his breast pocket and lit the prince's cigarette. He extinguished the match and lit a separate one for Gloria and Will.

"Do you helmet dive as well, Miss Hollister?" the prince asked.

"I'm getting used to it."

"She's being modest, Your Highness. She's taken to it quite easily," Will said.

Governor Bols joined their conversation seeking Dr. Beebe for introductions.

"How goes it?" the governor asked hoping Prince George was enjoying his evening.

"A splendid event, Your Excellency," Prince George said. "Wonderful occasion. Professor Beebe and his pretty assistant are sharing their experience with helmet diving."

"Well, Dr. Beebe. Maybe we let the young people have a moment while I introduce you to the Tuckers. I think their long-standing Bermuda connections will do you some good."

Will knew the Tucker name was prominent in Bermuda, so he accepted the opportunity to get acquainted.

Prince George took Gloria's hand and implied they walk. "You work in a man's arena as a science assistant, Miss Hollister. As a beautiful woman, are you taken seriously?"

"I don't know. I hope I am. My cancer research was serious. My male colleagues were slow to accept, but by the time I was ready to join Dr. Beebe they were sorry to see me leave."

"When Professor Beebe takes me helmet diving," Prince George said, "I sincerely hope you go too."

Gloria stopped. She studied Prince George's handsome face. "Are the rumors true?" she asked. "Have you experimented with heroin?"

"Don't hold back, Miss Hollister. Say what's on your mind," the prince said laughingly. "Are you asking because you'd be interested in trying it?"

"No thank you; not necessary. My work provides excitement. My dog entertains me. And now I work for a man who trusts me regardless of my gender. I have all I need."

"Then your question comes from trepidation. Can you trust me, or do I turn from Dr. Jekyll to Mr. Hyde assuming I've injected drugs into my veins?"

Gloria had no response. She considered his viewpoint. Perhaps she had made an unfair judgment based on hearsay.

The prince took his cue seeing a British officer give him a familiar gesture.

"It appears that once again I have to execute my duties as the King's son," he said. He took Gloria's hand, bowed, and kissed the back of it. "The music sounds quite inviting. I will make my rounds of royal babble, but then I look forward to a dance," he said. "You will be staying longer, correct?"

Gloria searched for a glimpse of Dr. Beebe before responding. "I can see Dr. Beebe is already on the dance floor, so I don't think I can escape. More than my boss, tonight he's also my escort."

Prince George bowed again and kissed her hand a second time promising to find her later.

Gloria continued to hold her kissed hand out feeling a shiver begin where his lips touched it. She watched him walk away strut ting a proud royal gait that exuded confidence.

Prince George made Gloria feel vulnerable notwithstand ing her guardedness. She saw Dr. Beebe gesture her way. She as sumed he wanted to dance. He had talked about it on the way to Hamilton warning her it was one of his favorite things to do. She entered the ballroom happy to take her mind off Prince George and to dance with the man who brought her.

CHAPTER 7

Eve of Thanksgiving
1928

Else Bostelmann worked to complete a series of pen drawings. She received a last-minute request from an advertising agency planning to run a holiday campaign in three New York newspapers the day after Thanksgiving.

Else, the rare artist who sacrificed holiday preparations to complete the assignment, drew the final line still anxious, fearing a messenger's knock before she added her last touches. She blew the ink dry.

A disappointed Hada Bostelmann sat in the front room with her sketchpad in her lap. Her heart was set on a short excursion upstate to visit her father's family, cousins near her age. She drew sad faces with tears.

"If the messenger arrives, have him come in," Else shouted to her daughter.

"I will, Mother."

"The ink is almost dry."

A coincidental knock brought Hada to her feet. It had been weeks since she had seen Bobby, the messenger whom she found handsome.

"Telegram for Mrs. Bostelmann," came an older man's voice from outside the apartment door. Hada opened it with excitement gone.

"Are you Mrs. Bostelmann?" the Western Union man asked.

Else appeared behind Hada. "I'm Mrs. Bostelmann."

"Your telegram, ma'am."

"Thank you."

The deliveryman left after a tip of his hat. Hada closed the door and stretched her neck to see
who sent the telegram.

"Who's it from, Mother?"

"The Zoological Society. I have an appointment with Dr. William Beebe next month."

Hada shared her mother's excitement. "Where did you say Dr. Beebe was going?" she asked.

"Bermuda. I found pictures at the library."

"I hope I get to go too," Hada said. She anticipated her mother's success with her interview.

"Continue to draw, Hada. Practice. One never knows what might happen."

Else and Hada heard footsteps outside the apartment door. Hada's excitement rose again when someone knocked. "Pickup for Mrs. Bostelmann."

When she pulled the door open, Hada saw Bobby with a teeth-glistening smile.

"Hiya, pretty Hada. Is Mother home?"

"I'm right here, Bobby," Else said peering over Hada's shoulder.

"Hello, Mrs. Bostelmann." Bobby's face changed expression when Else caught him making eyes at her daughter.

"Come in, Bobby," Else said while walking to her drawing-room to retrieve her artwork. She brought the pouch out and saw the boy and her daughter shuffling nervously.

"Here." She handed the pouch to Bobby who stood reluctant to leave. "Are you spending Thanksgiving with your family?" she asked Bobby.

"Yes, ma'am."

"Mother and I will have turkey and potatoes here. Just the two of us," Hada whimpered.

Else looked at Hada. "I will let you talk, but I know the agency is expecting the pouch soon."

"Yes, ma'am. I will get it to them on time," Bobby assured Else, who returned to her drawing-room to clean her pens and straighten her art supplies.

Hada waited until Else was back in her room before turning to Bobby. "It's good to see you again."

"It's good to see you too, Hada. How've you been?"

"I've been well. We just got good news."

"What's that?"

"Mother has an appointment to interview with William Beebe at the zoo."

"Oh, I know who he is. We talk about him in our night class at the college. He writes wonderful stories about his adventures. All the fellows say they want to be just like Dr. Beebe."

"It does sound exciting. Maybe I'll get to go too," Hada said.

"Really, Hada? That would be something." He looked at Hada sadly. "I better get this delivered to the agency."

"Maybe they'll have another project for Mother. You can come back then."

"Maybe, Hada. Happy Thanksgiving, pretty girl."

CHAPTER 8

Eureka!

December 1928

Will Beebe felt a tickle in his throat, a sure sign winter had arrived in New York City. He hated cold weather. Since childhood he fought congestion and lung disorders, so the onset of freezing temperatures, snow, and driving winds made Will tired and somewhat irritable because he knew he was vulnerable to sickness.

Still, he braved the elements and worked long hours at the zoo preparing notes for lectures to pay for his next adventure. He also used the time to meet with dozens of business associates and prospective employees for his Department of Tropical Research.

John Tee-Van sat next door scheduling a full agenda for his boss's day beginning with a pair of interviews. First, a young man wanted to present an idea for a submersible vessel.

Tee-Van popped his head into Will's office. "Are you ready for your interviews, Will?"

"Fill me in, John. Who's the first one?"

"His name is Otis Barton."

"Do you know Barton?" Will asked.

"I don't but I spoke to him on the telephone. He says he can make it possible for you to dive a mile deep in the ocean."

"Many have said that. Every jokester from here to San Francisco has sent me sketches a schoolboy would recognize as foolishness."

"I know, Will. You and I looked at several drawings about this same time two years ago."

"As Teddy Roosevelt warned me, it has to withstand tons of pressure. Has to have a window, otherwise, no sense going down. Who recommended him?"

"Madison Grant from the board."

Will thought again about the different designs he and John viewed. "What did Madison say?"

"He said the man has solid credentials. A Columbia man as well. Harvard for his undergraduate degree, then Columbia for engineering."

"Harvard! Sounds like trouble."

"It's too late to cancel. He'll be here soon."

"We'll make the best of it, John. What else do you have for me?"

"Mrs. Bostelmann is coming later."

"Mrs. Bostelmann…?"

"The artist I told you about."

"Oh, excellent. Enthused to see her work."

The phone on John's desk rang. He left to answer. After hanging up, John yelled to Will, "Barton's here. Going to get him."

Will looked at a picture on his desk of he and Elswyth while in Bermuda. The weather there wasn't perfect challenged by the open sea. The season for diving was shorter than at the islands in the Caribbean, but the climate was better for Elswyth.

Their marriage had turned out to be a good partnership. Their interests weren't always aligned, but he never expected it to be like what he and Blair Rice had. They did everything together and passion dominated their interactions. This marriage provided mutual benefits that made love simpler. He hoped more lasting.

He put down the papers he had been reviewing and leaned back in his chair. Thoughts of his early career with Blair Rice discovering things as a science team stirred his emotions. He missed that closeness. Having Miss Hollister helped restore his sense of partnership at work, but Will Beebe's passions needed around-the-clock nurturing. He didn't have that. Hadn't had it since Blair left.

John Tee-Van gave Will a courtesy knock and stepped into his office followed by a tall young man dressed nattily in a blue suit. When the man removed his hat, it revealed a bald head belying his age. He was as bald as Will.

"Hello. I'm Will Beebe."

Will reached out and took Otis Barton's hand, gave it a firm shake, and directed the silent, nervous individual to a chair in front of his desk.

John Tee-Van excused himself and closed the door between his and Will's offices.

Will circled his wood desk and sat in his chair folding his arms. "Tell me your name again," Will said to Otis.

"Otis Barton."

Will saw in Barton a six-year-old boy visiting the zoo for the first time. The young man gawked at Will's wall of books, his collection of stuffed critters, a signed picture of Teddy Roosevelt on his desk, and a slew of celebrity photos scattered throughout. But the man said nothing.

"So, you know Mr. Grant?" Will began.

"Who?" Otis asked still enchanted by Beebe's naturalist décor.

"Madison Grant from our zoological society board."

"I met him at the *New York Times* offices. Alice Greenbrier introduced us."

"Yes, I know who she is," Will said. "She's published newspaper articles about the Department of Tropical Research."

"She and I met at Columbia when I worked on my engineering degree."

Otis Barton had written to Dr. Beebe several times but received no reply. He used Greenbrier to acquire an introduction to Dr. Beebe, his idol. Her stories about Will's adventures increased his envy and sparked the idea to use her as a go-between.

Born June 5, 1899, Otis and his younger brother grew up in their mother's home after Otis, Sr. died of a heart attack. Young Otis was six. Mrs. Barton's family–mostly women–helped provide the boys with comfort.

He attended Groton, a private school north of Boston, where he did well. His sharp memory earned him excellent grades with little effort. He fantasized about adventures to Africa, South America, and the Far East where William Beebe had already been, and about which Beebe had written several books. Otis read them all.

Modeling Beebe at an early age, Otis donned a diving helmet and walked underwater. He and his brother took turns pumping air through a hose while the other dropped to 30 feet with weights aiding their descent.

Otis felt connected to Dr. Beebe as though a kinship already existed. He and his idol were among an elite group diving with copper helmets. Hoping to be a bon vivant naturalist like Dr. Beebe, welcomed into prestigious social circles, famous for daring travels, friends with the rich, Otis pictured himself surrounded by beautiful women like William Beebe when featured in the newspapers' society pages.

"I understand you have a submersible design to show me," Will continued.

Otis sat forward in his chair and unraveled a blueprint. He stood and laid it on Will's desk.

"The best design to withstand water pressure a mile below the surface is a sphere," Otis said.

Will looked at what Otis laid out. At first, he thought the man presumptuous, using his desk when an empty table sat in front of his library shelves. But the sudden realization that the hollow-ball design in front of him was ingenious changed his mood.

Will had already concluded it would take too long for inventors to devise a self-propelled submarine that could dive as deep as he wanted to go, so submerging in a tethered submersible represented his only hope. But his mind was stuck on the shape of a submarine. Until now.

Although not mechanical, Will was familiar with geometric shapes; a ball meant equal pressure pushing from all sides. The revelation caused a surprising epiphany, even a flash of anger at how simple it was.

Will stood over the blueprint realizing this awkward stranger had laid in his lap the answer. He excitedly yelled for Tee-Van to join them.

With John in the room, Will began to pepper Otis Barton with a series of questions. What is it made of? How big is it? How big are the windows? How do you breathe? How do you stop the windows from fogging?

Will Beebe knew from his helmet dives what problems happen underwater. A submersible ball would have many similar problems only more critical if sunk deep in the sea.

"There can be no air hose, but I guess you know that," Will said to Otis.

Otis reached across the blueprint each time Will raised a concern. He pointed to where the air tanks would sit inside the ball.

"Let's do it," Will said. "Can you have it ready by June? We'll take it to Bermuda."

Otis Barton gave Beebe and Tee-Van a glazed fright. "...by June? June '29?"

"Yes, of course. I'm ready to dive to see what's there."

"I'll, ah, I mean I can do my best working with the engineering firm I've hired to build it, but there are still things we need to work out," Otis said.

"Certainly. I understand the business side of things. Work them out, Mr. Barton. Let's get started," Will responded.

"Dr. Beebe, I have the resources to build the sphere, but I have one condition."

"What's the condition? There's always a condition, Mr. Barton. Spit it out," Will insisted.

"I want to dive too."

"Do you have a science background? For instance, are you an ichthyologist as well as an engineer?"

"No, Dr. Beebe. I'm not a scientist, but I love adventure."

Will Beebe looked at John Tee-Van whose excitement rose and dipped in a matter of minutes. John's knowledge of marine life made him the logical dive partner.

Will again looked at the drawing. "It's five-feet wide, correct?"

"Yes, sir."

"I'm six feet tall and you look that or taller. Can we both fit inside?"

"Yes, sir. We'll be snug, but I've tried the space and it works."

"Well, Mr. Barton, if those are your conditions and you're willing to cover your costs to build the sphere, then we have a deal."

A stunned Otis Barton left Dr. Beebe's office thrilled but also worried. In truth, he had no idea whether he could do what Beebe asked; build his steel vessel in 180 days.

John Tee-Van escorted Otis to the zoo grounds and returned to find Will drawing circles and putting stick figures inside.

"Why couldn't we see this, John?" Will rose and walked to the window as though searching for the answer in the chilly outdoors.

"We simply failed to adapt," John replied.

"I have to stop doing that, John. Correct me when I get stuck in my thinking."

Will walked back to his desk. "When will the artist be here?"

"She's here now. I asked her to wait in the lobby. I wanted a moment to talk about Barton's proposal."

"We have to do it his way, John. He gets to dive with me because he's picking up the cost. That's what he wants out of this arrangement."

"He's an engineer, not a scientist, not a zoologist or ichthyologist like Miss Hollister, Will."

"If we had a choice, you'd be the person I'd want with me," Will told John. "The solution fell into our laps with conditions. I don't like them, but I'm not willing to search for another."

"I know, but…"

"…the cost is right. He said he'd build the steel ball with his own money. One problem solved. The timing is right. I'll find a way to include you in dives when I can," Will said. "Let's meet the artist. What's her name?"

"Bostelmann. Her husband's father, mother, and siblings are musicians. That's how I met her through Helen. They share the same friends."

John returned to the building lobby and greeted Else who carried again her large art folder. John coached her about meeting Will. He told her the Department of Tropical Research director can be blunt.

"I'm German, Mr. Tee-Van," Else told him. "Blunt is the only communication I know."

"I didn't mean he's rude; he just says what's on his mind."

"I'm not rude and I say what's on my mind too. Will he like me or not?"

John opened Will's office door without answering Mrs. Bostelmann's question. "Dr. Beebe, this is Mrs. Else Bostelmann, an artist interested in turning our science images into art."

"Welcome, Mrs. Bostelmann. I'm eager to see your samples."

Else walked straight to the table she used when she showed her work to John Tee-Van several weeks earlier. She had arranged the art to emphasize her *Plein Air* experience. She said she loved drawing and painting nature and loved the challenge of doing it quickly.

As she was setting out her art, John Tee-Van's telephone rang in his office.

"Please excuse me, Mrs. Bostelmann. I must answer my telephone. Will, can you view her work and share your thoughts?"

John left. His voice echoed in the background as Will approached the table and began to leaf through Else's pictures, some in pencil, others in pen and ink, and still others in watercolors and oils.

Will showed little emotion, but Else could tell he was engaged. His eyes moved across the art exactly how Else wanted a viewer to follow lines, light direction, and colors. She could see the crinkles dancing across his brow.

"What do you think, Dr. Beebe?"

"Your work is very good, Mrs. Bostelmann. You understand nature."

He pointed to a tree she had drawn. "Do you remember being here, Mrs. Bostelmann?"

"Yes. Near the zoo in Leipzig."

"It's an elm that reminds me of France where I flew during the European War."

Else sat quietly. She heard John Tee-Van say "good-bye" right before he re-entered Dr. Beebe's office.

"Mrs. Bostelmann, I plan to take Department of Tropical Research staff to Bermuda in the spring. I want you to join us once we're established with our laboratory. Are you able to do that?"

"I would enjoy it, Dr. Beebe. I have a few questions," she responded.

"Ask away…"

"What are the business arrangements?"

"We provide a fair income for the talents you provide," Will said. "I will have John work out the specific details if you agree."

"I have a daughter, Dr. Beebe. I'm teaching her art while she completes her general studies…"

"That's fine, Mrs. Bostelmann. Bring her along. I will make her an intern assistant. She can use her art. She can assist you or we can assign her to another artist."

"Thank you. How long will the work last? I have to notify a few agencies for which I am doing current work."

John Tee-Van said he would prepare detailed plans. He estimated they would return to New York in October.

"There are uncertainties, Mrs. Bostelmann," Will said. "It's not always work you can count on. I hope you understand."

"I'm an artist. I understand perfectly."

"Very well. You are now part of my art team. I know you and John have discussed what that entails, so I thank you for coming and I look forward to seeing you and your daughter—what's her name?"

"Gertraude Hadumodt, but we call her Hada."

"I look forward to seeing you and Hada in Bermuda."

CHAPTER 9

Nonsuch
March 1929

Will corralled John and Gloria into a small boat just big enough to maneuver the waves from St. George's Harbor through Ferry Reach and into Castle Harbor. His unannounced destination: Nonsuch Island.

While entertaining England's Prince George with helmet diving in October, Will had deepened his friendship with Bermuda's Governor Louis Bols. The governor directed Will to Nonsuch Island and made a strong pitch for the naturalist to consider the island as a base for his research operation. Nonsuch Island fit most of Beebe's requirements.

Will started the boat as John untied a rope and pushed the stern. Although still groggy from a short night of rest, he jumped into the boat with rope in hand. Gloria used an oar to push the bow away from the dock.

The strong smell of gasoline and oil fumes stung their nostrils. Exhaust clouded John's vision until Will sped up through the noxious nuisances into the harbor's open water.

"Where to today, Dr. Beebe?" John asked with a choking cough and rubbing his eyes.

"Nonsuch. I received a telegram this morning from Governor Bols."

"Did the Assembly approve us using the island?" Gloria asked.

"Full steam ahead."

"I wish this boat used steam, Will. The petroleum fumes are making me sick," John complained.

"Are you pleased? When can we set up our laboratory?" Gloria asked.

"Now. And, yes, I'm pleased. But it took somewhat longer than I expected."

The small island was located at the southern lee of Castle Harbor south of St. George's and St. David's much larger islands. Past Nonsuch, Bermuda's shorelines opened to the Atlantic Ocean.

The island's 25 acres included cedar trees, palmetto, and olivewood that were native and exclusive to the Bermudian archipelago. Lantana scrub and flowering grasses blanketed the ground and laid an emerald carpet of welcome.

When showing Dr. Beebe Nonsuch, Bols escorted Beebe and Prince George to a small grouping of solid structures sitting at the island's volcanic summit. The buildings were hospital shelters for island patients with deadly contagious diseases.

However, the hospital infirmary was used only twice in the previous two decades, so Bols with His Royal Highness's blessing—was willing to grant the New York Zoological Society's Department of Tropical Research permission to set up laboratories and housing on the grounds.

A caretaker team of husband and wife kept the Nonsuch facilities in prime condition and agreed to stay while the researchers used the island. It added further appeal to the location.

Bermuda's governing assemblymen concurred with their governor if Beebe vacated should the need arise to isolate the islands' sick.

The morning telegram gave Dr. Beebe a final blessing. He could move his scientists to Nonsuch. Will was eager to see the island's accommodations again.

As they cut through the harbor's glassy waters, Will told John and Gloria about the hospital, which he described as ideal for their workstations. "The location is perfectly situated for bringing in specimens from the Atlantic," Will added.

With Spring of '29 only days away, trawling conditions seemed superb. The Beebe plan for diving in Otis Barton's steel ball also looked promising.

Before departing New York, Will told tycoon friends Harrison Williams and Mortimer Schiff he expected the expedition to produce many rewarding discoveries for the zoo. Those conversations produced more money and enabled Will to plan a full summer of oceanographic research.

Will knew the clincher would be successful dives with Barton's invention. It would give him a way to prove his theories that marine life existed deep in the abyss. Until then, he would pull from the Atlantic Ocean whatever life came up in his trawling nets.

Among Governor Bols' enticements, Will had gained use of a small fleet of vessels—all past their prime—but a tug called the *Gladisfen* was at least seaworthy. Using funds from Williams, Schiff, and their wealthy friends to purchase trawling nets, he targeted an eight-mile diameter south of the islands where the seafloor dropped abruptly.

Will steered the small powerboat onto a narrow beach on the western shore of Nonsuch. That's where the guide had taken Governor Bols, Prince George, and Will. He, John, and Gloria climbed a cliff and hiked towards the set of buildings.

"How much equipment do we need to bring up this rocky terrain?" John asked.

"I'm working on a better path," Will said.

"Good, because if we have the interns carry *my* stuff up the way we just came, they'll quit before they get to *your* equipment, Will." Gloria laughed in agreement.

Arthur Tucker and his wife spotted the three guests approaching the old hospital. They remembered William Beebe and had already heard the news their island would have new occupants. They greeted Will as though he had already been a long-time friend.

"It's good we have a doctor to look after," Arthur Tucker said to Will jokingly, "rather than sick people others don't want around."

"Arthur, offer our visitors a cup of water to drink," Mrs. Tucker told her husband, already displaying some embarrassment at her husband's crassness.

"How long have you been caretakers here?" Gloria asked.

"Many years, my dear."

"My, but you're pretty, young lady. It'll be nice to have *you* here," Mr. Tucker said to Gloria. "You're coming with Dr. Beebe, aren't you?"

"Arthur, behave yourself. Forgive him. We don't have many people stop at Nonsuch, especially with its history, so he forgets his English manners."

"It's all right, Mrs. Tucker. I can handle a little flattery."

"Can you give us a quick look at the buildings?" Will asked.

"Certainly. Follow me."

"Would you like some breakfast? I'm short on supplies. It's a day before we do our shopping in St. George, but I can fix some eggs and coffee," Mrs. Tucker offered.

"Would you have Grape Nuts and milk?" Will asked.

"I'm sorry, Dr. Beebe. I'm familiar with Grape Nuts, but that's not something we keep."

"Not our cup of tea," Mr. Tucker added.

"Eggs and coffee would be wonderful, Mrs. Tucker, after we see the old hospital," Will said.

Arthur Tucker guided the three scientists through the hospital's vacant floors. There were a few beds, tables, and chairs in some rooms. Others were empty. Will assumed John was already scheming where to place lab equipment and put staff members.

The space was less conducive to living quarters than they expected. The halls were open, which was ideal for setting up the lab, but not for providing personal privacy.

"We can solve that problem," Will told John after the walk-through ended. "We'll pitch tents. We'll need all the space for working area."

"Are you ready to sleep in a tent, Gloria?" John asked her when walking back to the Tucker's living quarters.

"I've done it many times, John, when my father took me hunting. I will have no problem."

Mrs. Tucker's scrambled eggs and coffee hit the spot. It comforted the trio learning the Tuckers chose to stay as caretakers. They were pleasant and accommodating.

"Let me ask, Mr. Tucker, how do you bring in your supplies?" John queried.

"Not the way you came, young man. There's a long path from the south, but it's easier than climbing the west cliff."

"I'm glad to know that."

"The south way isn't as easy as my husband makes it sound," Mrs. Tucker said with a scolding for Arthur Tucker. "Trudging through the sand and thick grass is tiring too, especially as I get older."

"How close to the shore can we get with a larger boat?"

"The south beach runs away, Dr. Beebe. Not very close, I'm afraid."

"Do you have any suggestions, Mr. Tucker?" Gloria asked.

"It depends on your funds, I suppose. If the governor approves, we can build a dock."

"How long would that take?" asked John.

"There's plenty of cedar and men willing to work, but we'll need other supplies hard to find in Hamilton. I'd say a month."

"We may need to find a different remedy, one we can execute quicker," Will said.

Gloria helped Mrs. Tucker clear her table and thanked her for her generous hospitality. She felt an immediate attachment to the grandmotherly and gracious Bermudian. But she also wondered how Mrs. Tucker adapted to a life of isolation.

Nonsuch Island was beautiful and peaceful. The sky vibrant and air fragrant. Gloria pictured setting up her lab and making Nonsuch Island a busy place, but the two men she'd be working with were both married. She worried that the island could also be a lonely summer home.

John Tee-Van felt excited about the prospect of living in the open air with Helen and doing the work he enjoyed most. He treasured gathering specimens, analyzing them, categorizing them, and taking back to the zoo new creatures from which they could learn new things about the planet and its unexplored life.

Will's curiosity and concerns about the Earth's environment had rubbed off on John. His passion grew with very little prodding. He shared with Dr. Beebe a goal to preserve nature as best they could. By identifying thousands of species at risk, including those in the sea, the Department of Tropical Research intended to have an impact.

"My goal is to understand everything we can about this tiny piece of Atlantic Ocean," Will told John and Gloria as they chugged away from Nonsuch.

Other science explorers identified species but placed little importance on the creatures' environment. Academic identification was important to William Beebe, but he also wanted to explore how life was sustained by its surroundings.

"We shall never be precise," he continued lecturing John and Gloria, "because there may be rare species that migrate in and out of our area of study, but the aim is to understand what is here, how does it continue to exist, and how is man affecting the environment."

"How thorough do you expect us to be?" Gloria asked.

"Our lives are not long enough to investigate every fathom of water, every acre of island jungle where unique life survives. No one has proven without a doubt that life swims a mile beneath the surface. Some still say impossible. Let's show the world those cynics are wrong; there *is* life and it can teach us extraordinary amounts about our evolution and our prospects for the future. How those lives survive is important to see. I'm counting on Barton's help."

CHAPTER 10

Arrivals

1 June 1929

John Tee-Van rose to morning light peeking over Soldier Bay. Eager to get the day started, he went to the kitchen expecting to find Will crunching his Grape Nuts. Instead, Mrs. Tucker was there alone preparing breakfast for staff and crew.

John and his wife Helen shared private quarters in the old hospital, now the DTR headquarters and laboratory. Will and Elswyth took the other private room, although Elswyth had already tired of what she called "rustic accommodations." She complained that the space was not conducive to her writing. She was making plans to move her things to the St. George's Hotel, where her mother stayed.

Will made no objections, promising to spend as much time as possible and all Saturday evenings at the hotel so they could attend church Sunday morning.

"Good morning, Mrs. Tucker. Did Will finish breakfast?" John asked.

"Good morning, Mr. Tee-Van. Yes, he and Arthur are looking over the South Beach shoreline. Dr. Beebe says he may have a better solution for bringing in supplies and your deep-sea catches."

John understood. Will and he met with the owner of a boat-leasing business. Governor Bols introduced them after Will asked the governor for advice on ways to dock boats at Nonsuch Island. The business owner recommended that the government move a sunken Navy supply ship, the *Sea Fern*, from St. George's Harbor to Nonsuch Island's beach. He said it would be the fastest way to create a landing dock.

John favored the plan because he knew a Navy supply ship would have secure chambers that would be ideal for flooding. He could keep the daily catches alive and safe from sharks and other scavengers. He hoped they could move the sunken *Sea Fern* soon.

He filled his cup with coffee and grabbed a strip of bacon Mrs. Tucker had just scooped from her cast-iron skillet.

"Careful, Mr. Tee-Van, that's hot."

John ignored Mrs. Tucker's warning and held the crackling pork fat between his teeth. Eager to hear Will's conversation with Mr. Tucker, he found them standing in front of a placid morning sea as though posed for a painting.

"Have either of you heard from Governor Bols?" John asked as he approached.

"Not I, Mr. Tee-Van," Arthur Tucker responded. "But a young sailor brought Dr. Beebe a letter this morning from His Excellency."

"What did the governor say, Will?"

"The Navy will salvage the *Sea Fern* from the bottom of St. George's Harbor on Thursday and deliver it to Nonsuch Island a day later."

"That's good news, Will."

"Yes, our capacity to record our findings will improve when we can launch our vessels faster and make our landings safer," Will said. "But today, John Tee-Van, could be the start of even greater achievement. And you're the man to greet the adventurous engineer who'll make it happen."

"I have the *Skink* ready, Will."

"I asked Mr. Tucker to listen to the local radio station this morning…"

"The broadcast report says the *Fort Victoria* is expected to arrive on schedule, Mr. Tee-Van," Arthur Tucker added.

"I'll be departing at eight o'clock then. But don't forget, Will. Besides Mr. Barton, I have Mrs. Bostelmann and her daughter to wait on."

The men agreed that it would take an additional hour for the ship to unload its passengers and their luggage. Will Beebe estimated that John would not have their new arrivals back to Nonsuch Island until well past the lunch hour.

John cranked the *Skink's* inboard motor to a noisy, fumy start. He pointed the bow west northwest across Castle Harbor. The waters remained calm as he aimed for the narrow passage between Ferry Island Fort and Coney Island, nearly four miles across the vast stretch of water.

Beyond the inlet, the Atlantic opened for John to cruise parallel to North Shore Road, the path used for horse-drawn carriages and buses. Bermuda law limited motor-vehicle ownership. It was one reason John chose the *Skink* to pick up his passengers.

When Tee-Van reached the open sea, he veered southwest. He could see two ships in the distance and assumed one was the *Fort Victoria*.

John Tee-Van grew up at the zoo. His father, Patrick, was a zookeeper who assisted caretaking birds, Will Beebe's department. Patrick helped his son get a job when Tee-Van was fourteen. That too was fortuitous because Patrick died soon after. Employed at the zoo while attending school, John helped his mother with family finances.

He studied zoology but also had an interest in architecture. He enjoyed drawing pictures of buildings. When Will learned this, he asked the young assistant to try drawing pictures of birds.

Will was so impressed with John's effort that he began to mentor the young man's career. When John was 20, Will took him to British Guiana on his first expedition for the zoo.

Tee-Van continued to work in the zoo's bird department for William Beebe until Will organized the Department of Tropical Research. John became Will's first DTR employee.

Helen Damrosch and John married about the same time. She joined DTR as an artist and researcher, but Helen came from a very different background. The daughter of a well-known musical family, a registered part of New York society, Helen earned her way into Will Beebe's graces through the family's generosity. Helen had been one of Will's interns when the family supported Will's conservation agenda.

John, grateful too for Will's introduction, fell in love with Helen from the moment they met. Through Helen and Will, John's social and business status grew.

John's loyalty to William Beebe did not blind him. He understood Will's critics who were quick to point to the differences between Beebe and other biological scientists. John saw they followed exact procedures and carefully recorded their discoveries in scientific journals. That became his job.

Will's approach was to share his information where everyone could read about his discoveries and where he could describe in colorful detail his excitement about something new that he felt mankind needed to value.

John endorsed Will's philosophy that *life persists in whole, not as separate parts.* He regretted it took so long for others to understand what that meant.

As John cleared the tip of the Pembroke Parish peninsula, he could see tugboats guiding the *Fort Victoria* into its landing pier. He became anxious about meeting up with Otis Barton. The stoic and non-verbal Barton had odd mannerisms. It was not what he expected from a Harvard- and Columbia-educated man.

After watching the ship dock, John floated the *Skink* into a pier where smaller boats and dinghies picked up passengers. He tied the *Skink* and headed to the debarking platform. He knew he'd be able to spot Barton's tall stature among the departing passengers, but he was less certain that he'd be able to pick out Else Bostelmann and her daughter. The ship carried nearly four-hundred people.

John stood in an open space at the gangway exit. He saw Otis among several men and women departing together. He was with first-class passengers. John lifted his hat in the air. "Mr. Barton. John Tee-Van. Over here."

Otis acknowledged John's shouts with a hand gesture, but no facial expression. When he descended the gangway, John held out his hand in greeting.

"It's good to see you again, Mr. Barton," John said. Age contemporary, they could have been college roommates reuniting for a vacation.

"Thank you. Did Dr. Beebe come?"

"No. He sends his regrets. We have other passengers, and our transport boat is small."

"Let the porter know where to take my luggage. I would like to say good-bye to a lady from the ship."

"Sure, Mr. Barton. I'll be standing here waiting for Mrs. Bostelmann. Did you meet her on while traveling here?"

"I don't believe so," Otis said. He quickly disappeared into the crowd to join a young lady in a crewmember uniform.

"Are you picking up Mr. Barton?" a ship porter asked.

"Yes, I've tied our boat to post number four," John responded.

The porter pushed a cart with several bags along the dock toward the *Skink*. John worried that all the luggage on his cart was Mr. Barton's.

"Mr. Tee-Van…?"

"Oh, hello, Mrs. Bostelmann. Thank you for recognizing me. I'm sorry I was looking elsewhere."

"That's all right, Mr. Tee-Van. I'm glad you're here to meet us. Do you remember my daughter, Hada?"

"Of course. Hello, Miss Bostelmann. Welcome to Bermuda."

"Thank you, Mr. Tee-Van. I am very excited to be here," Hada said.

"Do you want to leave your luggage here, Mrs. Bostelmann? I'm waiting for Mr. Barton. He will look for me here."

Else and Hada agreed. They left John to get in line for their crates with art supplies. It took only a few minutes.

They followed John as he walked a few yards carrying their cases. Else and Hada set their art supplies down as John boarded the *Skink*. He placed the Bostelmanns' luggage next to three cases the porter left for Mr. Barton. *Only three; what a relief.*

Else handed John a smaller case that he set under the center bench. She kept a purse over her shoulder. Hada repeated her mother's actions.

When his passengers were comfortably seated on the Skink, John told them he needed to locate Mr. Barton.

"We saw him on the ship," Else said.

"We sat with him at dinner last night," Hada added.

"Odd. I asked Mr. Barton if he met you on the ship. He didn't remember doing so. At any rate, that's who we're waiting for, Otis Barton. He seems to have made another acquaintance, a crewmember," John said.

"The pretty one?" Hada asked.

"I suppose so. I could see very little with so many people departing the ship."

Otis reappeared from the thinning crowd. He climbed aboard the *Skink* and mumbled, "Thank you for waiting." He then found a space and sat.

"I understand you met the Bostelmanns at dinner last evening..."

Otis looked at John and then at Else and Hada.

"Mrs. Bostelmann, Miss Bostelmann, this is Otis Barton," John said.

"We sat with you last evening. How do you do, Mr. Barton. I'm Else Bostelmann, and this is my daughter, Hada."

Otis tipped his hat but said nothing. The blank expression proved to John that Mr. Barton had no memory of the Bostelmanns although they were at the same table.

"The trip will take an hour, so I hope you enjoy the ride. It's a good view of Bermuda," John said. "We'll be traveling along the north coast."

"Is Hamilton the capital of Bermuda, Mr. Tee-Van?" Hada asked.

"That's correct, Miss Bostelmann..."

"Will you please call me Hada?"

"Yes. Hada. This is Hamilton, the capital." John pointed to a tall structure in the center of town. "That's where the Assembly meets. We'll go into St. George too, which the British made the seat of government in the early 16-hundreds."

Hada listened attentively.

"… Once the British settled the islands," John continued, "Bermuda's governor opened the new capital here in 1815. The city was named after a previous governor who served in the late 17-hundreds."

Although trying to listen, Else and Hada also gawked at other travelers loading trunks and suitcases into horse-drawn taxi carriages. John surveyed the docking canal searching for adequate clearance. He placed the propeller in gear, puttering slowly into the Hamilton Harbor.

"Have you learned a lot about Bermuda, Mr. Tee-Van?" Else asked.

"I suppose I have, Mrs. Bostelmann. But there's still a lot more I don't know."

"Is it always warm and sunny?" Hada asked.

"It's been warm in the months I've been here, Miss Bostelmann. Excuse me… Hada. However, we're in hurricane territory. The weather can get stormy surprisingly fast."

"Dr. Beebe stated in his last letter that our private quarters are outdoors in tents," Else said. "Is there a plan if we know a hurricane is coming?"

Otis lifted his head at the mention of tents for private quarters.

"Yes. Our laboratory space is a sturdy building. There's room to move personal items inside if a storm threatens."

Conversations remained light as the *Skink* cruised the shoreline bucking waves pushed by the cooling breeze from the north. Else and Hada never took their eyes off the land and the carriages traveling along North Shore Road. A few houses dotted the cliffs; a few more appeared under construction.

When they had been at sea for about thirty minutes, John took the boat in closer to land.

Hada pointed to a tall fortress ahead of them. "What's that, Mr. Tee-Van?"

"The large structure is Martello Tower. The Brits built it in the 1820s to defend the islands and stop invaders from entering Castle Harbor, which we're about to do."

"Is that a bridge under construction, Mr. Tee-Van? Is it a road for motor vehicles?"

"No, it's for a railroad to carry people and cargo between Hamilton and St. George. The islands don't permit motor vehicles except for emergency transportation and for those who have special privileges."

"Not us?" Hada asked.

"No, I'm afraid not."

John looked for a reaction from Otis. "Were you aware of motor car restrictions, Mr. Barton?" John asked.

"I read about the law," Otis responded. "I imagine it won't last much longer."

John steered the *Skink* under the unfinished bridge and across Castle Harbor. The water was calmer than the Atlantic, but it stayed choppy as the midday winds picked up. Otis and the Bostelmanns could see the harbor's shorelines on both sides.

As they neared Nonsuch Island's western landing, they saw a group of people starting to descend a winding path along a rugged cliff that headed to a level opening.

"That's your welcoming committee," John told his passengers. He pointed the bow at the island landing and slowed the motor.

"Oh, my…" Hada uttered.

"So that's Nonsuch Island where we'll be working?" Otis asked.

"Yes. It's a perfect location to launch your diving ball, don't you think?"

CHAPTER 11

Breaking Flesh

Will knew John would arrive soon with Otis Barton, the man of the hour, the man with the solution to Will's dilemma: How to conquer the ocean's depth?

Will was eager to tell the world about his exploration plans. He wanted to prove that there's life deep in the sea, life that exists without light and under enormous weight that would crush the human body. It was an achievement necessary to enlighten people about their planet, the importance of co-existing, of interdependence humans share with nature. He wanted it so others would join him in preserving nature, especially its living creatures.

By pulling specimens from the ocean's abyss, Will had already disproven the long-standing belief that nothing lived more than a few hundred feet deep. Disfigured and nearly liquefied by the extraordinary pressure change, the slimy bodies—a few surviving the ascent—confirmed that life was there, odd-looking creatures that lived as much as a mile deep.

Will's trawling discoveries increased his desire to investigate the mysterious environment in which organisms survived where man could not. His curiosity was more than a scientist seeking truth. It was a passion beyond explanation.

Recognizing the *Skink* in the distance, Will shouted for everyone to follow him. He wanted them to greet the arriving guests at the western landing.

He bounded over shrubs and branches like a schoolboy, nearly slipping on the sandy soil at the western cliff. He skidded down, his heels digging into the rocky earth and stirring a miniature avalanche.

He saw Otis Barton at the bow, his body twisted and looking in his direction. He saw Mrs. Bostelmann and her daughter bundled against the sea breeze.

"Ahoy. Welcome to Nonsuch Island," Will shouted.

Mrs. Bostelmann's daughter and John waved. Otis shifted on his bench and squared his shoulders to watch several people running down to meet them at their landing site. Will surprised Otis with a hero's reception.

Two interns—college boys in swim gear—bounded into the shallow harbor water and took the rope lines from John as he steered the boat parallel to shore. The boys took excited glances at the young woman sitting properly in the center of the *Skink*.

"Greetings, Mr. Barton." Will grabbed the younger man's hand and shook it vigorously. He then turned quickly to the Bostelmanns.

"Mrs. Bostelmann, Miss Bostelmann, welcome to Nonsuch, the home of New York Zoological Society's Department of Tropical Research. DTR as we refer to it."

The staff, some still descending the island's western cliff, applauded Will's welcoming comment.

"I won't take time now to introduce you to everyone. I know you're tired from your travels, and you still have a small mountain to climb before you can rest." Will had turned his head towards the cliff. "So, boys, please take our new staff members' luggage, and let's begin our ascent."

"Is this your bag, Miss Bostelmann?" a freckled boy asked Hada. She nodded, her cheeks turning pink.

The boy lifted her bag from the *Skink* as though it weighed nothing. Patten Jackson and another chap bumped him purposely when reaching for Mrs. Bostelmann's gear. The lad with eyes on Hada stumbled but regained his balance. Hada smiled at the freckled boy pretending to ignore the playful taunt.

"Be careful with those bags, gentlemen," Will scolded, turning quickly to swallow a laugh.

William Beebe, soon to be 52, nearly pushed Otis Barton up the incline. Chiriqui rode Will's shoulder, squawking and clinging to Will's neck.

"We're very excited to have you here, Mr. Barton. Our helmet dives and trawls have been productive, but all of Bermuda awaits your submersible ball."

"I received a telegram from Captain Butler while on the ship. He said the foundry is molding the sphere this week," Otis reported, huffing his way up the hill.

"It's June, Mr. Barton. Are they going to be able to deliver in a month?" Will asked.

"That's the promise, Dr. Beebe."

"Good. Then let's get you acquainted with Nonsuch Island and the staff."

Will's impression of Otis Barton had not changed since their first December meeting in his office. He recognized in the younger man an inability to communicate effectively, maybe because he was star struck. Will's popularity as a celebrity made some people nervous when meeting him.

Will tried hard to make Otis feel comfortable by spending time with him and the Bostelmanns. He paraded Otis around the island introducing him to every team member and the island caretakers, Arthur and Mrs. Tucker.

John followed Will and Otis and took notes when Will thought of something new to discuss. They walked the island's entire twenty-five acres. Will led Otis into the main building–the old hospital quarters–where the staff and interns were working. Most were sitting at tables near windows where they dissected flora and fauna from the sea.

The interns wrote while staff examined species under microscopes and dictated observations. The afternoon warmth held the pungent odor of fish and decaying specimen.

Will directed Otis to Gloria Hollister's laboratory table illuminated by the large windows.

"Glo, can you show Mr. Barton what you're working on?"

Gloria lifted her head and adjusted her strained eyes. She had examined a dragonfish.

"Will, I'm pleased with the way the whole fish body reacted to the potassium hydroxide."

"Please show Mr. Barton your technique. I need to check with Mrs. Tucker about dinner plans."

Will departed, leaving Gloria to entertain Otis, which made her uncomfortable.

"Is the fish transparent?" he asked. "What is it?"

"It's a dragonfish. Some call it a viperfish. They're not transparent but I made this one appear that way."

"How?"

"It's a chemical reaction. I use potassium hydroxide. I coat the fish and allow the chemical to make the scales and flesh reveal the skeleton. It helps us study and classify each species."

Gloria carefully lifted the tiny body eight inches long. "Would you like a closer look?"

Otis reached for the fish, which was not what Gloria intended. The texture surprised Otis. He twitched and broke the tail section from the body. He chuckled a nervous laugh and handed the damaged specimen back to Gloria.

"That's an ugly creature," Otis said.

Gloria said nothing. She stared at the rare and damaged dragonfish that was once the only flawless example of the species. She stood motionless trying not to scream or shout obscenities.

John entered the laboratory with Else Bostelmann. He saw the expression on Gloria's face and knew something was wrong.

"Gloria, this is Else Bostelmann, the artist I've been telling you about."

Gloria remained still. Else and John could see the fish body and a tail section in Gloria's hands. They knew they came upon a problem.

"I've been studying pictures of unusual fish to prepare myself for this assignment. I don't recognize the animal you're holding," Else said to break the uncomfortable silence.

"It's a dragonfish, Mrs. Bostelmann," John told her. "It was intact the last time I saw Miss Hollister working on it. What happened, Gloria?"

"I'm afraid I'm the guilty party," Otis confessed. "The tail broke when I was looking at the fish. It feels as awful as it looks."

"Really, Mr. Barton? I'm fascinated by it," Else offered. "I'm sorry you broke it. Do you have others like it, Mr. Tee-Van? If you need to see how I approach my work, I would like to begin with this specimen."

"No others, Mrs. Bostelmann. It's difficult to bring fish up from the deep and have them as good as this specimen was. It's why Dr. Beebe is excited to explore the ocean depths in Mr. Barton's submersible ball."

"Then I shall work with this sample. Can you tell me about its habitat?" Else asked Gloria, who remained comatose, still stunned, still silent.

"Gloria will set you a workspace next to hers," John said. "I'll take Mr. Barton to introduce him to our school interns. Do you have what you need, Mrs. Bostelmann?"

"I have watercolors I carry with me. I have brushes and paper. I just need a half-liter of water."

John put his hand on Otis Barton's shoulder and guided him away from Gloria Hollister's workspace. Gloria carefully set the fish onto a smooth board at her desk. She placed the broken tail on the board and aligned it with the body.

"Can you tell me about the fish, Miss Hollister?"

"I'm sorry, Mrs. Bostelmann. I'm very upset about what happened."

"I can tell, and I regret that Mr. Barton was so clumsy."

"We work hard to keep all of our specimens in pristine condition. That's important to Dr. Beebe and all of us working for DTR."

"I understand. So, tell me about this fish. What does it eat?"

"Shrimp, mostly. But they scavenge too."

Gloria described all she could about the viper dragonfish, information recorded during Dr. Beebe's recent outing.

"The *London Times* told of a British ichthyologist who discovered a new *Chauliodus* species in the Bathyal Zone," Gloria continued. "Oh, I'm sorry, you may not know about the Bathyal Zone…"

"I *do* know about it," Else said. "It's the underwater area between 250 and 2,000 meters."

Gloria stopped her preparation and looked at the artist.

"...I've been an amateur naturalist, Miss Hollister. I spent many years in an isolated part of Texas studying science and nature. It interests me so I'm eager to create images that may help you in your work."

"I'm very pleased to hear that, Mrs. Bostelmann, especially at this moment. Let me clear this table so you can begin."

The two women worked together clearing space next to Gloria's workstation. Regaining some enthusiasm, Gloria pushed a straight-back chair up to the table.

"Do you have enough light?" she asked Else while moving the dragonfish to a porcelain coated pan and placing it in the center of the table.

"Yes, it should be plenty. Do you have a magnifying glass?"

Gloria walked to Dr. Beebe's desk and retrieved his. "It's Will's, but I know he won't mind."

Else examined the slender fish's large head. The long-pointed teeth, almost transparent, were wicked looking needles longer than one might assume based on the size of the fish.

"I should explain something about the fish," Gloria said. "The skin is black. I've altered the color with a chemical so we could see inside the creature."

"Did you photograph it before you treated it with your chemical?" Else asked.

Gloria reached across her table, pushed some papers to the side, and uncovered a black and white photograph, five by seven inches. She handed it to Else.

"The white pan may make it look darker in the photo than it is," Else said. "Describe what you remember."

"It was more charcoal than a deep black. The skin was still glistening when we brought it in with the nets. But it faded to a very dull color by the time I had it on my lab table."

"The teeth are an incredible feature; very… very intimidating. Would you agree?"

"Yes. And the jaw opens very wide because it's hinged. Its prey would have little chance of escape."

Gloria poured water into two 500-milliliter beakers. Else moved the pan around on the table to select the best light reflections. She studied the photograph and then began.

Else dipped one of her larger brushes into a beaker and lightly covered an oval area she had drawn on a tablet. She dipped a smaller brush, touched dark blue pigment, and set the point of the brush against the moistened oval. Gloria saw the paint bleed to the edges.

"This will take me a few minutes. You may watch but if you have other things to do, please do not wait on me, Miss Hollister."

"I'm sorry. I've seen John's wife and others paint pictures of our specimen, but for some reason I felt an urge to look over your shoulder, Mrs. Bostelmann. You seem surer of what you're about to do. May I ask your age?"

"Yes, but an odd question…"

"I'm sorry, Mrs. Bostelmann. I don't mean to offend you…"

"I'm not offended. I'm forty-seven. Is that too old to be Dr. Beebe's artist?"

Gloria laughed. She knew by Mrs. Bostelmann's tone she was playing with her.

"You're not too old to be our artist, but maybe too young to be our mother. We could use a mother; the youngsters helping us."

"…including my own. I've already heard about the need."

In a more serious voice, Gloria added, "My mother wants to be here. Elswyth's mother is living in St. George. Will's father has been here too, so we have had plenty of parenting, but not the kind an organization like ours needs. Perhaps. Maybe. I don't really know."

Else listened and saw Miss Hollister's face. She knew distress and how to recognize it in others.

"Forgive my ranting, Mrs. Bostelmann. I'm still upset by Mr. Barton's carelessness."

"Does the dragonfish swim alone?"

"No, not like a barracuda. But not in schools either. Perhaps with one or two other vipers close by."

Else continued to paint for thirty minutes while Gloria cleaned her workspace.

"Have you already put Mrs. Bostelmann to work?" Will asked when entering the laboratory with usual briskness.

"She volunteered. We had an emergency," Gloria responded.

"I don't like that word, *emergency*, Glo. Fill me in later. Let's see what our new artist is doing."

Else Bostelmann leaned back away from her watercolor painting. She had done more than draw the fish in a pan. She had put it in chase of a shrimp with a wide-open mouth and hunger glistening in its eyes.

"Oh, damn. Did you beat me to the ocean floor, Mrs. Bostelmann? You didn't tell me you'd already seen a viper chasing its prey."

CHAPTER 12

Shuffling Affairs

Will Beebe went along with Elswyth's plan. She had tolerated the rugged life of a naturalist for as long as she could. She packed many of her things–clothes, undergarments, toiletries– and moved them to the St. George's Hotel, a twenty-minute boat ride from Nonsuch Island.

Will joined Elswyth in St. George Saturday evening after hosting a staff gathering to introduce Otis Barton, Else Bostelmann, and Else's daughter. Will got out his best whiskey and rum and poured a shot for all who wanted to drink.

Otis chose whiskey and was the first served. He added a splash of water.

They offered Else Bostelmann the second pour, but she covered her glass with her hand. "I prefer Riesling," she told the gregarious host in her best German accent.

Will laughed a full belly laugh, which brought laughter from others.

"I think we can accommodate, *Frau* Bostelmann," Will said.

While imbibing, Will invited Otis and Else to join him for a Sunday afternoon helmet dive following church services. Otis told Will he had done helmet dives since he was a teenager. Else had no experience. Will explained that it was an opportunity to go on an underwater adventure that could help her when she began to paint for him.

"Monday, if the weather permits, we'll have the *Gladisfen* crew take us on a hunt for deep-sea fish," Will said.

The staff party ended the day for the Department of Tropical Research. John Tee-Van readied the *Skink* to take Will to St. George while Gloria helped the Bostelmann women settle for the night.

Will offered Otis his and Elswyth's room since they would be at the St. George's Hotel. As he walked into their hotel suite, Elswyth greeted him with a familiar announcement. "I've invited Mother to join us. I hope you don't mind, Will."

"Of course not, El. Do I have time to bathe? It's been a long day."

"Yes but be fast. I'm hungry."

Will Beebe was fast at everything. He was ready for dinner in twenty minutes. With a tie. He escorted Elswyth and her mother to the hotel restaurant where they were seated at the center table.

"Did Mr. Barton and the others arrive on schedule, Will?" Elswyth asked.

"They all arrived as planned, yes indeed."

"Did Mr. Barton bring his diving ball, Dr. Beebe?" Mrs. Ricker asked.

"They'll ship it in a month I'm told. The steel is being poured into a mold at a foundry in New Jersey. Then they'll take it to another plant where they'll put in the windows."

"Are you nervous about it, Will?"

"Excited, El. Not nervous. I'm eager to dive as deep as the ball will take us."

"And how deep is that?" Mrs. Ricker wanted to know.

"According to Mr. Barton and his engineering partner, the winch and drum we brought from our work on the *Arcturus* can hold three-thousand four-hundred feet, which means we can dive more than a half-mile."

"My goodness, Dr. Beebe. Are you intending to go under the water a half mile?"

"That's my hope, Mother Ricker."

Elswyth sat up straighter. "Will, Mother has an announcement to share."

"Really? What is it?"

"It's about my name, Dr. Beebe. I think since Elswyth is using my maiden name, her middle name, for her writing, then I should use it too. It will be less confusing to people."

"So, I should begin calling you… Mother *Thane*?" Will asked.

"I'd prefer you call me Edith, but Miss Thane is fine too. I would like my identity linked to my daughter."

"Are you comfortable with that, Will?" Elswyth asked.

"I believe so."

"There's more, Will…"

"More names?"

"No, Dear. I want to go back to England and begin my research. My publisher says sales are doing well. I will have plenty of money."

"When? When do you want to leave?"

"Soon, Will. I don't like the heat. It makes me ill."

Will let Elswyth's proclamation sink in. "I encourage you to do your research, El, but I will miss you. Probably more than you realize."

Elswyth's shoulders settled as the tension trickled from her body. She had been nervous to tell Will she had moved up her departure because of her opportunity.

"You'll be fine without me here, Will. You have a way about you that attracts people. You'll be busy. You won't miss me as much as you think."

"I will go with her, Dr. Beebe, and take care of her."

"You're wrong, El. I will miss both of you, but I want you to write and be successful."

"Thank you, Will."

Elswyth's revelation did not come as a total surprise. Elswyth fell in love with the British monarchy when they visited London. She said she wanted to write about the Royal family. This could be her first step.

With dinner and wine consumed, Will and Elswyth walked Mrs. Ricker–now Miss Thane–up the stairs to her hotel room next to theirs. After saying good night, Will opened the door for Elswyth.

"I wasn't honest when I implied I don't worry about you," Elswyth said as Will closed their hotel door. "I worry constantly about you diving into the ocean."

"No need to fret over it. It hasn't happened yet and who knows if all the people working on Mr. Barton's design can build a safe submersible."

"You're not helping…"

"I don't intend to be naïve."

"You will test it first, I hope…"

"Yes, of course. My goal is to live to tell the world it's full of creatures that were probably here long before we began to walk on soil."

"But you don't have to be the one to take all the risks. Someone can describe to you what they saw and how it behaved. Send Mr. Barton if that's why he's building a submersible ball."

"I can't, El. Mr. Barton is a dreamer…"

"…as you are."

"No, he dreams of adventure. I dream of finding the truth. I have to see the fish that make up our planet. I need to discover how they survived."

"I give in, Will Beebe. You will do what you intend just like you always have. Obstacles mean nothing to you."

"There's danger, El, but only if we become careless. I'm not careless, Elswyth."

"Will, I'm from Iowa. I don't know a lot about boats. I don't like them. But when I look at the boats Governor Bols gave you to use, I see vessels that are barely afloat. I see old, rotten wood, steam engines that burn oil inefficiently, and crews that spend more days playing dominos than they do sailing the seas."

"Every task comes with challenges. If things important to accomplish were easy, then people would have already done them…"

"Oh, Will, for heaven's sake…"

"…the war in Europe would have ended much sooner. Man would have run a mile under four minutes. There'd be airplanes to fly us to Bermuda. Accomplishments don't happen easily; they're hard. No one wants to put in the effort, show the courage."

"I know I cannot make my point any better than I have, Will Beebe. You're my husband. I shall worry for your safety every minute I am in London just as I would if I were standing on a rickety boat and watching you descend. I trust you. But hear me, you're still putting yourself at risk and I don't think it's necessary."

Will sat on the bed and removed his shoes. He slid them underneath the bed, stood, took off his tie, and unbuttoned his shirt. He looked at Elswyth.

"After church and lunch, I'm going to take Mr. Barton and Mrs. Bostelmann on the *Skink* for a helmet dive. Would you care to join us?"

"Do they know how to helmet dive?"

"Mr. Barton said he's done it. Mrs. Bostelmann does not."

"You take them, Will. I'm sure John and Gloria will go. I have a chapter to edit, so I will use the quiet to do that."

Will hung his clothes and went to Elswyth who had gotten into bed. He laid beside her. "You're a good woman, Elswyth Thane. And soon, you'll be a well-known author."

"I will be thrilled if you're right."

She put her head against his chest.

Will held Elswyth as memories raced to another time. He did not want Elswyth to leave although he told her to go. In truth, her announcement gave him instant heartache.

CHAPTER 13

Coffee

Else Bostelmann slept much better than she expected. The women's dormitory was a small room, but dark and well-suited for sleeping. Hada stayed in a tent the same as other interns.

No one stirred as Else made her way across the grounds. She had personal things to put away in the tent where Hada slept. She opened the tent flap and nearly tripped on shoes and clothes Hada left piled carelessly. Else regained her balance and tried to search quietly.

Hada had spent her Saturday evening with her new friends. Else saw them sitting around a bonfire, singing, and telling stories.

Most interns were college students, but a few were still in high school. Some were looking for inspiration to help them shape their futures. Almost all came from wealthy families.

Else tied a tent flap back to let the first morning light help her see. A breeze caught a welcoming smell of coffee brewing. She whispered, "Guten Morgen, meine Lieblingsbohne."

"Mrs. Bostelmann. Are you in there?"

The voice startled Else, but she recognized it as Mr. Tee-Van's.

"Yes, you surprised me, Mr. Tee-Van." Else pushed the other tent flap and stepped out. John Tee-Van had a towel over his shoulder. His thick dark hair lay wet and flatter. His body dripped from a morning swim.

"I thought you might be up. Are you ready for Mrs. Tucker's coffee?"

"Yes, the aroma is making me very ready."

"Good. Please join me and let me introduce you. She's a native Bermudian."

Else followed John into Mrs. Tucker's kitchen. Mrs. Tucker seemed excited to have a woman who was much closer to her age than the others. She poured Else's coffee smiling broadly.

"What are your plans for the day, Mr. Tee-Van?" Mrs. Tucker asked as she moved the coffee pot to his cup.

"Well, I hope we can help Mrs. Bostelmann and Mr. Barton become comfortable because we want to involve them quickly in our activities."

"Is Mr. Barton ready for coffee too?" Mrs. Tucker asked.

"I don't know. Have you seen him this morning, Mrs. Bostelmann?" John asked.

"Not yet. I have seen only the two of you so far. The island is very calm compared to our arrival."

"You will learn, my dear lady, some Sunday mornings are much busier than others," Mrs. Tucker explained. "When Dr. Beebe has taken his staff to Hamilton for dancing and partying, I brew coffee to settle them down as they arrive home in the early morning hours, not to wake them up."

"I don't believe you will be settling me at this hour, Mrs. Tucker," Else said. "I prefer to wake with my coffee."

"Will plans to take Mr. Barton and Mrs. Bostelmann helmet diving this afternoon," John continued. "Tomorrow, the *Gladisfen* will take them on a trawling exploration."

Else and John gave up their chairs as some younger staff members invaded Mrs. Tucker's kitchen for breakfast. It took the gentle caretaker away from her conversation with the new lady.

Before separating, John told Else the plan: They would board the *Skink* later in the day for a series of helmet dives. He described how young staff members would pump air through the hose so the diver could walk on the sand.

"Should I put on swimwear under my clothes?" Else asked.

"Yes. Be prepared for any opportunity," he told Else. "It will be a full day."

John explained many days are spent exclusively in swimwear. He tried to prepare her for Dr. Beebe's outdoor lifestyle.

Otis Barton lay in Will Beebe's bed, appreciating the privacy but irritated by an uncomfortable night's sleep. The bed was hard. The air was stale. And the mosquitoes large and aggressive.

Still, it was Will Beebe's bed. He had accomplished an important goal. He had created a partnership with his idol, the famed man who enthusiastically awaited Otis's diving ball. Together, he and Dr. Beebe would descend to sea depths unthinkable and ascend into fame. One night of discomfort was worth the fulfillment of his dream.

Morning light penetrated thin curtains in Dr. Beebe's small living quarters. Otis swung his legs from the bed and planted his bare feet on wood planks, a texture harsher than Otis anticipated. He winced.

He moved slowly to a dresser basin. He poured water into the bowl and splashed his face.

His scratchy face made him wonder if the small island had a barber. A warm wet towel and lathery shave would feel good about now.

He picked up his safety razor and wondered if he could stand to shave with it. He decided if no barber, he'd rather go unshaven.

He pushed his arms into a long-sleeve denim shirt and pulled on khaki trousers. He was tying his canvas shoes when a knock at the door was followed by a young man's voice asking if he was awake.

"I'm awake, yes. Who's asking?"

"My name is Patten Jackson. I'm one of the interns."

"What do you want, Mr. Jackson?"

"Would you like breakfast, Mr. Barton? I have coffee from Mrs. Tucker's kitchen."

"I'll take the coffee. No breakfast, thank you."

Otis went to the door and accepted a steaming cup of coffee from the tall, thin, wavy-haired boy. He wondered if the lad was expecting a tip for delivering his coffee. Patten stood grinning in the doorway.

"Is there anything else?" Otis asked.

"No, sir. Well, yes."

"What?"

"I heard you created a ball you and Dr. Beebe are going to use to go to the ocean's bottom. Is that true?" Patten asked.

"We won't reach the bottom. We hope to go down more than half a mile, though."

"Gee, how did you come up with the design, Mr. Barton?"

Otis opened the door a little wider. "Common-sense physics. A sphere is the only shape where pressure applies equally from all directions." Otis held up his hands and shaped them as though he held a ball between them. "Therefore, the pressure from a point on the right is equalized by the pressure from a point on the left. If the sphere is perfectly round, seamless, and made from cast iron, then it should withstand a great deal more pressure than objects without the spherical qualities."

"Holy smokes, that's smart. You're pretty smart, aren't you, Mr. Barton?"

"I'm educated. Education and curiosity are a good combination. You should know that if you're working for Dr. Beebe."

"Did you discover this thing about the sphere, Mr. Barton?"

"No. What did you say your name is?"

"Patten…"

"Yes, of course. *Patten…*"

"…yes, Mr. Barton?"

"No, Patten. Archimedes set the stage for understanding the significance of shapes in nature. I just listened to my college professors and applied what they taught."

"College is a good thing, don't you think, Mr. Barton. I'm thinking about Princeton. In New

Jersey."

"Yes, college is good. I'm not so sure about Princeton."

"Gee, really, Mr. Barton?"

"No. I'm having fun with you. Princeton is a fine place to learn."

"I think I'd like it there. There are some really good athletes there. Do you like sports, Mr. Barton?"

"I do, but I need to get ready for my day, Patten. Thank you for bringing the coffee."

"You're welcome, Mr. Barton. I'll see ya later then."

Otis closed the door and sat at Will Beebe's small table. He looked around the sparsely decorated room, noticing more books than shelving to store them. Many were piled on the floor. Will also kept a small microscope in a wooden box that sat on the floor by the table.

Otis Barton's impression of William Beebe was changing. He seemed more common than Otis expected. He reminded him of a hot dog salesman at the ballpark. Constantly moving. Energetic but ordinary with a Brooklyn accent.

Despite the middle-class character, Otis could not deny Dr. Beebe's mastery of people and situations. He was king of Nonsuch Island, that was evident. The entire staff worshipped the man.

Otis walked to the window that faced St. George's and St. David's islands. On the grounds below were a scattering of tents and staff scurrying with chores. The sun cast deep shadows around the clusters of native cedars. Patches of intense sunlight speckled the ground.

Otis decided to venture outside. He closed the door and tried locking it. He struggled with the old skeleton key. The lock seemed rusty and stiff.

John Tee-Van came out of his room, his hair wet but neatly combed. He pushed his glasses higher on his nose with his right index finger. "Having trouble, Mr. Barton?"

"The lock seems gummed up."

"Not surprised. None of us use them. Don't even know if they work," John told Otis. "Have you had breakfast?"

Otis shoved the key into his pocket. "No. Not much of a breakfast person. A boy brought me coffee. Extremely chatty."

"The interns are a good bunch. Most work without pay, not that they need money. Their parents are zoological society patrons, mostly because of Will. They make large donations to our expeditions."

"The interns' parents pay for the expedition?"

"Some of it. In return they want their sons and daughters to get up at sunrise and learn the value of teamwork, respect, and hard, physical labor."

John chuckled when thinking about the parents. He told Otis he pictured them sitting by their pools, sipping forbidden alcohol, and living a passive, luxurious lifestyle. Odd, he said, that they would want their children to experience tent living and early morning chores. He tried to explain the irony to Otis who showed no interest.

CHAPTER 14

Helmet Awe

"Hello again, Mr. Barton."

Patten Jackson was one of three young men standing on the narrow dock at the west side of Nonsuch Island when Otis picked his way down the steep, rocky slope. The boys were there to assist Dr. Beebe, Gloria, and John in launching the *Skink* for Mr. Barton's and Mrs. Bostelmann's first Bermuda helmet dive.

Else carefully walked the decline, dodging loose rocks that tormented ankles and knees. Hada Bostelmann followed her mother, hoping to catch her if Else slipped.

Will Beebe carried Chiriqui on his shoulder. Gloria scolded Trumps for darting between Will's legs while barking at the laughing monkey.

When they reached the dock, John Tee-Van's head popped up from inside the *Skink*. He had fueled the boat and loaded diving equipment, except for Dr. Beebe's helmet. Will carried it to protect the glass windows from getting scratched.

"Are we ready to launch, boys?" Will asked the young men.

"Aye, Captain Beebe," Patten replied, jumping into the *Skink*.

"Good. Help the ladies aboard, mates," Will commanded.

Patten and the other two lads assisted Mrs. Bostelmann as she stepped into the *Skink*. Hada stood behind the boys watching.

"Please be careful, Mother," she said.

"If I drown, Tochter, you know who to blame."

"Don't make jokes, Mother."

"It's no joke. I'm the responsible party, young lady," Will said. "But I assure you, your mother will return wet but alive."

"Thank you, Dr. Beebe. You must know she is foolishly brave. She may try to show off her courage."

"I'm the only one who gets to show off. Your mother must follow my rules. She will understand when she walks on the sand at three to four fathoms."

"Hear that, Mother. Follow the rules!"

Hada spoke so Else could hear her above the revving engine as the *Skink* pulled away. Still worried and clinging to Trumps' leash, Hada waved a weak good-bye.

Two boys stood beside Hada and Trumps envying their buddy Patten. Seeing their pained expressions, Patten gave a humble thumbs up.

The boat did not travel far. John steered it around the southwestern tip of Nonsuch and guided it east towards Soldier Bay at the southern tip of Cooper's Island.

"Did you have time to attend church with Mrs. Beebe?" Else asked.

"Yes. The minister gave a fire and brimstone sermon this morning, Mrs. Bostelmann."

"Was there a reason?" she asked.

"His ancestors are Portuguese, Mrs. Bostelmann. I think he's still angry with the English. It gives him an excuse to scold them."

Will Beebe knew where there was a shallow and level opening less than 20 feet under the surface and less than 100 feet offshore. The water was clear and warm, but a cool current brought in a variety of fish and microscopic critters upon which the coral feasted.

"Let's anchor in that light green patch, John," Will said. "The sand bottom gives us a good view through the box. You and I will go together, Mr. Barton," Will said. "Use the helmet next to Mr. Tee-Van."

"Your helmet looks a little banged up, Dr. Beebe," Otis commented, "would you rather I use the older one?"

"No, those nicks are reminders of some harrowing times, Mr. Barton. My copper helmet and I have been through a few rough events together."

"Yes, sir. Can you tell me about the marks? What were you doing when you got those dents?" Otis asked, pointing to the deep scars on Will's helmet.

"Each one has a story, I suppose. This one, for instance, I did when I banged into some black lava in the Galápagos. This one when I became twisted in my air hose near Panama."

"May I see your helmet, Dr. Beebe?"

"Certainly. It's copper with brass here and there."

Otis Barton handled Dr. Beebe's dive helmet as though made of gold. He peeked inside at the glass window through which Will Beebe had seen underwater life he wrote about in his last two books. Otis felt the padded arches that sat on Dr. Beebe's shoulders.

Gloria, who said nothing since boarding the *Skink*, watched Otis fondle Will's helmet like a kid touching a baseball signed by Babe Ruth. She looked at Will and rolled her eyes. Will squinted an acknowledgment. John saw the quiet communication and turned his head to hide his smirk.

Otis handed the helmet back to Dr. Beebe, moving more cautiously than he did when looking at Gloria's delicate viper specimen. She shook her head and closed her eyes, angered with Otis's patronizing worship.

John pulled back on the *Skink's* throttle and coasted the boat over the glistening bluish-green water. Else looked over the side at the sand below. *A touch of lemon yellow, white, and a speck of red,* she thought to herself.

A few small fish swam near the bottom, cruising slowly. "They're enjoying rays of sun, Mrs. Bostelmann. They won't stay long," Will said.

"Oh, I hope they stay, Dr. Beebe. I want them to come close to me. Don't scare them away, Mr. Barton."

Gloria blurted a hefty laugh as John turned his back again so he wouldn't be caught joining her.

"Glo, give Mr. Barton a hand with his descent," Will instructed. "I'll enter the water from the starboard bow. You take the port stern, Mr. Barton. Glo, help him."

"I'm fine, Miss Hollister. Just hand me the helmet when I'm in."

The two men rolled backward together, splashing into the bay. When Otis emerged, he lifted from the water on the chain ladder. Gloria placed the helmet over his head. John did the same for Will.

Patten readied the hand pump in the boat's center and began his task. The pump fed both air hoses.

John and Gloria handed their respective divers a weight belt. Otis strapped his on eager to show the crew he was an experienced helmet diver. As Else Bostelmann watched Otis handle the helmet, belt, and his descent, she became nervous. She leaned toward the starboard side and saw Dr. Beebe's feet touch the sand.

"They appear to be in a contest, Mrs. Bostelmann, something men do to impress others, but I'm not certain who," Gloria said.

"I recommend you take your time descending. You will need to swallow several times as you go down, which is hard to remember when you have the heavy helmet on your shoulders and you're nervous about the air."

"Do I just breathe normally, Miss Hollister?"

"Yes, don't hold your breath. Breathe normally the moment I place the helmet on your shoulders even before you descend. Get used to it quickly."

"And why do I need to swallow?"

"…because the pressure increases as you lower yourself in the water, which can create pain in your ears, especially if you go too quickly without allowing them to adjust to the pressure change by swallowing," Gloria explained.

"I suppose I should have asked these questions much earlier."

"It wouldn't have mattered, Mrs. B. Is it okay if I call you Mrs. B?" Gloria asked.

"Please call me what you wish, young lady, just explain why it would not have mattered."

"…because instructions mean nothing on dry land. Now is when your attention is on diving.

You're learning much quicker now."

John nodded in agreement. Else looked at him and then back at Gloria. "Go through the steps, Miss Hollister."

"It's Gloria. Will calls me Glo, which you can as well."

"I'm old fashioned, Miss Hollister. Tell me each thing I need to do."

"The first is to relax. Look at the men walking on the sand. The water is heavier than air, so each step takes more effort. Go slowly and feel every sensation. It's amazing."

"Okay, assume I'm relaxed. What next?" Else asked.

"Get into the water, so you're used to it," John Tee-Van said.

"…after that, swim to the boat, lift yourself on the chain ladder, like Mr. Barton and Will did. I'll lower the helmet over your shoulders," Gloria continued.

"Never stop your normal breathing," John repeated.

"I'll hand you your weight belt, which is about twelve pounds based on your size and inexperience.

Else stopped her questions with her mind racing: *Auch du liebe Güte! Wodrauf habe ich mich eingelassen.* Her courage faded but she knew she had to prove herself, nonetheless.

"They're coming up," Patten shouted.

Gloria and John went to their respective divers and assisted by taking their weight belts first, then helping with the dive helmets. When they were lifted, Patten stopped pumping.

"Good show, Mr. Barton," Will said.

John and Gloria looked at each other, John lifting an eyebrow because Will's tone was sincere. He didn't offer sincere compliments very often.

Otis Barton said nothing, but his physical demeanor gloated. He had just made his first dive with Dr. William Beebe, the man he hoped to succeed as the world's most celebrated naturalist.

The enlarged ego filled the boat and quieted conversation. It even affected Else and air-pumping Patten.

Otis dried his puffed chest unaware of his effect on others.

Will saw Mr. Barton's ego bring on unfriendly thoughts from Gloria and John, which he worried might hinder their future dives in the sphere.

Despite Else Bostelmann's anxiety, she followed Gloria and John's instructions. She entered the water, swam a few strokes, and allowed her body to adjust to the temperature. It felt refreshing. Stimulating.

She swam to the chain ladder swaying in the water but struggled to hold on so she could place her foot on the first rung. Eventually she stepped up and controlled her balance. She timed the ladder's rhythmic bobs, caught the rung she wanted, and rose enough to grab the belt from Gloria. She leaned against the boat and wrapped it around her waist.

Else then closed her eyes as Gloria set the helmet into place. Her first sensation was an eerie hollow sound from the encapsulation. She opened her eyes, stepped down, and peered through the glass window at the underwater world climbing over her head.

Gloria said something but it was too muffled to hear. Else lifted her eyes to see Gloria's face distorted by rippling water. The colors and lines blended into indistinguishable light.

Else applied pressure to the breastplate with her left hand as she let gravity and her weight belt pull her down the anchor rope. She let the anchor rope slip through her right hand as she descended. Descending slowly, she held her breath, something Gloria and John warned her not to do.

Finally, she let it escape her nostrils then sucked the first gulp of air through her mouth. Nothing different. Her lungs filled. Her breathing was the same as if she were still on the boat. *The air is musty, but perfectly fine.*

But then pressure built in her ears. Gloria had told her if that happened to grip the anchor rope to stop her descent. She did. She swallowed several times, which seemed to help, and continued down.

Else assumed she was nearly eight meters below the boat when her feet touched the sandy bottom. She clung to the rope for the first minute while she got her bearings. The streaking sunlight illuminated a variety of objects, some waving in the distance. The yellows, faded reds, and oranges stood out against the bluish-green water.

She let loose of the rope and took her first step towards the closest coral grouping. A peacock flounder the size of a dinner platter tossed aside the sand in which it hid. The sudden movement startled Else who watched the flounder wiggle across the sand in search of a new resting spot.

Else turned 30 degrees to aim her helmet to her right. She spied a barracuda suspended halfway between her and the bay surface. It appeared to be a meter long and very menacing. Its lower jaw locked in anger while a few bottom teeth anchored like stalagmites caught the sun's rays. Else knew the fish was not a real threat, but its stare was unsettling.

When she turned to work her way toward the coral, a faint shadow in the sand signaled a large animal approached. Again, startled, it took Else a few seconds to realize Dr. Beebe had joined her on the sea bottom. He could see the fright in her eyes.

Will Beebe motioned for Else to continue to approach the coral. He reached out his right hand and Else took it.

They walked a few steps before Dr. Beebe released her hand. He stopped and turned towards her to get her attention. Else responded.

Will took a zinc-laminated tablet dangling at his left side. He scratched a message and turned it for Else to read: *"Look close at coral."*

Else did a slow nod and watched Dr. Beebe point to a tiny fairy basslet only six centimeters long. It peeked its bluish-lavender head from between a ribbon coral sitting atop a waist-high star coral. Will touched Else's arm to get her attention again. She looked into his helmet. He motioned for her to watch.

She started to lean in so she could get a closer look at the magnificent colors covering what looked like two large etched rocks. But Will stopped her.

He held up his right pointer finger and moved it closer to the tiny creature. As his finger approached the fish, the little tree-like forms on the coral suddenly folded and disappeared, leaving the fairy basslet naked against the pocked coral shells.

Else turned toward Dr. Beebe who was laughing about his underwater magic trick. She smiled and asked, "What just happened?" She forgot Dr. Beebe couldn't hear her, at least not well enough to understand her question. She whispered in German, *Wie dumm von mir.*

Else and Dr. Beebe pulled their way up the anchor ropes after a few more minutes of exploring. When Will popped from the water, John was there to help. Will climbed the chain ladder quickly and turned to help Mrs. Bostelmann board the boat.

Excited by the adventure, she sat in the boat's middle still huffing. She pulled a towel over her shoulders. "Can you explain about the coral, Dr. Beebe?" Else asked, wrapping the towel tighter.

"You know, Mrs. B, coral are animals. Each coral polyp produces calcium carbonate. After hundred of years, the carbonate shapes the mounds we saw."

"Were the little trees live coral?"

"They're called Christmas tree worms; sea worms with the formal name, *Spirobranchus tricornis.* They make themselves at home in the coral skeletons. They disappear when danger approaches."

"There were so many shapes, Dr. Beebe. Do you know all the different corals?"

"Some of what you saw weren't corals. They were sponges, sea fans, anemone..." Gloria said.

"They're all animals, not plants," Dr. Beebe added. "Yes, I've learned much about coral over the years. However, my knowledge of zoology began with birds."

"You became famous as an ornithologist," Otis Barton said, joining the conversation. "I read your books, your travelogue searching for pheasants all over the world."

Will thanked Mr. Barton for knowing about his long history as a naturalist. And yes, he was best known as an ornithologist, becoming curator in the Bronx Zoo while still in his twenties. He proudly talked about designing large displays where birds could fly under enclosed netting.

"I saw them," Else added.

"Where to next, Dr. Beebe?" John asked.

Will directed John to a dive site nearby, deeper with more species. Parrotfish, squirrelfish, sergeant majors, four-eye butterflyfish, bar jacks, and schools of wrasse and hamlets. The fish swam through a forest of coral, sea fans, barrel sponge, and giant tube sponge.

It was common to see a squadron of squid floating by in perfect formation. Larger fish—groupers and yellow jacks—swam in the distance waiting for their mealtime.

Otis Barton again dove first, but this time with John Tee-Van. Will took over the pumping duties so Patten could get a breather.

Gloria dove with Else. The two women connected much better than the men while exploring underwater.

When the *Skink* docked, John, Gloria, and the intern jumped off and secured the boat. Otis gathered his things and stepped ashore. He said something.

Will and the others picked up their gear and straightened the *Skink* to be ready for the next outing. They didn't notice Otis's departure. Finally looking up, they saw him already near the ridge.

Gloria looked at John, who shrugged his shoulders.

"Is he a genius and socially naïve, Will?" Gloria asked. "Or is he just rich and rude?"

Will didn't respond. He pulled his gear together and quietly led his team up the slope.

CHAPTER 15

Departing Shots

Will was up early Monday morning and swimming in St. George's Harbor before sunrise. Chiriqui sat on the dock eating berries, squawking at Will to hurry. He got even louder when Will emerged, grabbed his towel, and began to climb the hill toward the St. George's Hotel.

Elswyth surprised Will when he found her sitting up in bed with a notebook in her hands. Chiri jumped from Will's shoulder and sprang onto the bed to greet her, but the monkey got an ambivalent reception.

"Are you feeling all right, Elswyth?"

"I'm fine, Will, but I spent this morning planning."

"Planning what?"

"I think Mother and I shall leave quite soon for New York. And then London. Do you mind?"

Will rubbed his bald head with his towel and walked toward his closet to grab his khakis and a shirt. "Did you have your plan in mind when we spoke Saturday evening?" he asked Elswyth.

"I had no plan, Will, but our conversation made me think."

He pulled the shorts over his swimwear and turned to face his wife, placing his right hand on her soft cheek. "I love you, Elswyth. Give me the sad news so I can prepare. When are you departing?"

"The *Bermuda* leaves for New York this evening," she said. "Mother and I will stay in Manhattan for three days and board the *RMS Olympic*."

"That soon? Shall I cancel my day's activities with Mr. Barton and Mrs. Bostelmann?"

"No, of course not. Let's have breakfast and say our farewells."

When Will Beebe boarded the *Gladisfen*, Elswyth's breakfast comment was on his mind. She said her publisher was meeting her in New York with arrangements set for London. *Maybe she's right. She didn't have a specific time, but things were in motion.*

Will and Elswyth knew from the beginning their relationship needed to be one of convenience, tolerance, and discretion. They built their attraction on intellectual admiration.

Intimacy comforted, but it was not a priority.

Edward Millett, the *Gladisfen's* captain, greeted Will when the naturalist set his gear on deck. "Where to first, Dr. Beebe?" Millett asked.

"Take us to Nonsuch Island, Captain. We'll pick up John and Glo and I'll introduce you to two new staff members. I want them to see how your crew trawls."

"Very well, sir."

Captain Millett shouted commands to a dozen mates and fishermen manning the sixty-five-foot tug. The boat had sea-worn wrinkles like the captain's face.

He steered his vessel around St. David's Island and into Castle Harbor where the rest of his passengers awaited.

Else Bostelmann stood on the small Nonsuch Island dock where the *Skink* was tied. Jefferson, the Bermuda native who helped by driving the boat, waited for his other passengers as they scurried down the cliff.

John and Gloria led the parade. They carried a few pieces of gear, Chiri riding John's shoulders and Trumps trailing behind Gloria. Hada followed with two boys tagging along. They said they'd help Hada with Trumps.

"I don't see Mr. Barton," John said to Else upon arrival. "Is he already here?"

"I've not seen him, Mr. Tee-Van."

Gloria turned to look back at the path. Otis Barton was not in sight. "Have you seen him this morning?" she asked the interns.

They shook their heads.

"I saw the *Gladisfen* through my binoculars," John said. "One of you better go get him."

The two boys looked at each other and both dashed toward the path. Trumps barked and chased them up the embankment. He stopped abruptly when he heard, "*Trumps!*" Gloria's voice had an edginess even John hadn't heard.

"The director hates tardiness," Gloria said, seething.

"Mr. Barton was up late, too," Hada Bostelmann offered. "We saw him when the interns were singing by the campfire around eleven o'clock."

"Yes, but you got up to do your chores," Gloria responded quickly.

"I didn't want to, Miss Hollister," Hada confessed.

"…but you did because you're responsible."

"Let's be prepared," John said. "Get in the boat, Glo. Start the motor, please, Jefferson. Are you okay for the ride to the *Gladisfen*, Mrs. Bostelmann?"

"Ready."

"Hada, take Trumps with you and let the boys know we're leaving in five minutes with or without Mr. Barton."

"I will, Miss Hollister. Come on, Trumps. Come with me."

Hada and Trumps headed up the embankment. They stopped when they heard John say, "There he comes."

Gloria mumbled something before encouraging Hada to go ahead. "Don't wait on Mr. Barton," she said for Otis to hear.

Otis, Hada, and Trumps passed on the loose stones halfway up the ridge. Otis said nothing, but Trumps growled when Otis stepped over him.

The boat ride south of Nonsuch Island, where water was deep enough for the *Gladisfen,* took only a few minutes. Things stayed uncomfortably silent until Jefferson pulled alongside the tugboat. John yelled for the ladder and grabbed it, pulling the smaller boat closer to the tug. He held it in place for the others to climb aboard.

"Go first, Mr. Barton, so you can help the ladies," John instructed.

"I'll go," Gloria said. "I can help Mrs. B."

Otis Barton stayed put until Gloria was on the *Gladisfen* deck and Else was climbing the ladder. When she reached the top and Gloria assisted her over the side, Otis began his climb. John followed, thanking Jefferson, who pulled the *Skink* away after John stepped onto the tug and the *Gladisfen* crew pulled the ladder up.

Captain Millett clanged a bell and aimed his boat southward. John and Gloria searched for Will Beebe, coordinator for the day's activities.

"I see him," Gloria said. "Starboard bow."

The director clung to the rolling ship's forward deck, mesmerized by something in the water.

"Bring me the 12-gauge," Will commanded a young sailor transferring ropes nearby. The sailor responded, pulling the Browning A-5 from a shotgun rack attached to the mast.

Will aimed the shotgun 20 yards in front of him with the tugboat cruising at about eight knots per hour. He fired, adjusted his aim to the right, fired again, and then five more times.

Else Bostelmann stood frozen in place while Otis Barton meandered toward Dr. Beebe cautiously. John and Gloria followed also wondering what their leader was up to.

Will turned to face Captain Millett. He set the shotgun down butt first, barrel at his side. "Put the brakes on, Captain. We have some prey to round up before the jacks find them."

Captain Millett did as instructed. He throttled back his engine, circled right, and shouted commands to his crew to man the long-pole landing nets.

Still stunned by the noise and scurry, Else twisted to see who was shouting, who was running, and what Dr. Beebe would do next. She had not moved her feet since boarding the tugboat.

"Could you see them?" Will asked John and Gloria.

"See what, Will?" John questioned.

"Belonidae."

"What?"

"Belonidae. Needle nose flying fish. I'm sure I shot three. Missed two. We need to find at least one of them, right, Glo?"

"They're so small, they will be hard to see in these waves," Gloria said. "Can you see them from your bridge, Captain?" she yelled.

"Starboard, two o'clock!" came a deckhand shout.

Will grabbed a pole-net from a crewmember and leaned his full body weight against the railing and shoved the net into the water. He pulled the fish up and quickly surveyed the body for pellet damage. Otis Barton hovered.

"Port, nine o'clock!"

"Come, take this one, Glo," Will directed. He handed the fish to Gloria and ran to the other side, thrusting the net at the floating fish. A jack scraped the surface and snapped at the net as Will pulled his wounded fish out of water. Again, Otis stayed at his heels.

"Amazing. Good shooting, Dr. Beebe," Otis said.

Else was now close enough to the action to see the wounded fish wiggling in Dr. Beebe's net. She had seen wounded creatures many times. Rabbits, deer, quail, animals people shot so they could eat, but it bothered her that Dr. Beebe shot the flying fish for sport so he could look at it.

She worried that he killed the fish not thinking about scientific discovery, just the challenge.

Captain Millett's crew dropped several nets during their demonstration for Otis Barton and Else Bostelmann. They trawled for an hour. Then Will requested they haul the nets in and return to Nonsuch Island.

It took another hour to retract the netting, which was delayed further by engine complications aboard the *Gladisfen*. It alarmed Will who warned Otis that an alternate plan needed to be considered. They discussed the problems with Captain Millett while watching the crew unload their catch. The haul was sparse but enough to show life existed at various levels down to one mile.

The *Gladisfen* had stayed in the eight-mile diameter Will designated for his continuous research. Although pleased with results, he now worried about the tug. He depended on the *Gladisfen* to pull Barton's sphere to sea. He encouraged Captain Millett to alert his colleague, Captain Jimmy Sylvester. Then he returned to describe for Else and Otis his goal.

"So far, science has been generic," Will explained. "It's not helping us understand ecology, how plants and animals co-exist."

"Explain that, Will," Gloria encouraged.

"These fish bodies, many of them ruined by the change in pressure as we pulled the nets up, are creatures found here in the

Atlantic north of the Tropic of Cancer. Do they exist elsewhere? Are they unique to the Sargasso Sea? While they may be from the same family as a similar fish in the Pacific, are they from the same genus, the same species?"

"When we understand the differences, we may learn something about our planet's way of surviving changes in our ecology," Gloria added. "That knowledge will help us secure the lives of all animals, including those that seem threatened by man."

"I'm pleased to hear both of you say these things," Else said. "I fear for my daughter's future when I see so many people doing bad things to animals."

"We understand, Mrs. B," John said.

"…so I must tell you I was dismayed to see you with a gun in your hands, Dr. Beebe. You are a hunter with nerves of steel, I can see it. I've seen it before. It didn't look like you were concerned about animal life when you were shooting the flying fish with such clear enjoyment."

John and Gloria laughed at Else's frankness. Otis Barton lifted an eyebrow.

"There's great irony in my actions, Mrs. Bostelmann, I will admit. I'm a hunter, true. I've killed many animals in my lifetime, many kinds of animals. I've stuffed their skins and put them on display in my office, because I love them and I'm going to make sure they're always around."

"I'm sorry, I don't quite understand. To kill and to rescue seem like opposite actions," Else said.

"I see your point, Mrs. B," Gloria told her. "Perhaps we need to think about what she's saying, Will.

"What's your opinion, Mr. Barton. Do you agree with Mrs. Bostelmann, that my killing the flying fish was the wrong way to do our work?"

"What was your concern, Mrs. Bostelmann?" Otis asked.

"Can a scientist dedicated to saving life from extinction justify killing?"

"I'm not sure science needs a conscience. It's about finding and showing by whatever means. Simple," Otis said.

Jefferson met the *Gladisfen* where he dropped his four passengers earlier in the day. He glided the *Skink* alongside the tug and caught the chain ladder.

John descended first followed by Gloria and Else. They waited once more for Otis Barton.

When Will told them he was returning to St. George's Hotel to gather his belongings and planned to return to Nonsuch Island to be with team members, Otis asked to have a private discussion with Dr. Beebe. They chatted while the others waited in the boat.

"Captain Millett says I'm to meet with Captain Sylvester next week," Otis told Will. "I'm to go over the apparatus that will lift the submersible chamber from the boat's deck into the water. It has to be a different plan from us using the barge Captain Millett intended to pull."

"The back-up plan could be our only choice," Will agreed. "Do you still expect the ball soon?"

"Yes, but that's not what I wanted to say."

"Speak, Mr. Barton. What's on your mind?"

"I think it would be best for me to stay at St. George's Hotel so I'm closer to the people I'll be working with."

"All right, we can switch places tonight if you like."

"Excellent, Dr. Beebe. I'll ride in the boat to St. George. What time would you like that to be?"

"Seven-thirty. It's still light enough to unload your gear."

Will leaned over the rail to wave to his colleagues after Otis climbed into the smaller boat. Gloria returned the wave as Jefferson pulled away. With the sun at his back, Will knew he was just a silhouette. He lifted his hand high in response so she could see.

Will had become dependent on Gloria. He longed to talk with her. "Your instincts about Otis Barton were astute," he said to himself.

Gloria had also become a warm and caring friend, a principal member of DTR who was intelligent and perceptive. With Elswyth gone, he considered Gloria to be the best person with whom to express his end-of-day thoughts.

Will Beebe returned to his hotel and looked around his room. It was colorless without Elswyth in it. It seemed less comfortable and almost dingy. He welcomed the chance to get back to Nonsuch Island and to be around his staff and young interns.

Otis Barton's disinterest in the camaraderie annoyed Will. Otis was near the same age as John and Glo. *Why doesn't he fit in?*

Despite the lack of personal chemistry, Will knew he needed Otis Barton, because the young engineer had come up with the craft and the money to pay for it.

A ringing telephone cleared Will's thoughts. The concierge said Mr. Barton was on the elevator, suitcases to follow.

"Dr. Beebe, it's Otis Barton," came his voice after a softly thumped door knock.

"Yes, coming, Mr. Barton."

Will pulled the door open and attempted cheeriness. "Good evening, you're right on time. I've just finished packing my bag."

"I had the desk put the room in my name. I will be happy to cover my expenses."

"Very well. I appreciate your generosity, Mr. Barton. And speaking of which, what have you heard from your engineer? Captain Butler is his name, correct?"

"John Butler, yes sir, of Cox & Stevens. Nothing new today, Dr. Beebe."

"Well, days like today when we're over a deep part of the Atlantic make me eager to see what's down there."

"I agree. I'm keen myself. We'll make history together, Dr. Beebe, I'm certain."

"It's seeing life in the ocean that stirs my blood. I think science has been wrong for centuries, Mr. Barton. Life is there but we don't know what it looks like. I want to find out."

"I understand the concerns, Dr. Beebe. The pressure at a quarter mile is more than 585 pounds per square inch. Much worse at half a mile. Logically, no animal we know could live under those conditions."

"Precisely, Mr. Barton. So our goal is to tell the world there are creatures swimming deep in the ocean that have lived a long time, but they live under very different environmental conditions."

"I believe I have the vessel to help us do that, Dr. Beebe. I will leave the science to you…"

"And I shall leave the engineering to you, Mr. Barton. I'm counting on you."

—◦◦◦—

Otis dined comfortably in the hotel restaurant. He walked the veranda smoking a cigarette and enjoying the moon reflections in the Atlantic Ocean.

He was relieved to be away from the primitive activities of Nonsuch Island. It reminded him of summer camp in the Catskills, which he hated. Dr. Beebe's Brooklyn accent reminded him of the bullies he tolerated at camp.

Otis had idolized William Beebe since he began reading about the naturalist's adventures. Now meeting the person, Otis found him to be less heroic. He lacked sophistication. His bombastic style was annoying. Otis expected someone more like himself. More refined.

It made Otis wonder if the legends he heard about Beebe's seductive exploits of young wealthy women were true.

"Mr. Barton?"

Otis turned to see the hotel bellhop with an envelope outstretched in his hand.

"…Here's the telegram you were expecting."

John Butler, the consulting engineer with Cox & Stevens, responded to Otis's questions about the diving vessel. Butler wrote the steel ball would be ready the first week of July as promised.

Otis heard Butler's laughter when he read the telegram. Butler joked about the irony. Cox & Stevens built expensive yachts that excelled at staying on top of the water. *Now you want us to engineer a craft that sinks?*

Butler and Beebe seemed to be similar in their outward behaviors, gruff and uncouth.

Otis Barton was eager to get the sphere delivered, dive with Dr. Beebe, establish his name on a plateau with the renowned explorer, and move on to more pleasing venues where he could make his own mark with more daring exploits than those of the famous William Beebe.

CHAPTER 16

Friendship

"Guten Morgen, Frau Tucker."

"Good morning to you, Mrs. Bostelmann. Are you ready for coffee?"

Else held a cup as Mrs. Tucker poured.

"What a beautiful morning, Mrs. Tucker. The pink and orange sky over Soldier Bay makes me want to grab a brush and paint," Else said.

Mrs. Tucker asked nearly every morning to see what Else had painted. Else always humbly obliged. She was proud of her work but didn't enjoy boasting or showing it off. To her, her skill was no more important than Mrs. Tucker's excellent cooking and warm care for all who came to Nonsuch. Else told Mrs. Tucker her art was simply her means of enjoying her time alive.

When not concentrating on DTR's collection of sea life, Else loved painting the island's wildflowers and angular cedar trees, one in particular that had survived many hurricanes.

"Your old cedar has become my favorite tree," Else told her new friend. "Time has scarred its soul. I suppose that's why I like it so much. It stands there triumphantly despite the pain it's suffered, like a gallant sentry watching over Nonsuch."

"I fear for my tree every summer, wondering if this year's hurricane will be the one that tumbles it over. I will be heartbroken when that day comes," Mrs. Tucker said, "assuming it goes before I'm the one to tumble."

"No one knows how long we or our trees get to live, Mrs. Tucker."

"Dr. Beebe seems to not care how long he will be here. He's very courageous to want to dive into the ocean in that thing Mr. Barton is making."

"Yes, I have wondered about Dr. Beebe's courage. He wants to see what's down there. And I suppose I do too," Else said.

"Oh, dearie. You're not planning to get in that ball too."

"I think I would if Dr. Beebe and Mr. Barton would let me. If they prove it can be done, then why not see in person the fish he wants me to paint?"

"Oh, my. We need to talk more about that, Mrs. Bostelmann. Some things men do are not for women."

"I might agree, Mrs. Tucker, on things that require strength, but not courage. Being strong will not matter if the ball becomes disconnected and sinks to the bottom of the ocean…"

"…you see, you're proving my point. It's too dangerous for man or woman. I hope you're not considering such a risk. You have a daughter who needs her mother."

The two women sipped their coffee. Else thought about Mrs. Tucker's point about Hada.

"It's a silly notion," Else said. "Mr. Barton hasn't delivered the ball yet, so no one may experience the ocean like Dr. Beebe wants."

"You're right, Mrs. Bostelmann. Let me think more pleasant thoughts."

"I will paint your cedar tree today, Mrs. Tucker, my way of thanking you for the way you serve others so graciously."

Hada Bostelmann had risen early. John Tee-Van assigned Patten Jackson and Hada the task of pumping fresh seawater into the holding chambers of the *Sea Fern* dredged against the southern shore. John engineered the old ship's isolated rooms as holding tanks to keep specimens alive and out of reach of mortal enemies.

Patten was headed for Mrs. Tucker's kitchen when he heard Hada's voice from behind. "Wait for me, please…"

Hada liked Patten. He looked older than sixteen. Still, she found him cute, well-mannered, smart, and willing to do any task asked of him. If he were older, like Bobby, she would be sweet on him for certain.

"Are you stopping for breakfast?" she asked him.

"I'm going to ask for toast and juice. You can have more. I'll get started with the chores and you can join me."

"You're so handsome when you say things like that, Patten. Will you marry me?"

"That's not a question a lady asks a man. That's the gentleman's question. But, yes, I will marry you if you can wait until I'm finished with school. And do you mind living with my parents until I can find a job?"

Patten hoped his retort ended her silliness. However, he enjoyed knowing the prettiest girl among the interns liked him more than the college boys.

Mrs. Tucker had the electric toast maker on her counter with freshly sliced bread ready for Patten. She had juice prepared for Hada and asked Mrs. Bostelmann if her daughter would want more.

Mrs. Tucker was unaware that Else's daughter learned her eating habits in Texas when food was scarce. Neither Else nor Hada would forget the privilege of having a good meal. Life is good,

Hada would say, when you can refuse to eat because you want to, not because you have to.

"Good morning, ladies," Patten said cheerfully.

"Guten Morgen, Herr Jackson," Else responded.

"Yes, good morning, Mister Jackson," Mrs. Tucker said as she pushed the bread into the electric coils. "Toast in a minute, young man. Are you ready for another day on Nonsuch Island?"

"Yes, ma'am."

"Guten Morgen, Mutter. Guten Morgen, Frau Tucker," Hada Bostelmann added.

"The juice is chilled in the icebox, Miss Bostelmann. Please help yourself."

"Thank you, Mrs. Tucker. You make our day begin with such joy."

Else smiled at her daughter's comment.

"You are too kind, young lady. Thank you for making me feel special," Mrs. Tucker said.

Else asked if Hada and Patten knew how to take care of Mr. Tee-Van's sunken tanks in the scuttled *Sea Fern*. Hada deferred to Patten's expertise, saying, "I just follow what the young lord tells me to do."

"A wise decision, Tochter. It's good to know when to lead and when to follow."

"Hada is teaching me to paint," Patten said in defense of Hada's acquiescence. "I wish I could draw and paint like she does."

"She has much to learn as an artist. But I appreciate hearing you like her work," Else responded.

"Oh, I do like it. I have no artistic skills. But I'm learning thanks to Hada. She's not only talented but very patient."

"Are you being helpful to Mrs. Tee-Van, Tochter?"

"She seems to appreciate my assistance, Mother. Like Patten, I'm learning. I enjoy the Tee-Vans. They're a wonderful couple. I hope I can find a partner to be like them," Hada said while look-ing at Patten with fluttering eye lashes.

"I know about marriage," said Mrs. Tucker. "It's easy to make it look good to others, but not so easy to make it feel good all the time. It takes work, not romance. That's the secret. You're indeed partners and partners watch out for each other and are always honest. They have two opinions, but they must behave like there's only one, which doesn't always turn out. That's what takes the work."

Mrs. Tucker's serious explanation of marriage caught Else, Hada, and Patten by surprise.

Hada said she wasn't in any hurry to build a relationship. She confessed, however, that she had just proposed to Patten who accepted. "He explained that we would have to wait until he graduated high school, and we would make our first home at his parents."

Patten's blush brought smiles to Else and Mrs. Tucker. Else played along by warning the young man he would need to tolerate her daughter's beauty habits, both at night and in the morning.

"I hope your parents have a large powder room where Hada can spread out her toiletries like she does at our apartment," Else added.

Patten appeared to question Hada with a glance.

"It's not true. She's exaggerating to frighten you off. She wants me to marry someone older and rich to take care of both of us. Someone like Dr. Beebe's friend Mr. Williams. I prefer you. Young, handsome, debonair. You'll save yourself for me, won't you?" Hada asked, looking into his shocked expression.

Mrs. Tucker roared startling poor Patten. "You'd better eat and start your chores before this young woman pushes your heart to a stop."

Patten inhaled his breakfast and drank some of Hada's juice. "I'll meet you at *Sea Fern's* first tank."

He scampered away, still uncertain if Mrs. Bostelmann teased him or shared a morsel of truth.

CHAPTER 17

The Weight of It

Will, John, and Gloria rose early and took the *Skink* to St. George with Chiriqui and Trumps in tow. Before the *Skink* could dock, the lean naturalist peeled his outer garments and plunged into the chilly harbor. His leap pushed the boat forward.

Gloria stepped from the boat and lassoed a sturdy piling. John grabbed another and tied the boat taut. Chiri jumped to John's shoulders and searched for Will in the dark water fogged by morning air.

Bored with looking, Chiri climbed down John's body and began his morning hunt for food.

"We're going to pick up the hoses and helmets," John shouted to the swimming director. He joined Gloria on the walk to the hotel where Will said to meet him for breakfast.

Trumps and Chiriqui sat together outside the hotel while John and Gloria went in. Moments later, Chiri foretold of Will's arrival with a screech. The restaurant waiter brought out Grape Nuts at the moment Will sat.

"You're no longer a guest and you're still treated like royalty," Gloria said.

The waiter stood by beaming with pride that he pleased the hotel's most notable patron.

"Have you seen Mr. Barton this morning?" Will asked.

"No, sir. Were you expecting him to join you?"

"Not necessarily. I'm to meet him at Darrell and Meyer. We have an issue to resolve."

"Yes, sir. May I bring you anything else, sir?"

"No, thank you. I appreciate the Grape Nuts and your excellent service."

"Thank you, Dr. Beebe."

Will instructed John and Glo to prepare the helmet-diving equipment. He would meet Mr. Barton with Captain Sylvester at the shipyard hoping the conversation would be brief.

Jimmy Sylvester, captain of the *Freedom*, another aged tugboat, had met with Will after the *Gladisfen* developed engine problems and needed other repairs. Will expressed his fear the *Gladisfen* wouldn't be ready for the diving ball when it arrived. That's when he hired Captain Sylvester and his tug to take its place.

Jimmy Sylvester stood on the *Freedom's* deck. He gave Will Beebe a welcoming handshake and looked over Will's shoulder to see if Otis accompanied him.

"Where's Mr. Barton?"

"I hoped he was already here," Will replied. "He would not have done well as a pilot or seaman during the war."

"Indeed not. We were up at 5:30 every day. The routine. Can't shake it," Sylvester said.

"The Gerry pilots came at us in the evening when they had the sun at their backs," Will responded.

"Did you see much action, Dr. Beebe?"

"No, not much. They kept me at the base in France. My age. Said I was more valuable as a trainer for the youngsters."

"How old?" asked Captain Sylvester.

"I was 39. Turned 40 in France. I flew because Ted Roosevelt encouraged me."

"The president. That Ted Roosevelt?"

"He liked my early books on ornithology and my early travels to Central and South America, so we met and discovered many similar interests. He was my most loyal supporter before his death."

"Hello… Dr. Beebe. Captain Sylvester…"

Otis looked like he'd just gotten up. Will saw bags under his eyes and a pillow wrinkle across his forehead. It gave a clear picture of a spoiled child sleeping in.

"Sorry I'm late. Have you discussed the winch?"

"No, Mr. Barton, we awaited your arrival," Captain Sylvester informed him.

"Good. Well, Dr. Beebe hopes that you can use his winch, the one he had on the *Arcturus* during a previous adventure. Have you read about his explorations, Captain?"

"I'm sorry, Dr. Beebe. I'm not much of a reader."

"It's all right, Captain. The winch, can you use it? It will save us time and money."

"It will depend on the weight of the diving ball. And the cable. How much do they weigh, Mr. Barton?"

"Look, Captain, you don't need me as you work out the engineering matters," Will said. That's this young man's forte. I'll leave you two to negotiate. I have some diving to do."

Although concerned, Will Beebe departed. He wanted to show Otis his willingness to relinquish decisions that fell more into his area of expertise. He bowed out despite his worry.

Captain Sylvester watched Will depart, nervous too about dealing with a young man who lacked experience and had crazy notions of submerging in a hollow ball.

"The weight?" he asked.

"Ten thousand pounds. It's two-inch-thick cast steel."

"The cable?"

"Roebling seven-eighths of an inch times thirty-four-hundred feet."

Captain Sylvester did a quick mental calculation. "That's another two to three tons."

"I know your concerns, Captain. So, I've come up with a plan to reduce the pull on the masts."

Otis had drawn a rough sketch on hotel stationery. He handed it to Captain Sylvester.

"This is what I propose, Captain. We reduce the torque on your mast and boom by setting up a series of pulleys about 30 feet from Dr. Beebe's winch, which we attach at the foot of your main-mast."

Otis stopped talking and allowed Captain Sylvester to study his drawing.

"No. It won't work," the captain finally said.

"But we've reduced the pull against the mast through the pulley system…"

"Won't work. Not connected to this tug's mast. You'll destroy my boat and you and Dr. Beebe will sink like an anchor to the bottom of the Atlantic. Bring me a better plan with less weight if you intend to use that winch on my boat."

Otis Barton had already mailed a similar drawing of his layered pulleys to Cox & Stevens. When he returned to St. George's Hotel, he composed a telegram telling Butler that Sylvester rejected the plan. Otis needed John Butler to propose an option for reducing the weight.

In New York, Butler understood Captain Sylvester's concerns. A former seaman, he had seen the salty Atlantic's cruelty to old wooden and cast-iron boats. "I hoped Barton and Beebe's dives would launch from a newer, sturdier vessel," he told co-workers.

Early in his career, Butler read about Beebe's ornithology studies when he and Blair Rice traveled to the Florida Keys on a shoe-string budget. He realized that Beebe was driven to make something of nothing. So, that meant the boat's physical condition mattered little to Will Beebe. He was likely to dive in Barton's invention regardless of risks. Failure wasn't an option for Cox & Stevens.

CHAPTER 18

Into the Cave

Will Beebe did not intend to brood about Otis Barton's news. Nor was he surprised by Otis's sudden departure. Barton had footed the bill and assured Will he would cover additional expenses to reconstruct a submersible that the boats and winch could handle.

Still, Will needed a diversion to take his mind off missed opportunity. *How can I turn the situation into a way to keep the zoo's patrons involved?* The zoological society's support was necessary if he intended to return to Nonsuch.

Will had told several reporters about Barton's invention, so he wondered if they would follow up. *That would be a good way to alert investors.*

Will looked for Glo to get her insights. He found her in the lab sitting next to Mrs. Bostelmann.

"Are you done with your work, Glo?"

"Nearly. Did you want to give me more?"

"No. I want to explore south St. David's. Let's see what's there. Plus, I want to hear your thoughts about Barton's news."

"I'll be ready in 15 minutes. Let me clean my table."

"Meet me at the *Skink.*"

Gloria finished anointing small fish in her potassium hydroxide. She placed them in porcelain trays and stacked them in a crisscross pattern. She peered over Else's shoulder. "Those are wonderful, Mrs. B. You're so talented. Did you want to tag along?"

"No, thank you. I have a few more to finish."

"Very well. Perhaps we'll find something new for you to paint."

Gloria pushed her microscope to the back of her table and stacked empty trays to the side. She carefully placed jars of tiny fish soaking in formaldehyde on labeled shelves. "I'll let you know how we do when we return, Mrs. B."

"Enjoy the search, Miss Hollister."

Will had the *Skink* running and untied from the dock when Gloria joined him. He held the boat steady while Gloria stepped aboard.

"Is John going?" she asked.

"He wants to finish his fish inventory in the holding tanks. Just us."

Will steered the *Skink* eastward toward the southern tip of St. David's Island. The late afternoon sea calmed. The boat ride was smooth and quiet except for the motor's rumble.

"What do you make of Mr. Barton's news, Glo? I know you have an opinion," Will began.

"I don't like the man, that's obvious, but I hope the engineers can salvage his sphere."

"Yes, that's my hope," Will said. "But what if they can't salvage it? Do I talk about it with reporters? Do I hint I'm looking for another submersible?"

"What has Mr. Barton told you, Will? Do you trust his engineering skills?"

"He said he'd rebuild the ball to accommodate Captain Sylvester's requirements."

"And what are they?" Gloria asked.

"Weight. Sylvester says his mast can't hold up under the ball and tons of cable, especially with the added pressure when we're submerged."

"How can Mr. Barton design it any lighter and still protect the two of you when you're three-thousand feet beneath the surface?"

"I'm depending on Cox & Stevens and John Butler to know the answer to that."

"When, Will? Many people expected you to dive this summer. Is that still possible?"

"I don't know."

"If you don't dive, are investors going to stick around?"

"Again, I don't know."

Gloria studied Will while he guided the *Skink* toward a narrow sandbar. Will's lean body tensed wrestling with his concerns. Gloria wondered if the setback was wearing on him more than he let on.

"What have you heard from Elswyth?"

"She and her mother leave for England this coming weekend," Will replied.

"Is she nervous about traveling without you?"

"I suppose not. She has friends to comfort her when she arrives in London."

Will pulled onto a strip of sand and jumped from the *Skink*. He drove a steel stake into firm ground, wrapped the tie line around the stake, and took a flashlight from Gloria. She leaped from the boat, landing firmly on the sand with Will bracing her waist with both hands.

"Thank you. I forget how high the *Skink* sits when it runs ashore," Gloria told him.

Will hung onto her waist to steady both of them. She lifted her chin and pulled in the aroma of nearby orchid trees and lady-of-the-night flowers.

"Wonderful fragrances, Will."

"Don't be fooled by the sweet smells. The lady-of-the-nights create deadly poisons."

"I'm smelling them. I don't intend to eat them."

Will looked at her charming smile as it caught the amber rays of the setting sun. He pressed his right hand into her hip to guide Gloria toward an opening in the jagged rocks.

He used his flashlight to search the shallow waters spotting ordinary shore fish: wrasse, blue and butter hamlets, and fairy basslet. A small octopus scampered from one rock to another, changing colors to hide within its environment.

Will and Gloria would normally chase after a mollusk, but they became more intrigued by an opening to a cave. Low tide made it appear magically. They bent to follow the light Will pushed ahead of them.

Inside they found a cavernous opening. There were signs other creatures used the den to capture trapped fish. The opening went back into the cliff. They followed it a short distance, spotting fossils embedded in the molten volcanic rock. The sighting ignited Will's enthusiasm. He shook with excitement as though he were ten and coming upon his first scientific discovery.

"You're so predictable, Will."

"What do you mean?"

"The smallest sighting and you become a child."

"It's life before there was man. Finding skeletal pictures of natural history is fascinating."

He looked at Gloria, her face illuminated by ricocheting light. He stepped closer to her. "Imagine if touching this rock could take us back."

He took her hand, closed his eyes, and put his other hand on the fossil. "How did life get here? What was the planet like? How did these creatures live and die?"

Gloria folded Will's outstretched arm between them and leaned into him. She kissed him.

Will's eyes remained closed. He did not move. Gloria felt the tension in his body escape as she held him. She whispered, "I don't mean to confuse you, nor do I want to hurt Elswyth, but I love you, William Beebe. I love your passion. I love your urge to learn and discover. You are my inspiration. But I'm sure you know that."

Will opened his eyes and put his arms around her. He pressed his lips against hers. They remained embraced for several minutes standing in ankle-deep water, the light fading.

CHAPTER 19

The Curious

Else Bostelmann quickly became an accomplished helmet diver. She had talked Hada and her young friend, Patten Jackson, into rowing her to Castle Island a few meters west of Nonsuch. They would be her pumpers when she took her zinc sketchpad and dove a spot Miss Hollister had recommended.

"What are you hoping to sketch underwater, Mother?" Hada asked after switching places in the dinghy so Patten could row for a while.

"Miss Hollister says there is a spectacular fan coral she and Dr. Beebe discovered."

Patten snickered when he heard Else say Gloria and Dr. Beebe's names together.

"Did I say something funny, Herr Jackson?" Else asked.

"No, ma'am." Patten sat up straighter and pulled the oars especially hard.

"He's laughing because he and I were up late last week and saw Miss Hollister sneak into Dr. Beebe's tent. We knew he was sleeping in a tent rather than his room in the hospital building."

"And how do you know that?"

"We weren't trying to spy on anyone; we just saw him out walking when we were looking at the stars. The sky shows many more stars here than in New York, don't you agree, Mother?"

"Don't change the subject, Hada. Dr. Beebe and Miss Hollister work many long days, sometimes well into the evening. Do not make up stories with your imagination. Dr. Beebe is married."

"But Mother, Dr. Beebe and Miss Hollister don't work in the dark. The dark is for other things."

"Hada!"

"Patten and I won't tell anyone what we saw," she reassured her. "It's our secret, isn't it, Patten?"

"It's our secret, Mrs. Bostelmann. I promise," Patten repeated.

Patten and Hada traded places rowing twice more before reaching the northeast corner of Castle Island where Miss Hollister told Else to look for a pylon sticking up in the water. She instructed Else to dive thirty feet north of the pylon.

Patten put the oars in the water and slowed the boat reaching the spot Miss Hollister described. Hada helped her mother prepare the helmet. She threw the rope ladder off the stern while Patten wiggled to the bow to balance the small craft.

Else slid into the water and swam a few strokes. She went to the stern and waited for Hada to hand her the weight belt and lift the helmet over her head.

Patten began pumping the air as Hada fitted the headgear over her mother's shoulders. Else gave the okay, clutched the helmet, and descended into the clear water.

Else saw the fan coral Miss Hollister had described. She had tilted the helmet enough to locate the sandy bottom below her.

In the shallow water, the fan caught the midday rays giving the illuminated side a lavender color while the fan's shaded part appeared a deeper purple.

After settling on the bottom, Else walked toward the fan. Coral surrounded it and attracted dozens of small fish, which used it as shelter from predators. The large fan appeared to be two meters wide at the widest point.

Else moved closer and studied the stationary object's soft tissue veins and tiny flower-like tentacles that captured phytoplankton for food. She saw patterns she began to etch on her zinc tablet when a shadow darkened her board.

She could not tilt her head back to look above her for fear water would fill her helmet. However, Else could tell from the shadow movement a large fish floated above her. She thought first about her daughter in the small dinghy, then about Dr. Beebe's characterization of sharks; they're not a threat to people, but they're curious. She decided she had no choice but to share the space with whatever was above her, although her concentration on the fan coral diminished.

Else's heart raced when she felt a tug at her air hose. Was it Hada signaling for her to ascend or the creature above her toying with her lifeline? Else felt perspiration begin to bead on her forehead just before the shadow left.

She leaned her helmet back as far as she dared and searched the water above her. She saw a grayish mass disappear away from the island toward the open sea, but she couldn't identify its shape or species. Another more urgent pull on her air hose signaled Else to rejoin her daughter and Patten in the boat.

When Hada lifted the helmet from Else's head, mother and daughter's eyes connected. Else could tell her daughter had been crying.

"Are you all right, Mother?"

"I'm fine, Hada. What happened?"

"You couldn't see it, Mrs. Bostelmann!" Patten said, his voice quivering.

"No. I cannot tilt my head with the helmet on. I would drown."

Else tried to hand Hada her weight belt, but her daughter had fallen to her knees in the boat and wept uncontrollably.

"I'm fine, Hada. Take the belt so I can get into the boat."

"Move to the bow, Hada!" Patten ordered.

He grabbed her arm and pulled her to the front of the boat so they wouldn't tip the boat over. He assisted her mother. He took the weight belt and tossed it to the center bench.

Else reached for Patten's hand as he guided her on board the dinghy. When she was in the boat, Patten collapsed on top of the belt.

"It was the biggest hammerhead shark I've ever seen! It just stayed there. Then it nudged the air hose with its head. I guess it wanted to see if it was alive," Patten said.

"I felt it," Else told them.

"Mother, it was twice as long as this boat. It could have eaten all of us!"

"It didn't, Tochter. You must calm down. We're okay. Dr. Beebe would say it meant no harm. I'm sure he's correct."

"He might be wrong for the first time, Mrs. Bostelmann. If it didn't mean harm, I wish it would give me back the few years of life it took from me just seeing it."

"I hope seeing the coral was worth it, Mother."

"It's an amazing form of animal life, Hada. You can see it from here."

"I don't want to see anything in that water right now. Let's hurry home. I'll paddle first, Patten. I can get us back to Nonsuch with a few strokes, I'm so frightened."

Hada Bostelmann learned quickly that nervous energy is not the same as muscle energy. She fatigued after a few meters and Patten took over the rowing.

Else described what she saw in the few minutes she was studying the coral. It was hard for Hada and Patten to listen. It surprised them how calm Else remained.

When their boat neared the dock at Nonsuch Island, Else reminded her daughter and Patten to refrain from sharing their story about seeing Dr. Beebe and Miss Hollister and speculating that there was something romantic going on.

"Whether you're right or wrong, telling others what you *think* you saw could do great harm," Else told them. "Do you understand the consequences?"

Hada and Patten said, "yes."

Patten took the diving helmet and air hose back to the storage room in the main building. He ran into two of his buddies who peppered him with questions about the trip. Patten could not contain his nervous excitement about seeing the hammerhead swimming above Mrs. Bostelmann.

The boys quickly spread the story among the DTR staff. By dinnertime, everyone knew Else survived quite an experience while diving near Castle Island. Remaining unconcerned and eager to tell Miss Hollister about the coral, Else said she looked forward to her next dive, although she wasn't certain Hada and Herr Jackson would go with her.

CHAPTER 20

Better News

Three weeks passed since Otis told Dr. Beebe the diving ball would not be ready for the 1929 season. Otis eagerly awaited news from Cox & Stevens about the following year. If the engineering staff failed to come up with a solution to reduce the sphere by summer 1930, he wondered if Dr. Beebe would stay interested.

That very day, a messenger delivered the letter Otis awaited. He opened it and read with relief Cox & Stevens could make changes that kept the submersible viable.

Captain John Butler confirmed the foundry would re-use the steel and give Otis a rebate of a thousand dollars and reconstruct the hollow ball six inches narrower still making it safe down to half a mile.

So, instead of a five-foot diameter, the ball would be four-feet-six, a tight compartment for two men over six feet tall. Further, they'd reduce the wall thickness to one-and-a-half inches rather than two. The changes would make the ball's weight shrink from five tons to less than two-and-a-half tons.

While the size shrank, the price grew. Otis needed more money from his grandfather's trust. Fortunately, the stock market supplied the trust what he needed. It was headed to an all-time high, so Otis worried more about the timing than the cost.

Barton shared his good news with Captain Jimmie Sylvester and Captain Edward Millett. They responded. They told Otis the reduced weight would enable the rigging to work with their masts.

Thus, the future became clearer. All Otis had to do was convince Dr. Beebe to be patient. He also needed John Butler's assurance that his team could rebuild his sphere without further delays. He pressed forward.

At Cox & Stevens, Butler contacted vendors who had a role in rebuilding the rejected diving ball. Primary among the team was Watson-Stillman and their chosen New Jersey foundry, Atlas. They had molded a perfect five-ton hollow ball of steel that was now being melted into ingots for the next attempt.

CHAPTER 21

Bull and Bear

William Beebe and colleagues cruised home aboard the *S.S. Bermuda* proclaiming the summer of '29 an outstanding success. Although the Department of Tropical Research didn't deep dive the Atlantic Ocean, Will said it was the *First Bermuda Expedition,* implying an intention to return.

The director filed reports with his boss, Madison Grant, elaborating on more than five hundred deep-sea hauls. He said the team collected more than two hundred species of shallow-water fish and prepared more than six hundred specimens for later analysis.

After detailing their findings, Will concluded the research had just begun. Among their captures were fish without eyes, some with eyes at the end of tentacles, and others covered with luminescent organs used to guide them in deep waters. Responses to Will's stories and news coverage helped bring in additional funding for more trips to the center of the Atlantic Ocean.

To enhance his position, Will also told Grant that his most loyal supporters visited Bermuda during the summer. Among them were Harrison Williams and Mortimer Schiff who had contributed thousands to make sure Beebe succeeded in his mission.

Will took Harrison helmet diving and gave him the grand tour of the Bermuda archipelago. The millionaire reciprocated with parties for Will's staff aboard his yacht.

The return to New York was triumphant. The excitement thrilled the zoological board, but the enthusiasm died as they neared New York Harbor. Awaiting them was anything but good news.

Will and John sat in Will's office early Tuesday, October 29. John wanted to hear Will's plan if Wall Street's looming financial turmoil spilled over to affect the Department of Tropical Research.

"I suppose I'm as disturbed by Wall Street's reaction yesterday as anyone," Will said.

"Have you spoken to Harrison? I presume he's in a vulnerable spot," John said.

"I don't want to bother him. I spoke to him Friday. He felt confident after the rebound."

"Will, I know very little about the stock market, but the 13 percent drop yesterday was all people were talking about on the subway. I've never seen so many glum expressions."

Will shuffled books and papers on his desk. "All the glee has been about the market up another twenty percent. Mellon warned people it couldn't last. He said speculating with borrowed money would catch up."

"It has," John said. "And what about Otis? Do you know his situation?"

"I don't. His money came from a trust, but I don't know if the trust sat someplace in cash or if the trust invested it."

"Even if it was in cash, Will, the *Times* says many banks invested people's savings. Could they have done that with his trust? What if the bank lost his money?"

"It'll be gone, John."

"What do we do if that's the case?"

"We beg, we grovel, we do whatever it takes. We have a story to tell. People want good news. They'll want to know we're still out there finding nature's secrets. Somehow we'll get the money to give them what they want."

Gloria rapped on Will's door and entered. "Mr. Osborn had this message delivered to everyone at the zoological park."

"What does it say? John asked.

Gloria opened the folded paper and read: "Because of the panic-stricken nature of the news from Wall Street, the park will be closed for the remainder of the day. We will plan on opening tomorrow one-hour late to give employees a chance to sort out personal affairs."

"That sounds ominous, Will," John said.

"Turn on the radio. Let's hear their reports."

Gloria went to Will's radio sitting among the books on the third shelf of his bookcase. The warming tubes illuminated the back of the shelf. The radio voice was Ford Bond's, a respected radio broadcaster at the new National Broadcasting Company...

Panic seems to continue on Wall Street. Reports from the floor this morning are that all shouts are to 'sell.' No one is buying. Prices are falling rapidly in search of anyone with cash...

"That's enough. Turn it off, Glo."

"I have less than one-hundred dollars saved, but I stopped by my bank as soon as I could," Gloria said, clicking off the radio. "People were already in line at the door. I waited. I took out my money, but I don't know what to do with it."

"You find someplace to hide it in your apartment, Glo," John said. "That's what I'm doing."

"Are our jobs safe, Will?" she asked.

"Yes. I think. I don't know."

The three looked at each other in silence.

"We control our destiny," Will eventually said. "I'm glad we're not like the eggheads who criticize me…who criticize me for hiring you, Glo; who criticize me for writing articles for *National Geographic* and *The Atlantic Monthly*. Those guys will run out of funds quickly. We have a popular voice. We're scientists… no different, except we tell our story in ways people can understand."

Will looked at the worried faces of his two most valued employees. "We'll raise our own money a nickel at a time if we have to."

Will understood the threat. Still, his commitment to complete a thorough study of life in the Atlantic Ocean never wavered. Willing to tighten his belt, he pledged to raise enough money for a return to Bermuda and to dive in Barton's steel sphere.

CHAPTER 22

Bad to Worse

Hada brought in a day-old *New York Times* she picked up on a bench in Central Park. She walked to her mother's drawing table and showed Else a front-page headline that read, "Department Stores Forced to Add Help."

"Maybe I can get a job during the holidays," Hada told Else.

"Maybe…" Else responded.

Hada took her newspaper and sat. "I don't understand why they need help. I thought the financial news was bad."

"It is. What does the article say?" Else asked.

"It says, 'New York City department store owners were unanimous in reporting yesterday that despite the stock market crash they were enjoying a large volume of business and that they were swelling payrolls in anticipation of an increase in holiday trade compared to that of last year.'"

Hada mumbled her way through the article until she came to a quote from a senior official at Macy's.

"Listen to this. The vice president of Macy's says '…at present we have 12,622 employees, representing an increase of 2,041 over the corresponding day last year.'"

"I agree with you. I don't understand. It's not smart to be spending money when the news is not good," Else said.

Hada leafed through the paper to find additional articles. She read to her mother another front-page story in which President

Hoover requested the 48 governors increase their public works spending so they could hire people forced out of jobs.

"It's sad when working people lose employment. They get hurt more than the rich."

"Many interns I worked with came from wealthy families. I heard them say their parents gave Dr. Beebe money for his explorations."

"Dr. Beebe is a resourceful man. We must have faith he will find a way to continue his research and want me to return to draw and paint for him."

"Should I count on it, too, Mother? Or should I look for other work? People in the park saddened me with their long faces. No one was smiling."

"Maybe this moment is for you to discover something about yourself, Hada."

Hada walked about their new residence on 75th Street aimlessly. She spotted Else's well-traveled book, Mary Baker Eddy's *Science and Health*.

"I know what I want to do, Mother."

"If you've decided, then that's good. Go do that."

"It's not that simple…"

A knock on the door startled Hada. Else walked past her daughter and put a hand on Hada's shoulder as she went to the door.

"Hello, Mrs. Bostelmann."

"Hello, Robert. How did you find our new apartment?"

"Your landlord was showing your old apartment when I stopped. He gave me your new address. I hope you don't mind."

"No, of course not. It's good to see you."

"Thank you, Mrs. Bostelmann. I miss stopping with assignments for you and picking up your artwork. Is Hada here?"

"I'm here, Bobby…"

Else pulled the door wider and stepped aside. Hada collected her thoughts and came to greet her friend.

"Hello, Bobby."

"Hi, Hada."

"Do you want to come in? We're still moving furniture around. Mother hasn't decided where she wants things."

Hada guided Bobby into their sitting room.

"I'll let the two of you talk. I'll be in my studio, Hada."

"Thank you, Mother."

"It was swell seeing you, Mrs. Bostelmann. I read about you in the newspaper. Working with Dr. Beebe. That must have been exciting."

"It was, Robert. I intend to do it again." Else slipped away.

"Are you okay, Hada?"

"It's nothing, just things on my mind. I don't like the news since returning. I'm fine though. I'm so glad you found us. I wanted to see you again."

"I'm glad too, but I have bad news of my own."

"Really? What's wrong, Bobby?"

"My dad lost his job. His brother wants him to bring the family to Virginia to live on the farm. He says he could use Dad's and my help. You know what I thought about when my parents told me."

"No, Bobby."

"I thought about *you*, Hada. I wanted to see you again. I don't want to leave New York City."

"Oh, Bobby, I don't want you to go either. I like you and could use a friend."

"That's what makes this so hard. I can't let my parents down, Hada. I have to go to help them. I may not have a job here for very long the way things look right now."

"I know. It's scary. But I understand. Your parents are lucky to have you as a son. I'm lucky I got to know you, Bobby. Will you write to me from Virginia?"

"Of course. I like you too, Hada. I'm going to miss seeing your pretty face."

"When are you moving? Can you have dinner with us?"

"I wish I could, but they need my help packing Dad's car. They've sold all our furniture, so now we have enough money to get to Virginia. As soon as we're packed, we're driving."

"Well, you were right, Bobby, this is bad news."

"I know. I need to go so I don't cry in front of you, Hada. But I had to see you before I left. Goodbye pretty Hada."

Bobby rose and left quickly. Hada watched the door close and sat weeping, tears flowing untouched as she remained motionless. Else entered the sitting room.

"I heard. I'm sorry, Hada."

"I hope all bad things are over. It's making it very hard to think about the future when the present is so gloomy."

"There are reasons things happen the way they do."

"I love you, Mother. We had such a good experience with Dr. Beebe. I want to return to Bermuda. But today, I'm not sure if that's what I should do."

"There's time to decide, Hada. And you will see it gets easier."

CHAPTER 23

Reflective Moments

Alice Greenbrier sat at the head table watching people enter the Plaza Hotel Grand Ballroom. As chairwoman of the program committee for the Newswomen's Club of New York, Greenbrier tapped into one of her high-profile newsmakers for today's presentation, Dr. William Beebe.

But it wasn't the famous explorer who she asked to speak. Instead, it was his assistant whose chemical methods of turning fish transparent that had captured the attention of the science community. That's who Greenbrier wanted her club to hear. A woman. Gloria Hollister.

The newswoman sent Dr. Beebe two tickets to attend as a thank-you for introducing Greenbrier to Hollister. Excited to hear Glo's presentation, Will still had to decline. He had promised Elswyth they would attend an afternoon gathering at Harrison Williams' Long Island home.

Williams was hosting a reception for Britain's Prince Edward, who stayed with the Williams when visiting America. Harrison invited the Beebes to join Mona and him at their private gathering to meet the heir apparent to Great Britain's throne. Harrison was thinking of Elswyth's fascination with British Royalty.

Will instead asked John and Helen Tee-Van to attend the Newswomen's Club event so they could support Gloria. And maybe peddle some of his books to raise money. They accepted.

The Tee-Vans recognized Alice Greenbrier. They approached the head table hoping to see Gloria so she would know they were there.

"Good afternoon, Miss Greenbrier. I'm John Tee-Van with the Department of Tropical Research."

"Glad to see you Mr. Tee-Van. Dr. Beebe sent me a note that you would attend in his place. So glad to have you here."

"Thank you. This is my wife, Helen. We both work with Miss Hollister, so we're excited and maybe a little nervous to hear her speak."

"We expect to pack the ballroom, Mr. Tee-Van. Not only journalists but folks from the science community, especially Columbia."

"Have you seen Gloria yet, Miss Greenbrier?" Helen asked.

"It's Alice. And yes, she's in a small room behind us. She's visiting with our club's president and other officers. They're asking her to join our club. Her articles in the zoological society's publication are good."

"Did she seem nervous?" John asked.

"Perhaps a little nervous. Pretty lady. Dr. Beebe seems to like pretty ladies and handsome men."

"Well, we'll find some seats where she can see us," John said.

"Check your tickets, Mr. Tee-Van. I'm sure they're reserved seats here in the front row."

Helen looked at the tickets. "They are, John. Our seats are right there."

"Thank you… Alice, for your thoughtfulness," John told her.

"You're welcome. I'm sure Miss Hollister will be happy to see you."

———❦———

"I'm so glad you arrived early, Else," Ida Bostelmann said to her sister-in-law when greeting her in front of the Plaza Hotel. "Hello, Hada. I'm sorry I didn't give you both more notice, but I wasn't certain I'd be able to arrange things the way they came together."

"Mother and I were so pleased to hear from you, Aunt Ida. News has been so depressing. I needed something fun to take my mind off my sadness."

"There's more than one surprise in store, Hada."

"What do you mean, Ida?" Else asked.

"Not only are you going to get to hear Miss Hollister speak, but Cecilia and Truman are meeting us to attend as well."

"How wonderful! I haven't seen them in so long, will they remember me, Aunt Ida?"

"Yes, they'll remember you. They're just as excited as you are. They're staying here at the hotel. We'll meet them in the lobby and then go to the ballroom."

Ida Bostelmann had a knack for surprising Else when she least expected it. Eager to hear Miss Hollister talk about their storied trip to Bermuda, now she would see her sister-in-law, Cecilia, and Truman Fassett, Cecilia's husband.

The Fassetts were among the first of Monroe's relatives to contact Else after Monroe's death. Like Ida, Cecilia was an accomplished musician. Like Monroe, Cecilia played the cello. In fact, for their rescue of Else and Hada from Texas, Else had given Monroe's cherished violoncello to her sister-in-law, which she played in concerts.

At the time the Fassetts helped Else and Hada, they were living in New York. They had moved to Florida where Truman improved his painting and received high praise for his work. Art critics considered him a rising star among America's artists.

The fact that she and Hada were to see Truman and Cecilia brought back memories for Else. She could never express the gratitude she felt for Cecilia and Ida. Her desperate need following Monroe's death made her too sad. She hoped now to express her appreciation.

"There they are, Mother!" Hada shouted after zooming past the bellman's opened door.

Cecilia embraced Hada with equal enthusiasm. They hugged and twirled. Truman stood nearby gloating at their joy.

"Hello, Truman. It's so good to see you," Else said.

Truman took Else's gloved hand and held it. "We're so proud of you, Else. Even in Sarasota the papers wrote about your artwork and how important it was to Dr. Beebe during his Bermuda expedition."

"You're kind to say so, Truman. Thank you."

"Else. You look wonderful," Cecilia said, pulling her into a hug.

"Thank you, dear sister-in-law. You seem to become more beautiful with the passing years."

"Your flattery is noted. Is there something you need? I will buy it for you."

"Nothing but a chance to hear you play the cello."

"I've written a new piece for you to try," Ida said.

"Excellent. When can I see it?"

"How are your daughters, Aunt Cecilia?" Hada asked before Ida could respond. "I'd love to see them."

"Like you, they are tall and beautiful, all three of them."

"I'm sure she will tell you it's the Bostelmann traits that make them beautiful," Truman said. "Wouldn't you expect that, Else?"

"I prefer to think it's the total Prussian heritage, Truman, not just the Bostelmann blood."

"Then I get to claim no part of my success in producing beautiful women, is that what you're all telling me?" Truman complained.

Hada Bostelmann grabbed her uncle in a bear hug. "You can have all the credit for their artistic talents."

"Thank you, Hada. That at least is a consolation." He held her close to confirm his gratefulness for neutralizing a no-win situation.

"Speaking of women, we need to go to the ballroom. Else's colleague will speak soon," Ida reminded them.

There were three women for every man entering the Plaza Hotel Grand Ballroom. Hada searched the dais for Gloria Hollister. Two ladies sat on the stage behind a skirted table but no Gloria.

Then a door behind the stage opened. Three older ladies paraded ahead of the tall, slender, beautiful Gloria Hollister. Hada beamed excitement and continued to look around the room while Else, Ida, Cecilia, and Truman located seats together several rows back. Their selection disappointed Hada. She went to them.

"I want to be closer so I can see Miss Hollister better," she told them.

"Go find a seat by yourself, Hada," Ida instructed. "We'll be here."

Hada did not wait around for the scolding from her mother. She walked boldly toward the dais.

Gloria Hollister spotted Hada marching through the center aisle. She waved at the familiar figure with the youthful gait, which drew head turns from John and Helen. They also caught Gloria's attention. And then Hada's.

Helen waved and pointed at the empty seat next to her. John stood and greeted Hada with a hug.

"Are these seats reserved?" Hada asked.

"I think so," Helen replied, "but sit anyway. Maybe no one will show up."

"How are you, Hada?" John asked.

"I'm very excited to hear Miss Hollister talk. Aren't you?"

"Yes. Is Mrs. B here too?" Helen asked.

"She's sitting back there with my father's two sisters and my uncle Truman Fassett."

"Your uncle is Truman Fassett!"

"Do you know him, Mrs. Tee-Van?"

"I know *of* him; I've never met him. His artwork is showing at several galleries in the city."

"Is that true? He's a very modest man. He's married to Aunt Cecilia."

"We must meet them after the program," John told Hada.

"Do I get to stay here with you?" she asked.

"…until someone wants the seat," Helen said.

"Ladies and gentlemen, good afternoon. My name is Alice Greenbrier of the *New York Times*…"

Greenbrier's blunt beginning drew a smattering of applause from a few members in the audience. Others squirmed. Hada wondered if that meant they worked for other city newspapers.

Greenbrier introduced the Newswomen's Club officers sitting at the dais. She said she had a responsibility to announce the date and time of the next club meeting, which she did. Then she told a story about meeting Dr. William Beebe, someone who attended her alma mater, Columbia University, and had become an icon in New York City because of his devotion to the zoo in the Bronx.

"I met William Beebe when I was a cub reporter. The newspaper sent me to the zoo with no other instruction than to come home with a story..."

The journalists in the audience laughed at Greenbrier's comment because they'd all been there, told to come home with a story and no further instruction. For women reporters, it had become an expected norm. Assignment editors always gave good leads to men because they were men.

"...anyway, I met Dr. Beebe. And that's all it took. I had a fistful of stories because that man can talk." That brought a broader chorus of laughter.

John leaned toward his wife, "She makes it sound like it's a problem. It's not a problem; it's our reason for employment."

"...So, I've learned over the years when my cigar-chompin' editor doesn't assign me a story, it's time to head to the zoo and find William Beebe. Well, I found him not too long ago sittin' in his office with this pretty girl to my right. He introduced us and told me she's smart, went to Columbia under Professor Gregory. He said the young lady came up with a solution to see fish bones through skin and scales without cutting them out. Now that's a story."

Gloria looked at her friends in the front row. She lifted her hands from the table as if to say there couldn't be a simpler way to describe what she does.

"...fellow journalists, members of the Newswomen's Club of New York, ladies and gentlemen, please allow me to introduce a female scientist with the New York Zoological Society, a journalist herself, an inventor and discoverer, Miss Gloria Hollister..."

More than four hundred guests applauded as Alice Greenbrier sat and Gloria Hollister found her way to the podium. She appeared nervous at first. She told about her experience at Connecticut College as an undergraduate and a female athlete. She expanded on meeting professors William Gregory and Henry Osborn at Columbia who introduced her to William Beebe in 1925.

"…I knew as soon as I met Dr. Beebe that I wanted to work for him. He seemed to know that one day I would. It took three years and wonderful experiences at Rockefeller Institute with Dr. Alexis Carrel doing cancer research. Then Dr. Beebe hired me to be part of his Department of Tropical Research in 1928.

"We're a good team. I'm proud to see other members here in the audience today. I'm most proud of the fact that some of them are women…"

Gloria's remark brought her first round of applause.

"…It takes courage for women to enter careers dominated by men. Journalism is one such field. Medicine is another. I wanted to be a doctor like my father. Even *he* discouraged me because he thought it was man's work.

"All fields related to science look down on women entering what has been man's realm. Dr. Beebe has taken unnecessary criticism for ignoring prior norms. He hired me and others because we brought with us skills needed to do the work."

Another burst of applause bolstered Gloria's confidence. She continued.

"…I consider Will Beebe a strong, honest man. I consider other men dishonest because they said the work was theirs until it became too boring, too tedious. They gave the work to women then and called it women's work: Factory work—sewing, sorting, packaging. Farming, gathering eggs, picking fruits and vegetables.

"...Research has taught me more about gender fairness than I wanted to learn. Traveling to poorer countries, I've gotten to see abuses women take because men require them to work long hours in poor conditions. Because they're women; for no other reason. But to live they must work.

"...Even here, women work alongside their husbands. Then the day ends and a meal is put on the table for the family. Who prepares the food... and who sits down with the daily newspaper?"

Several women in the audience yelled "women!" after Gloria's first question, and "men!" at the end of her second.

Hada Bostelmann twisted in her chair and searched over the top of the engaged audience to find her mother and aunts. She wondered if they shouted. She turned and looked at Helen and John. They were looking at each other, acknowledging Gloria's observation.

Gloria continued.

"I work for a man who I consider enlightened. Not perfect, but he understands that women have a place beside men in many more situations than we allow. There is nothing about science that makes a man wiser than a woman..."

Cheers went up from a small section of young women from Columbia University. Alice Greenbrier applauded and pointed in their direction to signify who her praise was for.

"...I suppose some would say my discovery of a chemical process that turns fish scales and skin transparent is evidence that's true. I did not experiment and discover this process because I wanted to prove something or promote women's rights, I did it because I love science, I love discovery, and I happen to be a woman."

Gloria Hollister received a standing ovation when she completed her presentation. It became more about the Department of Tropical Research and its discoveries than gender inequalities as she talked. She concluded with a plea to support Dr. Beebe's work. But she admitted too, people facing difficult money matters after the stock market crash may find it hard to support science discovery if they're having a hard time feeding a family.

"Still, we know there are people who believe in our work and have money, they just need the willingness to help us."

Hada Bostelmann was so inspired by Gloria, she jumped to her feet when the club president concluded the presentation by thanking Gloria for her remarks. Hada ran to the dais and told Miss Hollister that she had never heard such a terrific speech. Hada's praise comforted Gloria whose hands shook and knees wobbled as she sat down.

Many others gathered, some asking for Gloria's autograph. Alice Greenbrier stepped in and told the gathering to let Miss Hollister have a moment. She said she would escort the speaker outside the ballroom where there was a table with Dr. Beebe's books for sale, the proceeds donated to the Department of Tropical Research. Miss Hollister would be happy to sign autographs there.

John appreciated Alice Greenbrier's tenacity. He and Helen brought Dr. Beebe's books. They were thankful for the push to get them sold.

When Hada heard the message, she dug her way out of the scrum and looked for her mother. She wanted to introduce her aunts and Truman Fassett to Gloria and the Tee-Vans.

Ida, Cecilia, and Truman had already worked their way out of the ballroom and walked up to the table with Dr. Beebe's most recent published books. Else stayed searching for Hada. She saw the Tee-Vans before she spotted her daughter.

"I had to think for a minute who that handsome couple was," Else told them. "You look different dressed so handsome and pretty. I'm used to seeing you in shorts and denim shirts."

"We could say the same, Mrs. B," John told her.

Hada came behind them with school-girl excitement. "Wasn't she wonderful, Mother? People liked what she said."

"Do you know the lady who introduced her, Mr. Tee-Van?" Else asked.

"I just met her," Helen injected.

"...I know who she is," John added. "She's written stories about Dr. Beebe for the *New York Times*. She's come to the zoological park to conduct her interviews. I've seen her there."

"Mother, she's walking Miss Hollister out front where there's a table set up with Dr. Beebe's books. Come say hello to her. Where are the others? I want Mrs. Tee-Van to meet Uncle Truman."

Hada got the family members introduced to the Beebe team. Gloria still seemed nervous. She, like Helen Tee-Van, already knew Truman Fassett's paintings.

Else and family stayed nearby while Gloria accepted congratulations and introduced people to the Tee-Vans. John watched book sales roll off the table, hoping he and Helen had brought enough to meet the demand. He was thankful for the hotel staff, which helped tote them in and managed the sales. John promised to give them each a copy of the book as a reward.

The Fassetts invited everyone to join them for an early dinner at the hotel. All accepted. Else cherished how well they all connected. Hada surprised her too by listening quietly. She saw Hada's pride explode when people walked by their table and noticed the mixture of celebrities.

PART II

SPHERE OF DISCOVERY

CHAPTER 24

Submersible
May 1930

People gathered at the wharf long before Otis Barton descended the hill from St. George's Hotel. They bunched in clusters chatting and trying to get a better look at the crew aboard a rickety barge several yards offshore. A retired sailor brought a telescope that passed from hand to hand so the most curious could get a better look.

When he reached the dock, Otis saw Captain Edward Millett and two sailors prepare a dinghy for the short ride to the *Gladisfen*. The tug anchored thirty yards in front of the barge.

"There seems to be great interest in your cargo, Mr. Barton."

"Yes, I see. Can you drop me at the barge on your way to your tugboat?"

"Climb aboard."

As Otis stepped into the dinghy, a shout penetrated the cacophony of shoreline conversations. "Captain Millett, is that white speck the thing we've been hearing about?"

"Aye. Not much to see, is there?" the captain responded.

"I hope you're not criticizing my invention, Captain," Otis whimpered.

"No, mate. But hoping the spectators can find something useful to do with their time."

Captain Millett's sailors pushed the dinghy away from the dock. The larger of the two sat at the center and grabbed the oars. He pointed the craft at the barge and stroked the water in that direction. Otis sat at the stern fiddling with his skull cap.

"Has Captain Sylvester seen your hollow ball yet, mate?" Millett asked.

"He met me in Hamilton aboard the *Freedom*, Captain. I had wired him to supervise the transfer from the *Fort Victoria* to his tug to get the ball to St. George. Instead, he pulled this barge and loaded it."

"A wise captain, my friend Sly…"

"…We discussed using the *Ready*—an ironic name, I might add… we discussed using the *Ready* as the launch platform," Otis explained.

The *Ready* was a rusted and rotting sea platform 130-feet long and less than 25-feet wide. It was rescued and resuscitated after serving as a tote barge for the Royal Navy.

On its uneven deck rested Barton's sphere. William Beebe coined it the *bathysphere* when reviewing the past season's deep-sea fauna, including one find: the *bathytroctes*.

The Greek prefix *bathy* simply meant deep. For Will, a perfect prefix for Barton's new submersible sphere. A *bathysphere*: A ball to submerge deep.

———

D TR staff and interns grooved new paths in the sandy soil around Nonsuch Island, a typical Monday morning march of activity. Else Bostelmann tied back tent flaps and shook her head at the trail of Hada's clothes leading to an unruly cot where her daughter slept.

Else, eager to start new sketches, was happy the spring's active socializing had slowed. Still, it was exciting having Rudyard Kipling and his wife visit and meeting Prince George when he returned to Bermuda. The young prince charmed everyone, but Else saw a noticeable interest in Miss Hollister.

"Good morning, Mrs. B."

Else didn't need to turn from her chores. She recognized Gloria's voice and Trumps' panting.

"Guten Morgen, Fräulein Hollister. Wie geht es Ihnen heute?"

"Wunderbar, Frau Bostelmann. Und selbst?"

"Es ist zwar noch früh, aber so weit so gut," Else replied.

"What are you saying to each other?" Patten Jackson asked as he walked past with an old broom handle concocted into a debris retriever. He stabbed the ground behind Trumps. The dog leaped into the air, twisting in search of the unexpected sound. Patten laughed.

"Don't scare my poor Trumps, Mr. Jackson."

"Sorry, Miss Hollister. He made me jump too."

Else asked the second-year intern if he stayed up late with Hada and the others. She said she heard them singing well past midnight.

Patten, who had added more muscle to his tall frame and a deeper voice, admitted that the young crew kept the campfire burning late.

"The stars were spectacular last night, Mrs. B. Hada was in excellent voice. I gazed and listened to her sing and thought this must be heaven."

"Oh, my word, Mr. Jackson, how you wax on..."

"I know, Miss Hollister. I'm practicing for college. The older boys say college girls fall for it."

"Don't let my daughter hear you talk about courting other women. I heard you pledge yourself to Hada last year, Herr Jackson. I'm expecting a college-educated son-in-law in four years."

The shock of hearing Mrs. B confirm her daughter's interest in marrying Patten made him stop his chores and search her face. He expected a smile.

Else remained solemn, but not Gloria who laughed hysterically.

Trumps barked begging Gloria to leave the conversation, which she did still chuckling. The dog jumped and frolicked down the path toward his morning hunting grounds. Gloria tried to keep up.

Will Beebe climbed the hill from the other direction. His clothes showed a watery shadow because of his swimsuit underneath.

"Swim done?" Gloria asked as they neared each other.

"The water's warming, Glo. Expect a change in our helmet dives."

"You're not thinking of helmet dives today, are you?"

"No, I'm so excited to see the *Gladisfen* pulling that barge this morning, I'm just babbling nonsense."

"I'm excited too. And nervous. I want us to succeed, Will, but that doesn't mean I'm not thinking about the danger."

"That's why we'll take our time, do our tests, and be thorough."

"Thorough and patient. We have the entire summer to do your dives with Mr. Barton. Do not let his impetuous urges convince you to be too hasty."

"I'm in control, Glo. Otis is an enigma, I agree. But he's delivered his promise despite a stock market crash. He's reworked the sphere at his personal expense. We need to pay him proper respect. Welcome him as a hero, because he is. An odd man but a hero to us."

Gloria said nothing. She agreed with 'odd,' but she reserved her judgment about 'hero' until she saw the bathysphere submerge and ascend with Will Beebe inside and safe.

Captain Edward Millett pulled a rope and let loose a foghorn blast that shot across a still Soldier Bay climbing the eastern cliff of Nonsuch Island. Will Beebe had already ascended to the top of the old hospital building so he could get an early glimpse of the tug with her cargo in tow.

He focused his telescope at the southern tip of Cooper's Island expecting the *Gladisfen* to appear. As the boat steamed around the island and Captain Millett sent a second blast in Will's direction, the skinny naturalist jumped. He yelled to staff and interns three stories below him, "It's coming. Here in fifteen minutes!"

He stabbed his eye into the telescope and searched the barge for his bathysphere. He saw Otis. Couldn't miss Otis. He stood in the center of the barge, his legs spread, his fists planted in each hip, elbows outstretched. He looked like a caricature of a swashbuckler.

"Can I see, Will?" John asked.

"Look at it, John!" Will exclaimed backing off the telescope so his protégé could look. "It's here, John. Otis did it."

John spent thirty seconds staring at Otis and the bathysphere. "He looks like he just institutionalized Kaiser Wilhelm, Will."

"I know."

John stepped aside and allowed Will to lunge back. "He's a proud young man. His ego will need more *ego* food when he arrives."

Will and John watched the boats approach Nonsuch Island for another five minutes before bouncing down three floors of narrow steps to ground level. The staff had surrounded the front entrance waiting for their leader.

"I expect Captain Millett will anchor his boats to the southwest where his dinghies can dock at the *Sea Fern*. Let's give the crew and Mr. Barton a joyous welcome," Will instructed.

Gloria looked at John, her face unyielding. Will knew he had work to convince his favorite researcher and secret lover that Otis Barton would be a worthy teammate.

Gloria feared people knew she and Will were carrying on an affair while Elswyth worked on her next book in England. The young staff who gathered at evening campfires were the spies about whom she worried the most. Their chatter and glances even when she and Will did legitimate research made her peek over her shoulder to see who was snickering.

Will told her she mustn't worry about other people's thoughts. He and Elswyth had an understanding.

Alone, Gloria enjoyed wrapping her long arms around Will's shoulders and pulling him close. She transferred passion for their work to her lust for his physical contact. He made a good lover. It took little for Will to succumb to her desires.

Gloria watched the throng migrate to the *Sea Fern*. She knew Will tolerated Otis, especially this time when he brought his diving ball, his bathysphere as Will called it.

Will stopped his march to the dock when he noticed Gloria had not moved from in front of the main campus building. He dodged the others so they could pass him, then walked back a few steps. "Are you coming, Glo?"

Gloria reacted instinctively to Will's voice and began to follow the rest to the *Sea Fern*. "I'm coming. Needed a moment, that's all."

Hada Bostelmann paused her trek down the rocky path and waited for Patten Jackson shuffling along with his buddies. Hada grabbed his arm and let the others pass.

"Did you notice?"

"Notice what?" Patten asked her.

"Dr. Beebe. Did you see who he went back for?"

"Yes. I noticed."

"Did the others?"

"I don't know, Hada. Golly, you're being such a girl."

"What does that mean?"

"They like each other, so what?"

"He's married, Patten, that's *so what*. You'd better not have an affair after we're married. I'll divorce you instantly."

"You can't. New York law doesn't allow 'instant' divorces. Besides, you're not serious about marrying me."

"I might be. But I'll change my mind if your attitude doesn't improve."

"What? My attitude? Let's get down to the dock or people will talk more about us than Dr. Beebe and Miss Hollister."

Patten took Hada's hand and pulled her resistant body. He jerked her the rest of the way down the hill.

Else went to the dock ahead of the crowd and set up an easel. She took pencils and watercolors to sketch the boats circling to anchor.

They were two hundred yards offshore in deeper water.

"There it is!" screamed an intern. She pointed to the center of the *Ready* where a tiny white speck caught the sun's rays.

Else lifted her body on tiptoes and strained to see the object. She exaggerated its size when drawing the barge and its cargo.

She saw Mr. Barton walking the deck toward a rope ladder that draped the *Ready's* side.

A dinghy with Captain Millett and two sailors rowed from the *Gladisfen* toward the ladder. Else flipped her sketching paper and began a new drawing.

As excited as the young staff, Else wondered what Dr. Beebe might discover when submerged in such a small craft. His daring new adventure was about to provide an answer.

CHAPTER 25

Otis the Great

Nearly a year had passed since Otis Barton first arrived at Nonsuch Island; eleven months since he departed. Otis didn't know if Dr. Beebe's team would welcome him back after his first sphere, too heavy for the boats to handle, caused palpable disappointment.

He got his answer when Captain Millett and his sailors docked the dinghy. DTR staff and interns were there to greet him with a boisterous welcome. He released an audible sigh.

A week earlier, Dr. Beebe and John Tee-Van visited St. George to see the bathysphere as it was being uncrated. They didn't open the 400-pound manhole cover. Instead, Will instructed John to stay with Otis to discuss several logistical issues, including how the two explorers would enter and exit the craft.

John and Otis went over the design and operating procedures calculating the time it would take to remove the four-inch emergency plug in the center of the manhole and ten bolts that held the manhole in place, the only opening where explorers entered and exited the steel ball. The manhole was positioned opposite three eight-inch window openings, two with three-inch-thick fused quartz glass and a steel plate over the third.

When they opened the ball, Otis and John climbed in. Struggling for space to put arms and legs, they looked for where and how to mount oxygen tanks, chemical trays, and a searchlight. They surveyed the hole at the top of the sphere where telephone and power lines would enter. When in place, they would plug the gaps with lead like a ship's propeller shaft stuffing box.

Otis appreciated the genteel nature Tee-Van showed when learning the simple but vulnerable aspects of the submersible sphere. Dr. Beebe's and his life depended on John Tee-Van's detailed focus each time the bathysphere dropped into the sea.

Otis endorsed Dr. Beebe's *bathysphere* name; it was a good descriptive name for the vessel, an engineering feat with a marketable story for scientific journals. It had the design to meet Dr. Beebe's expectation and now a title that told its purpose.

Following the reception for Mr. Barton, Will marshaled John, Gloria, Else, Helen Tee-Van, and the two men who would assist John with the bathysphere launches. He instructed them to board the *Skink* for a short jaunt to the *Ready*. When aboard the barge, Otis joined them.

"Welcome, Dr. Beebe," Captain Millett said with an outstretched hand to pull him aboard.

Will glared at the white ball seated in the middle of the deck. Gloria followed.

"Thank you, Captain," she said when accepting his assistance. "Oh, my goodness! It looks so small, Will."

"Try to move it, Gloria," John said after climbing onto the deck. "You won't think it small when you hear the winches struggle to lift it and plop it into the water."

"You make it sound like a fishing weight, John," Helen said as she grabbed her husband's hand to step aboard the old barge.

"She said it's small. I can't imagine us managing anything bigger," John explained.

When all the *Skink's* passengers had boarded the *Ready*, they circled the bathysphere, walking around then standing close. The ball sat on two steel feet so it would remain stable on flat surfaces.

"I want a look inside," Will Beebe commanded.

"Have your people stand away, Dr. Beebe. My crew needs to move in a hoist to lift the hatch," Captain Millett said.

Only three nuts temporarily held the hatch in place. John picked up a large wrench and began loosening. When he had the three off, he grabbed the hook hanging from a steel cable overhead. He secured it to the front of the hatch door and asked two sailors for help. They guided the door off the ten bolts as the cable tightened. The winch operator goosed the engine when the men set the hatch free of the bolts and guided the door away from the bathysphere.

Will lurched forward as soon as the hatch door swung by him. He thrust his head inside the darkness of the bathysphere hull. It took a few seconds for his eyes to adjust to the reduced light, but he could see and smell the effects of molded steel.

"What do you think, Dr. Beebe?" Otis asked.

Will pulled his head out. "We need to bathe before we get inside your contraption, that's what I think, Mr. Barton. And no beans before we launch."

Everyone chuckled at the obvious truth. They all took turns peeking inside the vessel, Else going last. She had sketched Dr. Beebe's butt and legs dangling from the mouth of the creature she now peered into. She imagined Jonah and the Whale.

"Well, Mrs. B?" Will asked.

"I think it needs a woman's touch. I would be glad to oblige."

"After me, Mrs. B!" Gloria responded quickly.

"Neither of you will enter the bathysphere until Mr. Barton and I have proven its sea-worthiness. I know I need not say this, but it's on my mind and I want it out there for everyone to hear. We are about to do something dangerous. I expect we're all nervous. I don't mind admitting that *I* am. But I'm also excited for the opportunity to discover. That outweighs my fears."

The group understood Dr. Beebe was setting a serious tone they all knew was necessary. They listened respecting the man about to take the biggest risk.

"This is an important moment for Otis and me. I cannot thank Mr. Barton enough for keeping his commitment despite personal misfortunes with the stock market and the necessary and expensive changes he made to his sphere—the *bathysphere*."

Will paused for a moment and looked into the eyes of each person standing with him.

"The entire world needs to know that life is everywhere on our planet," he continued. "Even twenty-thousand leagues under the sea as Verne described it—twice the circumference of the world. Nevertheless, the point is this: There is life at depths never imagined. Verne did well to get us to think of that possibility. That is why our world needs more self-acknowledgment. The planet Earth is an amazing place in the universe. Everywhere on Earth is amazing. Including deep in the sea. But equally important is the need to preserve it, not abuse it and allow it to decay, but preserve it so that life—all things flora and fauna—can continue on land and in this vast body of water that lies before us."

Heads nodded. Everyone agreed with William Beebe. That's why they loved what they were doing. That's why they rose at sunrise and worked until he said stop. They believed in his mission to explain that things existed even where others said they could not. Further, they agreed; *all* life had value worth preserving *ad infinitum*.

While discussions ensued about plans for the first unmanned submergence of the bathysphere, Else sketched and thought about Dr. Beebe's impassioned comments. She stewed over things she learned about some of Dr. Beebe's ardent supporters, the Zoological Society's leaders–Osborn and Grant–the founders of the American Eugenics Society, the Boone and Crocket Club, and New York's American Museum of Natural History.

Eugenic Society's philosophy was not one of preservation but annihilation. Members found fault with specific cultures and people. They devised plans to stop procreation for citizens descending from what they perceived to be inferior cultures. But simultaneously Osborn and Grant insisted on conserving animal life and putting creatures on display so it would inspire others to join them in their conservation crusade.

Else considered eugenics abhorrent and the Zoological Society's preservation efforts essential. How could diametric purposes come from the same minds? And what did Dr. Beebe think when around such influencers, including a former United States President?

She knew her role was to observe, draw, and paint. It was not to evaluate, fret, and criticize. Still, she couldn't stop her internal struggle.

Although eager to work with Dr. Beebe as he attempted to dive in the bathysphere because she believed in the mission, nevertheless she fought the philosophies she feared affected Dr. Beebe's passions.

Is Dr. Beebe being honest with me? With himself? Did he want to preserve life as he said? Because his colleagues seem more interested in manipulating it.

CHAPTER 26

First Tests

Otis Barton watched longshoremen bolting the Lidgerwood winch to the deck of the *Ready*. It was the winch Dr. Beebe used aboard the *Arcturus*, the boat used when Dr. Beebe explored the Caribbean and coast of South America.

Although mid-morning by the time Otis arrived, he came dressed for labor. He stepped in and used his long-body leverage to assist the team maneuvering the winch into place.

John Tee-Van supervised the installation. He had worked with the apparatus aboard the *Arcturus*, so his experience helped.

"Go over one more time how you see the winch and pulleys working together," John encouraged Otis.

"The aim is to reduce the stress at any point, including the winch, by setting up a series of pulleys," Otis replied. "Each point and each distance between points limits the overall stress on power."

John and Otis continued to instruct workers as they ran the Roebling cable through the pulley system and out the swiveling boom designated to lift the bathysphere over the side of the ship. The crew fired up both boilers, the one powering the Lidgerwood winch and the other that moved the arm from center-to-side allowing the sphere to drop into the ocean.

When they finished the testing, Otis told John he was ready for Dr. Beebe to set a time for their first unmanned trial.

"Will intends to be here this afternoon," John said. "Let's hear from Captain Millett too."

Will, Gloria, Else, and the two staff members Will put in charge of the winch and pivot mast, Phil Crouch and Arthur Hollis, arrived at St. George's wharf at one o'clock.

"I want the first drop to be where the harbor enters the sea," Will said. "If anything goes wrong, we need to be close to shore but where the water is deep enough for our test."

"Otis and I determined that we'll need eighteen able-bodied men besides the *Gladisfen* crew when we go to sea," John said.

"What about today? Can we manage with the deckhands already hired?" Will asked.

"If we're only pulling the *Ready* to the edge of the harbor, I should think so."

"Where's Otis now?" Gloria asked.

"He's meeting with Captain Millett to check the weather. If our test today goes well, we want to know when we can take the bathysphere to Dr. Beebe's designated area south of Nonsuch Island," John explained.

Within half an hour, the *Gladisfen's* boiler was producing adequate steam to chug its tow where Will Beebe directed. Will, Gloria, John, Else, and Otis gathered near the bathysphere while the crew prepared the clevis atop the steel ball for the cable attachment. The workers had piled sufficient steel cable on the deck to allow winch operator Crouch to test his gear without affecting their other duties.

The smaller steam engine hooked to the angular mast designed to pivot the bathysphere over the *Ready's* side also was being tested. Art Hollis and a native Bermudian Hollis picked from the deckhands practiced moving the arm until Art was comfortable with his assigned duty.

By the time Captain Millett pulled the *Ready* to the harbor's deeper sea edge, Will declared the operators fit to hoist the ball into the water. John climbed atop the bathysphere and Otis slipped inside. They worked together to seal the area where electrical wires and telephone lines wound together and entered the submersible ball.

John threaded the patented Okonite heat-sealed wires through a three-inch steel nut, sending it into the interior of the ball. Otis pulled the wires through a brass nut fit from the inside.

"It's through," Otis shouted.

John used a large wrench to turn the steel nut while Otis held the brass nut from inside. The brass threads circled the Okonite tube and grabbed the inside of the steel nut, pulling the two pieces together against the bathysphere's hull and interior.

John and Otis applied packing flax liberally from both sides. Captain Butler of Cox & Stevens told Otis it would never be a perfect seal but pressure from the sea would close it tighter as they descended.

John gave Will a signal they had completed their task. He stayed on the bathysphere's top while Otis climbed through the narrow egress, grabbed the cable end, and handed it to John. Tee-Van attached it to the clevis, signaled winch operator Crouch to pull the slack from the cable, and checked its firm hold.

Will raised his hand and looked at Captain Millett in his wheelhouse. The captain gave an order for the *Ready* to drop anchor. He shut down the *Gladisfen's* engine and twirled his wheel hard to the left. The tug leaned and curled the seawater as the captain steered alongside the *Ready*. His crew roped the barge and pulled the two vessels together on port sides.

With the boats tied, Captain Millett boarded the *Ready* and took charge of both ships' crews. The practice launch was standard procedure for a seaman like Millett, but aboard his barge was a celebrity and an important scientific team. He wanted them pleased and the setup flawless.

The captain walked by each steam engine to make sure the men Dr. Beebe assigned stoked them well. The plan was to drop the bathysphere seven to eight fathoms, let it rest in the water a few minutes, then bring it up to see whether the seals kept the craft's internal chamber dry.

Will checked the cable that looped from the *Arcturus*-Lidgerwood winch to the first set of pulleys thirty feet down the deck's length. It circled back to another pulley at the foot of the Lidgerwood, up the angled mast, and down to the bathysphere. Will looked at Art Hollis who gave him a thumbs up.

"Let's button the hatch and send her down," Will said.

John started a gasoline generator that motored a small hoisting rope draped above the manhole through which Will and Otis would climb. But this time the door was being swung into place to cover an empty bathysphere. John goosed the generator and pushed a bar that put the hoist in gear. It lifted the four-hundred-pound hatch even with the manhole.

Two crewmen and John guided the hatch into place, aligning the ten holes with the ten bolts protruding from the rim of the manhole. Once in place, the men spun huge nuts on each bolt. A third crewman stepped in with a large wrench and tightened each bolt. John came behind with another wrench and a sledgehammer, pounding each nut as tight as he could make them. The pounding reverberated across the deck of the *Ready*.

Satisfied that he had the hatch tight, John stepped back and looked at Will who was standing between Gloria and Else. Otis stood on the other side of the bathysphere also with his eyes on Will. The director nodded and John yelled, "Let's go!"

Phil Crouch placed the winch in gear and sped up his steam engine. The cable tightened against each pulley making the angled mast creak from the strain. The bathysphere rose and swung toward the winch, then back toward John, who took a step back.

"That's two-and-a-quarter ton," Captain Millett shouted, "give it some respect."

"Get it over the side," Will shouted to Art Hollis, who had already begun moving the pivoting mast toward the starboard side where they had removed railing to allow the ball to swing without causing damage.

"Don't let it swing back against the side," Will cautioned. "It'll put a hole in the *Ready* and sink us all."

Already nervous, Hollis wiped the sweat from his brow. It took an agonizing minute to swing the bathysphere over the side and free of the ship.

"Let it down, Phil," John said from his new position against the remaining starboard railing. He stood fifteen feet from the dangling ball, which looked extremely vulnerable at the end of the thin Roebling cable.

Crouch reversed the winch and allowed it to release more cable from the massive drum. The bathysphere began its drop toward the water. Crouch gave the winch more freedom allowing the ball to drop quicker. It hit the water with a forceful splash.

"Take it easy, Phil!" Will shouted.

"Sorry, Dr. Beebe."

After blue-green waves swallowed the sphere, Hollis swung his angled mast back into the boat letting the cable and Okonite hose drape the open side of the barge.

"It'll be at forty-five feet when the yellow marker on the hose goes over the side," Otis instructed.

Will, Gloria, and Else moved to the starboard railing next to John.

"The marker's coming," Hollis yelled to the others.

"It's barely visible, Will, but I think I can see occasional reflections," Gloria commented.

"Stop it, Phil, when the marker disappears," Will decreed.

"I see it, Dr. Beebe." He watched the yellow flag crawl over the deck and jerked the throttle back. The cable stopped.

"Let it sit there a few minutes. How do things look to you, Captain Millett?" Will shouted to the wheelhouse where the captain had returned for his bird's eye view of the happenings.

"Everything seems in order, Dr. Beebe. While it's resting there, it might be a good time to think about procedures when we send the ball deeper. Weather looks good for tomorrow if your sub comes up clean."

Will agreed with Captain Millett. He asked John if the order of actions was the most effective way to launch the bathysphere.

"We've done the easy steps, Will. We have communications to practice and safety procedures to rehearse. We need a few more empty dives before I feel ready."

"What do you think, Mr. Barton? Are you satisfied so far?"

"I'll know better when we lift the bathysphere and inspect it, Dr. Beebe."

"There's not much pressure at 45 feet. I'm not sure we'll learn about the seals. This was to make sure the crew can launch us and bring us back."

Will Beebe watched the crew on both boats stay busy. He saw them occasionally peek from their vantage points as they performed routine duties. They searched the water hoping for a glimpse of the submerged odd-looking vessel. He noted the irony. Earlier, he had picked up sarcastic comments about the bathysphere as the men were preparing for the test.

Otis Barton walked the deck of the *Ready* inspecting the winch as the cable unwound and now sat taut against each pulley. He appeared both anxious and annoying to Gloria Hollister who watched him behave like a military commander showing his authority. It irritated her because she felt he was attempting to steal the spotlight from Dr. Beebe who leaned over the railing as though he was a young boy waiting to reel in the fish he just caught.

"It's been ten minutes, Dr. Beebe," Phil Crouch reported.

"Bring it up," Will ordered.

"The arm needs to swing into place first, Dr. Beebe," Captain Millett announced from his perch.

"Move the arm, Art."

Crouch and Hollis worked their respective steam engines in coordination. The ball ascended about a foot every second, so it took less than a minute to break the surface throwing water like an orca emerging for air.

The winch and pivot-mast groaned as the bathysphere lifted into the air. Hollis swung the sphere aboard once Crouch had it lifted above the deck. The craft swung like an uncontrolled pendulum as it neared the deck.

John had moved back to his position where he wanted Crouch to set the bathysphere. He signaled to Art to stop the arm and waited for the sphere to settle its sway before he yelled to Phil to let it drop slowly.

The sphere plunked onto the deck with a thud. Will hurried to the front of the bathysphere and stuck his nose against the center quartz window. Otis stood at his heels asking if he could see anything.

"Too dark. Let's get it open, John."

Tee-Van had already picked up his tool to grip the center disc, the four-inch opening in the center of the hatch plate. He and a crewmember forced the opening to turn. He wrenched the nut off then spun it loose. Light from the opposite side gave Otis a better view when peering through the window Will vacated.

"It looks dry, Dr. Beebe."

"Then we're ready for the next step," Will asserted.

Else Bostelmann leafed through sketches she had shuffled together and kept in her carrying bag. She considered her drawings to be practice in the same way the crew had practiced its skills.

She was satisfied with results, especially her speed. There was nothing she cared to show anyone but a few she wanted to fine tune and fill with watercolors because she liked the composition.

Else reviewed the dynamics at work. Nothing surprised her although she marveled at the continuity. Dr. Beebe had a way of making everyone around him rise to challenges and excel.

John Tee-Van, a quiet and humble man, exuded authority. Gloria Hollister waited for no instruction. She studied, wrote her notes, and knew to prepare for future tasks without Dr. Beebe's guidance. Phil Crouch and Arthur Hollis also demonstrated abilities they had not exhibited before.

Else admired the images of people doing things beyond assumed capabilities. She attributed their accomplishments to William Beebe's leadership. But Dr. Beebe was a puzzle Else had not pieced together. He was complex. His motives to push himself and others to do more made her curious. Why? Why was he relentless? Why so courageous, a man in his fifties? Was his thirst for knowledge, his passion to discover so consuming that he could think of nothing else?

Else knew her role. She was to paint the life that Dr. Beebe and his staff studied. They were attempting to explain that each specimen they captured represented an important cog is life's wheel of perpetual motion, so it was necessary to view species in their environment.

However, Else saw a human dynamic at work as well. It was not part of her job to analyze and explain it. She knew that. It was not something she could paint, but it was something she felt important to understand to be effective with the people who depended on her artistic skills. A new role she made up just for her.

CHAPTER 27

Tangled

Although he spent a restless night, Will rose at his usual hour and went for his morning swim. He entered Mrs. Tucker's kitchen and asked permission to turn on her radio. He hoped the local station had weather information.

"It's going to be a perfect day, Dr. Beebe. I can feel it," Mrs. Tucker said.

"I hope you're right, Mrs. Tucker. We need to take the bathysphere to deep water so we can test it. We need to check our crew."

Else entered the kitchen with her standard German greeting for Mrs. Tucker. She spotted Dr. Beebe with his bowl of Grape Nuts. "Are we ready for another day?"

"I'm ready, Mrs. B. I did not sleep well thinking of all we need to check before we enter the water."

"Coffee, Mr. Tee-Van?" Mrs. Tucker asked when John entered her kitchen.

"Thank you, Mrs. Tucker."

"Did you establish a time to start?" Will asked John.

"Captain Millett said he could have the crew ready and the boats to Nonsuch by eight o'clock. I've made sure Crouch and Hollis are up. Glo already went for a swim and the interns are taking care of the fish tanks, so we all should be able to go by the time the *Gladisfen* and *Ready* are here."

Will had less than two hours to finish his chores.

Else took her coffee and walked to the tent she shared with Hada. She hoped Hada was one of those Mr. Tee-Van encouraged to take care of the fish so he could focus on checking out the bathysphere.

Hada was gone but her trail of yesterday's clothing lingered. Else grabbed her sketching supplies and headed to join the others.

Captain Millett settled in Castle Harbor west of Nonsuch Island at eight o'clock. Will had his staff aboard the *Skink* and motored toward the *Ready*.

Hada Bostelmann, Patten Jackson, and a team of interns stood on the dock with Trumps and Chiriqui. The animals barked and screamed at the departing crew.

Otis Barton stood on the *Ready's* deck guarding his bathysphere. He walked portside and threw the ladder over. Within minutes Will, Gloria, John, Else, Phil Crouch, and Arthur Hollis had joined Otis and circled the bathysphere to hear the day's plans. Else left and found a vantage point to draw.

She watched the *Gladisfen* as it pulled the *Ready*. It rose and fell bucking five-foot waves. She began to feel nauseous, so she moved away from the bow and focused on the cluster of islands shrinking beyond the stern.

Will lifted his voice over the group and called to her to join them. She picked up her bag and walked toward the bathysphere. She wondered if they created a new job for her.

"Mrs. B, this is how things will happen," Will said. "They will affect you, so I wanted you to hear."

"Of course, Dr. Beebe."

"Glo will wear a telephone headset. Mr. Barton or I will have a headset inside the bathysphere, not today, but when we dive. I will describe the life that I see as we submerge. Glo will write my descriptions. She'll give those notes to you. That's how we'll create the pictures."

"Very good. I understand, Dr. Beebe. When you're not describing things you're seeing, how does Miss Hollister know you're still alive?"

The question brought a chuckle from Hollis and Crouch.

"We've thought of that, Mrs. B," John began.

"…I'm insisting that Will say something, or cough, every five seconds, so I know they're okay," Gloria continued. "Did you hear her, Will? Mrs. B is saying what I told you. You cannot go down in the bathysphere in silence," Gloria scolded.

"An important communication Mr. Barton and I will need from the deck is our depth; how far we've descended," Will said. "That's one thing we can practice today."

"We've placed some markings on the Okonite line every one-hundred feet," John said. "Each time a deckhand sees a mark nearing, he'll alert Glo so she can notify you of the distance."

Will insisted on walking the *Ready's* deck. Staff and crew said little with tensions mounting. The director then moved to the bathysphere and rested a hand on it.

The sun climbed high in the east by the time the captain slowed his craft and allowed the *Ready* to settle in the waves. He had navigated his tug to the designated longitude and latitude Dr. Beebe specified keeping the towline taut while his crew reeled the two craft closer together.

A few deckhands, mostly descendants from shipwrecked slave ships a century earlier, assisted Crouch with the steam engine. Others worked with Hollis to manage the Okonite line. It lay near the opening in the deck rail where it could unravel easily.

"What's our goal, Dr. Beebe?" Hollis yelled.

"Two thousand feet," Will and John answered together.

"The boats are as stable as they're going to be," Captain Millett shouted from his perch on the *Gladisfen*.

"Send it in, John," Will ordered.

John and Otis stood next to the bathysphere. They tightened all ten nuts on the fourteen-inch manhole cap, screwed in the four-inch safety plug, and added packing lead to the communications cable stuffing box at the bathysphere apex.

Everyone was ready. The bathysphere swung like a wrecking ball with damaging force. Once over the side, it dropped and hit the water.

"That needs some practice," Will told the crew.

"Let it sink slowly, Phil," John shouted. "Slower still," he commanded.

Hollis had retracted the swivel boom. The Okonite hose and Roebling cable uncurled from their separate piles and sank. After nearly four minutes, the second mark on the hose slid into the deckhand's loose grip. Gloria wrote on her tablet. "That's two-hundred-feet, Will, at four minutes eleven seconds from the order to lower the bathysphere."

"Are you certain you want it to descend two-thousand feet?" Otis asked.

"We need to test the hatch, the quartz windows, and the packing around the utility hose to know they can withstand the water pressure. If the bathysphere comes up without leaks, we'll be ready to dive," Will replied.

After forty-five minutes, the deckhand guiding the Okonite line notified Gloria that the twentieth mark was approaching.

"We're at two-thousand feet," Gloria shouted.

"Stop the descent!" John yelled to Crouch, who instantly halted the winch drum. "Let it sit."

Whispered conversations spoke volumes about the tension on the boat. On the *Gladisfen*, Captain Millett pulled his head back into his wheelhouse and checked the sky to the southeast.

He dialed in his shortwave radio and listened for weather reports. The captain knew if it took forty-five minutes for the ball to descend, rested at two-thousand feet for ten minutes, and took another forty-five minutes to come back up, the midday heat would pull storm clouds closer.

Will fought the urge to pace. He didn't want to display the nervous feelings that were churning his stomach. Otis had little else to do, so he walked from bow to stern along the rail. Time passed slowly.

Will finally broke the tension. "John, bring it up."

Art Hollis cranked the boom mast toward the starboard rail. It creaked under the ascending weight. After a few minutes a shout from a deckhand reeling in the Okonite hose got everyone's attention.

The deckhand struggled to separate the hose from the cable. The lines had twisted together. The Okonite hose gripped the cable and approached the boom pulley. It clung in twisted knots.

"Stop the winch!" John yelled to Crouch. He leaned over the starboard side and noticed the hose and cable wound together as far down as he could see. "We have a serious problem, Will."

Beebe, Barton, and Hollister peered over the side at the disastrous entanglement. The bathysphere had spun during its descent twisting the hose around the cable. The crew wrestled with the two lines as Crouch inched the ball up.

"The twists in the Okonite sheath may have broken the electrical line or telephone connection, Will," John said.

"Glo, put on the headset and see if you can hear any noises coming from the bathysphere," Will instructed.

Gloria went to the table where she placed her telephone equipment. She unfurled the wires and placed the earphones on her head. She increased the volume.

"Anything, Glo?" Will asked.

"There's static. But I can't tell if that means anything."

"It's a mess. This will take some time to separate," John moaned.

Captain Millett saw the desperate efforts and once more dialed in his weather reports. There were storms to the east. Winds had increased to fifteen knots, which made grappling with the bathysphere's cables more difficult.

"Time's critical, mates!" the captain screamed from his wheelhouse.

Larger waves made the *Ready* rock. By the time the crew could see the top of the bathysphere they had untwisted more than thirty Okonite line revolutions around the cable.

Otis watched frozen in despair. Will approached him while John directed the efforts.

"We'll figure this out," Will said. "No one thought about the turning and twisting enough to guide the wires."

Else sat in the cool breeze looking westward. The setting sun painted the disintegrating storm clouds with a rainbow of warmth. Gray billows in the foreground created a perfect and ironic umbrella over Castle Island as though shielding it from further torment.

Else quickly sketched the massive shapes and used her watercolors to imitate the radiant beams of light. She was intensely focused, so sounds of crackling twigs nearby startled her.

She turned to see Dr. Beebe and Gloria Hollister in an embrace. Else ducked her head into the evening shadows. She felt uncomfortable, but she was frozen by a fear of being discovered, which would make them all feel more uncomfortable, so she stayed silent watching and listening. Though their voices were inaudible, their passion said a lot.

When lips parted, Will took Gloria's hand and continued walking.

Guilt troubled Else. Although her spying was inadvertent, she wished she hadn't witnessed what many rumored to be true.

Seeing the kiss made Else sad. She felt alone. It was something she tried to manage.

To be loved is good. Am I jealous of Miss Hollister? She is held and kissed, touched and wanted; those are what Mrs. Eddy says are God's gifts of human joy.

"Mother? What are you doing out here?"

Else jumped. "I'm looking at life and putting it on this small piece of paper, Tochter. What are *you* doing out here?"

"Hello, Mrs. Bostelmann."

"Guten Abend, Herr Jackson."

"Pat was complaining about feeling ill," Hada said. "I told him he needed fresh air and a walk. That's what you always told me when I complained about having an ache."

"Has the fresh air cured your pains, Mr. Jackson?" Else asked.

"I feel better when walking with Hada, that's true."

"Won't he make a marvelous husband, Mother? He always says the right thing."

"Am I being flattered or ridiculed?" Patten asked.

"It's just my teasing, Pat. Tell us about the day, Mother. Was the test of the bathysphere successful? We heard that it didn't go so well."

"The submersible came up with only a little water, so that pleased Dr. Beebe since he sent it to two-thousand feet. But there were problems with the cables," Else explained.

"We heard that Mr. Tee-Van is working at St. George's wharf tonight, trying to solve issues they hadn't expected," Patten said.

"The poor man works very hard. I hope he succeeds," Else replied.

"Mother, can you see the *Sea-Fern* dock from here?"

"It's getting so dark now, I don't believe so."

Dr. Beebe and Miss Hollister walked toward the *Sea-Fern*. Else suspected Hada had a purpose in asking.

"We saw them go that direction," Hada said.

"Who?"

"Dr. Beebe and Miss Hollister."

"They have plenty to talk about. Miss Hollister has many responsibilities when Dr. Beebe and Mr. Barton dive in the bathysphere."

"Your answers are so predictable, Mother."

"And your behavior is unbecoming a twenty-year-old woman. Our business is art and intern duties, not spying on others and creating stories."

"Your mother's right, Hada. We need to go back for the campfire and music."

"The other interns know what I'm up to, Pat. You don't need to worry."

"Hada! Leave me," Else demanded. "Both of you. I'm losing my light."

Will and Gloria rested their heads against the *Skink's* life jackets. They lay hidden from view on the boat's floor looking at evening stars that peeked from behind a few remaining ocean-bound clouds.

"The day was partially successful, Glo," Will said weakly.

"John will figure out the cable issue," Gloria answered. "I'm glad to learn the power and communications lines didn't sever."

Gloria rolled on top of Will. "We're not here to talk about how our day went. The day is over, William Beebe. This is my time to be alone with you. Let's talk about us."

She pressed her body against Will's. They kissed. Will slipped his hand under her loose blouse stimulating their passion. He pushed Gloria's shoulder and rolled on top. Gloria responded with willing acquiescence.

They made love and remained in an embrace; Gloria eager to talk.

"I want our furtive meetings to make me happy," she said. "And they do because I love you. But I would enjoy our time together more if we could be open."

"I'm not afraid of our team knowing our relationship, but there are canons the zoological society expects me to uphold," Will said. "Having an open affair while my wife is in England doesn't fit those canons."

"I've played second fiddle before. I'm used to it. That's why I love sports because in sports I win. I beat men, I beat other women. So as a woman, I don't care about 'canons' as you call them. I care about you and the work we do. That's all. If you can't love me as a wife, then it's okay to love me as your admirer, your friend…"

"Glo, I'm not putting labels on our relationship. I'm charmed by your beauty and intelligence. I have a wife who has an affair too with her ambitions. I understand that, but it's not physically satisfying. Time with you is the most pleasure I've enjoyed in twenty years."

"Oh, Will, I know better. You can have any woman you desire. I've seen how they swoon when you dress in a tuxedo, chatter,

and pose like a politician. You could bed any of them and probably have."

"And your beauty, doesn't it have the same effect on men?"

"You're wrong, Will, but I don't want to end our evening ar-
guing over who is luckier with the opposite sex. It's time to dress,
separate, and retire for the evening. How sad and ironic."

CHAPTER 28

Practice Dives
5 June 1930

John and Helen Tee-Van met Captain Millett at the Darrell & Meyer Wharf. They had spent the evening at St. George's Hotel after John worked well into the evening unraveling the prior day's disaster.

John feared the entanglement broke the wires, but the sheath's flexible strength survived the ordeal. He had both cables ready and a new strategy for preventing the unanticipated chaos —connect the cables with ties every 100 feet.

Captain Millett asked the Tee-Vans if they had seen Mr. Barton yet.

"Very few people at breakfast so we would have noticed if Otis was there," John said. "I'm sure he slept in after the disappointment yesterday."

"Did you sleep in, Mr. Tee-Van?" the captain asked.

"He did not, Captain Millett," Helen replied for her husband, "and thank you for observing the difference between my husband and some other members of our team."

"Those *others* make it easy to see differences, Mrs. Tee-Van."

John used the time to explain the new cable and line procedures to Captain Millett and his crew. Further, he said Helen brought a message from Dr. Beebe. With the problem solved and a good weather report on the radio, Will wanted to test the cable and do their first dive.

"The tug and barge are ready, Mr. Tee-Van. As soon as Mr. Barton shows we can head to Nonsuch Island. I'll raise the flag so Dr. Beebe knows we're on our way."

Captain Millett concocted the simple signaling method with Will. The director told the captain he could see St. George through his telescope from his "penthouse" island bedroom. A colorful red flag raised against the green palm and cedar trees was all he needed.

The flag went up.

Otis sauntered down the hill from St. George's Hotel. He went directly to the *Ready* with a coffee cup in one hand and his sweat-soaked leather skullcap in the other. A crewman told him today might be his first bathysphere dive with William Beebe. Otis grinned.

A telephone call at the wharf sent a messenger out to the dock to retrieve John Tee-Van. "Dr. Beebe's calling," the messenger said.

John hurried to the phone. "Good morning, Will. This is John."

"I'm loading the staff into the *Skink*, John. Tell Captain Millett I want to test the bathysphere at the closest deep water."

"We need enough depth to clip the two cables together for a reasonable test," John commented.

"I agree, John. We'll drop it as deep as you need. I want to hear you say you're satisfied the crew can do its job with the ties you've created."

The *Gladisfen-Ready* tandem waited for Dr. Beebe's team to board. Captain Millett took the craft where he knew the depth exceeded one-hundred-fifty fathoms.

They worked quickly to keep their minds off the stress. Otis grabbed two oxygen tanks, each just shy of eighteen inches, and Will scooped soda-lime into one tray to absorb carbon dioxide and calcium chloride into a second tray to absorb moisture.

John attached the small hoist to the front of the manhole cover. He lifted the four-hundred-pound cover and Otis climbed into the bathysphere. Will handed him the oxygen tanks and the two chemical trays. Otis placed the tanks on welded hangers and the trays on two shelves.

Will climbed through the narrow opening squeezing by Barton. Their knees rested on the cold, curved steel bottom of the ball. Will pivoted to stick his head out the manhole. "Seal us up and send us down about two-hundred feet, John."

It took several minutes to attach the ten nuts. John hand-tightened the nuts and pounded them with his sledgehammer, sending loud reverberations through the bathysphere. He screwed in the center plug, the emergency safeguard that opened quickly so Will and Otis could get air if needed.

John then waved to Phil Crouch at the cable winch and Art Hollis at the boom. Art waited until Phil had the bathysphere elevated and stable before he began to swing the boom toward the starboard opening. Gloria had her headset on and was trying to get Will or Mr. Barton to respond to her voice. Otis finally did.

The bathysphere swung over the sea's relative morning calmness and began to approach the water. John leaned over the deck's open edge and watched the ball push the grayish-blue sea aside. It sank into murkiness.

Hollis brought the boom back over the deck as two deckhands grabbed the Okonite line and prepared to clip it to the cable. When the hundred-foot tag slipped into their hands, Crouch stopped the winch. The crew snapped the clip around both lines and Crouch restarted the descent.

"Are they seeing anything, Glo?" John asked.

Gloria shook her head.

When the final hundred feet and clip touched the water, John halted the winch. "He's at two-hundred feet," John told Gloria. "More than thirty-three fathoms."

Gloria relayed the information.

"Will says to hold him there for a few minutes. He can see a few fish from his window. They're getting used to the interior space."

"Any leaking?"

"John wants to know if there's any leaking," Gloria said into her cone-shaped microphone clinging to her neck. "Otis says there doesn't appear to be any."

"We'll wait for Will's order to pull them up," John said.

Gloria once again demanded one of them utter a sound every five seconds. She asked Otis to test the light signal. One flash meant they were okay. Three flashes meant to pull them up. It was a backup in case the communications line failed.

At ten minutes Will had Otis tell Gloria to bring them up. She signaled to John.

Compared to the fight with the entangle cables, this ascent was over quickly. The boom had swung out and lifted the bathysphere from the water and nudged it toward the *Ready's* deck.

John stood near the landing spot where he wanted Crouch to set the bathysphere. He placed both palms against the wet ball and helped it settle its swaying motion as Phil lowered it into place. It jarred the deck as it plunked down.

Gloria stood over John's shoulder eager to see Will's face when the hatch door lifted.

John removed the center disk then loosened the nuts and spun them until all ten were off. He put the small hoist hook on the front of the manhole cover. Hollis had come over to assist him and goosed the generator engine to keep the small boom cable taut as John pried the hatch door off the ten bolts, pulled it, and pushed it out of the way.

Will Beebe, smiling, stuck his head out of the fourteen-inch hole. Saying nothing, he climbed from the ball putting his hands on the deck and lifting his legs out gingerly. Otis followed.

Will and Otis stood together. Connery took their picture. They seemed to giggle. Will reached out and Otis took his hand chuckling as though Will had shared a joke.

"We won't call that our first official dive. It was a good experience but not a real dive," Will said. He acted as giddy as a five-year-old holding his first caught fish.

Gloria noticed. She knew the symptom. "You need to make one adjustment, Will."

"It worked well, Glo, perfectly fine. I don't think we need to do anything. I think we're ready to dive," Will turned toward the *Gladisfen* and shouted, "Captain, let's go for the big one!"

"What's wrong, Miss Hollister?" Connery asked.

"Oxygen intoxication," she replied. "They need to figure out how to moderate the flow. See how much they used, John."

Tee-Van reached into the bathysphere. He unbuckled the tank with the control apparatus and pulled it out. "Doesn't look like it moved at all, Glo."

"Well, they can't be getting juiced in under twenty minutes, or they'll ruin this experiment for everyone," Gloria said.

"You're correct, Glo. Sorry," Will said. "I'm feeling a little dizzy and getting a headache. Too much oxygen. One more thing to monitor as we submerge."

"Are you all right, Dr. Beebe?" Connery asked. "Are we calling it a day?"

"No. I mean, yes, I'm fine. Disappointed in myself but fine. We'll rest and Mr. Barton and I will drink some water. Let's take the bathysphere out to sea for another empty test."

Captain Millett heard Will and before John could provide instructions, Millett had shouted orders to his crew. "Fire engine. Ease out the tow line!"

The *Gladisfen* churned ahead until the thick hemp rope lifted from the water and tightened like a clothesline. The *Ready* lurched ahead then eased into a calm cruise behind its sea partner.

"We'll drop the bathysphere then decide," Will told staff and deckhands gathered around the white sphere. "If it comes up clean, we'll dive."

Will looked into Barton's eyes to see if he flinched. Fighting a sudden headache, Will couldn't summon the energy to properly read Otis.

John took over preparations. He ordered Crouch and Hollis to check fuel supplies at all engines. He glanced at Gloria who already knew her role. She twisted the cap and looked at the small generator's gasoline line. It provided power to the bathysphere's thousand-watt lamp and her communications system.

John directed the deckhands to stretch out the Okonite cable along the port deck to free any knots, curls, or binds. They carefully rewound the cable and moved it to the starboard side near the boom engine.

Will strolled to Gloria's side while she worked. "This begins something important, Glo. Keep good records."

Will knew she would. Still, he wanted her to understand how critical she was to him and the success of the entire DTR exploration. She had expressed her desire to be in the bathysphere rather than on the deck. He wanted her in the bathysphere too, because she understood the science and significance. Otis dove for the glory. And because Will made a promise.

CHAPTER 29

Brilliant and Breathtaking

The empty bathysphere went over the *Ready's* side at John Tee-Van's directive. The hired deckhands worked with Hollis to organize the brass clips. Art swung the boom back to the deck to put the cables within reach.

The bathysphere disappeared leaving only a trail of foam as it sank. The team watched the cables unravel, looking for the first hundred-foot marks. When within a few feet of the edge, John yelled to stop the winch.

The crew pinched the thick cables together and slapped the first clip in place. Gloria wrote the time by her one-hundred-foot notation. She nodded at John.

"Start'er again, Phil," John said. And the cables moved.

Forty minutes later, Will shouted over the din of the winch, "That's good enough, John."

"Stop the descent!" John yelled. "Let it sit for three minutes then bring it up, Phil."

The bathysphere hung at two-thousand feet.

The minutes crept. Otis paced and Captain Millett lit the stub of a cigar watching from the wheelhouse. Will walked toward Gloria. Her hands covered her earphones, which she pressed against her ears. She listened for sounds from inside the bathysphere. Will said nothing; just studied Gloria's face.

"Three minutes!" John blurted. "Bring'er up."

The engines growled and the cables began moving. Water dripped to the deck as cable wire wrapped the huge winch.

John sighed relief as the cables came up unencumbered by tangles.

The top of the submersible emerged soon after the crew removed the final hundred-foot clip. The dripping ball swung and settled.

Soon it sat and the cables slackened. The team rushed to touch it. Gloria, trying to stay calm, removed her headset and trailed the others.

Will poked his nose against the center fused quartz glass. Light through the other window was too weak to allow him to see much but enough for him to know it was relatively dry.

"Get it open, John," Will demanded.

ee-Van, Hollis, and Connery worked quickly to wrench the nuts loose. Crouch moved the smaller cable to the front of the heavy manhole plate and hooked it. He took out the slack so the other men could pull it and lift it off.

Will had moved 180-degrees around the sphere and shoved his head inside the ball. "A little water," he said, "maybe a quart or two." He stepped back so Otis could confirm. When the engineer leaned back, he looked at Will. They both smiled little smiles but kept their eyes on each other. Then Will nodded. "We will dive," he said. "Let's get it ready."

Conversations over the next thirty minutes were brief and pointed. No wasted words. Will said little deferring to Tee-Van, the man in charge. John broke the silence with barked instructions.

Gloria disguised her worry by making certain the telephone line sounded clear, her notebook set to a clean page, and the emergency light functioning well.

Otis climbed into the bathysphere and placed the oxygen canisters against the chilled, curved wall. Will reached through the manhole with the first tray, the soda-lime, which Otis strapped to a small platform under the oxygen tank. The second tray, calcium chloride, came next.

Otis returned to the open air when satisfied the internal workings were in order. He looked at Will and John who had huddled with Gloria and Jack Connery. "We're set up inside," he told them.

"I spoke with Captain Millett," John reported. "The weather's stable; the ocean seems to be leveling, so the captain's prepared for the sphere to enter the water. Should I gather the crew, Will?"

Will shook his head. "I have no speech to make. It's time to dive. Let's just go."

John did a pirouette and shouted, "We're diving. Everyone in position."

He looked to the *Gladisfen's* wheelhouse where he could see Captain Millett leaning from the window listening.

"Keep it tight, Captain!" John yelled.

Millett waved.

Deckhands stood near their assigned stations next to the winch, at the boom, and with the Okonite line. Will remained stoic. He bent over, stuck his arms and head inside the bathysphere, and pushed his way inside.

Otis followed once Will wiggled clear. He pulled himself to the right. When inside, the two lanky men squirmed for comfort and maneuverability.

"I need a cushion for my knees," Will said.

John Tee-Van sent a crewman on a hunt. He came back empty-handed. "There's nothing on board the barge to offer you, Will," John reported.

"Then seal it up," Will ordered.

John signaled to Hollis to lift the manhole cover into place. Art revved the generator engine and the iron disk rose from the deck. John and a crewman guided the cover toward the ten bolts. They slipped it in place and John hand-tightened two nuts to hold it.

The bathysphere darkened. Light entered only through two six-inch wide quartz-glass windows and the four-inch center hole in the cover, the emergency opening Otis designed to allow air before the deckhands could remove the nuts and lift the cover.

Will and Otis continued to jockey for space and untangle legs while the team scrambled outside the tiny capsule. Otis tweaked the oxygen valve and watched the gauge settle.

John's voice became muffled. Noises disguised other sounds and people.

Tee-Van leaned into the center hole: "We'll tighten the nuts now," a warning the loud pounding was about to start.

John used a large sledgehammer to rap the end of a wrench he locked onto each nut. The echoing noise put the two bathysphere passengers in the middle of a gigantic church bell.

When it stopped, tinnitus-like sounds reverberated in Will's ears. He leaned toward the small opening, the last circle of connection to those who controlled his and Barton's fate. He could see Tee-Van lean toward the opening. "Good luck, Will," John whispered.

Will Beebe thrust his right hand through the opening and shook John's. He retracted it and told John, "Send us down." Otis copied his idol with a handshake for Tee-Van, after which John plugged the center hole, screwed it in snuggly then pounded the wing bolt tight.

"That infernal noise will stay in my ears this entire descent," Will complained.

The two men settled into the bowl of the bathysphere; Will on his boney knees, head pressed against a window, and Otis on his butt with legs crossed underneath him. He adjusted the microphone connected to Gloria Hollister.

"Testing," Otis said. "Can you hear me, Miss Hollister?"

"Yes, over," she replied.

"Our communication works, Dr. Beebe," Otis reported.

"Good. Tell Glo to have John get this sphere moving. The sun is cooking us."

"I heard him, Mr. Barton. You're about to go," Gloria said.

With her words spoken, the tension on the Roebling cable jarred the bathysphere from its perch. It lifted into the air. Without pause, the derrick swung toward the starboard. It carried the white ball high enough to clear all things in its path.

Four deckhands grabbed the bottom to slow its pendulum forces. They and Hollis eased the glistening sphere off the starboard side. It hovered over the water for an instant and then hit the surface hard sinking from sight.

"Are you okay, Will?" Glo asked. "Did you feel that?"

"We felt it, Miss Hollister," Otis answered. "We can see the foam rise around the windows."

"Tell her the sight is amazing, Barton," Will said.

"No need to repeat, Mr. Barton. We'll be stopping you for the first cable clamp."

"She says we're stopping so they can clamp the two cables together"

The foamy bubbles disappeared. Will searched for the bottom of the Ready as they tethered one-hundred feet below the ocean's waves.

"What a sight," Will said. "Coral clinging, weaving seaweeds dangling like mistletoe, tubular sponges hanging on like stalactites in a cave. Tissue-thin pearl shells; all seaworthy one might say."

"Does the director want us to hold longer?" Gloria asked.

"Do you want to stay here or are we ready to descend, she wants to know."

"Down; send us down."

"I heard, Mr. Barton," Gloria responded. She gave John a hand signal.

The bathysphere began its first official deep-water descent passing twenty-five fathoms and sending both ships' hulls out of Will's view and below the maximum distance he had gone with his copper helmet. Chills covered his thin arms as he began to lose himself in awe.

Otis monitored oxygen flow rather than Will's excitement, thinking more about his submersible craft suspended by a less-than-inch-thick cable. He fanned the air with a palm leaf to keep it circulating, his body hot and sweating.

"We're doing it, Otis. We're in your engineered sphere descending into history saying goodbye to superstitions that previously ruled science."

Otis smiled and nodded.

Gloria surprised Otis when she asked with concern, "Are you two all right?"

"Yes, yes, we're fine, Miss Hollister. Dr. Beebe was saying farewell to old science."

"Remind him you need to talk to me. You're stopping for another clamp at two-hundred feet."

"She says to remind you we need to talk to her; now at two-hundred."

Will told Otis at that distance, they were deeper than Commander Ellsberg when he gallantly attempted to recover thirty-three sailor bodies aboard the Submarine S-51 that sank off the coast of New York in 1925.

Otis and Gloria exchanged periodic utterances as the bathysphere continued downward. When the craft neared three-hundred feet, Otis let out an expletive, deafening Gloria.

"What? What's happening, Otis, for God's sake?"

"We're leaking! Water! It's coming in at the hatch!"

"Calm yourself. It's a trickle," Gloria heard Will say.

Not satisfied, Gloria demanded an answer, "Tell me what's going on!"

Will heard her voice from the headset strapped to Barton's ears. "Tell her we're fine; continue the descent. Drop us faster. The deeper we go the more pressure will push against the manhole cover and the seepage will stop."

Will wiped his finger across the drip and saw the trickling inside the bathysphere. He remained confident it would get no worse. Otis settled back but kept his eyes on the leak.

Will's attention went back to the deep blueness of the Atlantic. He mumbled, *we're ten miles off the coast of Bermuda, sinking into Davy Jones' locker, too far from any touch of earth.*

He saw the temperature inside the bathysphere was seventy-eight degrees.

"Has the drip stopped?" Otis asked.

Will looked. "It appears so."

At that moment, they halted abruptly.

"What's the problem?"

"No problem, Mr. Barton," Gloria responded. "You're at four hundred feet. We're attaching another clamp to the cables. Any sign of life?"

"Miss Hollister asks if there's any sign of life. We're at the four-hundred-foot stop."

"Turn on the searchlight, Otis. I'm seeing glistens of light in the distance."

Otis put his palm leaf at the bottom of the bathysphere bowl. He grabbed the back of the bulky lamp and flicked the switch. A burst of light filled the bathysphere. Otis aimed the lamp out the center window. Will saw the light's yellow spread through the blue ocean.

"Life is sparse, Glo," Will shouted. "But I've never seen blue so magnificent."

Otis pulled the headset and microphone from his body and handed it to Will. He tried to maneuver the light closer to the center window and shifted the beam from left to right. The electrical wire sparked.

"Watch it, God damn it!"

"What's wrong, Will? Speak to me!" Gloria demanded.

"Otis moved the lamp. He made sparks jump. Disconnect it, Otis!"

Otis tried but fumbled. He pulled the cord to straighten the kinks. The sparks stopped.

"Will, you must tell me what's going on. Do I have to bring you up?"

John now hovered over Gloria trying to understand if the divers were in trouble. Others on the *Ready* saw John's concern and froze in silence.

"Will, this is John," he shouted at the microphone still hanging from Gloria's neck. "We're about to abort and bring you up."

"No, John. We're all right."

"He says, no," Gloria relayed quickly. "He wants to continue."

"We're having a problem with the light," Will said. "It's under control."

"A problem with the light; under control," Gloria relayed again.

Otis gripped the electrical wire, pushed it against the back of the light, and coughed from spark fumes.

"Is he okay, Will?"

"Yes. We need a few minutes."

"And I need to hear your voices. Stay in touch. You have problems, but I don't know the nature. Are they serious?"

"We're doing fine. It's brilliant."

"What? What's brilliant?"

"The ocean. The blueness. It's dark, but it's a blue like nothing I've ever seen."

Will's chatter bothered Gloria. He sounded disoriented, which made her concerned about their oxygen levels.

"Absolute splendor. Amazement."

"Damn it, Will. What are you seeing? Is there life? Are you okay?"

"Of course, Glo. I'm seeing things that are breathtaking; brilliant and breathtaking."

"Will, I'm not understanding. You're past four-hundred feet. You say it's *brilliant*?"

"The color. Brilliant."

"Color from the searchlight, Will?"

"No. From the water. A shocking brilliance. Please continue our descent."

At five hundred they stopped, then six hundred and seven hundred and more stops. Will's eyes fixed forward as though hypnotized by the sea. He and Otis had descended well beyond all critics' expectations.

"Thousands of men have been here before, Otis, but we're the only ones alive to know its beauty and serenity."

"What did you say, Will?" Gloria asked.

"Thinking, Glo. We're where there's little distinction between day and night. There's life we see in flashes, but those creatures know nothing about circling the sun, spinning like a top so that half the world is bright and half is dark. I think they know only the brilliance of the sea's blueness. They know eat and be eaten."

Otis Barton had toyed with the light while Will chattered. He gingerly fed more wire into the light's housing. He tightened the clip that held the wire in place so it wouldn't spit angry sparks. But his hands were now numb from tense exhaustion.

"Will it work?" the director asked. "I'd like to see what's out there."

"You're nearing eight hundred feet, Will," Gloria reported. "Do you see fish? Is that what you're seeing?"

There was no reply.

"Will? … Will. Respond! Over."

"Stop us at eight hundred," Gloria heard him say.

"You're there, Will. You're stopping for the clamp."

They felt the jolt.

"Bring us back. We aren't going any deeper today."

CHAPTER 30

Thinking It's Love

That evening, Else ate an early dinner then returned to her art easel in the DTR laboratory. Dr. Beebe requested her skills for the evening.

Hada was excited, but also worried about her mother, because Else had been spending long hours at her easel trying to please Dr. Beebe. She went to her mother to offer help. Else loaded her down with rolled-up watercolors and a 12x16 framed canvas she had just completed in oil.

"Put the oil painting on the tripod in front of the tent. Bitte, Tochter. It's wet, so be very careful."

"I will, Mother. Did Dr. Beebe say how long you'd be working tonight?"

"No. Don't worry. I spent evenings on advertisements for the newspaper many times when you slept. You can't begin your worry now."

"Yes, but you're older now…"

"…and you're older too. You should know better than to use my age. I am not old, simply older than I was. Take this art and go."

Hada obeyed without further protestation. She left Else alone allowing the artist to clear her work area and prepare for the task ahead.

Fifteen minutes later, voices filled the hallway outside the team's lab. Else took a deep breath as the door handle turned.

"Good evening, Mrs. B," Will said. He marched toward his desk at the other end of the long laboratory. Gloria and the Tee-Vans followed.

"Guten Abend, Herr Professor Beebe. Congratulations on your first dive in the bathysphere. I regret that I was not on the *Ready* to see the event."

"And I regret assigning you so much art that prevented you from joining us. I saw your daughter carrying one of the completed paintings—in oil I believe—and I came to tell you I'm impressed once more. I will use the painting to win over new support."

Else thanked him for liking her work, reminding him the oil will take several days to dry. "I hope the time will not be a problem."

"Of course not, Mrs. B." He said it was for a prospective donor. "Today's dive made me more nervous than I expected," he told Else. He said he was glad the first dive was over.

"Tell me what excited you most, Dr. Beebe."

Will said his biggest thrill was seeing the overall luminescence of the fish and color of the sea. "It's not something I expect you or anyone to replicate on canvas, Mrs. B. I don't know that any pigment could capture the magnificence I experienced."

"I'm jealous, Dr. Beebe. You've gone where few dare try…"

"…or the means that Mr. Barton gave us. Mrs. B, I viewed a glorious *Aurelia aurita*. Do you know what that is?"

"The moon jelly is the English name, a jellyfish. I've seen them helmet diving, Dr. Beebe."

"But none as big nor as beautifully docile when floating all alone in the stillness. Can you sketch it and add your watercolor? I'd love it as my first vivid and personal memory."

"Describe the sighting, Dr. Beebe," Else urged.

"I have to say it struck me silent. I said nothing to Glo, so there is nothing in her notes to help me."

"I could not read your mind, Will," Gloria said defensively.

"It wasn't a criticism, Glo. The fault was mine. I was alone with my thoughts and an image of utmost natural beauty. It amazed me with its size and grace. I found solace simply looking at nature's creation."

Gloria sat at her desk with research documents from the Hamilton library. She stopped and listened to Dr. Beebe's impassioned description.

John and Helen Tee-Van also stood stunned by Dr. Beebe's entranced reminiscence. Else simply drew. The Tee-Vans eventually said goodnight and slipped away unnoticed by their colleagues.

Will watched Else sketch. He moved in close and put his hand on her shoulder. The touch caught Else by surprise, but she continued after a quick and quiet breath.

"You alarmed me, Will," Gloria said. "When you said to bring you up, I wasn't expecting it."

Will was slow to react. When Gloria's comment registered, he pulled away from Else's drawing table. "I've had moments like that before. I know when it's time to stop, time to change what I'm doing."

Else heard a new tone in Dr. Beebe's voice. "Do you know the word, clairvoyance?" she asked. "In German, Hellsichtigkeit."

"I'm influenced by science, Mrs. B," Will said. "I'm not clairvoyant, but I'm a creature like those I study. I have an instinct for danger."

"I find that amusing…" Else responded.

"…and I do too, Will," Gloria added. "You're always doing things people say are dangerous."

"I'm not saying dangerous; *danger*, Glo."

"You said it was large; how large?" Else asked.

Will turned back to Else's sketch. "The diameter, eighteen inches. The four pinkish luminescent gonads, two inches. It was though the creature was lighting up and doing a ballet for me."

"At the moment you spotted it, please tell me what you were doing," Else requested.

Gloria Hollister put aside her work. She had not heard Will talk about any helmet dive the

way he was discussing his first bathysphere dive with Mrs. B.

"Mr. Barton continued to struggle with his light. We were both jittery, so the light helped warm us and gave me a chance to look out farther into the abyss. I asked Barton to shut it off so I could see jelly's bioluminescence. He complained, but he did it. He was so focused on his gadgets that he missed the beauty."

Else erased some of her pencil lines and drew a large oval.

"Yes, that's good," Dr. Beebe confirmed. "The creature was above the bathysphere and to my left. The sun sent a touch of yellow as we ascended. The jelly undulated a slow rhythm. It tried to stay above us. We gained on it, but it worked hard to be where I could see it. I noticed other jellies now appearing higher in the water; a school awaiting its more inquisitive leader."

Else glanced at Miss Hollister whose eyes were glued to Will Beebe. "If we're looking from your perspective, at what angle were the other jellies?" Else asked.

Dr. Beebe laid a short pencil on her sketch pad, pointing at thirty degrees from center-left to the top of the pad.

"That's how I remember them approaching my window as we rose in the water. They seemed to flicker lights as the bathysphere rose closer to the school. They waited for the larger jelly. It stopped and we passed the entire school."

Else drew more oblong circles. "Did the others appear bigger or smaller than my ovals?"

"I think you have the right proportions, Mrs. B," Dr. Beebe responded. He looked at Gloria. "I don't remember saying anything, even then. Glo…?"

"You said nothing, Will."

"Close your eyes and tell me now how close were they to each other?" Else asked.

Will's eyes shifted under his lids.

"They were close and equidistant from one another." He opened his eyes. "I'd say less than a yard apart."

"Will, if you don't need me, I think I'll let you and Mrs. B finish," Gloria said. "I'll be up for an hour if you finish and want to talk."

"Very well, Glo."

"Gute Nacht, Fräulein Hollister."

"Gute Nacht, Frau Bostelmann," Gloria replied.

While Dr. Beebe stood gentlemanly, straightening to watch Gloria depart, Else studied his reaction.

"She is a remarkable young scientist, Dr. Beebe."

"Indeed, Mrs. B."

"I can tell you've grown fond of her."

"I try not to be obvious in my loyalties to people. Have I failed?"

"I am a blunt person, Dr. Beebe. Yes, you've failed. But I understand how hard it's been. Miss Hollister is fond of you." Before he could react, "Were there other fish in your vision of the jellies?"

He hesitated. "No. I didn't notice."

Dr. Beebe's eyes were not on Else's pad but her. "You notice things more than most, Mrs. B…"

"My professors trained me to observe, an important trait that most artists acquire over time. I have your principal jelly the focal point. It will be the largest image. Do you like where it is? Does it look familiar?"

"Yes. What do you know, Mrs. B?"

"I know Miss Hollister has more than an infatuation with her boss, Dr. Beebe. She loves you. Do you know that?"

"It happens in the workplace, Mrs. B, when a woman becomes enamored with a man's skills. She thinks it's love. It's admiration, but I'm not sure it's love. It's an understandable weakness."

"Weakness, Dr. Beebe? Respect and admiration are not weaknesses."

Will listened to his own words echo through his thoughts. They embarrassed him. They were words he might have heard in a tennis-club locker room. Now they presented a painful revelation.

"I'm afraid you have me, Mrs. B. I shall think before I utter such comments. I know Glo loves me. I'm happy when she loves me."

Else had a clear outline of the *Aurelia aurita*. It was perfect and more than Dr. Beebe hoped for, even without her watercolor.

"I will finish this before morning, Dr. Beebe. You have time to share with Miss Hollister now. You needn't spend it with me."

"On the contrary, Mrs. B, I look forward to spending many hours with you."

CHAPTER 31

Party Time

The next morning, Mrs. Tucker had Else's coffee cup filled and sitting on her kitchen work island when the artist arrived. Steam waved over the cup in the cool morning air.

"I hear there's a party later today," Mrs. Tucker said when Else entered.

"Yes, I hear the same. Dr. Beebe wants us to dress up as pirates."

"How much pirate jewelry did you bring, Mrs. B?"

"None that I think a pirate would wear. Do you have any suggestions on how to dress as a swashbuckler, Mrs. Tucker?"

"No, ma'am. But maybe start with blousy pantaloons and something tied around your head. That's the image I have of a pirate."

"That's where I'll begin, Mrs. Tucker."

Preparing for the evening costume party took the entire day. Staff and interns discussed nothing else. The only question circulating: Did Dr. Beebe have enough rum for the entire crew?

Among Will Beebe's hidden talents—hidden with his athleticism, musicianship, and love of poetry—was his ability to throw extraordinary costume parties. He spared no imagination nor put limits on the ridiculous. It was an opportunity to cut loose and reward staff.

When he declared the event, he told everyone their chores and daily tedium were simply meant to prepare them for raucous revelry.

Pirate costumes, Else would learn, were among Dr. Beebe's favorites. She sought further advice from her daughter.

"Do not spend time thinking about it, Mother," Hada told her. "It's not about looking perfect. Patten says people dress outrageously to make others laugh."

"I'm not sure I want people laughing at me, Tochter."

"Oh, Mother. Don't be a fuddy-duddy. Picasso will try anything, so should you."

"Mrs. Tucker says, 'blousy pants and something around my head.' Do you know where I find such pants?"

"Yes, Mother. I know exactly where you find them. You make them on the sewing machine. You have time. Make a pair for me too."

It did not take Else long. She made several pairs of pirate pantaloons before her shift on the DTR sewing machine ended. They were popular among the young interns.

Being an impromptu seamstress consumed much of Else's day. She had little time to fret about what she would add to her costume to authenticate her pirate appearance.

Else couldn't imagine Dr. Beebe, Miss Hollister, or the Tee-Vans spending time like she had done. Their Sunday was for rest.

She was wrong. It was a matter of pride to see who could create the most memorable outfit even among Gloria, John, Helen, and Dr. Beebe.

Will knew exactly what he intended to wear, so he spent an early morning hour at his desk writing to Elswyth. He hadn't spoken to her by telephone in more than a month. Letters were important.

Will missed Elswyth. He missed their evening conversations about literary matters. When together, he read poems to her and recited lines from Kipling's writings.

He asked how she was doing with her research. He inquired about her mother; how they were adjusting to London. He shared more about his success with his first dive; how he and Otis crammed into the bathysphere and responded as total opposites to the adventure. He told her about the pirate party he proposed.

Will finished his letter and sealed it. He placed it in the box where Mr. Tucker picked up the mail when he went for supplies.

With Elswyth still on his mind, Will walked the DTR campus to think and spy on his staff as they put together their clothing for the festivities. When he saw Patten Jackson and Hada Bostelmann parading colorful materials and laughing hysterically, he knew his spontaneous party proposal was working.

It had been a long time since Else Bostelmann felt tipsy, but she did as the evening wore on. Dr. Beebe, dressed as a silly and generous tavern hostess, flittered around the bonfire in a skirt with his ukulele in one hand and a bottle of rum in the other. He poured into her empty glass and others at every opportunity. He made sure fresh apple cider and grape juice were available for those who didn't want alcohol.

Else monitored her daughter. Prohibition in the United States made young people Hada's age inexperienced with alcohol. A little made quick intoxication. She did not want Hada sick. She found her daughter with her arm around her buddy Patten.

"Are you being good, Tochter?"

"Yes Mother. I'm having fun. I love Dr. Beebe's parties singing his old songs."

"Hello, Mrs. B!"

"Guten Abend, Herr Jackson."

"Guten Abend," Patten replied, giggling and anglicizing his words.

"Are you feeling the alcohol, Mr. Jackson? You may not like it in the morning if you don't slow your consumption."

"Mother, let him learn on his own. You don't have to be *his* mother too."

"All children need mothering; a good time for Mr. Jackson to receive mine."

"I miss my mother, Mrs. Bostelmann," Patten said more soberly. "She's a good mother. Like you."

"Then she would warn you, Mr. Jackson, that too much alcohol can make you miserable when you awaken, so please do not drink too much tonight."

"Yes, ma'am."

Else left the young group and saw Miss Hollister, her face reflecting the fire's warmth. Else sat with her and the Tee-Vans.

"You looked like you were having a parental discussion, Mrs. B," Gloria said.

"I'm certain Hada would have preferred I stay away, but they are not used to liquor. I needed to remind them of its effect."

"I never had alcohol as a teenager, Mrs. B. My father, the doctor, didn't allow it. He might have been a Prohibitionist. I wouldn't have known. But I don't recall seeing it in our home."

"…and when you went to college?"

"There were parties and liquor, even drugs at some parties. Heroin, cannabis hash. Did you know that Prince George offered me heroin two years ago?"

"No. Do you suspect the young prince uses such drugs?"

"Yes, I'm certain it's true."

"I'm grateful I grew up when I did," Else said. "I don't like the way things are going in this modern time, Miss Hollister. I do not envy you being young and having to deal with it."

"There are many issues we must face in the twentieth century, Mrs. B. However, I don't believe Prohibition is an answer. We've seen that it creates crime far greater than drunken disorder."

"Yes, moderation and self-discipline are things learned in good homes with responsible parents. They are not things a government can force on people."

"I agree, Mrs. B, do you think we'll ever see a time when people understand that?"

"We can hope. And pray. Do you believe in prayer, Miss Hollister?"

"I do. Is that an odd thing to admit when I stand here with a glass of rum in my hand?"

"There is never a wrong time to confess your beliefs."

"I'm glad to hear you say that, Mrs. B."

"To your health and long life, Miss Hollister." Else held her near-empty glass for Gloria to clink.

"…and to yours, Mrs. B."

CHAPTER 32

Proof Gets Deeper
11 June 1930

Will and Otis inspected their repainted bathysphere interior. They painted it black to cut down on glare that grew worse when they used the light. They hoped it would reduce the time their eyes took to adjust to the outside darkness.

Captain Millett slowed his tug and let the *Ready* settle over a two-mile drop in the ocean. John Tee-Van and two deckhands pulled smelly squid from a five-gallon bucket and baited a variety of hooks dangling from the conspicuous submersible.

Will looked over the crew's effort eager to get the second dive underway, anxious to test the dark interior. He went to Else who was standing well out of the way.

"Please, come look inside, Mrs. B."

Else dodged the workers and stood with Dr. Beebe in front of the open manhole.

"I'm not certain I would fit," she said.

"You would, but you don't have to worry. I won't make you get in."

"...and if I wanted to. I would be grateful to descend with you to see what *you're* seeing."

"I applaud your bravery, Mrs. B, but I won't let you, because you have a daughter who needs her mother."

"I understand, Dr. Beebe, but we all need you. Our livelihoods depend on you, which means my daughter's future is tied to *your* good fortune as it is to mine."

"You know, Mrs. B, there are very few people with whom I've lost a debate. I'm grateful you never challenged me."

"I must return to my station away from this activity," Else told him. "It's making me nervous to be in everyone's way."

"I want to see new fish and observe the bioluminescence that caught my imagination last week. I'm going to share my sightings with you as soon as we can sit together."

Else smiled and zig-zagged her way back to a position on the deck where she could watch without being in the center of activity.

"The morning's wasting, John," Will said. "Mr. Barton and I are ready to dive."

"Get in, Director," John replied. "It excites those of us on deck to put you and the smelly dead squid over the side."

Will laughed and climbed in first, scraping his boney shins across the lower bolts. When he had squirmed to the far side of the ball Gloria Hollister, with her headset already on, looked inside.

"Are you bleeding, Will? That looked like it hurt."

"I'm fine, Glo. Just a scratch. No blood. Send in Otis. And, Glo. Happy birthday."

"Otis is right here," she answered. "Thank you, Dr. Beebe."

"I have a present for you later."

Otis, broader than Will and twenty years younger, squeezed through the manhole placing his hands on the cold steel bottom of the ball and lifting his legs noticeably higher over the bolts fearful of duplicating Dr. Beebe's graceless entry. The two six-footers twisted, stretched, withdrew extremities, and finally settled.

John had the cover in place, slipping it over the protruding bolts. Only the four-inch hole in the center of the heavy disk gave the explorers their last stream of sea air. Otis set the oxygen to a liter an hour. Once John put the core into the manhole disk, Otis increased it to two liters per hour.

Pleased that the second launch of their submersible was going smoother and faster, Will still winced at the pounding of the wrench. Both men suffered severe ringing in their ears.

When in the water, Will pressed against the left quartz window thanking Otis for the black interior paint. "It significantly reduces reflections in the glass."

Will spent so much energy thinking about their depth and vulnerabilities during the first dive, he said it was difficult to remember what he saw until they ascended. That's when the flashes, colors, and intensity registered. He promised to do better this dive.

Gloria noted Will's comments about the color changes as they descended. Reds disappeared first, then yellows, and at three hundred-fifty feet, only blue-violet shown. The colors left according to their spectrum wavelengths.

Descending, Will's attention shifted again to the amazing sea. He chattered at Gloria as though she were aboard: "Note, Glo, how different the sea looks from under the splash of our sphere. Rather than waves rising and pushing away from our plunge, they appear from below as smooth, rounded indentations."

"Any creatures yet, Will?"

"Only our common helmet-diving friends, Glo. Bonitos in trios. A triggerfish darted from the sargassum and looked me in the eye. I suppose spotting a foot-long larval eel wiggling nearby at twenty fathoms surprised me."

"Any jellies?"

"Yes. A school. They seem lost but happy to be throbbing along. See that, Otis?"

"What, Will? What are you seeing?" Gloria insisted.

"I thought we were seeing an evening cloud at four-hundred feet below the surface. It appears to be a thick school of Pteropods. Flying snails. A pair of flapping wings. I could imagine them sounding like hummingbirds."

Otis Barton peeked and saw the small critters ricocheting off the center window. He continued to monitor gauges.

The stop at five-hundred feet came abruptly. Both men's bodies sank in the bathysphere as it stopped.

"I'm not too pleased with the elevator operator, Miss Hollister," Otis said. "I nearly lost my cookies."

"Oh, please, Otis. Don't suggest sea sickness aboard our craft," Will implored.

"My point is they could slow us to a stop better than they did."

"We'll do better with the stops," Gloria asserted. "Report your sightings, please."

"Carangids, pilotfish mostly, some long strings of salpa, lace-like. Oh, make note of this, Glo…"

"What? What are you seeing?"

"Lanternfish. How amazing to see them alive and swimming. We've netted many, but to see them now is quite different."

"Describe their behavior, Will."

"The one I'm watching is small – maybe six inches – dark, but seems to have light on its skin, flashing, then disappearing, then flashing again. He's drifting out of my view, but his full armor is intact and sparkling. Not like the ones you've worked on, scales missing."

"Anything else?"

"There's a silvery bronze eel slithering by, and a pufferfish. Didn't expect to see him at this depth."

"He's surprised to see you, too, Will," Gloria said with a chuckle.

"That's good, Glo; very good. Write it down. I'll use it in an article."

Will also saw squadrons of squid swimming in formation. It reminded him of his flying days

in France. Military science learned from flocks of transient birds flying in formation that the front bird created a draft. It gave the following birds an easier path. Geese, ducks, cranes, all took turns in the lead to relieve the harder work at the front.

But in the sea, was the lead squid sharing a pull that made the followers swim easier? Did the squid have an instinct like the birds? Did the birds bring the habit from the sea?

Although astounded by the coincidence between air and sea, more important to Will was spotting the mysterious giant squid.

As the submersible dropped to eight-hundred feet where Will had stopped their descent on the first dive, Gloria Hollister held her breath. "You're stopping at eight hundred for the clamp," she told him.

"Oh, Lord."

"What, Will?"

"You must see it, Otis. Verify that I'm seeing one alive."

Otis wiggled his body to the center window and saw the fish for which Dr. Beebe needed his witness.

"Talk to me, Will Beebe!" Gloria screamed into her microphone.

"The hatchetfish, Glo. Another creature you've had under your microscope in pieces, but here it's whole and at home, absolutely magnificent."

"Just one, Will?"

"No. I see three. How about you, Otis?"

Otis Barton looked and sat back in the bathysphere, checking his gauges and fanning the air with his palm leaf. "I saw the one, Dr. Beebe. Interesting. Mean looking and ugly."

"Do you have the headset on, Will?" Gloria asked.

"Yes."

"I heard Otis. Such enthusiasm. Could I please trade places with him?" she asked, revealing her frustration.

Will pressed the headset against his ears so her anger wouldn't leak out. "There's something else, Glo, but I can't make it out. It's too far away. I can tell it's large, much larger than the bathysphere..."

"Are you seeing a whale?" Gloria asked.

"I shall never know. It's gone. But the farther we go down, the greater the number of lights. Some flashing. Some colorful..."

"You're seeing bioluminescent fish, Will?"

"Yes. As though I'm flying through the galaxy searching for our next planet. It's astounding, Glo. The cosmos is in front of me."

"What fish are you seeing?"

"I don't know. Otis, let's try the light again."

Otis Barton put down his fan and a gauge for measuring their oxygen level. He aimed the light through the center window and turned on the beam. It filled the blackness with a yellow cast and reflected off several species, some darting away, but most lingering.

"The light is on. I see a few lanternfish, hatchetfish, bronze eels in the distance. A school of elongated fish like trumpetfish swimming vertically with their tapered tails dangling."

The marker-clamp stop at twelve-hundred feet came quicker than expected. A short distance later, aquatic life vanished. Even the large ghost-like figure that Will swore began following them at six-hundred feet was no longer visible.

Bored by the empty sea, Will used his time to inspect the interior with Otis: Manhole hatch bone dry; stuffing box held tightly; cable wire stable.

Before the stop, though, he told Gloria he spotted yet another new species, a pair of Macrourid-like fish with bright green bioluminescent lights. At least six lights on each side.

"When they vanished, Glo, my eyes readjusted as though I was caught looking into the sun."

Will Beebe stared into the darkness with his mind racing. *Oceans of such blueness cover the planet, but so little is known— important but mysterious. We dangle in an eight-mile section of the Atlantic, a spec in the vastness, hanging by a wire connected to a rotting barge. Our adventure would shock the bravest of men. I'm in shock knowing where I am and how I got here.*

Will searched again for life, for any flash of light, for the ghost creature lurking beyond his vision. He wished for a supernatural sighting. He wanted anything to halt his racing worries.

The bathysphere stopped.

"You're at thirteen-hundred feet. You'll pass a quarter-mile as soon as we attach the clamp and drop you twenty feet more," Gloria told Will.

Just hearing Glo's voice ended his racing thoughts. He saw flickering lights. He imagined he was looking across a nighttime summer yard covered with fireflies.

"Any sightings, Will?"

"Copepods; so small I can only see them because of the bioluminescence. Some are hitting our window. There's an arrow worm too. The milky sagitta."

"How are your chemicals? Your oxygen levels?" Gloria asked.

"Otis has said nothing, so I'm assuming our chemicals and oxygen are fine." He looked at Otis Barton, who prepared the light, and nodded. "Yes, we're doing well. The temperature inside the bathysphere is currently seventy-two degrees."

As he spoke, three squids crossed the beam of light that Otis turned on. They swam out of the light, then returned. Their colors alternated between black and pale white.

The water temperature had dropped, which chilled the inside of the bathysphere. The wall dripped from condensation. Otis added more chemicals to absorb the moisture. Will used his handkerchief to wipe his window.

The bathysphere slowed to another stop, pressing the two men into the floor. Gloria's voice announced, "Fourteen hundred feet."

Excitement and anxiety had exhausted Will and Otis. Their second dive ended at fourteen-hundred-twenty-six feet.

One of the last visions Will described for Gloria was a platoon of large shrimp. They surprised Will. He didn't expect to find them at a quarter mile.

Ascending, Will told Gloria his biggest thrill was seeing the large creature in the distance, too far away to determine whether it was a fish, squid, or whale. It didn't matter. The mystery, said Will, did not differ from landing on Mars and seeing evidence of life, but with no tangible proof of what he saw when returning to Earth.

CHAPTER 33

Symbiosis at Sea

Will, Gloria, Trumps, and Chiri walked the island to take in the setting sun and evening breezes. When Gloria sensed there was no one around, she stopped, pulled Will close to her, and kissed him.

"Thank you, Dr. William Beebe, for the bracelet and a marvelous experience today."

"I know I'm late, but I hope you'll remember your thirtieth birthday forever, Glo."

It would be hard to forget after climbing into the bathysphere with John Tee-Van and dropping four-hundred-ten feet. She became the first woman to dive in the bathysphere setting a record and bragging rights for female explorers.

Will and Gloria held hands and continued their walk. The pets scampered ahead, finding young interns to pester. Among them were Hada Bostelmann and Patten Jackson. Trumps jumped into Hada's arms. Gloria let go of Will's hand.

"You can tell him, 'No,' and he won't do that, Hada," Gloria said.

"It's all right, Miss Hollister. You know I love Trumps."

"Is Mrs. B resting this evening?" Will asked. "She's been painting nonstop lately."

"Resting? Oh, no. Not Mrs. B," Patten said. "She's at her drawing table."

"Will, tell her to quit for the evening."

"I'll tell her, Glo. I'll see you in the morning. And I expect to see both of you then too," Will told Hada and Patten.

"Yes, sir," Patten replied. "We have to meet Mr. Tee-Van in the morning. He has new fish in the *Sea-Fern*. He says they need special feeding instructions that he wants to share with us."

"Excellent, Mr. Jackson. I know John appreciates the way you and Miss Bostelmann have taken on his chores."

"It's been an extraordinary opportunity and education for us, Dr. Beebe," Hada answered. "I'm not sure I've thanked you enough for allowing me to be here with my mother and to make friends with *Herr* Jackson. I'm waiting for his official proposal any day now."

"Hada!"

"Really, Patten?" Gloria asked. "You still haven't proposed?"

"Miss Hollister, I just learned to tie my shoes. I'm not ready to marry."

Will laughed so hard Chiri jumped and grabbed his leg, clinging tightly. That brought a chorus of chortles from the others.

When the laughter calmed, Gloria, again, said goodnight and departed.

"I better go to your mother, Miss Bostelmann, and turn out her light so she can get some rest. Do you think she'll get the message if there's no light to paint by?" Will asked.

"I'm sure she has a candle nearby, Dr. Beebe. You may have to take away her matches."

"I'll look for them. Goodnight, Miss Bostelmann; *Herr* Jackson."

"Goodnight, Dr. Beebe," they said in harmony.

Will detected light bleeding from the window closest to Mrs. B's drawing table. He entered the building and went to the laboratory. Else kept her concentration on her brushwork when she heard the lab door squeak.

"Has someone come to criticize my work?" she asked without looking up.

"Not to criticize, but I wonder why you're working at this hour, Mrs. B."

"Goodness! I'm sorry, Dr. Beebe. I assumed it was Hada checking on me."

"No apology needed. I saw your daughter just now and learned you were here. Gloria insisted that I come dismiss you from whatever you're doing. It can wait until tomorrow."

"Well, I've finished. No need to punish me. I was doing some final details on your parrotfish."

Will approached Else's desk and looked over her shoulder. "That's it. You've either captured what I saw or seeing your watercolor makes me conjure what I wanted to be there."

"I think you flatter me, Dr. Beebe, but I'm not sure."

"It was, indeed, flattery, Mrs. B. This will be a picture I include with the article I'm preparing."

"Are you writing about your expedition? Do people know you've completed several dives in your bathysphere?"

"I wrote an article for the *New York Times*, which the newspaper printed on the front page. The editor surprised me."

"Did you receive any reaction from the zoological society?" Else asked.

"I did. Director Blair is coming in July for a visit."

"The director is traveling to Bermuda because of your successful dives?"

"I'm uncertain, Mrs. B. Director Blair has never endorsed my work, so I'm perplexed by his timing. Maybe he just wants an excuse to vacation on the islands."

W. Reid Blair, Beebe's boss who succeeded founder William Temple Hornaday, turned out to be among Will's leading critics. Although he held the title *director*, his voice cowered to that of Henry Osborn and Madison Grant. Will remained valuable to the zoological society because of his ability to communicate the mystery of science through his writing style and speaking skills, which also made him the leading fundraiser.

"Are there others who will print your story?" Else asked.

"I've told the editors at *National Geographic Magazine* about this year's expedition. I think there's interest, Mrs. B. They want to see photos to know what we're doing. We've sent Mr. Connery's pictures of the bathysphere to New York. I'm awaiting a response."

"That's exciting, Dr. Beebe."

"Yes, I've just begun an outline of things we must report. Your painting shows one observation that might seem trivial to ichthyologists, but to *National Geographic's* growing readership, I think it will be interesting. You've done it well. It helps me explain things in nature that translate to human characteristics."

"It's about the relationship, I presume, Dr. Beebe."

Else's painting depicted a large blue parrotfish floating vertically, buoyant, and surrounded by a dozen wrasse nibbling at the mouth of the larger fish.

"There's both science and symbolism in your painting, Mrs. B. The science is within the symbiotic relationship between the two species of fish. The wrasse eats and cleans the parrotfish of coral particles."

"And what about the symbolism?"

"Your picture shows the nature of the sea. Life exists in harmony, and it has for centuries because the fauna and flora co-exist symbiotically. And as predator and prey…"

"…which is the goal of your research, if I've understood it, Dr. Beebe, to see and record the nature of the sea."

Will confirmed but added that it was also to make people aware of the ocean's vulnerabilities.

"I want people to learn the deep sea supports life. We can't afford to spoil our oceans."

"Humans spoiling nature has been my concern since childhood."

"Yes, there's reason to be concerned. If we damage their environment with industrial waste that many nations allow to flow into the sea, it will affect them, and through them, us too."

"Dr. Beebe, I made you think about your methods of capturing nature's creatures by using your gun…"

"…because my methods disturbed you, Mrs. B, I've revised my message. People know I'm a conservationist. I'm a sportsman too, which means I hunt for sport, but that also helps manage the population of certain wildlife. Hunters don't kill every animal and bird."

"I've met many people who were farmers with a dozen babies by the time they were 35 years old," Else said. "They told me they did that so they would have plenty of help. I thought that wrong—having babies to build a workforce for the farm—just like I remain against killing for sport. For food, I understand. And one other concern I must express, Dr. Beebe, while I'm speaking my mind."

"Let me sit first…"

"I have read Mr. Grant's book on eugenics. How can men today reason that they are better than other human beings because of their bloodline?"

"They're good men," Will answered. "They want what's best for nature and this country…"

"…but they promote bigotry, Dr. Beebe. Do they know you use native Bermudians born of African ancestors? Grant finds them inferior and wants them sterilized."

"People misunderstand Henry Osborn and Madison Grant, Mrs. B. They want political leaders to acknowledge the importance of intelligence."

"I thought I left such thinking when I departed Germany."

"Is it bad if one's interest is to better our nation by improving our genetic strength, Mrs. B?"

"It's not man's role to *be* God but to be *with* God. Love puts all men into the world as equals…"

"I agree, Mrs. B, we have equal importance in the world. I could not succeed without our crew. It's their lack of education and life experiences that prevents them from achieving better fortunes…"

"God does not lower the value of their lives, Dr. Beebe. Man does. Grant does."

"My point is that we depend on one another like the parrotfish and the wrasse."

"Do we depend on one another out of love or because one man thinks he's superior to the other, and therefore, expects the other man to praise him with more respect? That is not the same as the parrotfish and the wrasse. *We* may think it foolish that the wrasse cleans the parrotfish because they *love* each other; respect each other equally, but it's not foolish to God. God calls it love, not symbiosis. We need to let in some of that love when we see people who look and behave different from us."

Will stood straight and studied Else. He didn't agree with all she said, but her candor and expressiveness stimulated his thoughts. He liked the challenge she presented. He put his hand on her left arm.

"I'm exhausted, Mrs. B. I need to sleep, but you've given me more to think about."

Else reached across her body with her right hand and covered his. She studied his face with apologetic eyes. "Dr. Beebe, I know I say too much. I'm not afraid of my words until after they leave me."

"You've not said anything I haven't thought about. I worry about the philosophy expressed by my friends, but I'm a naturalist. Discovery is my mission, not politics or philosophy. Osborn and Grant have directed my life to where I am today. I may have blinders when it comes to my loyalties, but I enjoy their friendships and intelligence. I would never speak out against them."

"They're just my observations," Else said. "Your discoveries are my mission too. Continue to open the natural world for people, that's what you need to do. And like the wrasse with the parrotfish, I will always be available when you need me."

CHAPTER 34

Miss Crane

The month of July sweltered. Will knew that Elswyth would have hated the rising heat, the afternoon storms, and the constant humidity. It was the cold that made Will sick and lackluster. He withstood the heat much better although his allergies acted up.

Will met Dr. Blair in Hamilton. The zoological society's director refused to visit the DTR compound on Nonsuch Island.

The meeting went as Will feared. Blair referred to the front-page article in the *New York Times* and accused Will of grandstanding in the press. He threatened to withhold zoo funding of further bathysphere dives.

Irritated by Dr. Blair's accusations, Will and staff worked even harder cataloging specimens and preparing live shipments for the zoological park in the Bronx.

Else completed dozens of watercolors, pen sketches, and a few larger oil paintings. And Jack Connery developed an equal number of photos that were sent to the magazines that requested Dr. Beebe's articles for publication, including *Harper's* and *National Geographic*. The latter magazine notified Will it would run his article, photos, and illustrations by summer 1931.

However, not all events served the staff well. On July 16, when trawling for additional deep-water specimens, the winch drum now aboard the *Gladisfen* cracked. It ended trawls until they could buy a replacement from New York.

It also ended bathysphere dives for the year, which pleased Dr. Blair. Will put the sphere into a shed at Darrell and Meyer's wharf.

Meantime, Jack Connery fell between the *Skink* and the dock, hurting his back and putting him out of commission.

Other bad news included the sudden death of Bermuda's Governor Bols. And later in the month, word came from the New York Zoological Society that Henry Fairfield Osborn's wife, Lucretia, died. She had been chairwoman of the Ladies' Auxiliary for more than twenty-two years and a staunch supporter of Dr. Beebe's expeditions.

But then, a few days before Will's fifty-third birthday and more party plans, a young intern appeared with surprising credentials. She came with William Gregory of the American Museum of Natural History, her mentor to that point and a long-time friend of William Beebe's.

After graduating from college, the young woman's mother, a wealthy socialite, gifted Will funds adequate to support her daughter and others. The new graduate's wish came true; she began work for Dr. Beebe.

At her introduction, she propped up Will with a flurry of flattery. "I've read every one of your books, Dr. Beebe, more than once," she said.

"Please tell us your name, again," Gloria instructed the young woman.

"Crane. Jocelyn Crane. And you're Miss Hollister. I saw the stories about your presentation to the women journalists in January. I wish I had been there. I'm quite envious of your work."

"Thank you."

"I was expecting you earlier, Miss Crane," Will said. "I received your letters and a telegram from your mother, a very generous woman."

"She is, Dr. Beebe. She knows how much I've looked forward to meeting you. I'm thrilled to be here and eager to be of assistance. I apologize for my delay. Dr. Gregory is to blame."

"I apologize as well, Will," Gregory added.

"Tell us your background," Gloria urged. They began moving toward the dining hall where Mrs. Tucker had dinner prepared for the staff.

"I was born in St. Louis. I just graduated from college on my birthday, the eleventh of June…"

"That's my birthday too, Miss Crane."

"What a coincidence, Miss Hollister. But that was also the day of Dr. Beebe's bathysphere dive to one-thousand, four-hundred-twenty-six feet. Were you there on your birthday?"

"I was. And so was Dr. Beebe."

"Of course he was. How funny. Then we'll always remember that date, won't we?"

"We shall," Gloria said while holding the door for the others to enter the dining hall.

"Your mother told me you attended Smith College," Will continued. "I spoke there recently."

"Yes. I was in the audience for your lecture. I sat in the front row, but many people attended, so I don't expect you saw me."

"I'm sure I admired your pretty face," Will said.

"You said you graduated on your birthday; did you turn twenty-two?" Gloria asked, sitting next to Will.

"No, twenty-one. I'm young for my age," Jocelyn said laughingly.

"At twenty-one, I was still in college playing field hockey," Gloria grumbled at Will.

"I'm sorry, Miss Hollister, I didn't hear what you said."

"Nothing important, Miss Crane."

"Do you have a job in mind for me, Dr. Beebe?"

"If you don't, Will, we can return to New York and I'll gladly put her to work at the museum with me," Dr. Gregory said.

"In fact, I do, Miss Crane. Since your letters show you studied zoology, and that was part of Miss Hollister's training, I thought I'd have you understudy her work. How does that sound?"

"Excellent!"

Else entered the dining hall and asked to join Dr. Beebe and Miss Hollister with their guests. She introduced herself to the young lady and Dr. Gregory.

"Are you joining the staff, Miss Crane?" she asked after introductions.

"Miss Crane is a new intern who recently graduated college," Dr. Beebe explained. "She'll be working with Miss Hollister."

"Then we'll be seeing a lot of each other, Miss Crane. My drawing table is next to Miss Hollister's lab. You'll be learning from a wonderful scientist."

"Are you the artist Miss Hollister talked about in her presentation to the women journalists in New York City?"

"Yes. She embarrassed me, but I was very proud of her that day. Were you there, Miss Crane?"

"No, but I read what she said. Our college newspaper reprinted the story from the *New York Times*. There was great interest in Dr. Beebe's research after he spoke at Smith College. I liked what you said about women in science, Miss Hollister."

"Thank you. We'll have an opportunity as women in Dr. Beebe's Second Oceanographic Expedition to further our cause."

"I'm so excited to hear you say that, Miss Hollister," Jocelyn said. "Dr. Beebe, I couldn't be happier!"

"Then we're thrilled too, Miss Crane, but I will warn you as these women will attest, we work very hard, and we work very long hours. But we also play hard when the opportunity arises, which is happening soon. It's *my* turn to have a birthday."

"I hope we get to use our pirate costumes again, Dr. Beebe," Else said. "I don't know if we have enough material for a new theme."

"Pirates or whatever strikes one's fancy. The ticket for entry is being outlandish."

"Oh, I've never been a pirate. I don't think I have anything to wear," Jocelyn fretted.

"Don't worry, Miss Crane. We'll be able to dress you," Else said.

CHAPTER 35

Walking the Plank
29 July 1930

William Beebe's birthday celebration took the sting out of the team's setbacks, discouraging news, and mishaps that had everyone on edge. Worries among the interns were about their parents' money and whether it might affect their college. Among the staff, it was about their jobs.

Will donned his barmaid outfit, picked up his ukulele and rum, rallied everyone, and started the party with, *we ain't got a barrel of money, maybe we're ragged and funny, but we'll travel along, singing a song, side by side…"*

Gloria walked Jocelyn around the campfire making certain all DTR members had met the new intern. Jocelyn was now on her own. Dr. Gregory had returned to New York.

Otis Barton also left, but before departing, he asked to have a private conversation with Dr. Beebe.

"I'll be back in August if repairs and weather make diving possible," Dr. Beebe. "However, I request that if you have further conversations with the press that you mention our relationship."

"I always do, Mr. Barton. You saw I told the *New York Times* in my very first sentence you were with me..."

"Thank you, Dr. Beebe. Yes, I saw what you wrote. I'm referring to the newspaper articles written from interviews you grant. It appears you don't tell them I had the bathysphere built and that every deep dive I'm with you."

"I do say that, Mr. Barton. I know we wouldn't be diving if you hadn't provided the Department of Tropical Research with your sphere. I tell reporters that every interview I give."

"Sit over here, Jocelyn," Gloria requested. "I need to warn you about tonight."

"Is something wrong, Miss Hollister?"

"Tonight, there are plans to surprise Will...

"Dr. Beebe?"

"Yes, Dr. Beebe. I wanted to alert you so you would know it's all in fun."

"I'm very curious now."

"It'll be entertaining. The interns and staff have some surprises cooked up."

"Thank you for putting me in the loop, Miss Hollister."

Will finished another sing-along with his ukulele when John Tee-Van stepped up and spoke. "Will, you have to share the stage for a few minutes. The gang has gone searching for more tiny creatures for you to evaluate. They put them in this cedar box. Since you've already admitted in song that we *ain't got a barrel of money,* your birthday gifts come to you from where things are *free*: Nature."

John made Will stand. He handed the director the cedar box. When Will lifted the lid, dozens of insects, butterflies, dragonflies, even two small hummingbirds fluttered away, surprising even the unflappable Will Beebe. Laughter flew too.

Before Will could respond, two large interns jumped up and grabbed Will by his shoulders and held him while Patten Jackson tied a bandana around Will's eyes. The two husky boys then guided the blindfolded Will on a long trail. He stumbled but the boys held him up.

They forced Will to walk an unsteady plank onto the *Skink*. Staff and interns squeezed into the boat while others boarded smaller craft nearby. Gloria, John, Helen, and Jocelyn joined Will on the *Skink* sitting next to him without speaking. Else and Hada bundled at the stern. The only instruction Will received came from Patten and the two pirate-attired thugs manhandling the director.

The boat ride was longer than Will expected. The pirates forced him to stand. They pushed him off the *Skink* onto a sandy surface. The air smelled familiar, but it didn't smell like St. George where he thought they had taken him based on the length of the trip. But they fooled him.

The boats took a circuitous route to nearby Castle Island. They could see Nonsuch to the east.

As Will stumbled across a sandy beach, music began to play. More revelers cheered. Patten pulled Will's blindfold to reveal the St. George's Hotel Orchestra. The boy-pirates pushed Will toward the castle moat and quieted the orchestra for speakers to praise their director with humorous anecdotes.

When the last of the long-winded jumped from the rock, the interns directed everyone's attention to an area where they performed a skit mocking Will's helmet dives. Will laughed the loudest and vigorously applauded the skinniest among the boys who played his role.

In the final routine, Patten pulled a floating bottle from the sea from which he produced a note. He tossed it to Will. Rather than written words, the paper was a map that instructed Will to find the X, suggesting a buried treasure.

Will found it and hoisted it from the loose sand. In it were gifts and bottles of rum, wine, and beer. The libations quickly spread to the hands of partiers.

John said it was time for Will to speak.

"Like many of you, I take stock of my life each birthday and measure the year in accomplishments, setbacks, but mostly in friendships. The past few weeks have been challenging, so your friendships have meant more to me than I can express. Our successful dives and good fortune finding new life in the ocean have been gratifying because of you. I lift my glass to all in thanks. May the coming year be as fruitful."

Will sipped his wine to shouts of "cheers." He felt emotional letting go of the stress. Dr. Blair's threats rang in his ears. He worried about Barton's money. He worried whether a new governor would be as generous as Governor Bols, and he worried whether the people of Bermuda still welcomed his adventures and stories about their islands.

Will watched the people for whom he felt responsible. He enticed them all with his drive and personality. Could he sustain their loyalty? Would there be a Third Oceanographic Expedition to Bermuda? They were questions he shelved because the second expedition had plenty to accomplish before October's departure.

CHAPTER 36

Anguish

Stormy weather, equipment repairs, and physical exhaustion made August just as strenuous as the previous month. The Department of Tropical Research churned out work from outdoor laboratories under tent covers. Staffers and interns who hadn't left for school, worked long days.

Every other Friday, Dr. Beebe encouraged all to go to St. George or Hamilton for relaxation and fun. Dances were popular. Young Bermudian women enjoyed seeing Dr. Beebe's handsome college boys, although the numbers thinned as August dwindled.

Gloria's opportunity to dance with Will also shrank as the summer neared an end. Jocelyn enjoyed dancing too. As long as Will spent his private time with Glo, she didn't mind, especially since she was among those suffering from exhaustion. Dancing became a physical chore.

Jocelyn proved to be a valued research assistant. Her college zoology background made it easy for her to identify fish, amphibians, mollusks, and other critters. The specimens came to them from net trawls, helmet dives, or gathered along shorelines.

Although young, Jocelyn was smart and well taught, her addition to the team fortuitous.

Gloria's exhaustion put her in the hospital. Jocelyn stepped up. She worked without Gloria's supervision and kept the team successfully categorizing fish.

Grateful, Will sent a note to William Gregory boasting of Jocelyn's abilities and thanking him for the introduction.

Once Gloria recovered, they returned to previously shared responsibilities. By September, they had caught up, but more setbacks befell the camp.

Hada walked to the *Sea Fern* early one morning to care for John's fish tanks, the task John assigned to her and Patten Jackson. John and Helen took the *Skink* to Hamilton for supplies.

Hada worked alone for half an hour wondering what happened to her steady partner. It was not like Patten to be late for any cause, work or play. She left the *Sea Fern*, putting a bucket in an obvious spot. If Pat walked a different route missing Hada, he would know she had been there.

When she called his name as she approached his tent, she heard him moan.

"Pat, are you in there?"

"Hada. I can't move. My guts feel like they're about to explode."

Hada pushed the tent flaps open and caught a powerful stench from Patten's body.

"Oh, my God, Pat. You stink."

"Thanks, Hada. I'm in a lot of pain."

Hada knew only one action; get her mother.

Else had consumed Mrs. Tucker's coffee and a plate of fruit. She headed to her drawing table when Hada called her name, her voice filled with desperation.

"What is it, Tochter? Are you okay?"

"Mother, Pat is sick. He can't get out of bed."

The two women rushed to Patten's tent. Else bent over his cot and felt his forehead.

"You're burning up, Mr. Jackson. Where's your pain?

"My intestines, Mrs. B."

Else gently put her hand on Patten's bare stomach. He grimaced at the touch. His body was hot. She bowed her head: "Lieber Gott, bitte mach, daß die Hitze weggeht und heile den Schmerz dieses Jungen."

"Mother, we need to get Patten to the doctor in St. George."

"I'm not sure I can move, Hada. My stomach feels awful."

Hada awakened the boys in the tents next to Patten. They helped him to his feet, but he couldn't stand. He bellowed and fell to the ground.

"Put him back on his cot, boys," Else instructed.

"We need to bring the doctor here," Hada cried. She ran for Mrs. Tucker, who called Dr. Paulina in St. George. He said he'd travel to Nonsuch to examine the boy, but it would take an hour to notify scheduled patients and secure a boat ride.

The women tried to cool Patten's body with wet rags. He became faint.

"We're here, Mr. Jackson. I want you to stay awake so you can describe your condition to the doctor."

Else kept Patten calm. She never took her hand from his stomach. With eyes closed, she prayed.

Distraught, Hada stayed outside Pat's tent so her worry wouldn't upset the young man. She asked Patten's buddies to take care of Mr. Tee-Van's fish.

By the time Dr. Paulina arrived, the entire camp was consoling Hada, including Will, Gloria, and Jocelyn. Else knelt by his cot, offering as much comfort as she knew. Hada explained over the telephone Patten's symptoms, so Dr. Paulina had medicines for food poisoning and indigestion in his carrying case.

"What are you feeling, Mr. Jackson?" the doctor asked.

"My guts. There's so much pain."

The doctor felt the boy's body-heat radiating. An infection had taken over.

He poked around Pat's intestines, eliciting shrieks the boy tried to hold back. The doctor noticed a scar near his navel.

"Did you have your appendix removed?"

"Small. I was small. They operated. My parents were there."

The doctor looked at Else. "This is very puzzling. His body shows he is suffering appendicitis, but if he has no appendix, it can't be that."

"What should we do?" Else asked, quite concerned for her daughter's best friend, but also upset that the doctor offered no better comfort than her prayers.

"We need to move him to the hospital in Hamilton so we can examine him there."

It took another hour-and-a-half for a boat to arrive. A nurse and two men in white uniforms placed the screaming Patten on a stretcher and carried him to the makeshift dock. The entire team followed Will and Else who had her arm around Hada. Her daughter's legs wobbled as she tried to keep up with medical personnel carrying Pat.

John and Helen Tee-Van docked the *Skink* at the *Sea Fern* as the two men lifted Patten's stretcher onto the hospital boat. The boy was still. He had passed out.

Will explained the situation and asked if there was enough fuel in the *Skink* for a return trip to Hamilton. "I need to take Patten's friends to the hospital," Will explained.

The medical staff and Dr. Paulina allowed Else and Hada to ride with Patten in the hospital boat. Else took Patten's right hand in hers. Trying to control her emotions, Hada placed a hand on Pat's chest. They worried, but there was less stress on Patten's sleeping face. The nurse held his left wrist monitoring his pulse.

More medical staff awaited the boat at the dock in Hamilton. They put Patten into an ambulance and took him the short distance to the hospital. Dr. Paulina and the nurse rode with their young patient.

By the time Else, Hada, and others walked to the hospital, the medical team had Patten in surgery. They waited to hear results.

Dr. Paulina came to the waiting room. His face somber.

"The surgeon opened the boy's scar. They had not removed his appendix as he thought. They did an experimental surgery at the time. Cleaned the appendix and removed the infection, but then sewed him up."

"What does that mean, doctor?" Else asked.

"The boy's appendix ruptured. He died on the operating table."

The entire DTR team heard the news. Hada gripped her mother with tears streaming from her eyes. The shock froze everyone.

Else rested her cheek against her daughter's head. Will put his hand on her shoulder. Else cried with her daughter.

Will Beebe had the uncomfortable task of calling Patten Jackson's parents from a phone in the hospital. It took several minutes for operators to connect them, the phone line weak. Will shouted into the mouthpiece so they could hear. When the word "dead" passed his lips, Will choked and listened to the silence.

Patten's father finally spoke. "I'm sorry, Dr. Beebe. This is shocking news. I don't know what to say except I love my son. I feel helpless and sorry you have to be there instead of me."

The hospital's medical staff prepared Patten's body for the trip home. Else, Hada, Dr. Beebe, and his staff went to Hamilton to see Patten's casket loaded onto the ship bound for New York. It was an informal procedure; the casket loaded as though it was just another piece of cargo except for the mourners watching.

———⊷⊶———

The start of October was dreary. In a few days, the entire DTR team, including the last of the interns, would travel home.

"I don't think I can come back, Mother," Hada said. "It will always remind me of Pat. I don't think I can be here without crying."

"You're too young to carry the weight of death."

Else saw Dr. Beebe listening to their conversation. She spoke to him.

"Sorrow is heavy, Dr. Beebe. I dislike seeing my daughter troubled by it. But for the young, there is time to recover."

"Does recovery mean a chance to forget?" Will asked Else. She could tell he was agonizing as well.

"No. It's simply Vaseline on the scar. Soothes the pain temporarily," she said.

"Mrs. B, I wish that it were true, that something could salve our sorrow, help us forget the pain of the heart. It would make life easier."

CHAPTER 37

Fannie and Noël

The holidays helped Will cope with the end of an emotional year. Elswyth regaled Will with dozens of stories about her experiences meeting royalty in London.

"Most of them, Will, were several steps removed from the crown, but they loved to talk about it, full of insights I treasured."

Will shared stories of his own. He told Elswyth he was delighted by the constant requests from newspapers and magazines for interviews regarding the bathysphere. He said he prefaced every conversation with accolades for Otis Barton, the craft inventor, but few articles mentioned the younger explorer.

"They quoted me describing what I saw when more than quarter-of-a-mile deep. I know Otis will be angry; he wants his name in print, wants to be a celebrity and make movies."

Will and Elswyth spent holiday evenings together at dances, plays, and dozens of parties where Will often took center stage. Early mornings found him traveling to his office at the Bronx zoological park. He worked alongside John, Gloria, and his newest permanent hire, Jocelyn Crane.

One afternoon he left early to write at his home where he expected the quiet to be more conducive.

"I have some news, Will," Elswyth said, interrupting the clicking of typewriter keys.

"What, Dear? Is it about the novel you're writing?"

"It is. How d'you know?"

"Because I heard you talking on the telephone with your literary agent."

"The publisher loves the idea of a novel about Elizabeth before she became queen, maneuvering her way to the top of a very political and tumultuous England."

"Did I hear you say you settled on a title, Elswyth?"

"… *The Tudor Wench.*"

"Clever. Did you come up with that on your own? It's perfect."

"Thank you. I've been so excited to run it by Fannie, I invited her down for cocktails before we dine. Do you mind?"

"Of course not. Have you heard what she's writing?"

"I'm sure she has more than one project. It'll be fun to hear her talk about it. She gets such wonderful write-ups that sell her books before they're printed."

Fannie Hurst was a frequent guest in the Beebe home. Although married to Russian-born pianist Jacques Danielson, Fannie kept a separate apartment. She lived above the Beebes and co-hosted events that included authors, actors, radio personalities, and journalists—the conversations always lively and entertaining.

Like Will, Fannie could talk. Readers found both of their quotes in newspaper gossip columns beyond New York City. She knocked on the Beebe's door carrying a bottle of Bordeaux hidden by a bouquet.

"Entrez vous, s'il vous plaît," Will said, his lingering Brooklyn dialect distorting his French.

"Hello, Will," she said, pushing past him to give Elswyth the flowers, hidden wine, and a kiss on the cheek. "Tell me everything about London."

Elswyth handed the bouquet and bottle to Will, wrapped her arm around the older woman, and escorted her into the living room.

Will took the wine to the bar where he had two flutes of champagne poured for the ladies. He served them and deferred to Elswyth.

"It was a marvelous summer, but I worked very hard and met dozens of people with ties to the British throne. It challenged me to keep their stories sorted, there were so many."

"Where are you with your draft, dear?"

"I'm not finished, but very near."

"Is it about Elizabeth?"

"Yes, but I'm concentrating on her early life, not when she was queen."

"Marvelous idea."

"Fannie, I've heard rumors," Elswyth continued. "Your next book is already in a second printing, and you haven't released it. When, when do we get to see it?"

"Soon. In '31."

"Can you tell us what it's about?" Will asked.

"My usual women's stuff, Will. Adultery, domineering men, and abuse of civil liberties."

Will lifted his eyebrows with a glance at Elswyth.

"Oh, for pity's sake, I know that look, William Beebe."

"Sorry, Fannie. I love you dearly, but your radical themes make me wonder about your childhood."

"…and you think what your friend Grant writes is mainstream? I think not."

"I'm not saying that. What bothers me the most is that both of you seem to have fervent followers, which means the two ends of the spectrum are crowded and wider apart than ever," Will said.

"My observation is the two ends are broadening and encroaching on the middle," Elswyth added. "I hope you make women's oppression more obvious to men, but I don't want men to ignore either of our books because they're incensed."

"You needn't worry about that, Elswyth," Fannie replied. "There are many sympathetic gentlemen in the world. I married one…"

"Are you sure you married Jacques?" Will asked.

"You can be such a charming prick, Will."

Fannie married Danielson in 1915. When the press discovered their marriage in 1920, some criticized Hurst and Danielson for maintaining two residences when there was a housing shortage. What she couldn't keep from the press were her dalliances with men other than her husband.

"All right, Fannie, tell us the title," Will demanded.

"*Back Street*. We won't be talking about it at our holiday party, Will. Mr. Grant will leave if he finds out this Jew is writing about abuses of Negros."

Elswyth laughed and toasted Fannie with her champagne. Will grinned. Fannie's spunk reminded him of Nettie, his mother. Their banter was fun. He would never let it be serious.

The holidays came and went. A beautiful snowfall covered the city for Christmas. The trees of Central Park sparkled white.

The cold weighed heavily on Will's health. He carried on nonetheless writing a dozen newspaper and magazine articles about his bathysphere dives. He spoke to business groups and women's clubs garnering funds for the Department of Tropical Research and its Third Oceanographic Expedition to Bermuda. But it remained uncertain whether the bathysphere would be deployed in 1931 mostly because of money, but also because the zoological society's director opposed any further dives.

Will's worst news came in late March. Temperatures had not risen above 60 degrees since November. Will felt miserable. Then one evening, Elswyth answered a telephone call. She held silent and hung up slowly without saying goodbye.

"Will, that was your father's nurse. Charles is dead, Will. I'm so sorry."

Days from departing for Bermuda, Will and Elswyth buried Charles Beebe next to Nettie in Glen Falls, New York, at the northern reaches of the Hudson River.

Elswyth plotted with Fannie to provide Will with a special audience that would entertain him, and they hoped, pull him from his depression before leaving for Bermuda. Several times the two women had heard Will's stories about England's Prince George and his near-death helmet dive.

Fannie learned her friend Noël Coward was in America and knew that Coward and Prince George also were friends. She invited him to her apartment for dinner. He brought acting legend Gertrude Lawrence as his date. They had recently opened Coward's play *Private Lives* on Broadway after a successful run in London.

Will and Coward chatted as if old friends.

"George carried on like a 12-year-old schoolboy about his experience helmet diving with the famous Professor Beebe," Coward said. "I was instantly jealous."

"No need. Come to Bermuda this summer. I'll show you how to dive and he won't be able to boast any further."

"Splendid idea, Professor Beebe. Maybe the island blokes would enjoy seeing Miss Lawrence and me in *Private Lives*. They have a theater there, do they not? Would you want to go to Bermuda this summer, Gertie?"

"Bermuda, Noël?"

"Yes, Bermuda. The King owns it. His Majesty, George III, used the islands to stage his ships when these upstart Yanks ruined our colonization."

"Yes, the history of the island makes it quite fascinating. A superb base for scientific discovery. And theater," Will said.

"England bullied Spain and Portugal to take over the islands four hundred years ago, Noël," Fannie said. "There are African, Spanish, and Portuguese descendants neglected and yet among the oldest citizens of Bermuda."

"Dear Fannie, you must bandage that bleeding heart," Coward responded.

"Are there rich men there, Dr. Beebe?" Miss Lawrence asked. "I'm looking for a new husband."

"I've met a few rich men. If you find one to marry, would you please encourage him to support our expedition?"

"Quid pro quo, so to speak," Miss Lawrence responded. "I used that line in an awful play once, Noël. I didn't understand what I was saying until the young actor I had to kiss explained it. He was a wonderful kisser."

"Do you see the fun we could have, Professor Beebe? Add our mutual friend, the young prince, and I think we could make Bermuda an outstanding destination."

"Mr. Coward, I couldn't agree more. I'm suddenly quite excited to return if for no other reason than to find Miss Lawrence's next husband."

The repartee lasted until four in the morning. Coward took over Hurst's piano. He and Miss Lawrence sang Coward's endless list of comedy songs while sitting on the piano bench, cooing as though they were teenage lovers.

Will, Elswyth, and Fannie laughed so hard, it brought neighbors to the door who stayed rather than complained.

Will stepped aside and watched the frivolity thinking about Prince George and the rumors he heard about Coward, widely known as homosexual. *Could the handsome prince who Gloria was instantly smitten by, also find the actor to be a good bed partner?*

In May, Will, Elswyth, and the DTR staff boarded a ship for Bermuda. As they climbed the steps, Will turned to look at the spot where his father stood in previous years waving farewell to his adventurous son. Once aboard the ship and in their private quarters, Elswyth asked Will how he was feeling.

"I will be fine, dear wife, when I have busy work to occupy my mind," Will said. "It is difficult at the moment because I miss him. I miss both of my parents."

"They would want you to do what you love, Will."

He and Elswyth hugged until a knock at their cabin door shortened their embrace.

"Telegram for Dr. and Mrs. William Beebe," said the voice behind the door.

Will signed for the envelope and read the message aloud: "Will and El, backstage with Noël and Gertie STOP Show extended STOP Can't do Bermuda this summer STOP NYC loves play STOP N and G send regards STOP Fannie."

"How wonderful for Noël and Gertrude," Elswyth said. "I hope you're not too disappointed, Will."

"No. I didn't think they'd come to Bermuda even if the play hadn't been successful. They love London and would have been busy with their next project."

"I suppose you're right."

"You should go see the play when you return to New York, Elswyth. Take your mother."

"I shall. But I'm hoping Bermuda stays cool enough for me to enjoy time with my husband, at least until he's too busy to pay me attention."

"I have plans, El, to spend time with you house hunting."

"Really, Will?"

"It's been more than 20 years since I owned a home."

"But we'll keep the apartment in the city…"

"Yes. I'm not saying we'll make Bermuda a residence forever, but it feels right for now."

"How exciting. I like the idea. I can't wait to see what we might afford."

CHAPTER 38

Mother's Love

Else Bostelmann had no desire to buy anything, but she put 34th and Broadway as her destination. After delivering three new oil paintings to the zoological park for Helen Tee-Van for review, she rode the subway past her apartment. She knew Hada had a half hour for dinner at six o'clock. Else wanted to join her daughter, whom she hadn't spoken to in several days, except to say goodbye when Hada left for her job at Macy's.

Else spotted Hada at the lingerie counter. She was waiting on a customer. Else looked at clothing while Hada finished her sale.

Hada Bostelmann used her good fortune to work at the prestigious Manhattan store to help her recover from a depressing year. First, the departure of Bobby, whom she hoped might stay in New York. And then Patten Jackson's unexpected death.

Although she teased Pat mercilessly, she considered the eighteen-year-old her best friend. She confessed to Else when they left Bermuda, she loved Patten. "I told him, Mother. I told him I loved him. I kissed him and said I was being serious. I would wait for him to finish college to marry him. I couldn't find a better friend to spend my life with."

Else worried about her daughter. She worked long hours, picking up overtime whenever she could. She secluded herself in her room until it was time to catch the subway.

"Hello, Tochter."

"Hello, Mother. You surprised me. I almost forgot what I was saying to my customer when I saw you."

"I'm sorry. But I was hoping to have dinner with you since we haven't been together in quite some time."

"That's very sweet. I have money so I can treat you."

"Unnecessary…"

"…I insist. Since I only have thirty minutes, let's eat at the cafeteria on the third floor."

"Das klingt gut."

They rode the elevator listening to shoppers chat about family issues and a mother trying to quiet a baby cutting new teeth. Hada led the way to the third-floor cafeteria.

They both selected a pasta dish, easy to eat quickly. Hada paid and they found a quiet corner.

"Are you finding the work suitable, Tochter?"

"The store people are nice. Sometimes the customers are rude, but they pay the bills, so I try to ignore their lack of manners."

"I leave soon for Bermuda. Dr. Beebe sent me a note. He said you're welcome to return with me. He'd like to have you supervise this year's new interns."

"I so admire Dr. Beebe, Mother, but I can't go back. It would be too hard. I need to find a career. People at Macy's are nice. I enjoy working here. I'm going to make friends and follow my intuitions like you've told me to do."

"I must learn to be independent, too, Tochter. I depend on you more than you realize."

Hada looked at her mother. "Are you telling me the truth, Mother? You depend on me?"

"It's not the same as a wife depends on a husband or a husband on a wife or a daughter on her mother. I depend on you because I love you and there is no one else I can say that to."

Hada took a deep breath. She fought the urge to cry. Her mother seldom shared words of love so sincerely.

Else could see the emotion churning. "I didn't mean to upset you. You have makeup on your eyes. Do not wash it away."

Hada laughed behind sniffles and padded the corner of her eyes with her napkin. "You are a funny parent, Else Bostelmann. I know you're here because you worry for me and want to see me happy, but you say things that make me feel like a lost child."

"I'm sorry, Hada. You're right. I should be better at understanding your sorrow."

"It's all right, Mother. I've met many young people here who tell me they do not understand their parents. I tell them I understand my mother, but I still want a life of my own."

"That's good to hear but a little sad."

"I know. I feel the sadness too. I have had too many losses this past year. I cannot leave my mother, but I also cannot stay dependent on her forever."

"No, you mustn't. I suppose I came to say that, and yet, to say I'm worried about you moving away from me."

"I can't leave, Mother. I still can't afford a place in New York City, but I don't intend to go anywhere else. I will keep your apartment clean while you're in Bermuda. I will be your *Tochter* forever, so please do not worry about me, because when you worry I do as well."

"Then we have an agreement. We go where we need to go, we do what we need to do, and we do not worry."

"Precisely, Mother."

CHAPTER 39

More Complexities
Summer 1931

When Else arrived in Bermuda, she went straight to the lab where she found Miss Hollister.

"The magazine editors loved your paintings, Mrs. B," Gloria reported. "They said your artwork pulled readers into Will's articles. I'm paraphrasing, Mrs. B, but they said they saw personalities in the faces of the fish and crustaceans, even the smallest creatures."

"The eye is the messenger on a canvas," Else replied. "A predator is excited; a prey is frightened. Our human instincts recognize emotions in the eyes."

"You're amazing, Mrs. B. I'm so glad to have you back at Nonsuch."

"Thank you, Miss Hollister. I'm nervous this year without Hada. It's the first time we've been separated for more than a few days."

"Is she doing well with her job? Did she tell you I saw her at Macy's?"

"She said she was so proud to introduce you to her store friends."

"Yes, the girls at the makeup counter fussed over me like I was a celebrity. I spent an hour with them. I could never repeat the way they made me up. But it was fun."

"Hada said the Macy's photographer took pictures of you. She said you looked stunning."

"Will handles that kind of attention much better than I do, Mrs. B."

John and Helen Tee-Van came into the laboratory carrying trays of new specimens.

"Look what we brought you, Glo," John said. "More dead things."

"Funny, John."

"Hello, Mrs. Bostelmann," Helen said, hugging Else after setting down her trays. "I just received a letter from your sister-in-law. She published another book of original music for piano."

"Ida is full of ambition. I'm proud of her."

John placed his trays on the table next to Gloria. He waited for Helen to let go of Else so he could kiss her on the cheek. "It's so good to have you back, Mrs. B."

"Thank you, Mr. Tee-Van. Is Dr. Beebe the one who gave you the new specimens for Miss Hollister to work on?"

"No. He and Mrs. Beebe are looking at a house in St. George's Parish," John replied. "They're thinking about acquiring it. Will is looking for a house where he can build his lab and set up pools to keep his catches."

"That would be so practical," Helen added.

"…and expensive," John continued. "We don't know how the money situation will turn out. Director Blair will not authorize any more dives, which hurts our possibilities of stories that produce donations."

"Then we need good artwork, yes?"

"Well said. I can paint a fish, Mrs. B, but I cannot produce a picture that tells a story the way you do," Helen confessed.

"You can, Mrs. Tee-Van. You have the skills; you just need to be with nature the way Dr. Beebe has allowed me. A copper helmet is a marvelous tool for artists."

"I'm not that brave, Mrs. B."

"You have enormous courage, Helen," Gloria said. "You married John!"

"No need for your contribution, Glo."

"Tell me more about the house hunting," Else insisted. "And, by the way, I didn't see Miss Crane at her desk this morning."

"She went with the Beebes," Helen responded.

John explained Dr. Beebe's goal was to have permanency. He wanted a way to show Bermuda's lawmakers and the island's science community that the Department of Tropical Research was completing a full scientific exploration.

Nonsuch Island had been ideal as a base for their dives, but their research depended on more than deep-sea discoveries. The plan was to understand a small section of the Atlantic and how life evolved through ecological adaptation.

"Will has his eye on a particular property just across the Swing Bridge. We can go to the roof and look across St. David's Island to see it on the other side of Ferry Reach."

"Is that a better location than here, Mr. Tee-Van?" Else asked.

"We believe so, especially since it's very near a building the locals are developing as their ocean research center. We might find it helpful."

"Dr. Beebe knows some of the scientists—ichthyologists from the United States—who are behind the center's development," Gloria told Else.

"With money tight and funding for science being reduced, working together might be an answer," John added.

"Will it happen this year?"

"Very unlikely, Mrs. B," John replied.

———∞∞∞———

Will and Elswyth made no deal to purchase or lease the house before Elswyth left for New York and then London. Further troubles plagued the DTR efforts, including a second crack in the winch.

The setbacks and Elswyth's departure did not slow Will. He used the lack of field productivity to increase his cataloging efforts. He pushed staff and interns hard to build lists and descriptive documents, filling long days with arduous work. When he had everyone near exhaustion, he would declare time for partying.

They loaded boats with extra clothing and dancing shoes to enliven St. George and Hamilton with gaiety reminiscent of the past decade's dance marathons. After exhausting locals, they cruised into a rising sun and collapsed for a weekend of recovery. Except for Will Beebe.

The DTR director often changed from evening wear to swimwear and took advantage of the calm waters surrounding Nonsuch. He swam, changed to his work clothes, and headed to his laboratory workstation.

After a short time of quiet progress, the door to Will's laboratory squeaked open. He turned to see Jocelyn Crane entering but trying to be unobtrusive.

"Sorry, Dr. Beebe. I didn't mean to disturb you. I can't sleep and saw the light on. Thought I'd come to get some work done."

"It's fine. Tell me what you're working on."

"Gloria has me grouping slides into family, genus, and species. I'm doing them alphabetically. I'm doing crustaceans. Working with crabs. I find the *Decapoda* order fascinating, Dr. Beebe."

"Maybe that will be your specialty, Miss Crane."

"I don't find all crustaceans that interesting, but the crabs intrigue me, I guess."

Will's eyes returned to his work, but his mind stayed with Jocelyn.

"Did you enjoy the dancing?" he asked her without lifting his head.

"I did. Yes. It was quite darb."

"Darb?"

"Yes. Terrific. Have you not heard that term, Dr. Beebe?"

"Maybe, but I don't believe in that context."

"The girls at Smith use it all the time. 'He's so darb; such a darb evening.'"

"So, you had a *darb* evening then?"

"I did. Thank you for dancing with me. You're pretty good…"

"…go on. 'For a man my age.' That's what you're thinking, isn't it, Miss Crane?"

"No. I don't know how old you are."

"We celebrated my fifty-third birthday soon after you began working with the department, remember? But does age matter?"

"I'm not sure. I haven't had the opportunity to be around many men in my life, Dr. Beebe. My mother kept me from them."

"I'm surprised they haven't found you. You're very attractive. Older men like attractive young women, because they keep them thinking they're still young."

"I wonder where I left the last set of slides?" Jocelyn asked herself, pretending she wasn't paying attention to Dr. Beebe's last comment.

"Do you need help finding them?"

"Well, maybe."

Will rose and went to Jocelyn's workstation.

"Oh, here they are, right in front of me."

She pulled a tray of slides from under an open newspaper.

"Let me see which set you're looking at."

Will reached around Jocelyn, putting his hand on her waist, his arm touching her back to balance his stretch. Their heads were close together. Jocelyn closed her eyes and smelled the cologne he splashed on his face after his swim.

"No, you really are a very good dancer, Dr. Beebe."

"Thank you, Miss Crane. I enjoyed dancing with you as well."

Else heard voices coming from the lab as she approached. She stopped before pushing the cracked door open because she could see Dr. Beebe and Miss Crane in an embrace. She waited.

When Dr. Beebe kissed Miss Crane, Else moved back a step from the door so her face would not pick up any light. She watched a moment longer, then left. She didn't want to embarrass them and nothing on her drawing table was that important.

As she ambled aimlessly across the campus grounds, her chin in the air to pull in the morning fragrances, she heard Trumps barking in the distance and hoped Miss Hollister was close behind.

Trumps came running to Else, tail wagging dog happiness. Else bent and greeted the terrier with equal enthusiasm. "Where's your master, Trumps?"

"I'm here, Mrs. B," Gloria said slipping past the trees that hid her. "Guten Morgen."

"Guten Tag, Fräulein Hollister. Wo waren Sie denn?

"Oh. Oh, I don't believe you've taught me that phrase, Mrs. B. What did you say?

"Wo waren Sie denn? It means, where have you been?"

"That's one I need to add to my German repertoire. And I need to teach it to Will. Can you repeat it?

"Wo… waren… Sie… denn? Do you have an answer?"

"Not in German. But I walked the entire circumference of the island. I saw Will after he finished his swim. I told him I might meet him at the lab after Trumps and I made the round and looked in on the Tee-Vans. Helen says John is not feeling well."

"Would you mind walking with me while I check on my flower garden?"

"Well… I suppose Will doesn't need me disturbing his work. Sure. Show me what you're growing."

Else kept Gloria interested in wildflowers she had planted from seeds she gathered at the end of their 1930 expedition. She called it a memorial garden for Charles Beebe and Patten Jackson, which also made her think of Hada.

Gloria put her arm around Else. "You're a wonderful woman, Mrs. B…"

"… Oh, I wish it were true, Miss Hollister. I try to be a good, honest person, but I don't always succeed. Mary Baker Eddy said, 'The way to extract error from mortal mind is to pour in truth through flood-tides of Love. Christian perfection is won on no other basis.'"

"Do you follow Christian Science, Mrs. B?"

"I try. I like reading her *Key to the Scriptures*. It's full of human wisdom, which I think is a good thing."

"Did you become a follower when you arrived in the United States?"

"Oh, no. Mrs. Eddy's teachings were quite popular in Germany when I was a young artist. Followers translated her writings into German. Her words seemed so gentle and honest, I read them over and over. They did not scold me like the priests that frightened me as a child. I could not imagine a God so mean and angry. Her God, the God within us, Miss Hollister, comes from love. I like that better."

"I can understand, Mrs. B. Will told me that his mother, Nettie, was a follower of Christian Science. Did you know that?"

"No, I don't believe so."

"I don't think he talks about it because his mother died relatively young from an illness she fought with prayer. I think Will may blame Mrs. Eddy's teachings."

"As a man with a passion for science and nature but who takes an animal's life without remorse, I can see that he has internal conflicts that are unresolved."

Gloria laughed. "Mrs. B, you're so perceptive. But I'm saying nothing more because Will is not alone with those conflicts."

"Any time you want to talk, Miss Hollister, I'm always available."

"I will not hesitate. I must go check on Will. He needs to get his mind off work."

Else followed Gloria to the main campus building, the old hospital, and into the laboratory. Else took a deep breath as Gloria pushed the door open.

"He's not here. Maybe he tired and laid down in his room. He could use some sleep."

"That might be where he's gone," Else concurred.

Helen Tee-Van entered the laboratory with a worried face. "Have you seen Dr. Beebe?"

"We just came looking for him, Helen," Gloria replied. "How's John?"

"Worse. I think I need to get him back to New York. His cough is so harsh. I'm worried his bronchitis will make him vulnerable to pneumonia. I don't want a hurricane to trap us with no power and John needing a respirator."

"Isn't the *Victoria* scheduled to depart Hamilton later today?" Gloria asked.

"Yes. I've asked Mr. Tucker to take us. I hope Dr. Beebe will understand."

"Go. I'll find Will and explain."

Helen scurried to Gloria and hugged her friend. "Goodbye. I'll send you a telegram when I get him to a city hospital. Goodbye, Mrs. B."

"Goodbye, Mrs. Tee-Van. Please take good care of John. I'll pray for him."

When Helen departed, Gloria looked at Else. "You *will* pray for him, won't you?"

"I've already begun. For him. For all of us."

CHAPTER 40

The Parade Begins
November 1931

John Tee-Van regained his strength by Thanksgiving. He added back a good portion of his lost weight eating turkey and dressing prepared by a caterer that Will and Elswyth Beebe hired for the entire day. It began with an early morning breakfast so everyone could walk less than two blocks to watch the Macy's Thanksgiving Day Parade go by.

Will and Elswyth's apartment grew crowded by eight o'clock. Among the early guests were Fannie Hurst and her husband, Jacques Danielson. Jacques sat at Will's piano after the parade's floats passed 67th Street and the street crowds dispersed. He played a variety of songs until the caterer had a full Thanksgiving spread laid out. People ate cafeteria-style, grazing throughout the day while partiers came and went.

Else and Hada Bostelmann were among those who made a late appearance. Hada found John and Helen Tee-Van at the buffet. After their greeting, Hada asked John about his health.

"I'm much better now, Miss Bostelmann. I didn't realize how sick I had become until Helen got me to the hospital. The way the doctors and nurses attended to me I began to think I might die."

"That must have been scary, Mr. Tee-Van."

"We missed you this past year, young lady," Helen said. "It didn't feel the same without your pretty face among the interns."

"That's very kind of you to say, Mrs. Tee-Van."

"How are you getting along at Macy's?" John asked.

"I'm doing well. I made my mother late today because all of Macy's employees had responsibilities during the parade. I've been up since three, and now I have to be at the 34th Street store for more events this evening."

"I'm sure you're tired, but that sounds exciting," Helen said.

"I am tired, but I feel fortunate to have a job, especially because I enjoy the people and my work."

"We're glad to hear that," John told her. "If you ever have free time, before the winter gets cold, please come out to the zoological park and visit."

"Thank you, Mr. Tee-Van. I will try to do that."

Will spotted Else talking to Gloria. He approached.

"I'm glad you could make it, Mrs. B. I see Hada talking to the Tee-Vans."

"Thank you for the invitation, Dr. Beebe. Hada has been working at the parade since early this morning, so I wasn't certain she'd be able to come. She insisted on being here."

"She is turning into a beautiful woman, Mrs. B," Gloria commented.

"Thank you, Miss Hollister. She tells me her friends at Macy's want her to invite you back for more makeup trials. They show your picture to customers and boast about consulting with you."

"I'm embarrassed, Mrs. B."

"You should be flattered, Glo," Will said.

"Please tell me what you heard from Mr. Barton," Else said. "You seemed concerned when I departed Bermuda."

"Yes, Will, tell her your latest episode," Gloria insisted.

"After donating the bathysphere to the Department of Tropical Research following our successful dives last year, Otis threatened to renege."

"I'm surprised by that, Dr. Beebe. His outward manners are not good, but I didn't expect him to be bitter."

"He experimented in the Caribbean with helmet dives and a cameraman he hired to shoot motion picture film. He wants to do movies about our dives in the bathysphere."

"That sounds exciting."

"When he notified us by telegram in late July that he was free to come to Bermuda, our problems had escalated, compounded by unpredictable storms, so I told him we ended the season, which upset him."

"He got mad too, Mrs. B, by the release of Will's story in *National Geographic*, which featured so many of your paintings," Gloria continued. "He didn't feel like Will gave him enough credit in the article."

"I'm sorry," Else said. "The article was so inspiring."

"I've written hundreds of articles, Mrs. B, but *A Round Trip to Davy Jones's Locker* is a piece I am proudest to point to because of your artwork. It inspired readers."

"You're too kind, Dr. Beebe."

"Not according to Otis," Gloria added.

"Well, I hope it doesn't affect your plans."

"I want to talk to you about the future, Mrs. B. Would you mind meeting me at my office at the zoological park next week?"

"Certainly."

"Let's say a week from today at ten o'clock."

"I will be there, Dr. Beebe. And now I must go say hello to the Tee-Vans and learn what my daughter is saying."

Will and Gloria waved to Hada when she looked their way after Else joined her with John and Helen.

Jocelyn Crane, assisting Elswyth with hostess duties, escorted a man for introductions to Dr. Beebe. She explained the gentleman was Fannie Hurst's special guest who came to meet Will. Fannie followed behind Jocelyn.

"Dr. Beebe, this gentleman would like to say hello."

"How do you do? I'm William Beebe. Welcome to our home."

"It's a pleasure to meet you, Dr. Beebe. My name is David Sarnoff."

"I've heard that name," Will said. "You're the one starting the radio network, correct?"

"Yes. We're underway, planning to do next year's parade for the first time so people from here to California can enjoy what we're able to see here in our city. It's become a celebrated event thanks to Macy's."

"Wonderful idea, Mr. Sarnoff. I'm sure Macy's will help you all it can."

"I'm counting on that, Dr. Beebe." Both men smiled. "But that's not what I wanted to talk about. I want to hear about your plans for the bathysphere next summer."

"Well, Gloria and I just began that discussion, Mr. Sarnoff. This is Gloria Hollister, my science assistant."

"How do you do, Mr. Sarnoff," Gloria said, extending her hand.

"Well, I can see I should be making a movie of your adventure. You've surrounded yourself with beautiful women as pretty as any starlet in Hollywood, Dr. Beebe." Sarnoff looked at Jocelyn and Gloria as he spoke to make sure they understood he directed his compliment at them.

"Thank you. It's true, outstanding gifts often come in beautifully wrapped packages," Will said.

"Oh, for pity's sake, Will," Fannie snarled.

"My purpose, Dr. Beebe, is to hear your interest in broadcasting one of your dives live to the world."

"Really? Do you think you can do that?" Will asked.

"I'm willing to try if I can have your cooperation. Yours and Miss Hollister's. I understand you have a telephone line linked to Dr. Beebe in the bathysphere."

Gloria nodded.

"Would you mind contacting me at the zoological park next week so we can set up a meeting to include my staff?" Will asked.

"Of course. A splendid suggestion. I will call you by telephone on Monday to make such arrangements."

When Sarnoff departed with Fannie Hurst, the broadcast executive wrapped his arm around the author and kissed her cheek. Will, Gloria, and Jocelyn watched them, then turned to each other.

"A radio broadcast from the middle of the Atlantic Ocean?" Gloria puzzled.

"I don't understand how radio works," Jocelyn said.

"Waves of energy," Will said. "But it takes power to boost it. I don't know if he can provide enough power from the boat to push a radio signal all over the world."

"Do people have radios everywhere?" Jocelyn asked.

"Those are questions we'll find out when Mr. Sarnoff meets us at our offices."

CHAPTER 41

Commitments and Disappointments
December 1931

J ocelyn Crane sat outside Will's office and greeted Else when she arrived at 9:45. "Dr. Beebe is on the telephone again with Mr. Sarnoff," Jocelyn explained.

"Do I know Mr. Sarnoff?" Else asked.

"You may have seen him at the Thanksgiving Day party. He has a radio network. He wants to broadcast from the barge when Dr. Beebe and Mr. Barton dive in the bathysphere this summer."

"Does that mean Dr. Beebe and Mr. Barton resolved their issues?"

"I'm not certain, Mrs. B. Maybe Will… maybe he can tell you when he finishes talking on the telephone."

Else sat in a chair across from Jocelyn, who filed documents in a cabinet near the door to Will's office.

"Are you still doing work for Miss Hollister?" Else asked.

"Yes, she's teaching me so much. We do well together, Mrs. B."

"I'm happy to hear that."

Will cracked the door to his office wide enough to see Jocelyn. "I'm off the telephone. Let me know when Mrs. B arrives."

"She's here, Will. Hiding behind the door."

Will pushed the door wider and saw his artist sitting, smiling. "Hello. You're early."

"My father said you're always on time when you're early."

"Come in, please, Mrs. B." Will held the door open. When she passed him, he said, "I've never heard you mention your father before. I like his wisdom."

"He also taught me to never waste time. I think you know that from my visit three years ago."

Will walked behind his desk and waited for Else to sit before he slid into his squeaky oak chair. "I remember that meeting. It's hard to believe it's been three years."

"Do you want me to go to Bermuda in the spring?" she asked directly.

"Yes, I want you to, Mrs. B, but I don't have the funds. The men who have bankrolled my expeditions for the past three years are running short. Mortimer Schiff's sudden death also came as a shock and a major setback. The depressed economy is lasting too long."

"I hate for our relationship to end, Dr. Beebe…"

"…it's not ending unless you want it to, Mrs. B."

"I do not."

"Then here is my plan and request of you; I shall continue to search for enough money to take the entire team back to Bermuda. If I fail by spring, then I will have to minimize my staffing to just my science team. However, I want you to go whenever I can raise sufficient funds. Can you promise me to be available, Mrs. B?"

"Dr. Beebe, I must make a living. My opportunities have improved because of the work I've done during your expeditions. Yes, I will make myself available. Now tell me about this radio man Miss Crane mentioned."

"Mr. Sarnoff. He runs a network of radio stations across the country that he calls the National Broadcasting Company. He's an important man at RCA."

"Does he want you to go on his radio stations?"

"More than that, Mrs. B. He wants to broadcast a live program from the *Ready* and listen to me describe what I'm seeing from the bathysphere like I'm describing things to Glo, but instead, transmitting it to all his listeners."

"Isn't that impossible, Dr. Beebe?"

"It's not impossible according to Mr. Sarnoff, but very challenging. He's willing to provide funding if we get the bathysphere ready."

"Are you and Mr. Barton on good terms? Does he know about the radio proposal?"

"He knows, Mrs. B. I promised him when he first brought me the bathysphere drawings that he could go on all dives he chooses. He wants the publicity because he has other aspirations."

Else asked if Will knew why Mr. Sarnoff chose the coming summer to do his broadcast. Will did not have an answer but assumed it was to prove to skeptics that the radio network could transmit from remote international areas.

His other theory was that Sarnoff intended to provide the nation a distraction from the emotional drain the stock market crash and subsequent economic depression created.

Broadcasting a daring achievement such as their bathysphere dive stirred excitement and national pride.

News that she wouldn't travel to Bermuda disheartened Else. She loved what she contributed to Dr. Beebe's expeditions and had grown fond of him and his staff. She prayed that things would work out for all concerned.

Otis Barton's money diminished along with other large fortunes. Still, he had no plan to work a regular job. Instead, his ambition was to convert his heroics into a motion picture that rivaled the drama of a James Cagney or Bela Lugosi film.

Because of Dr. Beebe's fame, Otis received generous donations of film when he purchased cameras from George Eastman. He envisioned setting up a film camera in the enclosed bathysphere. But that meant he might need to install the spare quartz pane in the third eye of the sphere. It remained plugged with a steel plate. It added risk to the project, but also put pressure on his budget.

Otis spun the situation one-hundred-eighty degrees. His gift of the bathysphere to the New York Zoological Society made it Will's dilemma to manage the craft's expenses. Otis went to Dr. Beebe lobbying for the third window so he could film.

Will Beebe's goal remained firm; he wanted to dive the bathysphere to half a mile. David Sarnoff wanted him to do it while broadcasting live on his growing NBC radio network. And now Otis Barton wanted to load a camera into the bathysphere to record their milestone on motion picture film. It was a matter of coordinating everyone's wish with very little money.

Will broke the bad news to Else Bostelmann when he and Elswyth traveled to Bermuda on another house-hunting mission. As much as he regretted it, he couldn't include her during the 1932 expedition.

While in Bermuda, the Beebe's also met up with Will's acquaintance and fellow researcher, Edwin Conklin. Conklin, a Princeton University professor, had a leading role in the Bermuda Biological Station, a cooperative research center established by

American, Canadian, and British scientists. The station was near the home Will hoped to lease or buy.

The New York Zoological Society and the Smithsonian were among supporters of the Biological Station. In fact, Conklin asked Will to take the directorship, which Will declined.

Although Will turned down Conklin's offer, he nevertheless asked Conklin to allow his staff to live at the station during that summer. The buildings had newer dorms and cottages for students, so Will wanted Conklin's organization to let his team use the space until he added facilities to the home he planned to acquire.

"Nonsuch Island has been a marvelous place for us to launch our work," Will explained to Conklin. "Governor Bols and Governor Cubitt have been quite generous in lending us the use of the island, but inadequate housing for staff, the island's vulnerabilities to high winds and rough water, and without a permanent dock, it's not an ideal long-term setting."

"I know what you're saying, Will. And, yes, we have sufficient housing for your staff, especially later in the summer when our American and European students leave."

"What about Elswyth and me?"

"Well, there's a cottage that will be available, but I doubt that it's what you're used to…"

"No, Professor. Will and I are used to four walls and a bed," Elswyth admitted. "Will sleeps and works. He pays very little attention to accommodations."

"But aren't you here to buy a home, Mrs. Beebe?"

"Yes. Will wants to renovate a property that would be ideal for his research. For my needs, a good window through which I can have light and a view to encourage my imagination."

"When do you need the rooms, Will?"

"I'm uncertain, Ed. May I contact you when I return to New York and set a schedule?"

"Very well. Let me know."

Speeches and public appearances kept Will and Gloria Hollister busy through the first months of 1932. The rigor took its toll. Will's chronic allergies weakened his system. He became so ill, Elswyth put him in the hospital.

It slowed plans, but he stayed hopeful of pulling the bathysphere from its shelter at Darrell and Meyer. He wanted to dive a half-mile and broadcast his report to the radio audience David Sarnoff promised.

CHAPTER 42

Biding Time
July 1932

Hada Bostelmann shooed her mother and Aunt Ida from Else's kitchen so she could continue preparing a meal for the three women. Hada was celebrating a year at Macy's and invited Ida to join them. She felt Ida had helped with both Else's and her careers.

While Else and Ida talked, Hada dropped linguini noodles into boiling water. She stirred two different sauces, a tomato-based meat sauce and a white sauce seasoned with butter, mushrooms, garlic, and two small anchovies.

Hada steamed vegetables the way she learned from the chef who did cooking demonstrations at Macy's. She had peas and carrots, which she loved to mix with the linguini when covered in white sauce.

Ida returned to the kitchen to tell Hada how wonderful everything smelled.

"It's the garlic bread," Hada confessed. "Chef Michael says it's the best way to impress dinner guests. Just pile some butter and garlic on fresh bread and toast it in the oven while you're cooking."

"He sounds like a smart man. How old is he?" Ida asked.

"Ida Bostelmann, come back into the sitting room and get out of her kitchen," Else shouted. "I don't want you match-making my daughter to a chef."

"Our dinner is ready, Mother. You can have your kitchen back as soon as we eat."

"I see your plan, Tochter. You expect me to do the dishes."

"Your mother is very astute, Hada. You didn't fool her."

Hada had the small dining room table set. She carried in the covered bowl of pasta and demanded Else and Ida sit. She went after the sauces, garlic bread, then the vegetables.

Hada sat and Else blessed the food: "Thank you, dear God, for watching over the three of us when so many women are suffering in our city."

"Amen, but I wish we had some Riesling to toast your daughter, Else. This is a wonderful meal. I'm quite proud of both of you," Ida told them.

They dined for an hour, chatting and picking at their food. They cleared the table and stacked the dishes in Else's sink. Hada promised to wash them later. With no work tomorrow, she said she was looking forward to sleeping until noon.

"No, there will be other chores to do tomorrow," Else told her. "You will not sleep past nine o'clock. I will see to it."

"So, tell me what you're working on, Else."

"The advertising agency assigned me newspaper ads to draw. It's boring, but they pay me twice as much now than before Dr. Beebe hired me."

"You're a famous artist, that's why," Ida bragged.

"I'm not famous, but they know my work. I'm much faster because of my experience with Dr. Beebe."

"You are famous, Mother. Tell Aunt Ida about the telegrams you've received."

"Telegrams, Else? Yes, please tell me."

"A store in Brooklyn contacted me. They might want me to do sea-life patterns and floral designs for dresses."

"That would be fabulous, Else!"

"That's not all, Aunt Ida…"

"Another scientist said he wants me to contact his office if Dr. Beebe no longer needs me on his expeditions. He said he wants an artist soon."

"Oh, Else, that is such good news. I've been worried your popularity might cause people to think you're too expensive."

"Worried, Aunt Ida?"

"There aren't many artists with names on the cover of a magazine telling readers there are eight paintings inside. Like I said, your mother's famous. Prospective clients might be afraid she's too busy and hard to hire."

Hada laughed. She knew her mother would never turn down a job because she was too busy or felt too important.

Else told Ida she appreciated her confidence, but there were dozens of artists in New York City with incredible skills. "Your friend Helen Tee-Van is a good artist."

"I know, but you have something special. Helen agrees. Dr. Beebe will want you on as many of his expeditions as he can afford to take you."

"Dr. Beebe has a very difficult job, Ida. He has to be more than a scientist or explorer; he has to be a salesman, almost like a pitchman in front of the carnival. The Zoological Society depends on him to give speeches and talk to every club in New York City."

"He's very popular upstate too, Else. But I don't think you realize how important your role has been."

"I do, Ida. Everyone in Dr. Beebe's Department of Tropical Research is important to him. He would not be successful without

Mr. Tee-Van or Miss Hollister. Even Miss Crane, a year older than Hada, is very smart and hardworking. I hope it can last because I believe there are few others thinking of the planet the way Dr. Beebe and his staff do."

"I love your passion, sister-in-law. I'm sure that's why Dr. Beebe insists that you work with him in the future."

CHAPTER 43

Adversaries
August 1932

William Beebe carried a machete as he guided John, Gloria, and Jocelyn from the house he hoped to buy to the Ferry Reach shoreline. He slashed through dense thickets and created a path to the water.

"We could build a dock here," Will said. "You can see across St. David's Island to Nonsuch from the veranda." He pointed southwest. "That's the Swing Bridge we crossed to get here. Ferry Reach goes to Castle Harbor that way and St. George's Harbor to the northeast."

"It's a beautiful spot, Will," Jocelyn said.

"It's convenient to the Biological Station," John added.

"Good to Nonsuch Island as well," Gloria said.

"Yes, I'm pleased, although there's plenty of work to do. I would open up the lower level and put windows across the length of the house, so we'd have natural light in our office laboratory. Then I would build a water system to circulate ocean water to the top of the hill with a pump and let it run down here."

"That's very ambitious," John said.

"Tell John about the letter, Will," Gloria encouraged.

"I told you Professor Conklin is president of the group that set up the Biological Station. He and I have common interests, so he agreed to have us set up temporary quarters on their campus. As you pointed out, it's convenient. I've hired local movers to transfer our laboratory equipment from Nonsuch Island."

"The letter, Will," Gloria insisted.

"Conklin hired a new station director, a job he asked me to take. I told him I couldn't leave DTR. The new director is an English zoologist, Wheeler. Wheeler sent me a caustic letter telling me I can't use the cottage Conklin assigned me. I heard he disparaged me in front of the board."

"Then are we using the station?" John asked.

"Yes," Gloria injected. "Conklin intervened. He compromised with Wheeler on which facilities DTR could access."

"I get a basic dormitory, not an executive cottage that Conklin intimated," Will said.

Conflicts with Wheeler continued but they were not Will's only worry. The weather made each day questionable. Late summer heat stirred the ocean. Money was in short supply. DTR had one-tenth the funds Will brought with him in 1930.

Rather than hire Captain Millett's *Gladisfen* and *Ready*, Will went to Captain Sylvester to use *Freedom*, slightly larger than the *Gladisfen*.

The winch and large mast for putting the bathysphere into the water needed to be transferred. Work began only two days before Sarnoff's radio crew arrived in Bermuda on the same ship with Otis Barton.

In late August, with pressure from David Sarnoff mounting, Will gathered all parties at the Darrell and Meyer storage building. Will and staff unveiled the bathysphere for the NBC crew: two engineers, broadcaster Ford Bond, and director George McElrath. The engineers created a telephone connection with the NBC studios on 5th Avenue in Manhattan so Bond could begin filing reports.

While the NBC crew enjoyed luxury at St. George's Hotel and Captain Sylvester supervised the repurposing of his tug, Otis began his work on the bathysphere. He removed the steel plug from the third eye of the submersible craft and replaced it with the spare three-inch-thick quartz-glass window. He built a mount for his film camera inside the cramped bathysphere.

When Otis finished his work, he and Will painted over the white sphere. It showed signs of storage—rust stains and dust-caked cobwebs. The new color was an aquamarine blue.

"I read your interview in the Boston Globe," Otis said while dipping his paint brush. "Did you tell the reporter I would be going with you during the radio broadcast?"

"I told him, and I said that you had donated the bathysphere to DTR. He used neither fact in his story, Otis. I'm sorry."

"I intend to film our adventure, Dr. Beebe. I need publicity so people will look for the movie at their local theaters."

"I'm aware of your goal, Otis. The reporters who talk to me are interested in science. They have covered my expeditions for more than twenty years," Will said. "They write about what they know. They don't know the motion picture industry."

"Then I hope you'll educate them next time. It will do us both some good."

With the new window occupying the third eye and his reputation at risk, Will worried about the world overlooking his shoulder. His confidence also eroded when several scientists at the Bermuda Biological Station joined Director Wheeler's Beebe bashing.

But the greatest concern became an approaching hurricane from the Caribbean. It bore down on Bermuda with heavy winds and torrential rains.

The DTR team redirected their energy to securing their rooms and laboratory at the Biological Station. They prepared for an impending storm while Captain Sylvester sought shelter for *Freedom*.

CHAPTER 44

Picture It Flowing
September 1932

A young executive appeared in the waiting room at the Oppenheim Collins, & Company Store in Brooklyn. Dressed in an expensive suit with his white collar starched stiff, Else Bostelmann noticed his tie pattern. It matched his pocket handkerchief. His shoes spit-shined to perfection.

Else assumed the young man was in his late twenties, maybe early thirties. The posture of an athlete. She stood when he approached.

"I'm Lance Irving," he said.

"Good morning, Mr. Irving. I'm Else Bostelmann. Thank you for your letter of invitation."

"You're quite welcome, Mrs. Bostelmann. I'm an avid follower of your art in *National Geographic Magazine*. I'm sure I've seen it elsewhere."

"Kind of you to speak of my art, Mr. Irving. Are you a collector?"

"No. Well, I mean I do buy art that I enjoy, but I'm not in the same league with the Rockefellers or Astors if that's what you're asking."

"Very few of us are. No, I was assuming from your introduction that maybe you invited me because you're interested in art."

"I'm interested in *your* art, Mrs. Bostelmann. I have an idea. Would you like to come to my office and discuss it?"

"Of course, Mr. Irving. I'm intrigued."

Else sat in a winged-back chair in a modest-sized office overlooking Fulton Street. She noticed several copies of *National Geographic Magazine* from June 1931 on Mr. Irving's desk, a few with pages of her artwork torn and paper-clipped to handwritten notes.

"Do those look familiar?" he asked when sitting.

"Yes. I'm embarrassed but flattered. They're among my first works for Dr. Beebe in Bermuda."

"So, here is my idea, Mrs. Bostelmann. I believe women's fashions are moving toward colors we find in nature. Shapes as well. Take a look at your first picture of the parrotfish with the bathysphere in the background. Those are the colors. And this picture of the eel..."

"...Yes, the Avocet-billed eel. Very unusual."

"It is. The movement is perfect for a flowing skirt. Can you recreate the shapes and build patterns from them?" Mr. Irving asked Else.

"Yes. It's not too difficult, but I would like to work with your designers to make sure I'm doing what they need."

"We have some of the best designers in the business at Oppenheim Collins, Mrs. Bostelmann. You will enjoy working with them."

"Then you are interested in hiring me to create pictures in nature for them to copy onto clothing patterns?"

"That is my wish, but I needed to hear your interest before I move my idea up the chain of command in our business."

"You are young and new, correct?"

"I am both, but I have good credentials and the manager is my uncle, so they are listening to my suggestions. Still, I need some support from others to proceed with my fashion ideas. Some things move quickly; some do not."

"I am a relatively patient woman, Mr. Irving. I'm excited about your ideas. I hope you have success. My daughter works in women's fashion at Macy's on 34th Street. This will excite her too."

"We're quite competitive with Macy's, Mrs. Bostelmann. I request you not discuss this with your daughter."

"Ja, wie dumm von mir. I'm sorry, Mr. Irving. I will say nothing to my daughter. I was not thinking clearly in my excitement."

"I'm thrilled to hear you say you're excited, Mrs. Bostelmann. That's encouraging news that inspires me to move forward with some alacrity. I shall be in touch with progress."

CHAPTER 45

NBC-sick

It took four days to recover from the storm's destruction. The *Freedom,* loaded with its famous cargo, had taken on water and sat low in the harbor. Captain Sylvester feared the bathysphere and its thirty-four hundred feet of steel cable made the sea-worn tug vulnerable. He was thankful his boat stayed afloat.

At the first opportunity, less than two weeks from when NBC said it would abandon its broadcast hopes, Will and Captain Sylvester agreed to test the bathysphere and *Freedom's* crew.

Sylvester took Beebe, Barton, and the others to a deep-sea destination at the north end of Beebe's expedition waters in the Atlantic. NBC's Ford Bond and George McElrath walked the deck and stuck their heads into the ball-shaped chamber.

"I couldn't do it," Bond said. "I'm too claustrophobic to even attempt to get into that thing."

"We're not sure you *could* squeeze through the manhole, Ford," McElrath commented, laughing at his friend.

Bond, a hefty gent, was much wider than either Will or Otis Barton.

When Captain Sylvester slowed his *Freedom,* John Tee-Van gathered a small crew together and prepared the unmanned bathysphere for its descent. They placed the four-hundred-pound plate over the manhole and pounded the winged center plug into place.

"It's ready, Will," John reported.

While John and his hired helpers were doing their tasks, Will, Gloria, and Jocelyn stood against the starboard rail, joking about Otis Barton circling the bathysphere with his sixteen-millimeter motion picture camera.

"Do you suppose Cecil B. DeMille looked like that when he was filming *The Ten Commandments?*" Gloria asked.

"No, DeMille never would have worn that ridiculous leather skullcap," Will responded.

Once John and Captain Sylvester dropped the bathysphere into the water, Will stepped away from the ladies and took charge. "Drop it to three-thousand, John," he ordered.

Bodies crisscrossed the deck, pacing away their anxieties. They listened to the winch unwind, clicking and whining an uncomfortable, unnerving sound.

After a few minutes, Gloria shouted, "One-thousand feet, Will."

After another half hour, Gloria told Will the bathysphere had reached his goal. The final indicator on the Roebling cable was visible on a near-naked winch drum.

John Tee-Van had sidled up to Gloria and Jocelyn while Will looked over the railing at the cable cutting two-foot waves. "Stop it, John," Will said.

"Shut it down, boys," John shouted across the *Freedom's* deck.

The noises ceased. Will kept his eyes on the cable playing in the waves. He turned to John. "Something's wrong."

"Look at the horizon, Will," John said. "We've heeled like a sailboat. Captain…?"

Captain Sylvester looked worried. His boat, patched from storm wounds, now leaned to the starboard enough to catch modest waves.

"It's taken on water, Captain," Will announced. "We need it up."

Otis put down his camera. He walked toward starboard while others staggered to port, hoping their weight made a difference in righting the tug. Worry was not just for the bathysphere. The concern now was whether the water-logged sphere might capsize the *Freedom*, its list so severe the deckhands bent knees and grabbed stationary objects to stop from slipping and falling into the sea.

After a torturous forty-five minutes, the bathysphere broke the surface ascending from a depth where pressure was more than nine-hundred pounds per square inch. Thousands of tons of pressure pushed against the steel ball from all directions.

The radiomen stood dumbfounded, wanting to see the bathysphere lift from the water, but afraid to wander starboard where the sea splashed against the deck.

"Who the hell assigned me this job!" an NBC engineer barked at McElrath and Bond. "I thought we were coming to paradise for some fun and relaxation!"

Jocelyn, also fearing for her safety, saw the radio crew clinging to anything that kept them upright, their terror visible. She went to them.

"We don't encounter this much drama every time we take the bathysphere out, but it is a dangerous exploration."

The men tried to act courageously, impressed by the young woman's calm demeanor under frightening circumstances.

"The only thing separating Dr. Beebe and Mr. Barton from crushing annihilation," Jocelyn told them, "was an inch and a half of steel. That's why it's important to test it before they go down into those conditions."

Clouds began to tumble across the sky. Otis moved in for a closer look at his steel masterpiece. It looked like a monstrous fish hanging from a line that could snap at any moment.

John coached Captain Sylvester to move the creaking boom with its heavy load to the center of his boat deck. The captain, sweating, knew if the line failed, the bathysphere weighed enough to break through the deck like an exploding bomb.

"Ease it down, Captain," Will instructed.

The bathysphere inched toward the deck and sank into the *Freedom* like a circus elephant sitting on a mattress. The crew gathered around the ball. It hissed an angry cat-sound.

Will could see water sloshing inside the sphere active under extraordinary tension. He went to the other side where steam-like mist escaped the crevices of the four-inch manhole plug. Its white packing lead oozed out like tiny volcanic rocks.

Otis moved in with a hand-held movie camera after winding the power spring. He stepped in front of John Tee-Van who stood opposite Will with the manhole plug in between them.

"Step back, Otis. It's under extreme pressure," Will told him.

Will looked to see where the manhole plug aimed. He stood to the side and hammered on the wing bolt that held the plug. It moved enough to throw off a louder screeching hiss and threatening mist.

Otis walked around the bathysphere and stood behind Will. John reached toward the plug.

"Easy, John. The pressure's keeping it tight. We need to get it off, but we have to do it carefully."

"Let me see if I can turn it by hand," John said.

"It's too dangerous," Gloria shouted.

Ignoring Gloria's warning, John and Will turned the wing a few degrees. The screech intensified causing the men to jerk their hands back. Will reached again, but with his slight touch, the plug exploded off the bathysphere and flew across the deck, pounding against the *Arcturus* winch. The resounding clang drove everyone back a step. They stared at a powerful stream of water shooting thirty feet across the deck like a fire hose.

Will checked his hand to make sure the plug didn't take his fingers with it.

The water continued with tremendous force. It lasted several seconds before it finally weakened, the stream pulling back to the sphere's plug hole.

All looked on dazed by the power of the compressed air and water. John and NBC's McElrath raced to find the plug. John hoped it wasn't damaged beyond use. McElrath found it, picked it up and moved it from hand to hand like a hot potato.

"It's very warm." He handed it to John and began searching for where it struck. "My God, it left a deep gash," McElrath said.

"The plug is repairable, Will. The rupture mangled the last threads, but I'm sure I can file them."

"Good," Will said. "It would have taken my head off if I'd been in front of it."

Gloria and Jocelyn surveyed the bathysphere through the quartz windows. "It still has water in it," Jocelyn said.

"The new window looks fogged, Will," Gloria said.

"Damnation," Will blurted. "You've got some repair work to do, Otis. Get that steel plug back."

Otis hid his eyes. His lip curled. He didn't deserve a reprimand from the Brooklyn bully.

PART III

THE DARK TRUTH

CHAPTER 46

The Broadcast
22 September 1932

Ford Bond and George McElrath asked their radio engineers for a conference aft away from the noises and DTR staff preparation. They had come up against David Sarnoff's imposed deadline. If the bathysphere couldn't submerge today, the crew had to head back to New York empty-handed. They clung to the sides of the *Freedom* hoping not to vomit.

Week-long weather was not good. The DTR staff had prepared twice but rough seas and stormy conditions turned them back.

The sea tossed treacherously for days, so Will ordered the bathysphere tied by five rope lines forming a star-shaped hold to prevent the ball from leaning with the sea swells, breaking loose, and rolling across the deck.

While the *Freedom* steamed to deep water, Otis and John readied the sphere. They had replaced the failed quartz window with the craft's original steel plate packing it with white lead and using large-bodied men to apply extreme force when tightening it in place.

When they tested the bathysphere and brought it up dry, Will declared the sphere ready for their radio broadcast dive. He had one last opportunity to talk to a live audience from hundreds of fathoms under the splashing surface.

George McElrath alerted Sarnoff by telegram late Wednesday that the bathysphere and tugboat were ready. The broadcast executive put musical programs scheduled for airing Thursday afternoon on standby. He brought all the musicians to the New York studios but said they might be pre-empted by an important live, remote broadcast.

NBC programmers milked delays as much as they could for several weeks. Now, when studio announcers promoted the live broadcast of Dr. William Beebe's half-mile attempt in the bathysphere, word spread throughout the cities covered by NBC's fledgling network.

Radio sets in America, Great Britain, and parts of France were linked to a boosting station in Bermuda set to receive shortwave signals from the *Freedom*. The signal was then routed to New York and London by undersea telephone cables, cables that William Beebe once misidentified as an enormous sea serpent crawling on the ocean floor.

McElrath had his broadcast associates, Bond and two engineers, well-rehearsed. But they fought the rolling ride the same as the DTR staff and hired crew. Many were sick.

When still on land, the radio producer coached Dr. Beebe's team, telling them how there would be two separate broadcasts, one to set up the event, and a second when Dr. Beebe descended.

At sea, with the situation already nerve-racking, the broadcasters put the DTR staff on edge every time they thrust the big, round microphone in front of their conversations. "Just testing," Bond would say.

Performing in dangerous circumstances they normally avoided, the DTR team was less guarded when barking instructions to one another. No one cursed as a habit, but they knew the words and let them fly hoping Bond was honest when he said the radio microphones weren't on.

Will found Captain Sylvester in his wheelhouse. They discussed the risks.

"I won't be able to hold the boat very steady, Dr. Beebe," Sylvester told him. "You'll have a bumpy ride."

"We'll do fine, Captain. This is an important day. You have thousands of people riding with you on this one."

"I hadn't thought of it that way. It's a hard thing to imagine for a crusty old sailor like me."

"We've both seen amazing changes in our lives, Captain. They're bound to continue."

"Good luck down there, Dr. Beebe."

"Thank you, Skipper. We're all in this to do our best."

Gloria sent Jocelyn to the bathysphere to test the microphone and headset inside the ball. Jocelyn, tossed off balance by the rolling *Freedom*, finally reached inside and put the earphones on and strapped the microphone in front of her.

"Gloria? Do you hear me?"

"Yes. It sounds good. Do you hear as well?"

"What's that?"

"I said, do you hear as well?" Gloria shouted.

"Yes. I was joking. I heard you fine the first time."

"That wasn't funny," Gloria yelled across the rocking deck.

John came over to assist Jocelyn with the communications equipment. He then searched for Otis Barton who stood near the winch with his camera on a tripod shooting film of the dangerous conditions.

"Time to put that away, Otis," John yelled.

"Bring it with you if you like," Will said loud enough for Otis to hear. He put his hand on John's shoulder and added, "but it's likely to bounce off the ceiling, and I don't want to be underneath it when it does."

John looked at Will with a grin hidden from Otis. "I'm nervous for you, Will."

"It's okay, John. Just don't panic. I know it will be rougher than we like, but we have to do well."

Ford Bond approached with his microphone extended. "The engineers down the line would like to hear a test of your voices, gentlemen. Just say your names and where you were born."

After the men, Bond did the same to Gloria and Jocelyn, who had huddled with notebooks and shared anxieties.

"Gloria Hollister, New York City, New York."

"Jocelyn Crane, St. Louis, Missouri."

"Thank you, ladies. We'll be on the air in a few minutes," Bond told them.

Otis Barton, Will Beebe, and John Tee-Van convened near the bathysphere manhole. The broadcasters joined them and reminded them when they went live the first time, it would be to set the stage. Both Bond and McElrath would have microphones able to pick up their conversations. McElrath told the men to carry on a normal conversation and ignore the radio apparatus.

Will knew in New York City the time was not yet eleven o'clock, but in Bermuda, it was approaching noon and the sea was restless. That made him restless too. He stayed busy looking over equipment.

At noon, Bond began his broadcast.

"Hello, New York, and all points, this is the NBC group calling from Bermuda. Ford Bond speaking to you from the tropical waters off the coast of Bermuda… to bring you an account of the

New York Zoological Society's deep-sea exploration, under the direction of William Beebe..."

The DTR staff paused, admiring how Bond rattled off information so effortlessly. It was entertaining to hear him speak. He made what they were about to do more glamorous than they thought it. Except for Otis Barton. He wanted to hear his name, but he didn't.

To the others it was science done the usual way on a shoe-string budget. Added were the extraordinary dangers Will Beebe battled compounded by a worn-out tugboat that now bounced in tall waves seven miles from land.

While Bond reported about the "attendant dangers," McElrath held a microphone near the bathysphere. Will, Otis, and John staged a conversation reminiscent of the first time they boarded the bathysphere. It now sounded hokey, but McElrath had said the radio audience would want to hear every detail, every nuance.

Bond continued... "We shall stand close to where Dr. Beebe's associates are working aboard the *S.S. Freedom* and hear the preparations being made for the descent. Later, when he has attained a depth approaching one-half mile, we shall listen in on his conversation with his associate scientist, Miss Gloria Hollister..."

Gloria felt a rush of embarrassment hearing her name and sensing others looking her direction when they heard it too. She felt even sillier later when Bond reported on her test of the emergency warning system with John...

"If Dr. Beebe's telephone goes out, then one flash of this light means things are okay; three flashes mean pull him up," Gloria recited.

"Right. Let's test it again," John said. John then reached inside the bathysphere and clicked the light switch. McElrath followed John's hand with the microphone to pick up the clicking noise.

Gloria leaned into Bond's microphone, "Looks good."

"That was Gloria Hollister and John Tee-Van," Bond continued. "Let us briefly as possible sketch for you a picture of the situation here…"

The broadcaster spoke to his audience for several minutes, describing what he saw and then preparing them for the second broadcast. He reported the details of Will and Otis climbing into the bathysphere and John's team closing the manhole hatch. McElrath held his microphone where it picked up the loud clanking of the hammer against the wrench.

Bond began to describe the boom picking up the "blue ball," when he went silent, startled by the physical strain that he hadn't noticed when the bathysphere was unmanned. Knowing that two human beings were inside and about to descend deep into the ocean with no possible escape should things go wrong caught up with Bond.

When the ball pivoted into his view, he saw Will and Otis pressed against the two fused quartz glass windows. He could tell they were not going for a joy ride. He told his audience their eyes expressed the demands and risks of the moment.

Bond spoke again when he saw the bathysphere disappear into the sea, rippling the water against aggressive waves. His rhetoric and timing dramatic, but his reporting less coherent, "… down, down into the depths," he uttered, "The bathysphere will be going down, down, down, down."

In the water, Will focused his eyes on the *Freedom's* rocking hull. He knew the descent would be rough. The turbulent surface controlled them.

After the cable-clip stop at one-hundred feet, Will the scientist determined not to fret over things he couldn't control. The world would be listening. He needed to think about the story listeners tuned in to hear.

"Is that the panic switch?" Otis asked. "Three to ascend quickly, correct Dr. Beebe?"

Otis looked pale. More nervous than any previous dive. He gulped for air tweaking the oxygen levels.

"Not too much," Will told him. "I want to be lucid when they tell us to talk on the radio."

Otis said nothing more but clung to whatever he could find that felt stable.

At the four-hundred-foot stop, Gloria spoke, "Hang on!" The bathysphere lurched, sinking Will and Otis deeper into the curvature of the floor. It bobbed left then right, causing the men to ricochet off the walls.

"What's going on, Glo?" Will shouted at the microphone horn that had flown from his chest.

With that, Otis heaved his breakfast, which included a shot of rum.

"Oh, God, Otis. Not now!"

The stench gagged Will for an instant. He turned to the window and gazed at the last glistens of sunlight disappearing above him.

"Will, everything okay?" Gloria's voice came from the concave floor underneath Will's foot. "Will, should we stop? We know the sea is making your ride uncomfortable."

"Not uncomfortable, Glo, violent. Otis and I are bruised."

"Sorry, Will. Do you want to call it a day?"

"No, but keep us informed of the sea and sky."

"Yes, Will."

Gloria covered her microphone and spoke to John and Jocelyn. "He said he's bruised, tossed against the side of the bathysphere."

"Otis too, I suppose," John said. "Did it damage his camera?" John knew Will had run out of patience with the young engineer who still showed no interest in the science, only the adventure. And now the film.

Gloria told her two colleagues what Will screamed, "Oh, God, Otis. Not now."

"That might make a good rallying cry," Jocelyn said. She repeated Gloria's phrase, "Oh, God, Otis! Not now!"

John and Gloria enjoyed Jocelyn's humor but also showed concern about the perils they were putting the director through so he could keep his commitment to David Sarnoff. Further, they knew Will wanted the broadcast to bring in needed money for future exploration.

The slow descent and constant undulation began to wear on both divers. Will tried to focus on the sea, searching for anything unusual to report to Gloria.

Captain Sylvester's crew stayed active with the winch, checking the boom and getting ready for the return.

The NBC foursome huddled to do a post-mortem on their scene-setter program. They reviewed their plan to cover Dr. Beebe's report from the abyss, the engineers listening to conversations between Beebe and Hollister, setting sound levels. Bond and McElrath checked in with Sarnoff and his studio producer in New York.

Gloria also took care of her requisite duties. She forced Will or Otis to utter sounds, words that gave her a clue to their survival in a bouncing and swinging bathysphere. She wrote notes from Will's observations and Jocelyn recorded logistical data: depth, temperature, and time. Otis seemed less useful than normal, constantly battling nausea and struggling to perform his tasks with the light. It made Will more irritated than usual.

"Will, do you have the headset on?" Gloria asked.

"I do, Glo."

"Will, we're about to go on the radio, you and me, our conversations. I'm nervous and your stress worries me."

"Don't worry, Glo. I've seen interesting things. I can describe them, and you can ask me questions."

"What? What do I ask?"

"Gloria! You've asked me a hundred questions on dives before. Those questions. Forget the microphone. Just talk to me and think about your notes."

George McElrath again used the shortwave radio to talk to his program producer in New York. The producer told McElrath they were dealing with angry musicians in the studio. They don't want to leave, he told McElrath. They say they made the trip downtown and set up their instruments. They expect to have their scheduled time to play for our audience.

"Sorry for your stress," McElrath said. "It's a breeze here. And I mean that in the literal sense. The wind gusts are troublesome. The sea is bouncing our tugboat like noodles in boiling water. I don't know how Beebe is surviving. I don't know if the noise will make Ford inaudible."

"How deep is Beebe now?" the producer asked.

"I heard Miss Hollister say he's at a thousand-five-hundred."

"We won't be able to use your shortwave to talk further. Prepare your stopwatch to start in fifteen seconds. That will give you five minutes until we go live. Ten, nine, eight…"

McElrath started his stopwatch to know when to give Ford Bond his cue. He instructed Bond to move closer to Gloria Hollister with his microphone. He asked John to step closer to him.

Gloria told Will they would be on the radio in about four minutes. Will relayed the information to Otis, who still fought seasickness.

⸙

E lse and Hada stopped their morning routine to listen to Ford Bond report from the *Freedom*. They laughed and giggled like schoolgirls each time they heard Dr. Beebe, Miss Hollister, Miss Crane, Mr. Tee-Van, or Mr. Barton speak. Else said, "I can picture them!"

When the first half-hour live broadcast from Bermuda ended, Hada prepared a light lunch. Listening to classical music on the radio, she boiled eggs, toasted bread, and sliced Braunschweiger.

Else sat at her watercolor table, glancing at her clock to make certain she didn't get so absorbed in her painting that she missed the second program. It was to begin at two.

Hada, meanwhile, carried a plate to her mother's studio, sat and ate with her, then washed and put away the dishes. As the time approached, the women moved closer to the radio.

We conclude our musical presentations and now return to Bermuda and NBC's premiere remote transatlantic broadcast with Ford Bond.

Hello, New York. I'm Ford Bond with the National Broadcasting Company speaking to you from the SS Freedom seven miles from the shores of Bermuda. For the past two hours, we have been witnessing one of the most courageous scientific explorations in human history. Dr. William Beebe of the New York Zoological Society has been placed in his bathysphere more than one-thousand-five-hundred feet into the Atlantic Ocean so far, still descending deeper as we speak to you. I'm watching the steel cable roll off a giant drum holding him, keeping him from dropping to the bottom of the sea and enabling him to tell us what he is experiencing. For attached to the steel cable is another cable, more like a hose that keeps an electrical wire and a telephone line protected from the ocean's enormous pressure. Through the telephone line, we will be able to hear Dr. Beebe in conversation with his science associate, Gloria Hollister. Dr. Beebe is not alone in the bathysphere.

Miss Hollister, standing a few feet from me on the deck, is wearing a telephone operator's earphones and horn-shaped microphone. She is in conversation with Dr. Beebe now. Let's listen.

"What are you seeing, Will... Dr. Beebe?"

"The color of the water is the bluest black imaginable, as dark as one might expect Hades," Will said.

"We've stopped you at one-thousand six-hundred feet to attach a depth marker. Can you see anything?"

"There's no sunlight at this depth. Without turning on our spotlight, I can only see fish and other life forms that create light. They use it to frighten enemies or attract prey. They dangle the light overhead and sucker the prey closer because it wants to eat them."

"Are you seeing fish with lights now?" Gloria asked. "Can you describe them?"

"A school of brilliantly illuminated jellyfish with pale green lights came within three feet of the bathysphere window. A group of eels, two or three feet long just went by. Maybe Zonichthys."

"Are there illuminated fish all over?"

"No. They're at different levels. We don't know why. A string of salpa just floated by. Thousands of lights. One might think I'm headed *to Mars, Venus, or Jupiter, with millions of stars in front of me, not a half-mile deep in the Atlantic. That's how many bodies with bio-luminescent cells are near the bathysphere. It looks like a moonless, starlit night."*

"Describe your conditions in the bathysphere, Dr. Beebe."

"We're in extremely cold water. The walls of the bathysphere are like touching a block of ice. But our chamber is currently at seven-ty-two degrees thanks to our body heat in a confined area. It was eighty-five degrees when we were on the deck of the Freedom. If we get too cold, Mr. Barton can turn on the searchlight so I can pick up the shapes of fish outside our sphere, but which also warms our quarters."

Else leaned back in her chair for the first time in several minutes. She let out a sigh.

"It was their voices, Mother. I knew it was Dr. Beebe and Miss Hollister because I've heard their voices so many times. To hear them over the radio and know that Miss Hollister and Mr. Tee-Van were on the tugboat, and Dr. Beebe was deep in the ocean… I just don't know how to describe it."

"Yes, Tochter. I'm sure people are listening who think it's a hoax. No one has ever done such brave things. No one has spoken on the radio for us to hear when they're doing those things. The world is moving too fast for me sometimes, Tochter. I don't know if I like the speed."

———

John Tee-Van had contained his excitement well past an explosive stage. Everyone was concentrating on their responsibilities.

He knew that but he also wanted to share his elation. William Beebe and Otis Barton had broken their depth record set in 1930.

John went to Captain Sylvester's wheelhouse during a lull when he was sure his deckhands had everything under control. He told Captain Sylvester he was now part of a record dive.

"Blow your horn, Captain. Let the world know!"

Captain Sylvester reached for the cord and pulled it. The blast startled all on deck, especially the radio crew.

"What's that?" McElrath asked Gloria Hollister.

"We've set a record, Mr. McElrath. Our tradition is to let people know."

The tugboat *Powerful* had joined the *Freedom* as a precaution because of the weather. Captain Sylvester knew recent hurricane damage and mere age weakened his boat. He tried not to worry the broadcasters by explaining that if things went wrong, the bathysphere's weight could drag his boat into the sea.

The *Powerful* followed its fellow tugboat with a blast of its own celebrating the record. No one knew yet at what depth the record would settle.

When John Tee-Van came down from the wheelhouse, he went to Gloria and Jocelyn and pulled them into a group hug. He shouted congratulations to the director through Gloria's telephone horn.

Will pulled back from his window, grinned, and sighed. "We have a new distance record, Otis. Does that settle your stomach?"

Otis shook his head.

The two divers continued downward. Will reported additional sightings, including "the largest fish I've seen yet." He described it as barracuda-like. Six feet long. There were two. Each had a row of bioluminescent lights, pale color, that reached from head to tailfin.

Will's reports to Gloria continued to be broadcast through the network. He had been describing his sightings for twenty minutes.

"We're at two-thousand feet. Five hatchet fish just past. *Argyropelecus*… The greenest light… I can see full outlines of fish. Loads of them. I don't know what they are."

Less than two minutes pass.

"You're at two-thousand one-hundred feet, Will," Gloria reported.

"The bathysphere is rolling badly," Will said. "Bigger fish in the distance. Two. Their lights coming and going. Pale creamy color. Four big fish are going by, and hundreds of others. I can see the upper and lower sides of a fish six inches long with a deep shape. Lights from photophores illuminate them. When it turned head-on to me, all illumination vanished. More jellyfish than anything else. Pteropods. Everything lighted up."

The bathysphere stopped at two-thousand-two hundred feet for a marker tie of the two cables.

"We must now conclude this broadcast," Will said. "Otis Barton and I bid you farewell from a depth of twenty-two hundred feet beneath the surface of the Atlantic Ocean…."

Will covered his microphone with a rag so his sounds would not carry. The broadcast from the abyss ended. He and Otis gave out harmonious gasps of relief.

Once again Will considered where they were hanging from a steel cable less than an inch in diameter and held in place by a worn-out tugboat seven miles from shore. He had talked nonstop for twenty-five minutes. Nothing new for him, but it was the first time he did it while bouncing like a Yo-Yo.

He looked out his window and observed the stillness and tranquility of the ocean, a picture no one could have imagined until he told them about it. While above them, nearly one-half mile, were a reckless wind, choppy water, and people about which the sea's creatures knew nothing.

On the deck of *Freedom*, broadcaster Ford Bond gave his farewell to listeners.

Down there in his bathysphere, he has entered a new world hitherto unknown to man. He is, at this minute, still at that depth. The microphones of the National Broadcasting Company have carried you with him, as a privileged member of his expedition...

We have seen this great scientist actually at his work, have heard his reports as they will be added to the total of human knowledge...

We wish to thank Dr. Beebe and his associates, the New York Zoological Society, the officials and people of the beautiful islands of Bermuda for the untiring hospitality and aid which they have shown to the NBC group...

We hope that we have succeeded in making the picture both clear and enjoyable to you. Now, good afternoon. This is Ford Bond announcing.

"They're off the air, Will," Gloria told the director.

Will removed the cloth he wrapped around his microphone. "Let us rest a moment, Glo. Otis and I both have headaches. The undulation motion is about all I can take."

"Are you ready to ascend?" she asked.

"Bring us back, Glo. We'll need some bandages and fresh water to drink. There's a gallon or two at our feet from condensation, but it's mixed with vomit."

"That's not a sight I care to imagine."

Will used his flashlight to look over the bathysphere. Otis still appeared greenish, his eyes in desperate need of sleep.

He pointed the light at the stuffing box where the electricity and telephone lines entered the bathysphere at the apex. Pressure had pushed the wires farther into the cavity. A few drops of water fell, but it did not pose a threat according to Will. Instead of further worry the director returned to his window.

"The big fish have returned, Glo. I'm putting the searchlight on them."

"Can you see them, Will?"

"Very ghostly. Jaws are shorter than a barracuda, but the shape is the same, except…"

"What, Will?"

"Fangs. Their teeth are wicked-looking fangs that seem illuminated from inside their bodies. Very eerie."

"You said before they had a string of lights along their bodies."

"A pale blue bioluminescent light, yes. Two long tentacles are hanging down as well. Lights at the ends. Globe-shaped. One red, the other blue."

"Enough, Will. Come home."

It took half an hour for the bathysphere to reach the surface and lift onto the deck of the *Freedom*. When the crew set it down and removed the manhole hatch, Will crawled out first. When his feet reached the deck and he straightened his body, Captain Sylvester gave another blast of his horn, which the *Powerful* again echoed.

Otis stumbled out, stood, and gagged. He tried his best to enjoy the moment, but his head pounded from the inside.

Both men received handshakes and pats on the back from staff, *Freedom* crew, and the NBC team.

"That was one marvelous broadcast, Dr. Beebe," Bond said. "I'm proud to have been a part of it. Amazing radio. One for the record books."

Will smiled and thought, *one for the science books as well.*

CHAPTER 47

World Distractions
November 1932

John Tee-Van carried a *New York Times* into Will's office eager to share several stories that caught his eye. "Have you seen the newspaper yet, Will?"

"I haven't had time, but there's a copy on my table."

"I have one, Will. The stories I want you to see are about elections, Prohibition, and the situations in Germany and Japan. There's so much going on the world Will, so much tension. It makes me nervous. I'm worried, Will, that people are ignoring our work..."

"Don't get excited over the news, John. We're making progress. I've received a dozen invitations to speak about Bermuda. Organizations from New York to Ohio. Chicago, even out in Sioux City, Iowa."

"I'm glad you're optimistic, Director. The newspaper put me in a sour mood."

Will looked at his reliable aide and saw his worry weighing heavily.

"Stand up straight, John. It's just life. Things we can't do anything about." He pushed away from his desk and put his feet up. "Tell me what's so upsetting."

"World leadership seems to be in such disarray. Germany re-elected Hindenburg, but his popularity is slipping, so he's contemplating naming a fascist radical, Adolf Hitler, chancellor, just to stay in office."

"That's Germany. I saw their tactics during the war when I was in France. But it won't happen again. Hoover will keep their economy in check."

"Are you going to vote for Hoover, Will? Do you think Roosevelt has a chance?"

Franklin Roosevelt was the very antithesis of his mentor, Teddy. Will, the scientist, naturalist, and conservationist, said before he had no interest in politics. His burning issue was the same as it had been since his early teenage years—seeing nature and its kingdom of animals and plants identified and preserved.

"I have no solution to offer you, John. Mrs. Roosevelt is not too fond of her late husband's cousin. She sounds like she will avoid the polls this week, so I may follow her counsel."

"It's our responsibility, Will," John pleaded.

"It's our responsibility to make a good choice, an informed choice. But I don't feel well informed, so my *good* choice is to pick no one. I will be loyal to whomever the country decides."

With no help from the director, John acquiesced, but before he left, he asked if Will had heard from Mrs. Bostelmann.

"She sent me a letter of congratulations when we returned. I responded by letter," Will said. "I asked her to contact me again in January. I should know by then our goals for '33."

"Were you being honest, Director? I thought we already knew the disappointing plans. Does Mrs. B know how desperate things became?"

"I did not tell her. I don't want to lose her to another job that would prevent her from returning with us if we can fix our finances."

"So, you never told her about our voluntary pay cuts—yours, mine, and Gloria's, and that you're paying Jocelyn from your own pocket?"

"No. Those were our decisions…"

"…But it would help her understand that we valued her work, but we just don't have the money."

"I will call her by telephone."

"Thank you, Will."

"Before you go back to your office, take this article. This is for *Harper's*. I'm talking mostly about diving. Proofread it for me."

"Yes, sir."

"And, John…"

"Sir…"

"Contact Mrs. B if you must. Ask her to come in for a visit."

"Yes, Will. I'll get her here as soon as possible."

CHAPTER 48

New Plan
December 1932

Hada arose early to prepare for another workday at Macy's. She boiled water for tea and made two cups, one for her and one for her mother.

Else dressed and entered the kitchen. "Does this look appropriate for a business meeting?" she asked her daughter.

"You look wonderful, Mother. Are you excited to see Dr. Beebe again?"

"It's been several months. I'm excited to see all of them. I want to hear about their experience on the *Freedom* with the radio people."

"I must get to work. Please tell them hello for me."

Hada sipped her tea, hugged her mother, and departed.

Else took her cup and saucer to her art table and looked onto the street below to watch Hada walk to the corner of Columbus Avenue for the trolley downtown. She prayed for her daughter's happiness.

Packing a few watercolors in her folder, Else thought about the past year and her last conversation with Dr. Beebe. She was hoping he would include her in his plans for the upcoming season in Bermuda. Thoughts of seeing Dr. Beebe and Miss Crane in a romantic embrace returned.

Jocelyn, near Hada's age, attracted Dr. Beebe with her flirtatious allure, but Else knew he was conflicted by feelings for Miss Hollister, and then, of course, his young bride of five years.

She understood they all adored Dr. Beebe. He charmed every woman he encountered, not with handsome features or physical stature. Dr. Beebe charmed even her with passion and confidence. She knew that because she compared Dr. Beebe's beguiling nature to that of Monroe. Both dreamers. But her late husband never fulfilled his dream the way Dr. Beebe did. His failed visions ate away Monroe's will to live.

Riding the subway north to the Bronx, Else kept thinking about the two men. She remembered her romantic feelings for Monroe, which she now considered wasted but for one exception: Gertraude Hadumodt Bostelmann.

Comparing the two men was not fair, but she couldn't stop. There was something in those thoughts that drew her closer to Dr. Beebe.

John was the first to greet Else when she arrived at the zoological park. The smell of animals, the sound of chirping birds from the aviary, thrilled her and took her back to the zoo in Leipzig and her first sketches of wild animals.

John gave Else a warm hug that made her feel welcomed and optimistic. Gloria also held tight to the artist.

Else was oddly nervous about seeing Miss Crane, but she refused to let her secret hold her back. They met with outstretched arms. Enormous energy radiated from Jocelyn, but old images still clouded Else's thoughts.

The three aides walked Else into Dr. Beebe's office. Will stood and welcomed Else with a tender hug.

"It's so good to see you, Mrs. B. How've you been?"

"Quite well, Dr. Beebe. Thank you for asking."

"Please have a seat at the table and let's begin."

John held a chair for Else who sat and put her art folder to her side. The two young women sat near the empty chair for Dr. Beebe. Will carried a pad of paper in his left hand and placed it in front of him as he sat.

"I have a two-year plan to discuss with all of you," Will began. "There is nothing in stone, but it's a place for us to begin."

"If you're looking two years away, then my hope for this summer seems to be fading, Dr. Beebe."

"Mrs. B, all of our hope for this coming summer has faded with this economy. I wish I could offer more optimism. I'm going to be honest and set expectations that encourage you to be available."

"Whenever you need me to go back to Bermuda, I will go."

John reached for Else's hand and squeezed it. Gloria and Jocelyn added their hands like children grabbing the thin handle of a baseball bat to see who got to hit first. They all smiled.

"You worried us," Gloria admitted.

"We thought you'd tell us to bugger off," Jocelyn added. "We want you to join us when Dr. Beebe gets the money together."

"I feel very fortunate," Else explained. "My freelance work has been steady. Hada is supporting herself well but living with me. Life is comfortable."

"So glad to hear that, Mrs. B," Will said. "I hope you'll tell your daughter we miss seeing her. I think of her and Mr. Jackson hoping that the next group of interns we take with us can be half as joyful as they were together."

"Thank you, Dr. Beebe. My daughter sends each of you her greetings as well. She wants to see you again."

The memory of Patten Jackson and Hada together caught the group off guard. They sat composing before Will spoke.

"Why don't the three of you give Mrs. B and me a few minutes to discuss how we stay in touch."

John, Gloria, and Jocelyn pushed back their chairs and stood. They smiled at Else. John bent and gave her another hug before departing Will's office.

"I miss each of them," Else said when they closed the door.

"It could not be more than they miss you, Mrs. B."

"You seem worried, Dr. Beebe."

"Oh, there is plenty to worry about, but we are doing fine. I'm sure I bear guilt because I want you to be part of our work."

"I understand. This is more than a shelter for the creatures we both love, Dr. Beebe. You must operate it like any business. You cannot spend more money than you take in."

"With your wisdom, Mrs. B, we should put you on the society's board of directors."

Else knew his compliment was in jest, but it made her wonder how difficult it would be to interact with men believing in eugenics that Else viewed as less than humanitarian.

"Please tell me the situation, Dr. Beebe. Do you intend to do further research in Bermuda? Is Nonsuch Island no longer important?"

"Money drives everything, Mrs. B. We found a supporter who gave us better shelter for doing our research. Elswyth and I also found a home that will become our future research center when we've completed renovations."

"Is Mrs. Beebe liking Bermuda better these days?"

"I didn't say we'd be spending any more time there together."

Else smiled. "Sorry, Dr. Beebe. I know Mrs. Beebe never felt comfortable on Nonsuch Island and never liked the heat in the summer. To allow you to set up a more permanent residence in Bermuda is um… unusual."

"We may discuss that at another time," Will said enjoying her lightness. "I want you to understand why I'm going back on my promise to you. The attitude in the zoological society is not favorable. To return to Bermuda last year, I cut my salary in half. I did the same to Mr. Tee-Van and Miss Hollister. And I paid Jocelyn with personal funds. We survived but I'm telling you because the zoological society made it impossible for me to add more staff. Unfortunately, it remains true now. The society's leader told me no further bathysphere dives."

"That's very disappointing. It's also surprising after your success with the radio broadcast." Else said then waited to ask: "You paid Miss Crane from your own money, Dr. Beebe?"

"She has a comfortable life, Mrs. B. Her mother is wealthy, so I didn't offer Jocelyn an income by which to live. John also has wealth comforting his lifestyle because of Helen. It was much harder for Glo. She told me the year depleted her savings."

"Then I feel quite fortunate that my art has been in demand thanks to your popularity. I will confess this too, Dr. Beebe, since we are being honest with one another. A researcher who saw my paintings in *National Geographic Magazine* contacted me. He wants me to call him when our ties have ended."

"Who may I ask?"

"I've promised not to say. I'm glad to postpone contact with him, but I'd appreciate knowing if you feel I'm too expensive for any future work. I could not join you for half of what you paid me in previous years."

"Your value is worth more than your expense, Mrs. B. However, I need another year to work on fundraising and changing the minds of a few powerful people who control my fate with the society."

"I can survive another year, Dr. Beebe, because your reputation improves mine. If neither of us grows in stature and your name fades from the newspapers, then I must consider the business offer on the table. I hope you understand."

"Not only do I understand, but Mrs. B, my respect for you increases with every conversation we have."

"I'm grateful and have many more things to say to you, Dr. Beebe, but I will hold my thoughts until we have more time. Do you know what you will do this summer?"

Will said the organizers of A Century of Progress International Exposition contacted him. The Chicago promoters asked to display the bathysphere in the same building with Auguste Piccard's gondola from his fifty-three-thousand-foot record-setting balloon flight. When Else asked if he had committed the bathysphere, he hesitated.

"If I commit," Will said, "then for certain, we won't do any deep-sea dives this summer. However, we've already made plans to bring the bathysphere to New York. Professor Osborn wants to display it at the American Museum of Natural History."

"That's in my neighborhood," Else said.

"Yes, that's correct, Mrs. B. Ironic, don't you think? However, it will take several days to pull the bathysphere from storage. Once we have it in the States, it will be much easier to ship to Chicago. But that's another expense I don't know how to cover at this point."

Else admitted her welfare was much easier to manage than Dr. Beebe's. She wished him well and restated her availability for another year.

"Before you go, Mrs. B, I have something for you."

Else followed Dr. Beebe with her eyes as he rose and walked toward his bookshelves. He pulled a book from a shelf lined with several of the same covers. He brought it to her.

"This is the book on Nonsuch. If you recall, I wrote to you for permission because I'm using a few of your paintings to illustrate things unique to our island paradise." Will handed Else the book. "Turn to page forty-four."

She did and smiled at what she saw. "The stunted cedar," Else said.

"It might be my favorite of all your paintings, Mrs. B, aside from the ones you do of the fish from my descriptions." Will laughed. He took Else's hand and guided her to her feet. He hugged her. "I'm very hopeful we'll see each other soon."

"Please let me know when you deliver the bathysphere to my neighborhood museum. I will bring Hada. She will want to see it."

"She is a good daughter, Mrs. B. I send her a warm greeting. Auf Wiedersehen, Frau Bostelmann."

"Auf Wiedersehen, Herr Professor Beebe."

CHAPTER 49

Reading Beebe's Book

Else finished the final page and closed the book. She looked up from her table at the evening light disappearing behind the city skyline. She closed her eyes and breathed deeply. Pride warmed her.

She could hear Hada's key turning in the lock, home from another day at Macy's. Else was eager to tell her daughter, her *Tochter*, about her day reading Dr. Beebe's book.

"I'm home, Mother," Hada yelled as she closed the apartment door.

"I'm in my studio, Hada. Come sit with me. Tell me about your day."

Hada removed her coat and hung it in the closet. She sighed an end-of-the-workday sigh and joined Else, wrapping her arms around her mother's neck. "Did you finish it?" she asked.

"I just now closed it."

"…and what did you think?"

"It's better than his previous book; written like others when you could tell he was in love with his subject. It captured me."

"Reviewers said he forced it in his previous book. I felt it too when I read it. Why do you think it true?" Hada asked.

Else pushed her artist's stool away from her table and walked toward the kitchen. She placed the teakettle on the burner and ignited the gas under it. Hada waited for her response.

"I've been wondering about that while I read this one, Tochter."

"What did you conclude?"

"I'm still thinking."

Hada watched her mother pull two teacups and saucers from the cabinet and place them next to the stove. She dipped her tea strainer into the tea-mint mixture, filled it, and placed it in the porcelain pot. Else waited for the kettle to whistle while Hada stood and looked at her mother's artwork.

"Did you do this quickly, Mother?"

"Why? Is it not good?"

"It's beautiful. No other artist can finish such work so fast."

"I was eager to read today, not paint," Else said. "But those are for clients, so I had to do them."

"You're amazing, Mother. You do what you love, and now you're able to do it with less worry about the money."

"I'm quite fortunate, it's true. I owe Dr. Beebe…"

"…and Aunt Ida…"

"Yes. Ida, Cecilia, Truman… I owe many for my good fortune. Our good fortune, Tochter."

"I agree, but I've taken you away from what you were thinking about – Dr. Beebe's book."

"I thought about Miss Hollister while reading."

"Did he talk about her?"

"No. He wrote about Nonsuch. He wrote about what he always does – nature, life, and coexistence."

"So, why Miss Hollister?" Hada asked.

"…because in every chapter, when he began a new observation about another fish, or bird, or animal he saw on the island, I could see her at his side."

"Do you think she still loves him, Mother?"

"I'm certain she does."

Hada hesitated. "What will they do, Mother? Do you think *he* loves *her*, too?"

"I believe he does, but differently."

"…but he's married to Mrs. Beebe. Doesn't he love her?"

"Yes, he loves them both."

"Oh, Mother, you sound like you know something I'm supposed to know, but I don't."

Else laughed a nervous laugh. Hada responded with a delayed smile.

"Dr. Beebe is an accomplished man. His confidence and success make him attractive to women…"

"Are you attracted to him?"

"…Tochter, are you going to listen or interrupt my thinking?"

"Sorry, Mother, but are you? You said confidence and success attract women. You're a woman. Are you attracted to Dr. Beebe?"

"I'm trying to explain that both women, Mrs. Beebe and Miss Hollister, love him, and he loves them, but in different ways…"

"You're not making sense, Mother. You said he attracts women because he's confident and successful. How could Miss Hollister and Dr. Beebe's wife be attracted in different ways?"

"You make this too difficult. I'm saying Mrs. Beebe loves Dr. Beebe because he's a success at writing. She loves writing. Miss Hollister loves Dr. Beebe because he's a success at science. She loves science…"

"So, you can't love him, because he's not an artist…"

"Du bist ein hartnäckiges Kind. You know what I'm trying to say, but you want me to say I find the man attractive, don't you?"

"I want you to be honest with me." She moved closer. "I do not want to share a man with another woman. How are they to be happy? I admire Dr. Beebe, but I don't understand why he can't be loyal to one or the other."

Else walked to her art table with her teacup in hand. Hada waited, but then followed her mother. She sat next to Else's table gazing at her mother's expressionless face.

"Do men love different from women, Mother? Am I to learn something about men from watching Dr. Beebe with his wife and science assistant?"

"I don't want you to conclude based on one situation, Tochter. I don't have an answer for *your* life based on what you and I see in another's behaviors."

"But I can tell it bothers you too. That's why I ask you if you love him?"

"I love who he is when we are working together. Alone. When I am drawing and he is directing me."

"Do you want to kiss him?"

"No. I just want to be there with him."

"Miss Hollister kisses him, I'm sure," Hada said. "And she does other things with him."

"…because she succumbs to the physical desires love creates. It cannot last."

Else finally offered Hada what she sought; a morsel of wisdom she felt her mother kept from her for reasons Hada didn't understand.

"It won't last because he's married?"

"It won't last because Miss Hollister wants more than Dr. Beebe can provide."

CHAPTER 50

On Display
January 1933

Will and Elswyth Beebe had a short layover in Baltimore as they made the long trip between New York and Scottsdale, Arizona. Scottsdale is where doctors recommended Will spend the winter because of his debilitating sinus infection.

They planned a stop in Chicago. Will wanted to meet with sponsors of the science displays at the Century of Progress International Fair planned to open later in '33. The sponsors were asking Will and the New York Zoological Society for permission to display the bathysphere.

When Will and Elswyth stepped from the train in Baltimore, a newspaper reporter greeted them, admitting he received a tip from Elswyth's literary agent that they were on the train. He asked the couple for an interview.

After a comment about *Nonsuch: Land of Water*, Will excused himself to find the station's telegram office. The reporter seemed delighted to have time alone with Elswyth.

"Can you tell me about your playscript?" the reporter asked.

"It's called *The Tudor Wench*," she responded. "Will and I are going to London this summer to see it open."

"I understand it's about Queen Elizabeth," the reporter said.

"…before she was queen. It's based on my novel of the same title."

"Of course. I'm familiar with your book. I'm intrigued. How do you tell that broad a story on stage?"

"Shakespeare did it. In iambic pentameter," Elswyth responded. "It's simplified. The play is more about how Elizabeth's personality and power develop."

"…and you and Dr. Beebe will be in London when it opens?"

"Yes, that's our plan. We're both very excited."

"I can imagine. Do you have a date for the opening?"

"Not yet. We hope it will be in July."

"Thank you, Mrs. Beebe. Or do you prefer to be Elswyth Thane? I intend to quote you in my article if that's all right?"

"I like Mrs. Beebe, but I'm sure my publicist would prefer Elswyth Thane."

"Who do you wish to receive the message?" the telegram official asked Will.

"Her name is Else Bostelmann."

"Her address."

Will pulled a piece of paper from his pocket. "It's 24 West 75th Street, New York City."

"What would you like to say?"

"Dear Else…"

"Else…"

"Yes, of course. Bathysphere at museum STOP…"

"Bathysphere? You're Dr. Beebe. Good to meet you, sir. I've followed your articles in the magazines. Boy, my wife is going to be surprised when I tell her that Dr. Beebe sent a telegram from my station."

"…the telegram."

"Oh, sorry, Dr. Beebe. I'm such a Reuben! You were saying 'at museum STOP.'"

"Free tickets at window STOP In Arizona next STOP Send comments END."

"Got it, Dr. Beebe." The operator counted the words. "That'll be $1.47 with the interstate charges."

Will pulled a handful of coins from his pocket and counted out the exact amount. He gave the man a new quarter for his trouble.

"Gee. Thanks, Dr. Beebe. That's not necessary." He fondled the quarter, "I won't spend it. I'll keep it forever."

Will smiled and walked toward Elswyth who was signing autographs for three young women. The newspaper reporter took a flash photo of the celebrity and her fans.

Twenty-two hours later, the train from Baltimore reached Chicago. Will and Elswyth made their way to the Palmer House Hotel. They gazed at the elaborate Louis Pierre Rigal painting centered in the towering ceiling. Ornate arched pillars framed the painting.

Awestruck, Elswyth offered Will a history lesson of the hotel. She explained that businessman Potter Palmer gave the hotel to his wife, Bertha, who befriended Claude Monet. Her fascination with French impressionism was obvious.

"She owns the largest collection outside of Paris," Elswyth told her husband.

While they signed the register and picked up their room keys, Will searched the lobby for the men he was to meet.

He checked his pocket watch. He and Elswyth arrived to the minute he told the exposition group they would be at the hotel.

"Dr. Beebe? Over here."

Will turned to see a man about his age rise from a chesterfield chair. He lifted his hand in the air. Three other well-dressed men completed the lounge setting.

"I'm Gerald Woolley. Thank you for interrupting your travels to spend a few minutes with my business associates and me."

"I appreciate the opportunity to learn about your plans, Mr. Woolley," Will said. "I'm told you're interested in bringing the bathysphere to Chicago to display it during an exposition."

"Exactly, Dr. Beebe. My friends and I feel your accomplishment with your sphere is worthy of public display alongside the Piccard gondola."

"Dr. Beebe, I'm Francis O'Rourke," a man said, standing and extending his hand. "I listened to your broadcast in September when you descended past two-thousand feet. Remarkable. We want that ball for the people of Chicago and all the city's visitors to see."

"That's quite flattering, gentlemen. But I must remind you, the depressed economy has put financial pressure on the New York Zoological Society just like it has the rest of the country. It will challenge us to come up with the money to ship the bathysphere and to care for it while in Chicago."

"We intend to cover those costs," Woolley said. "We just need to know that you can afford to leave it here for several months. We're hopeful for a long exposition and fruitful attraction to our city."

"We're backing the exposition, not the city or state of Illinois," O'Rourke added. "Entrance fees will help."

"I can't give you a response for at least a week," Will said. "To be perfectly honest, I've contacted *National Geographic Magazine*. I'm told publisher Grosvenor has some interest in sponsoring another series of dives. I just made the contact, so I don't think he expects it to be this summer. When I confirm and get a blessing from the zoological society's leaders, I will give you an answer."

"We ask nothing more, Dr. Beebe," Woolley responded.

"Where is the sphere now, Dr. Beebe?" O'Rourke asked.

"The American Museum of Natural History in New York City," Will answered. "Their display opened within the past few days."

"Do you have a lengthy commitment?" Woolley asked.

"Only a handshake and a day-by-day trial. Museum and zoological society officials are many of the same men. The two entities are quite single-minded."

"Look, you have our request and financial commitment to support the bathysphere for as long as you can leave it with us," Woolley said. "Now, I'd like to invite you to join us for a cocktail, but Prohibition still has a grip on us. We hope not much longer."

"I concur. Thank you for the thought, but I see my wife is waiting for my help."

"Would you mind if we met Mrs. Beebe?" O'Rourke asked. "My wife sent me with Elswyth Thane's recent book. She gave me firm instructions to get her autograph."

"He might sleep elsewhere if he fails," another said, followed by laughter.

Will signaled across the spacious room for Elswyth to join him. She nodded, turned to the hotel clerk, and then turned back, walking toward her husband.

When she joined Will, he introduced her as the famous author and now playwright, Elswyth Thane. They all stood as Elswyth stepped in front of each man and held out her gloved hand. Each man took her hand and bowed.

"Mr. O'Rourke has a copy of *The Tudor Wench*," Will began.

"...it's my wife's copy," O'Rourke interrupted. "Would you mind autographing it so I can get back into my home tonight?"

"...or at all," Woolley added, generating another round of laughter.

"It's my honor, Mr. O'Rourke. "Please tell your wife I'm grateful for every reader."

Following the ceremonial signature, Will and Elswyth shared their gratitude with the men and returned to the lobby desk. They led a bellboy carrying their overnight luggage to a room on the twenty-second floor.

Elswyth went to the window. Below was the intersection of Monroe and State streets. The busy crossing was ablaze with lights. A snowfall gave the scene a holiday glow as people hurried to their destinations.

"Perhaps your doctor was wrong, Will," Elswyth began. "Maybe the weather in Chicago would help your sinus condition," she said. "We could stay right here while you work on bringing the bathysphere to the exposition."

CHAPTER 51

An Artifact
February 1933

Else left for the museum two hours early, stopping along Central Park West to sketch scenes of mothers pushing blanket-covered strollers. The sidewalks were clear, but patches of snow reminded everyone that winter was in full command of the neighborhood.

The artist wore specially knitted gloves. The thumb and forefinger were free to grip a pencil, pen, or brush.

When time neared the hour Hada promised to join her mother, Else packed her gear and continued her short hike to the museum. Waiting for Hada at the ticket window, Else heard a familiar voice…

"Hello, Mrs. B. Will sent a message to look for you."

"Hello, Mr. Tee-Van."

"Hello, Mother." Hada's voice made its way through the crowd gathering at the entrance. "Holy smokes, Mr. Tee-Van. What a great surprise."

John hugged the young woman and admired Hada's stylish attire. "Look at you, young lady. You look like you came off Macy's catalog."

"She's not the same girl feeding your fish," Else admitted proudly.

"Not in these clothes," Hada said. "But I'm happy to change if you need me to."

"Wait 'til Helen and your aunt Ida see you," John said.

"Ida! Is she coming to the museum?"

"Helen, Ida, and her husband Edward. They should be here within the half-hour."

"How fortunate, Mother. I'm excited to see them."

"Me too, Tochter."

"They'll be thrilled to see both of you as well," John said.

"You look healthy, Mr. Tee-Van. How are things at the zoological park?" Else asked.

"It's more of a struggle with the economy still in recession. Our patrons are less generous, but we understand why. So, we spend less and hope that our country's new president can deliver on his campaign promise to put people back to work."

John walked Else and Hada into the museum. He told them it surprised him when Otis Barton showed up at the opening of the bathysphere exhibit.

"Was Dr. Beebe here too?" Else asked.

"He was. A photographer took their picture together. Will and Mrs. Beebe boarded a train for Arizona the very next day," John reported.

Else and Hada showed their tickets. The museum staff recognized Mr. Tee-Van.

John guided the ladies to an elevator that took them to the third floor. He walked them through several sections chatting about the harrowing experience during the radio broadcast.

"The *Freedom* is a larger tug than the *Gladisfen*, but still cramped quarters," John said, "especially with the radio equipment and the extra bodies that sometimes got in the way."

"I told Dr. Beebe in December I heard stress in his voice," Else said. "He admitted he was nervous."

"I felt they were in constant danger when we listened to the broadcast," Hada added.

"Near the end of the dive, the boat swayed so much I felt the danger too, Hada," John said. "We would never have sent the bathysphere down if it weren't for the radio broadcast. It was an enormous risk that turned out well."

John told the Bostelmanns that Will and Otis did several short contour dives to finish the season. He said he dove with Will too when Otis and his cameraman tried to shoot pictures of the bathysphere entering shallow water.

"They put on the helmets and went underwater with their cameras," John said. "They wanted film of the bathysphere plunging into the water from underneath."

"Did they get what they wanted?" Hada asked.

"I don't know. They didn't develop the film until later, and Otis said nothing when he showed up for this opening."

Hada spotted Ida and dashed to give her aunt a welcoming hug. She did the same for Helen Tee-Van and then held out her hand to Mr. Cobb. He looked older, more mature than the first time they met at the concert three years earlier.

Edward Cobb pushed past her extended hand and wrapped his arms around her. Everyone greeted Else with the same warmth.

"This seems like an unusual setting for a reunion but I'm very happy to see everyone," Else announced.

"You look wonderful, Mrs. B," Helen told her.

"You call my sister-in-law Mrs. B?" Ida asked.

"That's what Will calls her, so it became her name. I never asked if you like it," Helen said looking at Else.

"It's fine. I think that's who I am now... Mrs. B."

John led the ladies and Edward to the first floor where the bathysphere sat on display. Scrubbed clean, it looked like something one would see in a Flash Gordon comic strip. It didn't look like a famed scientist's capsule for record-setting dives at the end of a thread of steel.

Museum visitors walked around the sphere, peeked through the two fused quartz windows, and walked away shaking their heads. What William Beebe and Otis Barton did defied logic.

CHAPTER 52

Bobby's Letter
June 1933

Waiting anxiously for her daughter to come home, Else paced from her drawing table to the kitchen and through the sitting area. She anticipated the sound of the key, which finally came.

"He wrote again," Else announced before Hada had closed the door.

"Who wrote, Mother?"

Hada knew exactly who her mother was talking about, but she needed time to take in Else's curiosity before she responded honestly.

"Bobby. You knew. Are you going to tell me why, after three years, the young man is writing to you?"

"Can I put down my things and change from my work clothes first?"

"If you must," Else said sarcastically. "Here's his letter." She handed it over. "He's a good, hard-working boy."

"Mother. For pity's sake."

Hada escaped to her bedroom and closed the door. Else continued her pacing until her daughter re-opened her door and entered the kitchen wearing pleated shorts and a buttoned blouse. She was barefoot.

Else peeked into Hada's bedroom and saw the opened letter spread across Hada's quilt. She wanted desperately to go in and read it but refrained. She followed Hada into the kitchen.

"Are you going to tell me about Bobby?"

"Yes, Mother. I will tell you everything. He's doing well. His father and he have been farming since they arrived in Virginia. He's growing tobacco. He says his uncle's farm is among the best tobacco producing farms in the state."

"That sounds promising for the young man…"

"He says his uncle died last year and willed the farm to his brother, Bobby's father, and him. He says he is very lucky. His uncle was a kind and good soul."

"Bobby is very sensitive…"

"He wants me to come to Virginia."

Else went to the cabinet where they kept tea. She pulled the tin box down and scooped a spoonful of crumbled tea and mint into a strainer. Hada had already begun heating water.

"Are you going?"

"Mother, he wants to marry me. No, I'm not going."

The blunt honesty caught Else off guard. She had watched Hada mature rapidly over the past two years, changing from a dependent child to a woman with clear intentions. Else saw Hada's personality imitating hers.

"Why? Why did you make that decision?" Else asked.

"I wrote to him. I told him that I could see us married. I liked him. I still like him. He's handsome, kind; he's funny, too…"

"Those are good reasons to try, Tochter…"

"I asked him to come back to New York. I wanted to see him. I said I thought we could make a nice home here."

"What did he say?"

"He said he likes his life in Virginia. He said I'd like it too," Hada continued. "He said the people are friendly, the air is fresh, and there's so much space. It's like Central Park everywhere."

"He made it quite inviting," Else said knowing her daughter was agonizing.

"I love my city, Mother. I think I can be successful here. What will I do on a tobacco farm?"

Flashes of Texas cotton fields overtook Else's thoughts—serenity and pain, beauty and loneliness. She understood and wondered if her daughter remembered the isolation.

"You can be a wife. You can raise a family. You can be a business partner. You're good at math, good at organizing, and good with people. Those are the only reasons I can give you…"

"…but they're not satisfying reasons. I'm a woman at a time when women need to be more than wives and caretakers of a man and his children…"

"It's a choice, Hada. That's all. It doesn't need to be a statement for women," Else pleaded. "Do you think Bobby is asking you to forfeit your independence? Do you think he wants you to throw away your life's experiences only to focus on his?"

"I don't know. Maybe. There's more confidence in his words. He's not the same person."

"Confidence is not bad." Else poured hot water over her tea strainer, filling the teapot. She poured two cups and handed one to Hada.

"Your father insisted I come to New York after he left Germany. New York was so different from Leipzig or Berlin. America was so different from Germany. The people seemed so boisterous, so overt and certain of success."

"I remember very little about Texas, Mother. A dusty house, listening to my father speak three different languages, wondering which one I was to speak. I remember people being angry with father when he spoke German, not English or Spanish."

"They were angry because their sons were being sent to fight against Kaiser Wilhelm's soldiers. Many of their parents had come from Germany and Austria too. They weren't angry at German people."

"I don't want to leave, Mother. I know I could love Bobby, but I don't know if I could love him if I were not here."

CHAPTER 53

An Unexpected Chance
Bronx, New York

Will convened his DTR team in his office. He was eager to lay out a calendar for the rest of '33 and to set more aggressive plans for the following year. They sat at Will's library table; John Tee-Van to his right, Gloria Hollister across from him, and Jocelyn Crane to his left.

"It's good to have you home, Will," John said.

"I like the feeling too, John."

"How was London?" Jocelyn asked. "Was Elswyth's play a success?"

"The play opening went well. She loves the Brits, loves London."

"The stories from Chicago show record-setting crowds are attending the Century of Progress Fair," Gloria added.

"It's a spectacular event, Glo. The promoters treated us well. Placed the bathysphere in the center of the Hall of Science. I'm sure most people attending get an up-close look at our submersible."

"The summer is passing quickly," John said to get the meeting started.

"It is," Will agreed. "We have some tasks ahead, but it won't involve deep dives. However, Edwin Chance wants to take his yacht *Antares* on a short expedition around the Caribbean. He specifically requested Glo and I join him."

Gloria Hollister wanted to shout "halleluiah," but she knew not to antagonize the others. She had been looking at the inside of dead fish for nearly half a year. Occasionally, she traveled to cities where she lectured about DTR expeditions, Dr. Beebe's deep-sea dives, and his importance to her and other women in science because of his rare male support of their involvement.

She looked forward to time with Will away from the others. She knew they'd work hard on the *Antares* because Will would want to show the New York Zoological Society's board he was productive while pampered by a wealthy supporter. But she also knew they'd play hard too.

Mr. Chance was both generous and gregarious. They always ate and drank well, and he'd insist on stopping at every beautiful lagoon to helmet dive with Will.

Gloria was too modest in her appraisal of the situation. Edwin Chance requested her company in part because she decorated his yacht well when working in her bathing suit. Bringing along Glo boosted Chance's admiration for William Beebe.

Will was not naïve. He referred to the *Antares* cruise as the seventeenth DTR expedition, a perk that took them from the West Indies around the tip of Florida. He told John to close offices in New York and head to Bermuda.

New arrangements with Edwin Conklin allowed John and Jocelyn to stay at the Bermuda Biological Station. Conklin convinced Director Wheeler that it would be a short season for the Department of Tropical Research. Wheeler agreed to the conditions when he learned Beebe wouldn't join the team until later when Wheeler intended to be on holiday at his home in England.

"Do you have research assignments for Jocelyn and me while we're there, Will?" John asked.

"No, I have supervisory tasks," Will said. "Elswyth and I put a deposit on the house, the one that overlooks the west end of St. George's Harbor."

"How exciting, Will. The house we explored last year?" Jocelyn asked.

"Yes. That one. We need the house put in shape. That's your assignment, Jocelyn. And you need to clear the grounds, John. There are about three acres. I want you to hire locals to cut enough to build holding ponds, which means you must figure out how to terrace the land to build them."

"Do you have an idea of what you want done inside the house?" Joselyn asked.

"The bedrooms on the third floor are useable, so the priority is the basement. You need to empty it, find better windows to install on the south wall, and improve the electrical wiring; add to the storage space. Hire people, Jocelyn. I don't expect you to do the lifting."

"Is there a kitchen?"

"Second floor. It needs upgrading."

"Do we have a budget to get this work done?" John asked.

"We'll go over the budget later, but I need part of the work finished by October. I'll have Mr. Tucker supervise the finishing work so the house and grounds can be our DTR campus when we go back in March of '34."

Gloria made sure Will hadn't misspoken. She questioned whether they could get the house ready in eight months.

"Mr. Tucker has already begun some of the work. By the time John and Jocelyn get to Bermuda, he'll have more done." Will said the project still needed supervision from his team.

"I would prefer to be in Bermuda supervising house remodeling than working in the office all summer long," Jocelyn said. "I'll get things done here. I think I can be ready to travel in less than a week."

"I'll do the same," John added. "Can you make the travel arrangements, Jocelyn?"

She agreed, got up, and returned to her desk outside Will's office.

"I believe she can do a good job," Glo told Will and John when Jocelyn closed the door. "She takes on any task I give her, and she does them all well. She knows how to organize. Better than me. And I'm good."

"I know," Will said. "I've observed the same thing. I didn't give her that assignment on a chance. I'll talk to her."

"We'll get it done, Will, but I can understand why she might be upset. I'm envious too," John confessed. "She idolizes you, Will. She'll work hard despite her disappointment."

"I'd like all of you on the *Antares*, but it's not my decision. Mr. Chance has invited his friends who he thinks have money to help us out. The yacht is full."

"I understand, Director. I'm happy to be going to Bermuda. I remember the slope of the terrain surrounding the house," John said. "I welcome the challenge to terrace the land and build holding tanks."

John stood and went to his office. It left Will alone with Gloria.

"Edwin Chance is your greatest admirer next to me."

There was a different tone in Will's compliment that shook Gloria's confidence. It sounded fatherly, not something he would have said to her a year earlier.

Will left the conference table and returned to his desk. "We leave for Philadelphia in three days. Can you have things in order here? Edwin expects to depart on the *Antares* Saturday."

"I can be ready. Should I board Trumps?" she asked.

"Yes. Make it easier on yourself."

Gloria pushed herself from the table, gathered her notebooks, and began to exit Will's office. "Is everything okay, Will?"

"Yes, everything's fine, Glo. I'm just frustrated by circumstances."

"Anything you can talk about?"

"I'd like to continue our work in Bermuda, but there's no money."

"Are you thinking we should abandon our work there?"

"Not at all. Sit down, Glo."

She walked to the chair in front of Will's desk and sat. "You're worrying me," she said.

"Do you remember the name Gilbert Grosvenor?"

"Editor of *National Geographic Magazine*. Yes. We worked with him when you wrote your first Bermuda story for the magazine."

"He's president of their society. I'm composing a letter to Grosvenor. I just read what I've drafted so far. I'm pleading with him to sponsor additional deep-sea dives next year. The New York Zoological Society leadership insists that any funds we solicit from members need to go into the general ledger. I cannot designate it for DTR exploration. That's one reason Chance is using his yacht to take you and me on a private expedition."

"What does that mean for Bermuda?" she asked.

"It means if I can't get the magazine to sponsor us, we must wait until finances improve whenever that might be."

Gloria wondered if Will's house on St. George's Island was ill-timed. She said if funding remained questionable for several years, what could they accomplish at an expensive laboratory?

Will listened to Gloria's comment, realizing he had questioned his decision in the same way but hadn't verbalized it.

"I have been lucky with money so far. I know it's a gamble but one I feel we must take. There are times you must fake success to gain success, Glo. This is one of those times."

Gloria wanted to offer Will encouragement, but doubts crept into her thoughts.

"Look, I intend to have a good time on the *Antares*," Will told Gloria. "Chance will make it fun. I don't know if he has the wealth or desire to back our dives next year but enjoying ourselves and giving him credit for our accomplishments can't hurt our cause. Meantime, I intend to press the issue with Grosvenor and hope for the best."

"Did he give you any sign he's interested? Is that why you're writing?"

"Only through an associate. He thinks Grosvenor will be receptive. However, he's traveling, so it's unlikely he'd see or respond to a letter that I would send now. We'll travel with Edwin Chance. I'll send the letter when I learn more."

Gloria went to her office. Although excited to get on Chance's yacht for six weeks and bask in the Caribbean sun, the romantic pang that struck her when Will announced the trip faded. Will's business-like instructions darkened the appeal.

She felt in competition for Will's attention. Jocelyn was not shy about her admiration, flaunting praise and hanging on his every word even after two years on the job. Gloria wondered if it disappointed Will that Chance chose her over the younger Miss Crane.

Despite the angst, Gloria decided she would turn the trip to her advantage. She worked on her business affairs and was ready to depart in three days.

CHAPTER 54

Missed Dream
August 1933

The streets of Manhattan were hot. People were eager to step into stores just to get out from under the sun. Among them was Else. She had used the cooler tunnels of the New York subway system to travel from 75th Street to 34th and Broadway carrying a bag with pencils, pens, and drawing paper. She wanted to sketch a lady who sold flowers at Penn Station.

The flower lady was a colorful character who spoke to everyone. She also sold some of the best-prepared flowers in downtown Manhattan.

Across the street from the train station was Macy's and Hada.

The noon-hour crowd had overtaken the store. Large fans stirred the air.

Else weaved her way through the throngs, keeping an eye out for her daughter. She saw Hada waiting on multiple customers at the lingerie counter. She stayed in the background, picking up garments, inspecting them, and returning them neatly folded. She tested fragrances and a young woman assisted with makeup, coaching Else on the proper color that would highlight her "gorgeous high cheekbones."

Else wandered for forty-five minutes, sitting occasionally near the dressing closets where she could catch glimpses of Hada at work. Approaching one o'clock, the crowd began to thin. Else walked toward lingerie.

Hada folded underwear and returned them to display shelves. It surprised her to see her mother's face pop into view.

"Oh, my word. Mother, what are you doing here? Don't you know it's hot outside?"

"It's August, Tochter. It's supposed to be hot."

"Is everything okay?"

"Yes, of course. I came down to sketch the flower lady at Penn. I thought I'd stop to see my daughter. Isn't that a good thing?"

"It's Friday. It's always busy on Friday at noon before the weekend."

"I watched you, Hada. You're very good with the ladies. And a few men. I saw some young men admiring you. Were they buying underwear of flirting with you?"

"Mother! Some of the girls are listening. Speak softly."

"Am I embarrassing you, Tochter?"

"Yes."

"Do you have time for lunch?"

"No, Mother."

Else stood fingering her folded handkerchief.

"Sorry. I didn't mean it to sound so harsh," Hada said.

"Es ist alles in Ordnung."

"It's not okay. I dislike myself when I speak disrespectfully to my mother."

"And I don't like myself when I'm being less than honest with my daughter," Else said. "Here. This came in the mail this morning."

Else removed a letter from her purse and placed it on the counter in front of Hada. "I sat looking at it for an hour hoping it would open by itself and I could know how my daughter's future might be."

Hada lifted the letter. "It's from Bobby…"

"I know, Hada. What did you tell him?"

"I said again I'd marry him if he'd move back to New York. I said I'd help him find a good job here."

One of Hada's friends approached Hada and put her arm around her. "Are you going to open it?" she asked.

"I don't know," Hada responded. "Maybe I should wait until after work."

"Please open it, Tochter. My heart is aching for you."

Two other young women joined for emotional support. Hada pried her finger into the seal and popped the envelope. She pulled the single-page letter and looked at it.

The other women stepped back to give Hada room to read on her own, but they returned when she put the letter on the counter. Else looked at the two-paragraph message upside down, hoping to read Bobby's answer.

"He says no," Hada whispered. "He can't give up the farm; can't leave his father to operate it by himself."

Hada's friends began to sob. They all put their hands on Hada to comfort her.

"It's okay. I'm fine," Hada said. "I didn't think he'd come back. I haven't seen him in three years, just his picture."

"I'm sorry, Tochter."

"I'm sad, Mother, but it's not the same sadness I felt when Patten died. Bobby is alive and happy with his life. I could see him again if I was willing. I'm just not. And I can never see my best friend in Bermuda ever again. That's real sadness."

"We love you, Hada," one friend told her. They all returned to their work areas where people were waiting.

"I hoped I was bringing you good news, Tochter, not bad news. If I tell you I'm sad too but relieved that you won't be leaving, will you understand?" she asked her daughter.

"Yes, Mother. You're part of the reason I can't leave New York. I would miss you too much."

Else sniffled. "Then I must go sketch my flower lady so I can cry where no one will notice."

CHAPTER 55

Rowdy and Raw Honesty

Edwin Chance directed his *Antares* to Key West to find a slip large enough to handle the one-hundred-thirty-foot yacht. Chance excitedly planned to entertain his guests at a Florida island hot spot.

After dinner, Will and Gloria headed to the dance floor as a local trio switched from dinner music to playing swing that Will couldn't resist. They danced until the musicians announced a break. Ready to rest up for round two, Will escorted Gloria back to their table.

Chance stood and applauded with the others for the couple's high-stepping performance. Three younger men also applauded and sauntered up to the Chance-party table.

Will guided Gloria's chair next to his as the three hovered around the woman closest to their age. They brought un-welcomed swagger.

"Why don't you join us, pretty lady," the taller of the three said to Gloria. "We're headed to Tank Island where there's a lot more fun than here.

"It's a snazzy place with a floating nightclub and free-flowing liquor," another lad offered. "Open all night."

"Ernie rows out there all the time for exercise," the third man chimed in.

"Ernie?" Gloria questioned.

"I'm sure he means Hemingway," the *Antares* captain told her. "He lives here."

"Ya, but he ain't here. He took his pretty wife and went to Africa to kill something," the third intruder continued.

"My name's Ferd... I'm mean Fred," said the first inebriated lad, laughing hysterically at his misspeak.

"If you don't mind, fellows, we'd like to finish our dinner," Will told the three men.

"Eat away, gramps. Got enough teeth to chew?"

Two waiters who had been serving the Chance party grabbed the rude drunkard and pushed him toward the door. The other two laughed but stayed by the table close to Gloria. Will stood.

"Put away those skinny sticks if you know what's good for you, pops," one said.

"You shut your mouth, son, and get the hell out of my restaurant," said the restaurant owner, holding a double-barreled sixteen-gauge shotgun aimed at the boy's torso. "Prohibition ain't over in Florida, boy. Get, or I'll get our sheriff."

The young men lifted their arms and stumbled toward the door. "You gonna shoot us?" Their bugged eyes stayed focused on the shotgun.

"BANG!" shouted a waiter with a hard slap on a neighboring table.

The young men jumped, thrashing arms, hoping to be first out the door held open by restaurant staff.

"I'm very sorry folks, young lady," the owner said when lowering his shotgun. "I have fresh Key Lime pies and homemade vanilla ice cream. I'll bring 'em right out. On me."

Will Beebe sat down, his knees wobbling. Ed Chance slapped his back. "Good show, Dr. Beebe. You got some balls."

"I hope I haven't soiled them," Will said, making everyone, including the waiters, laugh.

The restaurant owner delivered his promised pies and ice cream, which the Chance party devoured. Edwin invited the man to sit with them.

"So, here's the question of the hour: Is Tank Island a good spot for us to visit? We'd like to do some helmet dives tomorrow."

"It's become a popular spot because it's only five-hundred yards off Key West. Pretty good natural beaches surround it. There's an old barge that a former barkeep made into a floating nightclub. Rumors say the guy brings in all sorts of entertainment from Cuba: liquor, cigars, and exotic dancers. Before the sun comes up, he brings all the drunks back to Key West and physically throws them off his boat."

"No first-hand experience, though?" Will asked teasingly.

"Say, my waiter tells me you're some hotshot scientist. Are you somebody famous?"

"William Beebe's my name. This is my assistant Gloria Hollister, and our expedition host Edwin Chance. We're very thankful for your swift action. Was that a Fox Sterlingworth?"

"Good eye, William Beebe," the owner said. "My favorite shotgun. Comes in handy as you can see."

"Good eye, indeed, Will," Chance said. "All I saw were two barrels and four buggin' eyes. How d'you have time to notice the shotgun brand during all that commotion?"

"It's much easier when the weapon is aimed at someone else," Will said.

The following morning, the *Antares'* captain and first mate steered the yacht to the far side of Tank Island and dropped anchor. The long craft rested inside a horseshoe-shaped cove. The water between it and the island glistened from the rising sun as it popped up over palm trees.

Will left Gloria's cabin with dance shoes in hand. He tip-toed to his quarters and stripped his clothes, stepping into a bathing suit. On deck, he spoke to the first mate still aft.

"Good morning, Dr. Beebe. Ready for a swim?" the first mate asked.

"Are we deep enough for me to dive in?"

"Twenty feet starboard; twenty-five port."

"Thank you, mate."

Will leaped from starboard, the side exposed to Tank Island. He swam one-hundred-fifty yards to the sandy beach. It remained darkened by tree shadows and a steep dune.

He walked toward the dune admiring undisturbed nature. But after a short walk and the thought of the first mate's coffee brewing, he chose to re-enter the water and get back to the *Antares*. He climbed the ladder and swung onto the deck where the first mate greeted him with a steaming cup.

"It can be a bit brisk after a swim," he said. "Thought you might like this."

"Very thoughtful."

"Yes, sir. There are clean towels in the deck locker if you'd like one."

"The air and sun will dry me soon enough."

"Already dripping wet I see," Edwin Chance said, entering the conversation.

"Good morning, Colonel Chance," the first mate responded.

"Morning, lad. Did you brew enough for another cup?"

"Yes, sir." He went to the galley to pour coffee for the yacht's owner.

Chance thanked Will Beebe for the umpteenth time for joining the cruise and entertaining his friends. Like Chance, both the man and his wife were in the banking business. They operated smaller-sized facilities in Pennsylvania with banks in Lancaster, York, Harrisburg, and Reading.

Chance said the couple avoided the crisis of Wall Street because they were good to their farming customers, most of them Amish or Dutch, who returned their loyalty by refraining from panic. The banks remained solvent and so did their customers.

"They're conservative investors, Will." Chance said. "I knew little about their wealth, so I'm thankful you agreed to go on this trip. I've learned more. Unfortunately, I don't expect them to be that generous. I wouldn't be surprised if they're holding the first dollar they ever made as a banking family."

"They're good people, Ed. Gloria and I have enjoyed them. We appreciate your hospitality and willingness to venture into some uncharted waters, both figuratively and literally."

The men turned when they heard a door to the cabins open. Gloria Hollister appeared. She wore her bathing suit, the one Edwin Chance admired.

"Good morning, beautiful lady."

"Good morning, Mr. Chance. How's the water, Will?"

"Invigorating. Calm and crystal clear."

Gloria said nothing more. She dove off the back of the *Antares*, swimming toward Tank Island's western beach.

"You're a lucky man, Will, to have such a beautiful assistant... And an understanding wife..."

Will turned to see a wily grin. Not a surprise, but the naturalist found it odd that his host sprung his knowledge at this point in their friendship.

"...My wife has threatened to have me castrated for a few flirtatious conversations with younger, unattached women. Yours seems to be okay with your intimate closeness to Miss Hollister."

Will bobbed his head and refused to give Chance any satisfaction with a response.

Chance's other traveling guests joined the men on deck. The first mate poured them coffee. They placed their cups on the rail next to Ed and Will and watched Gloria glide through the glistening calm waters of the horseshoe lagoon.

"Did you already swim, Dr. Beebe?" Chance's friend asked.

"I made the same trip Glo is doing now," Will said. "Went to the shore, walked around in the sand, and swam back."

"It must be what keeps you so trim," the wife observed.

"Skinny. The man is skinny," Ed Chance said. "I don't know how he eats so much and stays looking like that."

Gloria reached the beach and rose from the water. She walked a few steps in the sand and turned toward the *Antares*. Ed Chance saw her look, so he waved. She responded with a meek salute.

Chance slapped Will on the back. "Quite a gal. A beauty even from this far away."

Later, when Chance asked the first mate to row his friends and him to Tank Island so they could hike the dunes and enjoy the raw acres of nature, it gave Will and Gloria an hour alone. They walked the deck and watched the boat cut a passive path through the still cove.

When the party landed and began to trek through the beach, Will turned to Glo and began to talk business. He mapped out how he planned to spend time in Bermuda.

First on his agenda was preparing the house, which he told Glo he intended to name *New Nonsuch*. He was proud that from the third-floor south windows, he could look across flat St. David's and locate the smaller, secluded island from which the Department of Tropical Research launched its Bermuda explorations.

Will's plan also included a greater study of the Sargasso Sea and its mysterious flying fish.

"Further, I want to build a laboratory at *New Nonsuch* customized for our work."

Gloria nodded agreement, but she showed no excitement, no verbalized endorsement.

Will ended his thesis and watched Glo sulk. "Am I boring you?" he asked.

"No. I agree with the plan. It's good. The house is perfect. And I know Jocelyn is going to turn the house into a wonderful home."

"It's a home for Elswyth, so she'll accept Bermuda. But more important, it's our laboratory. It's a place that will quiet my critics. They'll see we're being thorough, so they'll stop claiming we're just vacationing in Bermuda."

"Do they really say that, Will? Or are you stewing unnecessarily?"

"Of course they're saying it. But we're doing serious research. We'll build a place that will set new expectations for science, a comfortable lab surrounded by the nature we're exploring. Science doesn't require sterile buildings and intense artificial light. It needs semi-permanent homes amid nature, places that blend into the environs."

"I agree, Will. You don't need to convince me. I'm your most outspoken proponent and advocate, and I've been your proponent from the moment we met, which is now eight years ago."

"Are you disappointed, Glo?"

"Yes. And no."

"I need an explanation."

"Will, I love you. But I realize you can't love me, Gloria Hollister, in the same way. You love me because I'm your protégé, a loyal and grateful understudy you reward with intimacy and sex. It's become empty, Will. And I know why."

Gloria's frankness hit hard. Will felt like he showed her love. And if she loved him, what was missing?

Although much younger than Will, Gloria saw his naïve expression and knew he couldn't understand her empty feeling.

"You're making me nervous, Glo," Will responded. "You're one of two people I treasure the most. I cannot complete this work without you."

"You're wrong, Will…"

"Wrong?"

"I'm one of *four* people you treasure and with whom you cannot complete the work. Do not lie to yourself," Gloria scolded. "Elswyth Thane is just as important. You need her idolization away from our work. Although maybe not as much as you currently need Jocelyn's."

"That's not fair, and quite untrue."

"I think it *is* true. But Will, it doesn't affect my loyalty or commitment to our goals. To John and you. We don't have to be lovers to be good together as scientists. I want you to know I'm not giving up."

Gloria gently touched his face. She then walked across the deck and disappeared into her cabin.

CHAPTER 56

Last Hope
February 1934

Surprised by how nervous she felt, Else Bostelmann walked from the trolley station at West Farms and entered the New York Zoological Park at Bronx Park South. John Tee-Van greeted her. He said he invited Else because he wanted to talk about Dr. Beebe's plans for Bermuda.

Else searched Mr. Tee-Van's face for a clue anxiously awaiting what he had to say. She wasn't certain he would ask her to return to Bermuda since newspaper stories about the zoo's attendance and finances were worrisome. Her last business visit to the zoological park ended in disappointment. Conditions seemed worse today than they were then.

John took her arm to guide her to Dr. Beebe's office. Will wasn't there, but Jocelyn Crane sat at her desk in the outer office. She jumped from her chair and wrapped her arms around the artist. "So wonderful to see you, Mrs. B. Are you excited for summer?"

It was the first encouraging sign Else received, so she smiled and nodded. Jocelyn wouldn't have asked about her excitement if there weren't plans to include her.

"Dr. Beebe is in the Midwest on a lecture tour," John told Else while holding the chair for her to sit at the round conference table.

"Thank you, Mr. Tee-Van. I hope… that is, if you need me, I'm eager to assist."

"Mrs. B, Will asked that you join the team again in Bermuda."

"I'm quite relieved to hear that," she responded. "I have to inform another scientist, someone who knows my work with Dr. Beebe. He has been waiting for a year to learn whether my tenure with Dr. Beebe has ended."

"Is that so?" John asked.

"He said he and Dr. Beebe know each other through the American Museum of Natural History."

"It must be Roy Miner, the curator of oceanography. They're friendly competitors."

"They seem to be alike," Else observed.

"In what ways do you see them alike, Mrs. B?"

"I read Dr. Miner married a woman half his age. I didn't know that was part of being an ichthyologist."

"It's not. Purely coincidental, I'm certain."

John enjoyed her humorous observation.

"The article I read said Mrs. Miner involves herself in science work too."

"Yes, she's likely to hold important positions. Her credentials and marriage to Roy make her a good candidate for jobs in academia."

"Tell me more about the summer plans, Mr. Tee-Van."

John explained that some staff will leave as early as March. Dr. Beebe requested Else join them a few months later. He said their new laboratory would be at a small estate Will named *New Nonsuch*.

Else asked for details about all that had occurred since she was last in Bermuda.

John obliged. He told Else about their activities at the new home, beginning with Jocelyn's supervision of work crews that installed new windows and made improvements elsewhere in the house. John said he worked with Mr. Tucker to clear overgrowth around the neglected landscape. They hired several young locals who did the labor.

"When Will and Gloria returned from their Caribbean expedition with Colonel Chance, we began building a water reserve and concrete pools to keep shallow-water fish. We installed an electric pump that pushes the water back up the hill to a large tank. It's a perfect system for keeping the water aerated."

"Did you have any time for exploration?"

"With funding still an issue, Will limited our research to one topic: He wanted to learn more about flying fish."

"I'm not surprised," Else said.

John said the DTR team discovered flying fish are abundant near sargassum seaweed, which is thick and widespread.

He said some story-telling seamen say the seaweed was the culprit in ship disappearances between the fifteenth and seventeenth centuries and the legends of the Bermuda Triangle. He explained the marine plant could stop older, smaller vessels by entangling rudders and grinding shallow hulls to a halt.

"What is the connection to the flying fish?" Else asked.

"Will wanted us to figure out how the fish reproduce." John said they discovered flying fish eggs cling to sargassum vines. The plant protects the hatchlings from predators until they're able to out-swim and outfly their enemies.

"A fascinating discovery," Else said. "I hope to see the eggs under Miss Hollister's microscope. Is she doing well? I hoped to see her today."

"She's on the road too, speaking, trying to attract more money for our summer's work."

The big news John told Else was about Will's contact with Gilbert Grosvenor, a name Else recognized because of *National Geographic Magazine*. Grosvenor had printed more than thirty of Else's paintings.

"The publisher responded to Will's request for National Geographic to sponsor this year's dives. Will asked for the full expense of twelve thousand dollars. Mr. Grosvenor countered at ten thousand and requested exclusive control of publicity. He said he'd supply a PR man for the summer. And Will accepted."

"Exclusive means we're not to talk to other reporters?" Else asked.

"Yes. The National Geographic Society publicist will handle newspaper and radio interviews. Will also has to write an article for the magazine. He can write for other publications too, but he's to credit the National Geographic Society for sponsorship."

"Where's the bathysphere?" Else asked.

"Still in Chicago."

"Are people viewing it?"

"The promoters told Will more than half-a-million spectators have stuck their heads inside the sphere."

"Oh, my goodness. I hope they didn't damage anything."

"That's funny, Mrs. B, because Otis arranged for an engineer from Watson-Stillman, the bathysphere builders, to inspect the ball. It needs repairs."

"Is Otis paying for those?"

"He gave the bathysphere to the New York Zoological Society in part so he wouldn't have that responsibility."

Knowing the tension still existed between Dr. Beebe and Otis Barton, Else asked if Mr. Barton committed to dive again.

John said Otis was in Central America with his cameraman planning to film near Panama for at least another month. "He wrote Will that he would return to help supervise the bathysphere's refurbishing and to dive."

CHAPTER 57

Improvements Requested
March 1934

Ataxicab pulled up to the Watson-Stillman Foundry. The young driver sighed, obviously happy to be at his destination after bouncing over unmarked cobblestone roads to find the facility. He turned to Otis Barton. "Here we are."

Otis tipped him a dollar. "Don't go anywhere. I'll only be a few minutes. I need to get back to the Upper East Side when I'm done."

Otis climbed from the cab and walked to the warehouse entrance. He stood at the front and lit a cigarette. He took a few puffs, dropped it, and drove it into the pavement with his foot. He was hoping he'd gotten to the foundry before William Beebe.

"Good to see you again, Mr. Barton."

A short, older man met Otis at the building entrance. "If you'll follow me, I'll take you back to the foundry where you can see the bathysphere," he said. "It was just delivered two days ago."

"Is Captain Butler from Cox joining us?" Otis asked.

"John? Yes. Expecting him soon."

The bathysphere looked small in the spacious foundry warehouse.

"Is Dr. Beebe here?"

"He's in our conference room with the others."

"Others?"

"There's a representative from General Electric, a gent from Bell Telephone, a salesman with the company that supplies the chemicals, and an official from *National Geographic Magazine*."

"Grosvenor?" Otis asked.

"I don't believe it's the publisher, no."

Otis walked around the ball. He looked inside, put his hand on the outside, and dragged his fingers across peeling paint. He didn't show emotion or concern.

"The team wants to discuss several proposals. We'll begin as soon as Captain Butler arrives."

The General Electric, Bell Telephone, and Air Reduction Company reps stood when Otis entered the conference room where Will sat in the key position at the head of the oval-shaped conference table. Otis stayed at the end closer to the door.

"Good to see you, Mr. Barton," Will said. "How was filming in Panama?"

"Film's processing in the lab, Dr. Beebe. I hope we have good footage."

The company reps peppered Otis with questions about his movie making. Glad for the spotlight, Otis said he planned to produce a dramatic documentary about deep-sea diving and the risks it entails.

Will remained stoic, especially when heads turned to see his reaction to Mr. Barton's story-telling. Will considered Otis's center-stage opportunity wasted. He was monotoned and uninteresting.

Shielding his opinion, he looked around the room and concluded others agreed with his assessment. The reps tried to disguise their boredom by lathering Otis with lifeless follow-up questions and insincere encouragement.

Otis enjoyed the attention although Will knew his bathysphere mate couldn't tell he was being patronized, a desperate wannabe with more money than personality or talent. Otis ended everyone's excitement when he opened his mouth.

"Gentlemen, Captain Butler has arrived," the Watson-Stillman host announced.

John Butler spoke as soon as he walked into the room. "I know you're thinking I'm making this grand entrance on purpose," Butler said. "It's not on purpose. A horse got loose in the Holland Tunnel. It stopped all motorists. Sorry I'm late," Butler said.

The host directed Butler to take the seat opposite Dr. Beebe then sat to the right of Butler. Otis was on Butler's left. The Cox & Stevens engineer wasted no time.

"The general condition of the casted steel ball is acceptable. The seals around the windows and portal Dr. Beebe and Mr. Barton use for entry and egress are *not* acceptable. Those will be the Watson-Stillman responsibility to remove and replace," Butler said. He looked at the man representing General Electric. "Tell me about the fused quartz glass."

"Time and changing atmosphere have produced minute cracks. We feel at the depths to which Dr. Beebe wants to descend the cracks might produce rupture."

"Can you create replacements fast enough to install by late spring?" Butler asked.

"It will challenge our subsidiary. However, they're willing to try."

Butler looked at the man from Bell. "I understand you have replacement systems ready to install."

"Yes, Captain Butler. Our only stipulation is that Dr. Beebe relinquishes the antique headsets and breast microphone for our museum."

The thought of Gloria Hollister and he using antiquated communications equipment brought a smile to Will's face. Others tried to quash their laughter, but the Bell representative heard the snickers, looked around, and began to laugh too.

"Well, we have other technical matters to address as we begin to re-assemble the diving ball, such as improvements to the logistical layout of the interior. I'll let Dr. Beebe and Mr. Barton address those concerns," Butler said. "But the other danger area that we must improve is the stuffing box. To me, it's the most vulnerable area of the submersible."

"I think Mr. Barton and I would agree, Captain Butler," Will responded. "Likewise, the rubber hose enveloping the electrical wire and communications line appears to be deteriorating. I hope someone can examine the hose when they check the stuffing box."

"So noted, Dr. Beebe," Butler replied. He looked at the Watson-Stillman staff sitting on the outskirts of the conference table. "What is a reasonable date to have the bathysphere ready to send to Bermuda?"

The Watson-Stillman leader next to Captain Butler looked around at his staff, then to Captain Butler. "We'll have the interior cleaned and shelving installed per Mr. Barton's new diagrams by the second week of April. We'll replace the portal seals with new copper and brass fittings by May first. Can we have the new windows by then?" he asked with a look at the General Electric representative.

A cautious nod confirmed.

"Good. I'd like to discuss the stuffing box and cabling issues with Dr. Beebe, Mr. Barton, and the Bell folks before I offer a deadline."

All agreed with nods and guttural approvals.

"Then let's begin with a delivery goal of June one. It's imperative we communicate any advances or setbacks that might affect that commitment."

The meeting ended in less than thirty minutes. The attending vendors gathered around Dr. Beebe and the National Geographic Society executive. They offered additional assurances on timing. Otis Barton said a few words to John Butler, but then departed.

The young cab driver was dozing in his taxi. Otis awakened him, thanked him for waiting, and instructed him to return to Manhattan.

Once back in his apartment, Otis called his cinematographer.

"They say they can deliver the bathysphere in June. It'll be July, I'm certain. Nevertheless, plan on departing the last week of May," Otis instructed. "I didn't tell Dr. Beebe what my goal is with the film, so don't say anything. Between Beebe and John Butler I'm dealing with a couple of tiresome bullies. I want the filming done before I tell Beebe about the movie."

CHAPTER 58

Else's Future

D r. Roy Miner sent Else a telegram asking her to meet with him. Through a letter, she advised him that Dr. Beebe hired her to return to Bermuda for a summer '34 expedition, which kept her commitment to inform Dr. Miner of her plans. Nonetheless, Dr. Miner wanted to talk.

Else entered the main door to the American Museum of Natural History and approached the information desk.

"Can you please guide me to Dr. Miner's office?" she asked.

"Are you Mrs. Bostelmann, the artist?" the woman asked.

"Yes, ma'am."

"Dr. Miner informed me you might come to my desk. I'm to alert him by telephone, but before I do may I tell you what a pleasure it is to meet you, Mrs. Bostelmann." She held out her hand.

Else reciprocated. "That's very kind of you to say."

"I've enjoyed Dr. Beebe's articles ever since he began publishing them. When I saw your artwork, it brought his colorful words to life. You're very talented."

"You're going to make me blush, Miss…"

"Spindler. My full name is Elizabeth Ann Spindler. People have called me BethAnn for as long as I can remember."

"Did you meet Dr. Beebe when he opened the bathysphere exhibit in January, BethAnn?"

"I didn't. This is my first day back to work as a volunteer. I have diabetes. I had been bedridden. I'm doing better, using a new medicine called insulin. Painful because I have to inject it twice a day. But effective."

"You're a brave woman," Else told her.

"I'm sorry to burden you with my health, Mrs. Bostelmann. I know Dr. Beebe... I mean I knew him when we were younger."

"Children?"

"We attended secondary school together. That's not the full truth. I was in my first year and Dr. Beebe was a senior."

"And where was that, BethAnn?" Else asked.

"East Orange, New Jersey. East Orange High School."

"Would Dr. Beebe remember your name?" Else asked. "I'll see him this summer."

"Well, I doubt he would," she said. "The difference in our age was so obvious then. I was a child and he was a popular senior. That's when he wrote his first published article for *Harper's Young People Magazine*, my favorite magazine. When I saw his name in the article, I yelled to my mother, 'I know him. William Beebe, the most popular boy in school.'"

Else laughed and touched the woman's hand. "My dear, he is still the most popular boy wherever he is. He charms us all. I'll tell him I met BethAnn from East Orange High School."

Else followed BethAnn's directions and found Dr. Miner's office on the third floor of the main museum building, his name printed on the frosted glass. She knocked.

"Come in," a female voice shouted.

Else pushed the door open and peered in.

"Mrs. Bostelmann? I'm Mrs. Miner. This is my husband, Dr. Roy Miner."

He lifted his head from behind several sheets of paper and waved.

"Please come in and have a seat," the young woman instructed. She turned to her preoccupied husband. "Finish that later, Roy. I didn't mean for you to review it now. Conduct your interview."

Mrs. Miner turned again to Else, "He's all yours, Mrs. Bostelmann. "I gave him some documents to review; I didn't mean to disturb your meeting."

"That's quite all right, Mrs. Miner. Glad to make your acquaintance."

The women passed each other as Mrs. Miner exited her husband's office. Else set her portfolio case against a chair leg in front of Dr. Miner's desk. She sat, knees together, and to the left, covered snuggly by her ankle-length skirt. She felt Dr. Miner's inspecting eyes.

Seeing Else settled, he began: "I admit that it disappointed me to learn Will Beebe had you scheduled again this summer. I need your artistic talents, or someone's, for my work. I've seen your paintings for Beebe, and you come with high marks from my friends at National Geographic."

"I want to be the one you choose, Dr. Miner. And I don't want to disappoint you, but I'm also loyal to Dr. Beebe. Without his trust in hiring me five years ago, I would not be sitting here meeting you. And, by the way, I thank you for contacting me."

"You're welcome. It seems like it's been several weeks since I wrote my first inquiry to you."

"Months, Dr. Miner. Your first letter I received months ago."

"That might well be true, Mrs. Bostelmann. Time seems to pass quickly. So, let's move from the past to the future. I've delayed my plans for an article because I believe you're right. You're the person I want for my assignment. The magazine wants me to author at least one, maybe two or more articles on sea creatures that play on our imaginations: Octopus and squid. Whales. To focus on those along our Atlantic coastline."

"When?"

"The first article is to publish by next summer," Dr. Miner said. "If they like it, a second the summer after that."

"How many paintings for your first article?" Else asked.

"Between eight and a dozen."

"Do you have an outline for your article, something I can read to prepare suitable sketches?"

"It won't be an issue, Mrs. Bostelmann. I'll give you precise details for the art," Dr. Miner said.

Else considered the implication. Would he be telling her how to paint the marine life he chose? It made her nervous.

Dr. Miner leafed through Else's portfolio. He lingered on her sketches of the copepods and cephalopods. "Have you already published these?" he asked.

"Let me see."

Dr. Miner turned and lifted the first page with sketches. He put it down and lifted a second page.

"No, I don't believe so."

"Good. I like these. They'd go well with what I've started."

Despite her trepidation, his compliments of her art pleased Else.

Dr. Miner repacked her portfolio. He told her she should contact him as soon as she returns from Bermuda. He would have his first story drafted. If she was available, she could begin.

Else left and felt sure of herself for the first time after an initial meeting. Ironically, the person she wanted most to tell was Dr. William Beebe.

CHAPTER 59

New Love; New Nonsuch
April 1934

W ill Beebe walked down the hill from the house on the estate he renamed New Nonsuch. When he reached the con-
structed dock along Ferry Reach, he peeled his outer garments
and dove into the water.

Still brisk from the Atlantic's winter currents, it caused Will's
body to shiver involuntarily. He drew a breath when his head re-
surfaced for his first breaststroke.

He swam to Swing Bridge, looped a piling, and circled
back. Chiriqui and Trumps had followed Will to the water's
edge making noises throughout his swim as though jealous of
his courage.

When Will got back to the dock, he untied the rope attached
to a small dinghy. "Get in," he shouted at the monkey and dog.
Each responded instantly. He held the rope and floated on his
back, kicking and pulling the small boat with the pets together on
the center bench, Trumps on his haunches, Chiri leaning against
the dog.

John, Gloria, and Jocelyn descended the hill to the dock in a
staggered single file, each carrying a cup of coffee and rubbing the
sleep from their eyes.

Trumps barked when he saw his master. He startled Chiri. The capuchin jumped to the back bench screaming obscenities at his canine buddy.

Will guided the boat back to the dock and climbed the ladder. Trumps and Chiri had already leaped from the dinghy and were scampering up the hill, followed by Gloria. "I have to pee," she told the others.

"Has the water started to warm yet, Will?" John asked.

"I think it's up one-degree Fahrenheit from yesterday," Will said jokingly.

John chuckled at his silly question. "I will test the pump this morning, Will. It did well yesterday filling the holding tank at the top of the hill," John continued. "I want to see if it can keep the tank supplied while gravity empties it into our holding ponds and troughs."

"I inspected the system last evening," Will reported. "I think it works well; nicely engineered, John."

"If you're satisfied, I can start transferring some of the live fish," John said.

"Do you have them corralled?" Will asked.

"They're in separate tanks at the Biological Station. I've heard Wheeler wants everything owned by the Department of Tropical Research moved before the first day of summer. He remains paranoid about our presence, Will."

"Yes, I'm certain Dr. Conklin regrets hiring the Brit. Wheeler's an ogre wearing a tight collar."

"I'll get our sea life transferred as soon as I can, Will," John said. "I'll take the smaller motorboat to the station now for a quick inventory."

John's departure left Will and Jocelyn alone on the dock. Jocelyn looked up the hill toward the house. She took Will's hand and moved him to the shadow of a large cedar.

"I'm so happy to have you back in Bermuda," Jocelyn told Will. "I felt myself longing to see you, to hear your voice, and feel your touch."

She took his hand in hers. She opened his fingers and laid his palm on her heart, closing her eyes. "Ah. That's better. Can you feel it beating harder? That's what you do to me when you touch me."

Will stepped closer to Jocelyn and wrapped his arms around her. He wanted to kiss her, but a motorboat turned the bend from St. George's Harbor. He held her tightly, his body shivering with passion.

Young Jocelyn had been on his mind throughout his and Gloria's expedition with Edwin Chance. He enjoyed Gloria's company, her friendship, her lovemaking, but Jocelyn stole his heart.

Gloria idolized Will just like Jocelyn, but it was Jocelyn holding him, feeding his ego, uttering the same love prose Gloria had spoken four years earlier when Will and Glo kissed in the misty cave.

Jocelyn added a fresh spark, an awkward spark, but one that renewed Will's excitement. He tasted a new elixir that quenched his ego and libido.

With fortune turning because of National Geographic Society's insertion of new capital, Will felt invincible. He lifted Jocelyn's chin and saw her desire. He ached to have her. He felt young and fierce, urging to take her. He kissed her; their heated bodies embraced. He steadied her as they became entangled in lust.

From the kitchen window overlooking Ferry Reach and St. David's Island, Gloria Hollister searched for Will. She was feeling emotional.

She saw John puttering the motor dinghy to the other side of Swing Bridge headed to Bermuda's Biological Station. John appeared to be alone, but he was too far away to be certain. The dock at New Nonsuch looked abandoned. Until a breeze lifted the cedar limbs and she saw feet entwined.

It took little imagination for Gloria to realize who and what was happening. She could see Jocelyn's right leg wrapped around Will's calf. She inhaled deeply and with her exhale: "Well, I enjoy a good competition. May the better player win."

CHAPTER 60

Renewed Joy; Returned Tensions
5 July 1934

A blast from the *Monarch of Bermuda* let everyone know it was safe to walk the gangway and safe to enter the capital of Bermuda.

Else Bostelmann was eager to disembark. Excited to be back in Bermuda for the first time in three years, the DTR artist lifted her smaller suitcase and joined the human parade traipsing toward the exit. She kept an eye out for the porter's wagon with her trunk. She wanted it quickly in case John Tee-Van was already waiting.

Unbeknownst to Else, there was another important passenger on the *Monarch* that Dr. Beebe sent John to look for: The bathysphere. The ship's crew buried the three-eyed iron ball deep within the cargo hold.

Otis Barton expected to go as well, but he was uninvited. Dr. Beebe told him John could handle it. Otis could concentrate on his film project, including keeping his cinematographer out of the taverns and away from Gloria and Jocelyn, comments Otis shared with his employee.

A high-ranking officer stood ready to escort John below to examine the submersible. The goal was to transfer the bathysphere to the *Ready*, the old British Navy barge that had been the sphere's launching deck in 1930.

The men's discussion continued as the officer guided John to the crew's private gangway. Else saw John when behind others standing in line. She recognized the ship's officer, so she hesitated to call Mr. Tee-Van's name, uncertain why he and the officer were marching together seriously engaged in conversation.

Else had plenty to do while she waited for Dr. Beebe's right-hand man. She shifted her focus to finding her trunk.

Meanwhile, John kept descending deeper into the bowels of the *Monarch*. He found the bathysphere encased in a wood-framed box; the general integrity of the submersible protected from the shifting and sliding of other cargo. The important fused quartz windows were padded and wrapped.

A crewmember supervising the cargo hold joined the ship's officer. He described how his crew would hook the bathysphere to pull it from the space and transfer it.

"Our hoists will lift the ball onto a rail wagon that will slide the load to the adjacent dock," the crewman told John. "It will take a couple of hours."

"Captain James Sylvester is in charge of the *Ready*," John said. "I'll alert him to the timing. I have a passenger I'm meeting at the dock. I need to go find her."

"I'll lead the way," the officer said.

Else tracked down her trunk in the luggage barn. She asked a porter to cart it to the dock where she found the *Skink*. "Pier four," she informed him. They were making the walk across the still-crowded wharf when she heard John's welcoming voice.

"Mrs. B, you made it safely," John said, enveloping her with a hug.

"I did, Mr. Tee-Van. I'm delighted to be back in Bermuda. I've looked forward to this expedition with more anticipation than ever before."

"There might be a good cause, Mrs. B. I've just seen the bathysphere below in the cargo area. They've refurbished it and updated it with new equipment. Will is thrilled about diving with the changes."

"The bathysphere was onboard the *Monarch*?"

"Yes. Two prized members of our expedition landed today, and you thought you were the only one."

"Kind of you to include me as a 'prized member,' Mr. Tee-Van."

"It's a fact."

"That's very flattering, but we must get to work. The porter is waiting for instructions on loading my trunk into the *Skink*."

"Let me carry your luggage then," John said. "No more delays."

⸻ ∞ ⸻

More than a week passed with the bathysphere resting aboard the *Ready* looking like a forgotten actress whose youthful glamour had faded.

The barge was tied to an old three-masted sailing ship, which, like the *Ready*, had seen better sea-going days. Its rusted hull was sunk deep in St. George's Harbor as though handcuffed to an uncomfortable bed. But now the old vessel had a purpose; it held tight to the *Ready* until Will Beebe beckoned its cargo. The barge and its freight were destined for Will's bull's-eye section of the Atlantic Ocean.

DTR staff had dozens of tasks to complete before the bathysphere could submerge. While they did the expected – painting and lettering the ball with the National Geographic Society's name below that of the New York Zoological Society – they tested and re-tested every piece of new equipment.

John, Gloria, and Jocelyn kept doing their research duties while also rehearsing for the hopeful dives. John fine-tuned the aeration of water through his complex system of tanks, pumps, waterfalls, and filters at New Nonsuch.

Jocelyn repurposed the ground floor of the house to replicate the DTR laboratory on Nonsuch Island. She oversaw installation of floor-to-ceiling windows that offered calming scenery, evening breezes, and daytime light for microscopes and artwork.

Gloria buried herself in ichthyology detail, memorizing species, their genus and family names, and creating elaborate catalogs. She sat closest to the artist's table, sometimes occupied by George Swanson who, for the first time, accompanied the DTR staff.

George welcomed Else Bostelmann because he was eager to learn from her. Among his first lessons was to give sea creatures personalities when drawn and painted.

That was Else's legacy and mastery. She made the sea animals William Beebe described take on human-like characteristics: mesmerizing eyes, frightening anger, and intimidating physical strength. *National Geographic* readers and gallery viewers said they could not stop gazing despite the chilling fear they spawned.

The National Geographic Society's support for Dr. Beebe's twentieth expedition and sixth summer in Bermuda boosted the Department of Tropical Research energy. It also legitimized Will's efforts in the eyes of doubting scientists, including those at the Bermuda Biological Station headed by John Wheeler.

Wheeler remained the staunchest of Will's critics, but the organization's founding president, Edwin Conklin, prevailed, welcoming DTR as summer residents once more while they made New Nonsuch their working headquarters.

Finding little rest, Will Beebe kept commitments to speak at Government House in Hamilton while still assisting his staff with physical labor. He made routine visits to check on the bathysphere.

As the second weekend approached since the bathysphere's arrival, Will overheard sharp words exchanged among staff. He announced in the evening it was time for a party in honor of his upcoming fifty-seventh birthday. He instructed Jocelyn to hire the musicians from St. George's Hotel and to invite the hotel guests to join them at Darrell and Meyer Wharf where Will wanted the floor cleared and swept for dancing.

The event turned out exactly as Will planned. The orchestra sounded better than ever and dozens of hotel guests and local dignitaries, including several young interns from wealthy British, American, and Canadian families working at the Bermuda Biological Station, joined in the fun. It gave everyone a chance to spiff up and feel good.

Will did his usual thing playing his ukulele and making everyone sing some of his favorite songs when the orchestra took a break. With the musicians' return, Will stepped down from the flatbed wagon the crew converted to a stage and was mobbed by people thanking him for throwing such a gala birthday event.

John stood with Else, watching the DTR director turn on his charm and captivate dozens of people meeting him for the first time.

"He has an amazing gift, Mr. Tee-Van. I do not believe I have known anyone like him with such energy and charisma."

"Quite unique, Mrs. B. Look at the people. What do you notice?"

"Most of them are women. That's what I notice first," Else said.

John took Else's hand and guided her to a table set up as a bar. "Would you like a glass of wine? I'd like to discuss something with you."

She took a white wine while John ordered a rum swizzle that Will had concocted himself in five-gallon containers.

"Cheers, Mrs. B," John said, tapping his glass against hers. "And let me say once more how pleased I am to see you back."

"I appreciate your kindness, Mr. Tee-Van. I'm quite certain I would not be here if it were not for your introduction."

John put his arm around Else and pulled her tight. "What a smart man I was then."

"Please tell me what you wanted to talk about. I doubt it was just to engage in our mutual admiration."

"True, Mrs. B. I'm worried we have the potential for jealousies that might interfere with our work. I want your keen observations to tell me I'm wrong."

"Well, to be honest, I shared your concerns when I arrived and noticed the beautiful smile gone from Miss Hollister's face."

"Exactly. Then you know what I'm implying."

"I know Miss Crane has an abundance of affection for Dr. Beebe. I saw them embrace during the end of my last tour with DTR…"

"That was in '31…"

"Correct. So, I've been wondering how things between Miss Hollister and Miss Crane had been working out. It surprised me when Dr. Beebe took Miss Hollister on last summer's expedition aboard Mr. Chance's yacht."

"Yes, that was surprising to me as well, but Will told me he had no choice. Colonel Chance is the one who insisted Gloria come along on the voyage. The Chances like Glo. They know she befriended Amelia Earhart during a lecture tour with the pilot. They love Amelia."

"I read Miss Hollister and Miss Earhart attended Columbia University about the same time."

"Yes, Earhart was there for a year before Glo worked on her master's degree. People compared them because of their extracurricular athleticism."

"So, Dr. Beebe would have preferred to take Miss Crane rather than Miss Hollister?"

"I'm only presuming, Mrs. B," John admitted. "Jocelyn acted vexed at first but then lost herself in preparing New Nonsuch. Even though we were working at the same home, we rarely saw each other except to share progress reports."

"And how was that?" Else asked.

"Well, I learned more about Will and Glo's adventure from Jocelyn than I heard from Will. She seemed to know where they were and what they had seen."

"This is awkward to ask, Mr. Tee-Van… Do you think Dr. Beebe and Miss Hollister were intimate during their travels aboard Mr. Chance's yacht?"

"They've been intimate before…"

"Mr. Tee-Van, we both know that Miss Hollister and Dr. Beebe have shared love for the past five years. Am I to assume that relationship ended?"

"Exactly my concern, Mrs. B. Gloria and Jocelyn must work closely for us to succeed and for me to guarantee the safety of our director and his co-pilot. Should I be concerned?"

Else watched the dance floor while the orchestra slowed its pace. Dr. Beebe had been dancing with a young woman Else recognized as a hotel guest. He bowed to the lady and looked for Miss Crane who stood conveniently nearby. Will pulled his assistant to his body with dramatic playfulness, but then slowed his waltz to a romantic pace.

"He's infatuated with Miss Crane, it's obvious," Else said. "He's not trying to disguise it."

"Do you see Glo's face?" John asked. "She's pained by Will's abandonment."

"Yes, I watched them dance earlier," Else said. "There was no emotion from either."

"Glo and I have worked closely now for six years. It hurts me to see her agonize."

"The irony, Mr. Tee-Van, is that we're concerned about Dr. Beebe's affairs rather than his marriage."

John shuffled uncomfortably.

"Do you have something else to tell me, Mr. Tee-Van?"

"It's always been a strange union, Mrs. B. People call it a modern marriage. I prefer to call it a complicated marriage, more of a partnership with pretend affection."

"Partnerships are important in marriages don't you think?" Else challenged.

"Of course. But so is affection."

"I will disagree with you that there is 'pretend' affection between Dr. Beebe and his wife..."

"Yes, I didn't mean to imply..."

"I know what you're saying. I understand some men value sex in marriage more than others, and I agree it can be important," Else continued. "But I don't believe it's important to Dr. Beebe and Mrs. Beebe in their relationship."

"Yes, you're right. And I've taken us off track. My concern is for us as a team. Do you have any recommendations knowing what you do about all of us? Can we work toward a common goal with the way things are?"

Else looked again at Dr. Beebe and Jocelyn, disguising little about their attraction. She glanced at Miss Hollister standing with two young admirers. Else could tell she listened only to her heart-ache, not their flirtations.

"Is Mrs. Beebe coming to Bermuda soon?"

"Not until October Will tells me."

"Miss Hollister wants to talk," Else said. "I've felt that since we arranged our tables next to each other at the new laboratory. I will learn what I can about her temperament."

"Gloria is my friend as well as my associate, Mrs. B. It's hard for me to help her when I know so much about her passions, professional and personal. I know who she loves—and who seemed to love her—and all the circumstances that surround their relationship."

"I understand, Mr. Tee-Van. It has put you in a difficult spot. I will help you because I know how important it is to you."

CHAPTER 61

Managing the Pain
8 August 1934

Gloria burrowed her eyes into the ocular lens of her microscope. She groaned from the sheer monotony and physical stress.

"You're straining too hard, Miss Hollister," Else scolded. "The morning is so young you need to pace yourself or your eyes will not forgive you."

Gloria leaned back and smiled at her mothering colleague. "Okay, Mum."

"Good. Now tell me what you're straining to see."

"Will insists that I explain how his flying fish lay their eggs in the sargassum weeds, and how the hatchlings survive."

"Can you explain it, Miss Hollister?"

"Yes, I'm certain I can, but I will not burden you with the details, unless you want to paint a tiny egg the size of a pinhead.

Will Beebe pushed his chair away from his worktable at the other end of the laboratory den and walked past John and Jocelyn to join Else and Gloria's conversation.

"Have you told Mrs. B about our progress with the bathysphere over the past two days?" he asked Gloria.

"We've both been busy, Will."

"I'm happy to hear that but I don't want our star artist to be left in the dark."

"I've heard from Mr. Swanson that you feel ready to dive, Dr. Beebe."

"Glad to know someone is keeping you informed," Will said, poking another jab at Gloria. "I wish we were going out today, Mrs. B, but the weather forecasts were not promising."

"So, you're ready?" Else asked for confirmation.

"Yes, but I'll let Glo fill in the detail. Captain Sylvester insists we undertake more tests. I'm taking John and Jocelyn to the harbor so we can check on Otis. He said he'd have the bathysphere interior spotless and the instruments re-arranged based on progress we made yesterday."

Tee-Van and Crane pushed their chairs away from their workstations, waved to Gloria and Else, and departed with their director.

"You can keep the story short, Miss Hollister," Else began. "I'm interested to hear if *you're* ready for these long-awaited dives."

"Yesterday was a pivotal day. Captain Sylvester wanted his crew and all of us to rehearse our roles as if it were the real thing."

"Meaning you sent the bathysphere deep?"

"…to three-thousand twenty feet."

"Did you bring up any concerns?"

"The bathysphere was clean. Otis had his film camera set up to shoot when he flipped a switch from the deck."

"Did that work?"

"He ran off four-hundred feet of film, but we don't know how well it exposed. I'm not sure he'd tell us if it did or didn't."

"So, Dr. Beebe feels confident in the submersible. And Captain Sylvester, how did he feel about his crew's preparation?"

"They did well. We're ready to go as soon as Will likes the weather outlook."

Else stacked her sketches to one side of her table and turned to Gloria.

"And you, Miss Hollister? How are you feeling?"

"Mrs. B, I think you're prying for something more than my readiness."

"You and I cannot hide much from each other, Miss Hollister. I want to know if your heart is ready for the way things are."

Gloria leaned back in her canvas deck chair and let out a sigh. She stared through the window rather than look at Else.

"I have loved Will Beebe for several years. Perhaps before I began working for him. Then he married."

"Did you know he was going to marry?"

"No, but I was working for Dr. Carrel, so my mind was no longer fixated on William Beebe. Except, I still wanted to work for him so I could get out of a sterile lab."

"Which you did."

"Yes, three years later and a year after he married a woman my age."

"But you still loved him."

"I began to love him more when I was around him, Mrs. B. He is a marvelous man with courage, charm, confidence…"

"I know his strengths. Do you know his weaknesses?"

"Yes, young women who idolize him…"

"…like you, and now Miss Crane."

"Yes, like Jocelyn. Pretty, smart, and clinging to every word he speaks."

"Do you think that describes you as well?"

"It did. No denying it."

"Did?"

"Will Beebe loves being loved. But he doesn't love back with his heart. He loves intellectually. Does that make any sense, Mrs. B?"

"Do you know why he can't love with his heart?"

"No. And it doesn't matter to me anymore. I just want to do my best to make him successful because he's earned that. He's earned it by putting up with Otis Barton. And he's earned it by trusting me and other women to be good scientists. Including Jocelyn."

Else put her hand on Gloria's, affecting her, causing her eyes to tear.

"Do you have any motherly advice, Mrs. B, especially for a woman who knows that someone she loves is not the right person to be in love with?"

A picture of Hada flirting with Bobby at her apartment door flashed. "Do you know the poem by Tennyson, Miss Hollister?" Else asked.

"I'm not much of a poetry reader, Mrs. B."

"The famous line from his most famous poem says, 'Tis better to have loved and lost than never to have loved at all.' Does that sound familiar?"

"Yes, I've heard it before. I didn't know Tennyson wrote it."

"It's hard for me to tell you how to react to the situation. But I know this. You're a strong woman with years of success ahead of you. You cannot let unrequited love influence who you are. You must let faith guide your path. Many opportunities and many people to love are in your future."

Gloria brooded a moment. "I'm thirty-four. I don't know if I want children or if I concentrate on my career. I probably shouldn't think about a marital partnership at all."

"What you need to think about is living with your eyes wide open. The God within you will show you the right path. Be open to the messages God sends you."

"I know you follow Mrs. Eddy's philosophies, but are you more religious than you've let us see?"

"I'm not religious, Miss Hollister, but I'm a believer in God. I believe in human beings who live as though God is with them every moment."

"I think I believe the same way, but I have lapses when I forget about God. I feel guilty when I do. Like now."

"You shouldn't feel guilt. You just need to renew your faith in yourself. That's where you'll find God. It will help you understand more with each passing day."

"Renew my faith in me…. That's quite a leap from where I am now."

CHAPTER 62

Ready Again

Weather forecasts were mixed. Some predicted clear skies and a calm ocean; others said late storms will result from increasing heat. Will Beebe gambled.

Like the very first time William Beebe and Otis Barton climbed into the bathysphere, the submersible sat on the deck of the *Ready* pulled to sea by the aging *Gladisfen*. They drew within a mile of the latitude and longitude where the bathysphere descended in 1930.

The staff congregated around the bathysphere. Else and George Swanson joined them. Else encouraged Mr. Swanson to observe Miss Hollister and Miss Crane as they eavesdropped on Dr. Beebe's instructions.

National Geographic publicist John Long also tagged along to see the story unfold. He hung out with Jocelyn and Gloria photographing the women. Mostly the younger woman.

The *Ready* floated deep in the water catching an occasional swell that splashed over the decaying sides. The crew scattered to avoid getting wet.

Will stood. He looked at Otis, who had shown flashes of seasickness. The stench Otis created before their radio broadcast returned to Will's nostrils, a smell of rancid rum. "How are you feeling, Otis?" he asked. "Still hoping to film?"

"I'll manage," Otis snarled.

The bathysphere engineer learned the film he shot from the unmanned submersion had few usable frames. He looked for reasons to blame Dr. Beebe.

Will signaled Captain Sylvester to settle the boats. He told John Tee-Van to prepare to lock the two explorers into their craft. Will's new personal assistants, Perkins Bass and William Ramsey, recent college graduates, took their posts at the steam engines powering their respective winches.

Else stood along the starboard railing explaining to George Swanson what was happening as Will and Otis climbed into the bathysphere. She pulled Swanson closer to Gloria who began talking to Dr. Beebe as John pushed the four-hundred-pound cover over the bolts. She made him listen to Jocelyn call out the time.

"Miss Hollister won't be able to talk to Dr. Beebe or Mr. Barton once they pound each bolt," Else explained. "The sound is deafening."

The process seemed much faster than Else remembered from her previous voyages with the team, which she knew had to comfort Dr. Beebe.

John looked to Gloria for a signal that Will was ready to go. She understood the look and asked the director, "Are you all set, Will?"

When she nodded, Jocelyn yelled the time. John waved to Captain Sylvester and shouted to Bass and Ramsey to stoke their engines.

The pulleys creaked and whined as the steel cable tightened. Then the bathysphere lifted and crawled a few inches across the *Ready's* deck rising slowly.

As it climbed to six feet, the boom began to veer two-and-a-half tons of steel toward starboard. The methodical control prevented it from banging into any part of the fragile barge. It dropped to the sea without sway.

Before it took its plunge, the crew and staff could see Will Beebe's face pressed against the center fused quartz window, his smile comforting everyone.

With the boom stopped and the cable reversing direction, the bathysphere and Will's face disappeared. The ball changed colors as it dipped below the surface. A trailing cut in the water reminded those watching from the deck of the exploration's unrepairable risks.

Jocelyn called out the time of contact with the water and once more when John reported the bathysphere beyond sight. Gloria asked Will how they were doing.

"My goodness, I'd forgotten the amazing sight," Will said over the telephone line.

"What are you seeing?" Gloria asked.

"Spectacular colors. Changing rapidly as we drop to one-hundred feet."

"We're stopping you for the first marker," Gloria told him.

"I can still see the *Ready's* hull. It's gained another layer of barnacles since we last dove from its deck, looking more and more like a miniature coral reef."

"It's been three years, Will, since you saw the bottom of the *Ready*.

"Thanks for reminding me how long we've been at this, Glo."

"Is Mr. Barton still with you?" Gloria asked sarcastically.?"

Will pulled his face from his window and checked on his co-pilot. Otis had his eyes fixed on his gauges holding his film camera in his lap. He looked up at Dr. Beebe. "Is everything alright?" he asked.

"We're doing well so far," Will responded.

Will told Gloria the reds and yellows disappeared from the spectrum. "The sea is full of copepods; swarms, Glo."

When the bathysphere passed through the third cable tie, Will said he saw several drifting siphonophores; Portuguese men-o-war.

Gloria wrote notes as fast as her pen could move. She wrote Will's words verbatim, or as close as she could make them.

"What are you doing down here and where's your host?" Will asked rhetorically.

"What's that you're saying?" Gloria asked.

"I'm talking to the pilotfish that just peered into my window. Many colleagues will deny what I'm seeing, Glo, a pilotfish at what, four-hundred feet?"

Jocelyn interrupted. "Four hundred. Mark. Time, 09:49:32."

"Did you hear her, Will?"

"Yes. Very authoritative," Will said with a chuckle. "More fish, Glo. More that will surprise most ichthyologists: yellow-tails and blue-banded jacks. What would they be hunting at this depth?"

"Can you answer your question, Will? Do you see any prey?"

"Dozens of silvery squid."

At six hundred feet Will reported the ocean was a dark luminous blue. No more green, no more light from the sun, but still, he said, there appeared to be light cast from the ocean.

At eight hundred, more copepods accompanied by arrow worms and round-mouth cyclothones. Then a school of lanternfish. All were visible because of their luminescence.

At one thousand feet, Will used his smaller flashlight and checked the stuffing box above him. He searched the seals around the manhole and windows. They were dry.

The small electrical fan that replaced the palm leaves for air circulation ran quietly, and the chemicals were controlling humidity and carbon dioxide far better than before. Will had yet to use his handkerchief to block his breath from fogging the fused quartz glass.

As the bathysphere descended deeper into the abyss, Will continued to report a series of unusual fish and siphonophores growing more bioluminescent as their craft went deeper.

"Glo, I'm about to turn on our fifteen-hundred-watt lamp. We're surrounded by fish, their yellow and blue lights flashing strangely." Will gave his report at 11:17. The bathysphere was below two-thousand feet.

"Oh, damn!"

"What is it, Will?" Gloria asked excitedly. "Everything okay?"

"I'm looking at a quartet of a thin and colorful fish. I don't know where to place them in genus or family."

"Describe them, Will. I have Mrs. Bostelmann listening on John's headset," Gloria instructed.

"Four inches. Maybe five. Bird-like beaks. Long. Slender. Stiff. Standing upright on a thin tailfin. Sharply pointed jaws. They're buoyant in perfect formation, unaffected by my light. Colors brilliant: scarlet head, blue body, and clear yellow posterior."

"Dr. Beebe, this is Else. In proportion to the body, how long is the 'bird-like beak?'"

"Mrs. B, I'd say twenty percent of the length," Will answered. "There's more, Glo…"

"Go ahead, Will."

"I'll call them Abyssal Rainbow Gars—I know they're not gars, but for describing, that's their name. They've swum out of range, their dorsal fins vibrating and waving ever-so-slightly as locomotion. Now, a much larger fish has caught my light beam. Amazing. Chilling. A fin from the center body to the tail, large and triangular. Like two sails; one up, one down."

"Color, Will."

"No color. Dead looking. But very alive. Oblong head; salmon-like. No teeth. Large eyes. Torpedo body."

The bathysphere with its encapsulated explorers had dropped to two-thousand five-hundred ten feet. It had been submerged for more than two hours.

As Will rambled comments about the various bioluminescent lights and how common they had become to Otis and him, Gloria and John looked at each other and knew fatigue was setting in. With encouragement from his staff, Will called for a halt. The bathysphere hung at that depth for a short time and then began its ascent.

At the first stop to cut the marker that tied the wire-wrapped sheath to the Roebling cable, Will called up another sighting. He saw a new anglerfish. "It came from this vast ocean right up to my window," Will told Gloria. "Is Mrs. B close?"

"John's giving her his headset, Will. Stand by," Gloria said.

"I'm here, Dr. Beebe," Else reported in.

"Good. It's an anglerfish, Mrs. B. Six inches long. Dark body but three tall tentacles dangle from the top of its body. Illicia. Each about two or more inches; each with a pale-yellow bioluminescent organ at the end."

Else sketched an oval as she listened and drew three lines upward from the body. She asked about eyes.

"Small."

"Anything else unusual," she asked.

"Two pear-shaped organs in front of the dorsal fins. Common *Cryptospharas*," Will said.

The artist continued drawing but removed her headset and handed it back to John when Dr. Beebe completed his description. She showed what she had done to George Swanson before pulling it back and continuing her sketching.

After more than three hours balled up inside the submersible, Will and Otis climbed across the bathysphere's sharp manhole bolts and fell to the deck of the *Ready*. The *Gladisfen* and *Ready* blew long blasts from their horns. Another tug that escorted them to sea sent a blast as well.

The two explorers needed help standing, their legs cramping, and their equilibrium affected by the swaying barge.

"What's the noise about?" Otis asked.

"You've set a new depth record," John said gleefully. "We're celebrating."

The crew and staff cheered when John finished his explanation. Publicist John Long snapped a dozen candid photos with his Kodak. He used Captain Sylvester's short-wave radio to inform the *Royal Gazette* in Hamilton of the record.

Long negotiated a deal with the *Gazette's* publisher to receive first notification if he also would send an immediate wire to Alice Greenbrier at the *New York Times* with his two-paragraph story. A reporter already wrote it. It just needed the official depth.

When Will had his balance and legs in working order, he went quickly to Else Bostelmann who stood near Gloria. "My notes, Glo," he ordered. "Let me see what you've drawn, Mrs. B."

They looked over Else's sketches of the three discoveries: the so-called Abyssal Rainbow Gars, the Pallid Sailfish (*Bathyembryx istiophasma*), which Will named, and the Three-starred Anglerfish (*Bathyceratias trilynchnus*), also a Beebe-named species.

The DTR director paid little attention to the noises and cheering carried out by staff and crew. He focused on getting his fish drawn and shared as soon as possible. He was eager to alert both the zoological society and Gilbert Grosvenor so they could enjoy their successful investments.

CHAPTER 63

Satisfied...

Dinner at the Bermuda Biological Station served as a platform for further celebration. Director Wheeler stayed away but most of the station staff and interns cheered the DTR staff when they entered the dining hall.

One of the British scientists who had criticized Dr. Beebe's showmanship, stood to offer a toast. In typical British fashion it ended with a call for three cheers that echoed through the hall and into Wheeler's office. He walked to his door and slammed it shut.

Will, always at ease in front of an audience, thanked the station staff for its generous reception. Although Otis returned to St. George's Hotel with his cinematographer and dined there rather than with the others, Will still acknowledged his dive mate and donor of the bathysphere to the New York Zoological Society.

He looked at each of his staff, Tee-Van, Hollister, Crane, Bass, and Ramsey, and thanked them with direct eye contact. He introduced John Long, the publicist, and young artist George Swanson, and thanked them for their work as well.

"I must eat fast," Will said. "I don't want you to think me rude, but I have work to complete at my lab. I have a dedicated artist in Mrs. Else Bostelmann, who expects my help. I identified three new fish today. That, to me, is as great an accomplishment as the two-thousand five-hundred ten feet we submerged."

The scientists applauded, although some did so as a courtesy, still skeptical that Beebe saw what he claimed. The dive, however, was witnessed by many. That was worth acknowledging.

John Long watched for those who seemed sincere looking for notable candidates from whom he could gather pithy quotes about Will's accomplishment. A distraction suddenly interrupted his concentration—Jocelyn Crane touched him.

Long had been admiring her, flirting occasionally, for several weeks. He lost consciousness momentarily when she grabbed his arm to get him to appreciate the station staff's applause for Dr. Beebe. It didn't matter why she touched him; it was the only thing he noticed.

Else Bostelmann's table was the only one illuminated in the New Nonsuch laboratory. She had sketched and partially painted watercolors that were now scattered over her work area and on the floor.

Clipped to wire hanging above Else's table were her drawings made on the *Ready*. They dangled more to push her onward than to recall Dr. Beebe's descriptions. Still, she glanced at them for confirmation.

Else had re-drawn each of the three species Dr. Beebe wanted to show the world as new. He told her when he emerged from the bathysphere that he made Otis look through his window as a witness to each discovery. But he admitted to Else that her artwork was more substantial proof than anything Otis Barton said.

Else worked each fish several ways looking for the visual trigger that would help Dr. Beebe remember what he saw. And if not, then they would adjust them until he was satisfied.

She was happily surprised when the door at the far end of the laboratory opened and Dr. Beebe appeared.

"How's the artwork coming, Mrs. B?" He marched with long strides to join her.

"I have a number of sketches for you to see, Dr. Beebe. I hope I've captured at least one frame of each fish that we can work with."

Will stepped around the artwork on the floor, seeing that they were paintings of the Rainbow Gars and Sailfish. He looked for the anglerfish.

Else pushed her chair back trying to avoid creasing her work. She bent and scooped them up and shuffled them into two stacks. She had the anglerfish drawings already assembled.

"I have them stacked according to my favorite followed by my second favorite and so forth," Else said. "Would you look for an image that is a good starting point? I know none may be suitable yet, but I thought this would help."

"That may take a few minutes, Mrs. B."

"I'll make some tea."

"Tea sounds good."

Else went into the back room, a small kitchen with a hot plate, sink, and older icebox that came from the main living floor above the lab. She put her teapot on the hot plate and plugged it into a socket. "Have you ever thought about what makes you climb into a ball of steel and drop into the ocean, Dr. Beebe?" she asked.

"I like this one of the Rainbow Gar," Will said, pulling the third one in the stack and moving it to the top. "I don't think about it, Mrs. B. If I thought about it for too long, I probably wouldn't do it."

"You're a brave man, Dr. Beebe. I think about your courage often."

Will heard Else put cups onto saucers and scoop tea with her spoon. "Really, Mrs. B?"

"It may surprise you, but I have a theory. Do you want to hear it?"

"Well, I'm curious now, of course, but a little fearful too. Are you going to be critical?"

The tea kettle whistled, which relieved Will. He heard Mrs. B pour the hot water over the tea infuser. She stirred each cup and brought them to her table, handing one of the saucers to Dr. Beebe.

"No. Not critical, but do you remember when I had you pose for a profile painting the second year we worked from Nonsuch Island?"

"I remember."

"I knew I wanted to do that painting before I left New York. I went to the library and read your books. I found newspaper clippings from 1913. I wanted to know you better before I painted."

Will sipped his tea. "So, you learned about my first marriage…"

"To Mary Blair Rice, born 15 June 1880. Married you in 1902. A pretty woman who traveled the world with you…"

"And then betrayed me in 1913."

"I think we start with your Rainbow Gars," Else said. "This one you think is good to begin with?"

"Yes. The proportions of the fish are correct but close the gap between them. The scarlet coloring on the heads ended abruptly. You have it feathered too much into the blue body, which needs to be lighter."

Else pulled a fresh page from her watercolor tablet. She sketched the four elongated shapes in tighter formation. "What were you looking for when you and Mary Blair were traveling?"

"Primarily birds. We finished our research on the pheasants after seventeen months circling the globe. It was a thrilling expedition that I could not have done without Blair."

"You called her Blair?"

"She preferred it, yes. We wrote two books together about our travels." Will paused, then continued. "You say, Mrs. B, that I'm brave. Blair was much braver. Her courage to sit with natives in British Guiana and Venezuela, each fascinated by her unblemished white skin, but distrusting our motives; only I understood the courage it took. We lived so primitively on a broken-down houseboat cruising the Amazon rivers."

"What were you looking for?" Else asked, listening but sketching.

"The truth. It's what we all want to know, Mrs. B. Why? Why are we here and how did we evolve into this menagerie of life?"

"I have asked many times, Dr. Beebe." She looked at him. "Did you find an answer in the Amazon?"

"I found an array of answers and four times the questions. There are so many forms of life, all of them dependent on other species, other flora, to sustain their lives. And we as humans, curious and destructive, are villains, enemies of nature."

"The irony of your words—your mission to find the truth in nature—still bothers me when I watch you capture or kill one of nature's creatures."

"I know. But to understand where we all came from, I must know how we are different. I couldn't explain it when you challenged me, Mrs. B, but I've thought about it many times since..."

"Go on, Dr. Beebe..."

"I must examine life down to its smallest detail–every form of life–if I am to set the stage for our answers..."

"Take a look at the gars. Are they spaced better? Does the light beam need a sharper edge?"

"Sharper, yes. You've spaced them perfectly. The eyes are smaller. Beady."

"Why did you and Blair begin your long expedition in search of pheasants? Is there something more revealing in the bird's evolution than in other life?"

"The principal reason we studied pheasants was because Colonel Kuser wanted me to and he was willing to pay for the entire expedition, which, as I said, took seventeen months."

"Who was Colonel Kuser?"

"Anthony Kuser, a millionaire, philanthropist, and an avid pheasant hunter…"

"More killing for sport; more irony, Dr. Beebe."

Will wiggled uncomfortably. "How are the Rainbow Gars coming?"

Else explained it was time to set them aside. She pulled up the Pallid Sailfish sketches and confirmed with Dr. Beebe which one was best to start.

"When did you begin your pheasant expedition?" Else asked.

"December 1909."

"I had been in America for two months," Else said. "I just married."

"An interesting coincidence, Mrs. B."

"Another time, Dr. Beebe. Where did you go first?"

"Our destination was Asia, but we left New York on the Lusitania…"

"The ship the German's sank during the war?"

"The same ship, yes. We landed in London, put together our supplies, sailed the Mediterranean to Egypt, through the Suez Canal, crossed the Indian Ocean and began our first adventure in Ceylon, headed for the Himalayas."

"You and Blair were established explorers by 1910 when you arrived. You spent seventeen months together doing what?"

"Finding, capturing, examining, and shipping pheasants—and other birds and animals—to the New York Zoological Park where my associates put them in cages for people to see."

"What knowledge did you gain about nature from your exercise, Dr. Beebe?"

Will waited to answer while watching Else shape the head of a sailfish centered in the beam of light. He told her it needed to be shorter and rounder.

"The trip solidified my belief that we must do all we can to rescue nature from human assault."

"Why do you think it's difficult to do that?" she asked.

"Our world population is exploding, Mrs. B. As we build homes, factories, cities, destroy forests to grow food, dig for coal and ores, and now drill for oil, we are upsetting the balance that existed in our ecological system for centuries. Certain species are already becoming extinct because of our haste to gorge our human needs, so if we don't pay attention, more animals and plants will disappear from nature."

"I can think of a few animals I would not miss. Rattlesnakes, for instance. They were all over Texas."

"Texas, Mrs. B?"

"Continue your thoughts, Dr. Beebe. I want to hear more about your concerns for our future."

Else held up her sketch of the sailfish. "The light beam crosses the fish from the top left to the middle right, correct?"

"Yes, that's correct," Will replied.

"So, like many things, my research has evolved from ornithology to oceanography and ichthyology quite naturally."

"Do you think your interest in the flying fish has anything to do with your passion for birds?"

"Yes, in fact, I think it does."

"In what way? Before she let him continue, she asked, "Does this color seem right?"

"More warmth," he replied. "Darwin upset many religious leaders and followers, including my own mother. But he made strong points about natural evolution. He concentrated on man, but at one point in our world's development, water covered the planet. There were no animals roaming on land, so there were no apes that became humans. Not yet."

"When was the Earth covered by water? And how old is our planet?"

"I don't think anyone can pin it down, Mrs. B. In the 1800s, Lord Kelvin said the Earth is one-hundred million years old. Then Marie Curie discovered radioactivity in 1898 that measured time through geological studies."

"And did that prove Lord Kelvin correct?"

"The opposite. Between Darwin's theories and Madam Curie's discovery, it was clear the Earth was much older. Some say as much as one-point-six billion years, sixteen times older than Lord Kelvin estimated."

"Could it be older?" Else held up the Pallid Sailfish for Dr. Beebe's approval.

Will nodded his consent. "I think so, Mrs. B. The universe had to exist before our solar system. Others have estimated the universe to be several billion years old."

Else reached for the pile of anglerfish sketches. "So, the world is covered in water, when does man appear? Perhaps the Bible is correct. God created Adam and Eve and placed them after parting the seas. Do you believe in God, Dr. Beebe?"

"I do. But let's step back to your question. Let's assume man appears along with thousands of other forms of life at an evolutionary pace. That does not mean God isn't controlling the pace, isn't creating man and his environment just the way He wants it…"

"…or She wants it." Else held up her new drawing of the Three-starred Anglerfish."

"Yes, that's the shape of the pair I saw pass the bathysphere window. Dark all around; their three stars bright enough to illuminate them."

"Go on," Else insisted. "How did we get here? And when?"

"I've been asking that question for the past twenty years, Mrs. B. And I have a theory."

"The fish and I are listening, Dr. Beebe."

"My thoughts brought me to the oceans for answers. It's why I want to explore the deep; why that anglerfish is so important to me."

"Do you hear that, Mr. Anglerfish…?"

"The new Earth, covered in fresh water with its core of hot gases and molten chemistry, nourished a single cell. Water and submerged rock produce a source of food for that cell. After time, the cell unites with similar cells to become an organism with the capability of pulling oxygen, sodium, and nitrogen from the water and rock. So, in the first billion years, living creatures begin to swim, evolve, and survive the Earth's violent guts that heave gases and more rocks from below the water. It created mountains that began to affect the flow of huge water masses."

"We know Bermuda is the peak of one of those mountains," Else added.

"It is. And continents formed as the water evaporated, receded and became salty. When that was occurring, living creatures from the sea found food sources at the land's edge. Vegetation grew from new cells that rose with the land. Animals in the sea soon left the water for short periods of time to gather this new food source. Maybe fifty million years later, they had legs and long necks to reach the vegetation that had gotten taller and bigger from the warmth of the sun and constant watering from the sky."

"Is this God's work you're describing?"

"Maybe so. What do you think?"

"I think God grew and evolved as well," Else said. "Notice the light on the back of the front fish reflected from its luminescent stars and bouncing from the face of the second fish. That's the way I heard you describe them. Do you like it?"

"Yes. Your pens and colors are inside my memory once more, Mrs. B. I don't know how you do it. You've given them life."

"I will improve them when I'm less tired, but I hope you can stay and tell me more while I clean up. I'm enjoying your story. It's believable. But when does man appear?"

"I will get there soon enough. What do you know about the surface of the Earth now?"

"It's two-thirds water."

"Correct. Do you know that you're made up of about the same percentage of water as our Earth?"

"I knew we were largely water, but I didn't realize the coincidence in the amount."

"A fish, on the other hand, is more water. You might expect that."

"How much more?"

"Eighty-three percent versus our seventy percent."

"You're getting to another point I can tell, Dr. Beebe."

"When animal life emerged from the sea to gather new food, it had to enclose its circulatory system, no longer using the ocean water for circulation. Humans can no longer drink sea water to survive, but we also can't put fresh water into our veins without risking death."

"But saline solution can be fed to our bodies as a substitute for blood for a short period," Else said. "That I know from my physical science studies thirty-five years ago."

"Yes, that was an important fact during wartime," Will commented. "As we pinpoint when salts of the sea were at levels that match the saline in our bloodstreams, we may learn when animals emerged from the sea independent of its life-sustaining waters."

"You're implying that life came from the sea. The only living creatures were fish at some point millions, perhaps billions of years ago."

"Yes, Mrs. B, and that's why our expedition in search of our deep-sea ancestors is important. That's why the evolution of pheasants was important. That's why preserving every creature is important. They are kin. They all fit in the cycle of life. When we force their extinction because of our human neglect, human greed, and human intolerances, God's planet is at risk of dying because man murdered nature."

"You seem to predict a doomsday, Dr. Beebe. I'm chilled thinking that it may be near."

"The more we learn, the better our chances of preventing it, Mrs. B. I'm not giving up on my fellow humans, but I've seen more events in recent years that alarm me."

"Like what, Dr. Beebe?"

"Like the war. Wars are destructive. They've never solved a conflict. They just prove who can build a better arsenal. Like poorly managed industrial growth. Governments are failing to regulate how factories build without consideration of waste, because money clouds good judgement."

"I'm feeling depressed, Dr. Beebe. What do we do?"

"Provide the skill of your art. Your skills mean the Department of Tropical Research and the New York Zoological Society can tell its story more effectively."

"Dr. Beebe, you're a wonderful man. I am pleased to help. Do you mind if I make an observation that is very personal?"

"Do I have a choice, Mrs. B?"

"You must not carry your heartbreak any longer. You are loved and needed by so many people. I must include myself. It hurts me to see you carry the memory of Blair in your soul."

William Beebe sat in silence for a moment unsure whether he wanted to discuss Blair with his artist. "Is it that obvious, Mrs. B?"

"What is obvious is that you fight to stay young and stay in love with women who remind you of your life with her. Miss Hollister, Miss Crane, even the current Mrs. Beebe have qualities and youth that keep you clinging to Blair's memory. They all love you, but you cannot love them all equally."

"I don't love them the same. But they are all important to me."

"Yes, they're important to you, but not as important as your work…"

Will frowned to express his disagreement.

"…They love you, Dr. Beebe, because you make life important. I worry that you increase your risks, you live too dangerously, because you're not satisfied. Live happy. You make others happy, so be satisfied, Dr. Beebe."

CHAPTER 64

Luminescent Lights

The Atlantic Ocean was calm for mid-August. The weather station in Bermuda said it would stay that way.

Will Beebe alerted Otis Barton at the St. George's Hotel and Captain Jimmie Sylvester at his favorite pub. They both appeared on time at Darrell and Meyer Wharf.

The crew departed at 7:25 with Sylvester at the helm of the *Gladisfen* and the DTR staff aboard the *Ready*, including Beebe, Tee-Van, Hollister, Crane, Bass, and Ramsey with Otis Barton, his cinematographer, and publicist John Long of National Geographic Society.

Captain Sylvester steered the tugboat and barge to the spot where Will and Otis completed their deepest record-setting dive of the past four seasons. Neither diver considered it their most memorable bathysphere experience, but it was still gratifying.

With the waters peaceful, Will set his goal for the day thinking about his last conversation with Mrs. Bostelmann. He appeared focused and more attentive to those around him.

The *Gladisfen* drew a semi-circle in the ocean with its bow aimed back at Nonsuch Island. The *Ready* followed while John directed preparations of the manhole cover. They cleaned the wing bolts and lined the threads with white lead.

Otis loaded chemicals for moisture control and carbon dioxide reduction. Will handed him the two oxygen tanks and stepped aside so Barton's cinematographer could hand Otis his sixteen-millimeter camera.

At 9:50, Will and Otis climbed into their submersible and wiggled around the concave bottom to find legroom and comfortable positions. Four-hundred pounds of steel eased onto the ten bolts and the pounding began.

With the noise reverberating inside the bathysphere, Otis began a diatribe: "The story about our record dive said little about me, Dr. Beebe. We did the dive together. We set the record together…"

"I know, Otis. I try every time I speak to reporters to praise you for what you've done for DTR and me…"

"Please try harder, Dr. Beebe. I'm trying to produce a film that talks about our exploits, but no one will pay to see it if they don't know I was with you during every one of these dives."

Fifteen minutes passed and the bathysphere lifted airborne on its Roebling cable. It swung as a matter of course toward starboard. When past the rail, the ball began its drop to the glassy surface below. The turquoise silhouette disappeared at ten fathoms.

"That might have been the smoothest entry we've ever made…" Will reported to Gloria.

The changing colors continued to thrill the director. The sunbeams danced around the *Ready's* hull, sending arrows of yellows, blues, and greens darting in every direction. They lasted only a few seconds.

Light inside the ball quickly faded. Only casts of dark green and blue hung inside until they too were gone. Outside the submersible, *Aurelia aurita*–jellyfish–floated as ballerinas, tranquil as the sea itself.

In preparation to film, Otis looked through his quartz-glass window spotting pteropods, swimming snails with little interest in the monster bathysphere. He turned on his beam that shot yellow streaks, leaving a lavender glow. Nothing extraordinary came into view as they descended past five-hundred feet.

At just below six-hundred feet, Will saw the first sparks of light like those of shrimp crashing into his window. A close explosion made Will jerk back.

"An abundance of copepods. Sagitta. Larval fish too," Will recited.

Plankton and copepods became so thick at seven-hundred feet, Will called them a "mist," describing the color as turquoise that ran half the length of their light beam.

Will reported seeing strings of salpa and siphonophores at eight-hundred feet. Then six cyclothones swam together, small fish about three inches long, which Will described as among the ugliest and most abundant fish in the sea.

He leaned against the wall of the bathysphere as he tried to follow the cyclothones' bioluminescence when he blurted, "Damnation that's cold!"

"Will, anything wrong?" Gloria asked.

"No. I touched the side of the bathysphere. The outside temperature must have dropped quickly. The wall is freezing cold."

He reported additional flashes of lights in the distance, but fish sightings declined as they dropped below one-thousand feet. At one-thousand one-hundred feet, another group of *Aurelia* surprised him.

Will told Gloria the descent through one-thousand five-hundred feet seemed ordinary. At sixteen hundred forty feet, the bathysphere entered a school of large shrimp. Comfortable seeing the species explode when the ball trespassed their territory, he was intent on watching more closely to learn what occurred.

Rather than looking at the front of the approaching body, he set his eyes behind the shrimp. When the crustacean exploded, Will noticed a cloud of debris discharged violently by the illuminated body. It reminded him of gunpowder sparks fired from a musket. The suddenness gave the shrimp time to dart away from danger, a magician's trick making the eye blink while jumping behind a curtain of darkness.

"That explains it," he told Gloria.

Two hundred feet deeper, Will reported seeing another small fish, but this one with teeth lit brightly. Black between the teeth. Then siphonophores, eight inches long, with bright bioluminescent lights. A mass of color and floating sea flesh, thicker, but with similar texture to jellyfish.

As the bathysphere approached two-thousand feet, Will told Gloria he saw several myctophids—lanternfish—that were five inches long providing bluish bioluminescence. In large numbers, they illuminated the area in front of Will's window without the divers' fifteen-hundred-watt light.

"Damn, that was startling!"

"What, Will?" Gloria asked.

"A lanternfish snuck up on a tiny red light, looking for food when this ugly head came from nowhere and grabbed the poor lanternfish in its long dagger-like teeth."

"What was it?"

"A great gulper eel. Had to be," Will said. "The mouth and head were wide, but the thin body was outlined in a faint green glow and circled in a floating string. Must have been four feet long when uncurled. The red light on the eel's tail lured the lanternfish."

Larger fish—twelve inches long—appeared at twenty-one hundred feet. Fully luminescent. Will described them as *Melanostomiatids*. That was the giant fish he saw during their

1932 dive. However, these were one-sixth the size with similar shape and similar lights across the sides of the body looking like portholes on a submarine. He asked Glo to remind him when he surfaced to search for the fish in his books.

A large, shadowy form appeared at twenty-four hundred feet. Will estimated the size at twenty feet long and seven feet thick. He couldn't determine if it was fish or cetacean—whale or huge porpoise. He begged it to come nearer.

"It's enormous, the largest figure we've seen at this depth," Will told Gloria. "But I can't trust identifying its species. Too far away, too clouded by distance."

At twenty-five hundred feet, less than two fathoms from their record-setting depth of four days earlier, Will and Otis did a check of the bathysphere.

"Pressure has pushed the electrical lines a quarter inch into the bathysphere," Otis reported. "Not enough to be concerned, Dr. Beebe. Oxygen level at fifteen-hundred pounds."

Otis looked at the gauges behind him. "Humidity sixty-three percent; barometer steady at seventy-six."

"The craft is good," Will told his associates over the telephone lines. "We're ready to go deeper."

Will and Otis felt the bathysphere move again. More shrimp bombarded their windows as they entered new underwater territory. Record territory.

"We're turning on the light to warm the bathysphere," Gloria heard Otis say in the background. "Our wires have pushed into about half an inch. No apparent risk."

Nearing twenty-eight hundred feet, Will saw a long, slender fish with a pointed tail swimming nearby. "This is a big fish. I can see that much."

When Otis turned off the spotlight, Will closed his eyes and allowed them to adjust to the darkness once more. He opened them to an array of lights and flashes. Then the larger fish, three feet long, swam slowly by Will's window.

"Crescent-shaped lights under its eye. Pale green. Swimming so slowly, I can make out its entire light pattern, close lines of lighted plates."

A loud metallic twang in his headset alarmed Will. It was followed by a series of screams and shouts from crewmembers aboard the *Ready*.

"Glo, what's happening?" He heard more background shouts then silence. "Gloria! Talk to me!"

Barton's eyes widened. "Is there trouble?"

"Gloria…!"

"It's okay, Will. The guy rope that helps the Roebling cable wind properly on the *Arcturus* winch snapped. Some of the crew were standing close. It frightened us when it whipped around."

"Anyone hurt?"

"No. But, Will, you're at three-thousand feet. Maybe four-hundred feet of cable left on the winch. I can see a few inches of core."

"Then stop us, Glo. Let us sit here a few minutes. Otis has the light on. Let's see what's here."

Captain Sylvester leaned out his wheelhouse window and yelled at Tee-Van. "No farther. Don't let that cable run out. That ball weighs too much at that depth and with that much cable exposed, we can't trust the winch to hang on."

The entire crew and staff heard the captain. They could hear the pulleys creak under the added weight. One crewman put his hand on the winch. "It's hot, Captain."

"Tell Dr. Beebe we need to bring him up," Captain Sylvester yelled to John and Gloria. "Get another guy rope on the winch. Now!" he ordered the crew.

"Will, we need to bring you up. We're concerned up here."

"Okay, Glo. I'm not in any hurry though. At these depths, the fish seem more willing to stick around the bathysphere. We're getting some of the best views so far."

The *Ready* crew worked swiftly attaching a new rope across the winch. The rope enabled three-thousand feet of steel to wind evenly onto the heavy spool. When the crew had the guy rope in place, they signaled the captain and Tee-Van.

"We're starting you up, Will," John said over his headset.

William Ramsey operated the steam engine that drove the *Arcturus* winch. "Everyone clear?" Ramsey asked before pushing the rod into forward gear. Without waiting too long, he made the winch tighten the cable, the pulleys and boom responding.

When they had the bathysphere at twenty-nine hundred feet to remove the marker tie, the guy rope snapped again. With the same frightening noise and violent whipping, the rope slapped against the deck floor. Ramsey froze the winch.

"We've had another break in the guy rope, Will," Gloria reported.

Captain Sylvester shouted orders to get another rope across the winch.

"The luminescent lights are as thick as I've seen them, Glo," Will said. "An eight-inch squid with pale blue lights just swam by. I could see the whole body from lights cast by other fish."

"They have the guy rope attached again, Will," John interrupted. "You'll be moving."

Ramsey revved the engine and pushed the rod. The gears clanged and the cable began its crawl onto the winch.

While the bathysphere rose, Will continued to provide narration describing additional sightings. Otis contributed commentary as well.

Ascending through twenty-five-hundred feet, Will said he saw a fish less than a foot long and "peppered with brilliant but small lights. It's like staring at a miniature cosmos."

Out of danger with another five-hundred feet of cable wound on the winch, Captain Sylvester let the world know William Beebe and Otis Barton had set another distance record under his command. He blew the *Gladisfen* whistle and soon had the *Ready* echo blasting.

"Can you hear that, Will?" John asked.

"What was the official distance, Gloria?"

"Jocelyn says three-thousand twenty-eight feet, Will," Gloria told him. "She says it occurred at 11:23."

"I show we're at 11:45 now," Will said, seeking confirmation.

"That's the time I have too, Will," John verified.

Will had his eyes on Otis, who was looking at his watch and nodding agreement.

"We set a new depth record of three-thousand twenty-eight feet, Otis," Will said. "Captain Sylvester's blasting his whistle."

"Congratulations, Dr. Beebe."

Will held out his hand. Otis shook it. "Congratulations to you. I hope your film picked up some of those illuminated fish. They were spectacular."

The *Arcturus* winch cranked steadily for an hour, winding the remaining twenty-five hundred feet of cable and lifting the bathysphere from the Atlantic. The boom swung out and pulled the heavy ball from the water. It swung easily across the deck before setting down.

John approached it quickly to loosen the four-inch center plug on the manhole plate. His hired crewmen worked on the ten nuts. They had the plate removed in five minutes with Will emerging first.

He reached his arms out to brace his awkward exit trying not to scrape his cramping legs across the sharp bolts. Otis followed, reaching and stumbling too.

When they stood and stretched out their cramps, publicist John Long made them pose next to their submersible and the words National Geographic Society. The two record-setting explorers offered tired smiles.

Long took several shots while Barton's cinematographer ran off a hundred feet of film. John, Gloria, and Jocelyn stood behind the photographers cheering.

Long made Captain Sylvester pull the *Gladisfen* alongside the *Ready*, anchor the two boats together, and jump aboard the barge. He took a full group picture with the DTR staff, hired assistants, and the captain's crew.

Captain Sylvester returned to his tug and steered it to the front, slowly letting out his towline and easing it tighter for the journey to additional dive spots. The crew aboard the *Ready* went back to work laying out the rubber-coated cable so it would be organized.

After additional dives, the boats headed north, sailing near the *Monarch of Bermuda*. Captain Sylvester, a drinking partner to Commander Francis of the *Monarch*, sent his friend a wire announcing Dr. Beebe's accomplishment. He said he'd give the *Monarch* passengers a close view of the bathysphere if Commander Francis would open up his ship broadside. Francis announced Beebe's record and his intentions.

Captain Sylvester aimed the *Gladisfen* at the luxury liner, then veered left so the starboard bow of the *Ready* opened to the waving passengers. At the maneuver, Sylvester blew his whistle, followed by a loud series of blasts from the *Monarch*.

Will Beebe waved to the passengers, many of them pointing at him and the blue bathysphere resting behind him. Otis waved from the stern where he stood with his filming associate. With camera mounted on a tripod, they filmed Dr. Beebe and crew in the foreground of the passing *Monarch*. They recorded cheers and the commander's horn blasts.

The luxury liner disappeared behind them as tug and barge turned back on course for St. George's Harbor cutting through the *Monarch's* wake.

Will kept busy reviewing Gloria's notes. When John joined him, Will told him there was no further need to dive beyond a half mile. His dive below three-thousand feet was enough.

"Are you suggesting we store the bathysphere?" John asked.

"No, we have sufficient budget for a few more deep dives. You need to go with me on at least one of them."

John felt a rush of excitement. He didn't want Will to disappoint him if the situation changed.

"Do you think the dive will satisfy Mr. Grosvenor?" John asked the director.

"I should think so," Will replied. "I have to finish my article for his magazine. I have plenty to write following this adventure. Three-thousand feet, John. It's not the mile I wanted to achieve when Teddy and I commiserated, but knowing what it takes to manage such depths, I'd say we accomplished something quite remarkable."

John glanced at Otis struggling with his camera and tripod and talking with his cinematographer. "It matters to him only because his name will appear in the newspaper, Will. He doesn't seem content with anything other than fame, but we wouldn't be standing here if he hadn't come to you with his invention."

"You're right, but I don't mind saying I'm just as disappointed in him as I am grateful. The voyages can be quite stimulating and educational. He missed those pleasures entirely."

An excited Jocelyn joined the men's conversation. Gloria trailed.

"Glo and I finished our clean-up chores, Will," Jocelyn said, then wrapped the director in a physical hug, nearly knocking him over. As she pulled away, "I was so nervous and excited when you reached three-thousand feet. I'm so proud of you."

"The three of you deserve more credit than I can ever repay. I have the deepest trust in my staff."

"We trust each other too, Will," Gloria said. "But I wasn't so sure of the equipment when the guy rope snapped the first time. It was so loud, I thought it was the cable."

"I did too," Jocelyn sobbed.

"I was telling John we do not need to achieve any further records. The life I saw at three-thousand feet I can see at two thousand, even fifteen hundred. We dive for discovery, for information, not because it creates a milestone."

"You're the boss," Gloria said. "We could discover more if we had two sets of eyes down there, rather than one set and an ego with a camera."

"I'll work on that, Glo. I will take John with me next," Will said."

"I would enjoy going again, Will," Gloria said. "But I'm not eager to dive with Otis if that's part of the condition."

"If he's not getting anything useful with his camera, I'm not sure he's interested in any further dives."

"It's a better use of our funds if he doesn't go," Jocelyn added.

"Be ready to dive, Glo. I'll see what Otis wants to do. And when we get back, I want you to bring your notes and sit with me while I work on a few new sketches with Mrs. Bostelmann."

Will handed Gloria's notebook back to her. She and John left Will and Jocelyn to help the crew as the boats entered St. George's Harbor.

"I could use another hug now," Will told Jocelyn. She responded without hesitation.

"That was so exciting," Jocelyn told him. "I admit I was terrified, though, when Glo told you she could see the core of the winch when you reached three-thousand. I looked at it and noticed the noises it was making, especially when Ramsey started to pull you up."

"I couldn't tell, but I'm noticing someone looking at us now."

Jocelyn quickly turned around. She saw John Long taking their picture.

"He has what Gershwin calls "a crush on you," Will said.

"He's cute, but he's not my type."

"And what's your type?"

She smiled. "Brave ocean explorers."

CHAPTER 65

Clearer Pictures

S ounds of success reached New Nonsuch long before the *Skink* bumped up against the Ferry Reach dock. Water splashed the pilings as the boat settled. A truck crossed the famous Swing Bridge honking its horn for Dr. Beebe and staff.

Else had her table cleared. She straightened her stacks of watercolor paper ready to begin her work. Excited and a little nervous to see Dr. Beebe, she twisted when the laboratory door opened. Gloria Hollister entered.

"Will is coming soon, Mrs. B," Gloria announced. "He sent me ahead to go over his notes. He made me dive with Otis this afternoon. I was so irritated, but I set a record for women. We stopped at twelve-hundred-eight feet. We barely talked. I would have enjoyed total silence. The sights, the fish were better than ever."

"Congratulations, Miss Hollister, for your record and your tolerance. How did Dr. Beebe do?"

"Will set a new distance record too. That's what the horns were about when we entered St. George's Harbor."

"I heard them," Else said. "I took the sounds to be good news."

"Three-thousand twenty-eight feet, Mrs. B. I thought he was going to run out of cable and we'd never get him back."

"Oh, Mein Gott! What did you do?"

"Captain Sylvester intervened. He told us we had to stop the descent and bring them up."

"I'm so glad, Miss Hollister. It would have been terrible if you couldn't do anything to save Dr. Beebe after all this."

"I know, Mrs. B. The steam engine on the winch sounded like it was going to explode it worked so hard to reverse the cable."

Else sketched nervously drawing the Lidgerwood drum that Miss Hollister put it in her mind, but Else had other topics to discuss… "I scolded Dr. Beebe."

"Scolded him, Mrs. B?"

"I told him I worried about his motives for doing courageous things.

"I'm not sure I understand…"

"I've thought about it. His expeditions place him in dangerous situations. They started with Blair when they traveled the world."

"His first wife?"

"Then Blair left him, put a note on the table and left him for Mr. Niles, their neighbor and Dr. Beebe's friend. She didn't even say goodbye. Do you know why?"

"No, Mrs. B. I've never talked to Will about his first wife."

"…He loved his work too much. He loved it more than he was able to love his wife. And he continues to love it more than Mrs. Beebe, or you, or Jocelyn. But he's attracted to all of you because you're young like Blair when she left him, when he loved her."

"Are you saying he's incapable of love? Because I've said something like that to him, but he's a good man, Mrs. B. He's been good to me; he's given me gifts and shared intimacy. He's a dedicated scientist, a good writer, a good everything…"

"Goodness does not mend hearts. I know what that feels like and how the pain torments the soul."

"That makes me sad, Mrs. B. What do we do? I can never dislike the man. He seems so satisfied, so excited with his success. And, yes, look what he's done for someone like me, a woman who would never have had an opportunity like this without him…"

"…yes, for me and Miss Crane too. He's a good person who cares for things we both appreciate. Nature and science. But his heart carries a burden. We must tell him he has achieved enough with his risks. He does not need to punish himself for failing to love enough."

"What do I say to Jocelyn, Mrs. B? She wants to be my friend, but she also wants Will to love her, love her more than me, which keeps me from the director."

"No one will take your place with Dr. Beebe. Do not be sad about losing love that was never enough to make you happy. That's the dissatisfaction Blair felt. You don't need to experience her pain, because Dr. Beebe does not mean to cause you pain."

"Are you sure, Mrs. B?"

"I'm sure of this: He loves his work the most."

The door opened to a quick-paced Will Beebe. "Have you talked about my new sightings, Glo?"

"No, Will. Mrs. B and I have been catching up on other issues."

"Show her your notes. Let's get started."

Gloria laid her notebook on Else's table. She opened it to when the bathysphere stopped to add the marker at twenty-nine hundred feet. "He wants to start here," she told Else.

"Is that where the gulper eel lured the lanternfish?" Will asked.

"Yes. Do you need me for this, Will? I'm tired. I have so many things to examine tomorrow. I think I'll just sleep on the cot upstairs."

"Go to bed, Glo. Mrs. B and I can work together."

"Thank you. Goodnight, Mrs. Bostelmann. Thank you for your advice. Goodnight, Dr. Beebe."

Will watched Gloria walk the length of the laboratory, open the door, and disappear. He turned to Else, "Has she been acting strangely to you, Mrs. B.?"

"No, Dr. Beebe."

Will accepted and picked up Gloria's notebook. "We stopped for a marker. We were more than three-hundred feet deeper than our record Saturday when this school of lanternfish came into our view. My eyes had readjusted to the dark after Otis turned off his light…"

"The background is dark blue…" Else began.

"…black. Maybe the slightest blue-black. I saw a faint dark red light. It looked like a scarlet arrow worm. The largest lanternfish, six inches long, approached the light, but before he could strike, an ugly eel's head, almost as wide as the fish was long, snared the fish. With its pointed phosphorus teeth sunk into it, the lanternfish glowed bluish gray. The light emitted allowed me to see the eel's thin body unfurling to a length of four feet, its tail still aglow."

Else had already sketched circles, ovals, and dashes of short lines. "Was the eel's head more round?" she asked.

"No, more oval. Oblong. Its jaw hinged low," Will explained. "The fish expressed fright."

Else drew and erased, drew more and erased again until she had the outline of the coiled eel and fish in its mouth. While searching his face for approval, she asked, "Were you thrilled to set a new distance record?" She kept refining the shape and filling in texture lines.

"My mind was on seeing these creatures in their habitat, Mrs. B. I think about where I am only to know at what depth the fish exist."

"I presume they're all carnivores that deep. No plants."

"Plankton. Small flesh. Life depending on finding flesh to eat, fish eating fish to survive."

Will looked over Else's shoulder at her progress. "I've thought about what you said last time, Mrs. B."

"What part, Dr. Beebe. We talked about many things."

"You implied that I live dangerously because I'm unhappy—I'm unhappy because Blair left me. I inferred you meant I don't use caution because life doesn't matter to me."

"Is that true, Dr. Beebe? I'm interested. Courage can look like a lack of caution. I don't think you've forgiven her. You haven't forgiven your young friend who fell in love with your wife and stole her."

"Forgive them, Mrs. B? They ripped the heart from my chest. Both of them."

"If you don't forgive them and forgive yourself for not seeing Blair's unhappiness because your work was more important, then you will carry pain in your heart to your death."

Will looked for a stool to sit. He pulled it up to Else's table. "Can't I be in pain and do my work?"

"Oh, Dr. Beebe. You sound like a martyr. Forgiveness is too easy."

"All right, Mrs. Bostelmann. How do I go about forgiving them when I'm still angry?"

"Dr. Beebe, I cannot answer your question. I had my own issue for which I needed help. My husband's death and abandonment angered me. I read Mary Baker Eddy's words and tried to forgive Monroe, so I could do what I needed to—care for myself and my daughter. My suggestion for you is to let go of resentment and trust the people you're with now."

"Referring to Mary Baker Eddy is worrisome, Mrs. B."

"Miss Hollister told me that your mother read Christian Science Key to the Scriptures."

"Tell me what happened, Mrs. Bostelmann. How did your husband die?"

Else recognized it was time to share her vulnerabilities to allow Dr. Beebe to be open to his.

"Monroe was a complex man, a handsome musician. A classically trained cellist destined to be among the best. His emotions were intense. I'm sure it made him a wonderful cellist. He felt the music and used his cello to express it…"

"…Monroe…"

"I know that's why I fell in love with him. He had some of your passions."

"Then I would have liked your husband, Mrs. B."

"…and he would have liked you, Dr. Beebe. I believe you would have understood him. I wish you'd met him in New York."

Will stayed silent for a moment.

"I'm sure I heard your husband play. We—Blair and I—had returned from British Guiana. It was late summer of '09. That I remember well. Blair struggled with her typewriter. Her wrist was not healed. She broke it falling from a hammock. Still, she typed. We were co-authoring *In Search of a Wilderness*. We had worked for fourteen hours straight. Robin Niles was our neighbor then. He knocked on our door around nine o'clock…"

Else put down her pencil and turned toward Will.

"…He said his friends were hosting a party in a pavilion across the street in Central Park. Robin chided us, said it was time for a break. He talked us into going."

Else recalled Monroe's letters in which he wrote about his string quartet. They played in Central Park during the summer's evenings.

"I remember the night well—a handsome cellist in the quartet, handsome and a superb musician. He had an aura, a way about him that made him stand out."

Else thought about Monroe's pleas for her to come to America so they could marry.

"Blair was beautiful. Even after a long day of work, her beauty survived. The musicians flirted. The cellist dedicated a song to her. Robin said I should tell the cellist that the pretty lady was my wife and that his dedication was disrespectful. He seemed upset. The musician flattered my bride. He didn't offend me."

When Else attended Monroe's concerts, she heard him dedicate music to various patrons. She thought it a kind gesture warranted to gain future employment.

"The musician came to our table and introduced himself. I had not recalled his name until you said it. Monroe. That was the cellist's name."

"I came to America to marry him in the fall of that year. He played in parlors across the city. Occasionally I was invited. I could see young women's admiration for Monroe. Perhaps lust as well…"

Will shifted on the stool and crossed his leg as Else continued…

"…When he came home late—perhaps better said, very early in the morning—I worried. But I thought I was pregnant, so I tried to put my jealousies out of mind. When he told me we needed to leave New York and that we were moving to Texas, I wondered if the cello was coming with us."

"Why did your husband choose Texas?"

"He had many interests. He tried to be entrepreneurial. He lost our money, so he decided he wanted to farm. Natural cotton farming. A musician from New York trained by the best in Berlin for twelve years, a prodigy now wanting to grow cotton near Waco, Texas, without the help of science."

"Didn't you object?"

"I was his wife. My English was poor. I followed him. We moved around the area, settling in a small town called Mexia.

People knew everyone in the community. Monroe spoke German fluently. We spoke German everywhere. The war started. Some wanted America to enter the war; some feared we would and their sons would be sent to fight. People complained about Monroe's politics. He defended the German people, not the Kaiser, but the people in Mexia didn't approve. Federal lawmen came twice to question Monroe's loyalty."

"Was he loyal to the United States, Mrs. Bostelmann? I was a pilot in France in 1917."

"He was a loyal American. His entire family, German descendants, were loyal to America. The government told the community, which didn't believe, so we struggled. He told me many times he was a failure. His soul was lost. He died in our car parked on a country road."

"I'm sorry, Mrs. Bostelmann."

"Such a proud man, so talented; confident playing his music. But he could not find himself and we will never know why. I became furious at him for abandoning us."

"Mrs. Bostelmann, I'm surrounded by friends, a successful wife, an outstanding staff discovering wonderful scientific facts. I've done well despite my personal anguish. Don't you think?"

"Dr. Beebe, you're separated from your wife half the year, you have trysts with young women, you take extraordinary risks to gain knowledge and fame, and you sell your accomplishments every opportunity so there will be enough money to do it all over again."

"You're making me sound villainous, Mrs. Bostelmann. I'm simply trying to record and preserve nature so we don't destroy our planet."

"The only person you could hurt is yourself, Dr. Beebe, and I fear you would if it helped your message."

Will looked at Else's sketch of the eel gripping the lanternfish in its teeth. "I don't want to be that fish. I don't want to be suckered and swallowed by something I didn't see coming."

"Forgive, Dr. Beebe. It's freeing. Love again trusting the person, not because she idolizes you, but because the partnership is fulfilling."

"All right, Mrs. Bostelmann. I will consider your advice no matter how uncomfortable it makes me."

"They're observations, suggestions, Dr. Beebe. You don't need advice; you need to listen to the God within you who can help you understand your anger."

Will stood. "There you go again using Mrs. Eddy's philosophy. I'll forgive you, Mrs. B!" he said emphatically. They both smiled.

"I told Jocelyn I would walk with her when I returned to the Biological Station. I'm late, Mrs. B."

"I will finish this tomorrow, Dr. Beebe. Do you have a boat? May I go with you to the station?"

"Yes, I have a small motorboat. Ride with me, Mrs. Bostelmann, but we're done talking about forgiveness and Mary Baker Eddy's teaching."

CHAPTER 66

Mein Freund
September 1934

Will kept his team busy throughout August and September although the deep-sea dives happened only twice more. On August 27, Will dove with John Tee-Van to fifteen-hundred-thirty-three feet. Will enjoyed watching John's excitement and child-like reaction to life in the deep-sea.

On September 11, he took Jocelyn Crane to eleven-hundred-fifty feet, fifty-eight feet short of Gloria's record for women. That same trip, he dove again with Otis Barton to fifteen-hundred feet. After that, Otis left Bermuda not saying anything more to his once-idol naturalist William Beebe.

Captain Sylvester's crew took the bathysphere off the *Ready* as summer came to an end. They placed it in storage at Darrell and Meyer Wharf until it could be secured for the trip back to New York.

However, it did not board the *Monarch of Bermuda* with Else Bostelmann. She had completed Dr. Beebe's paintings that he eagerly awaited to show *National Geographic Magazine's* Gilbert Grosvenor.

John carried Else's luggage loaded with her art supplies. He stepped carefully down the path to the dock ahead of Else who had a heavy carpetbag over her shoulder loaded with some of her favorite pens, brushes, and art books. Her trunk from the Biological Station was already aboard the *Skink*.

"Watch your step, Mrs. B," John instructed. "Our path has new rocks. They're still loose."

John loaded Else's luggage next to her trunk. She took a seat while he went to the helm. He started the engine as Perkins Bass unleashed the boat from the dock and jumped on.

The *Skink* plowed through the calm Ferry Reach waters, went under the Swing Bridge, and slipped into the ocean. Their destination: Hamilton and the luxury-liner docks.

Will arrived at New Nonsuch on his bicycle. He had come from the Biological Station ready for additional lab work.

Gloria sat at her table. She wiped tears from her eyes after watching the *Skink* pull away. She heard noises outside the lab door and peered into her microscope to look busy. Will entered. He saw Mrs. Bostelmann's cleared workspace.

"Glo, where's Mrs. B?"

"She left, Will. John's taking her to Hamilton."

"I wanted to say goodbye. I may not see her again."

"Are you going to let her work for Dr. Miner?" Gloria asked.

"It's not something I want, Glo. Roy's budget is bigger than ours. He can afford her."

"I understand budgets, Will, but her pictures.... People talk about them wherever I speak. They're irreplaceable reminders of what we accomplished."

"I agree, Glo."

Will picked up the jacket he had just thrown over his chair. "I may be too late, but I'm going to make an effort to thank her."

The director saw William Ramsey working at the dock. "Mr. Ramsey," he shouted from the house. "Is the motorboat fueled?"

"I think so, Dr. Beebe."

"Start it," Will said. "I want you to take me to Hamilton."

Will ran down the path to the dock. "How long ago did the *Skink* depart?"

"It's been at least ten minutes, Dr. Beebe. We'll never catch them in this boat if that's what you wanted to do."

"We'll do our best, Mr. Ramsey. Do our best."

John circled the peninsula at Pembroke Parish and entered Hamilton Harbor. Else could see the *Monarch's* three smokestacks. The sight was comforting but sad to look at too.

A few minutes later, John had the *Skink* against an open dock. Bass jumped out to attach the boat. John leaped out and offered his hand to help Else climb out. A porter pushing a hand cart approached and asked if she needed her luggage carried to the check-in station.

"Thank you, young man."

Perkins Bass vaulted into the *Skink* and handed Else's luggage first. With help from John, they got her trunk onto the porter's cart, who toted it toward the station.

Else thanked Mr. Bass for his aid and gave John Tee-Van a long hug.

"I hope to see you soon, Mrs. B. Please give Hada my best."

"I will do that, Mr. Tee-Van. You tell Mrs. Tee-Van we're thinking of her. You're wonderful people. But go now. I don't want to be emotional, and I know you have things to do."

John kissed her cheek. He turned and climbed back into the *Skink* while Perkins set it free and jumped in behind John.

William Ramsey had the throttle wide open. The engine whined and spewed oil fumes as it chugged through the Atlantic shoreline rocking dangerously.

As the boat neared the point at Pembroke, Will spotted the *Skink* heading the opposite direction. He stood, knees bent, waving for John to see them.

"John! Slow down. Come here," Will yelled.

John eased back on the *Skink's* throttle and let it settle in the water. Will directed Ramsey to pull alongside the larger boat.

"Switch places with me, Mr. Bass. You ride back to New Nonsuch with Mr. Ramsey. I want John to take me to the Hamilton docks."

Bass and Ramsey held tight to the two boats as they bounced in the water. Will climbed into the *Skink* after which Perkins Bass swung his legs into the smaller craft.

"Slow down now, Mr. Ramsey. Stay closer to the shore where the water is smoother," Will said. "Please get me to Hamilton, John. I want to say goodbye to Mrs. B."

John sped up the *Skink* and whipped around the boys, sending a wake that rocked them as they waved to the director.

The *Monarch* was scheduled to leave Hamilton in an hour. People boarded so they could find their cabins, drop their carry-on items, and climb to the upper decks for the view.

Still on the dock, Else completed her check-in and put her claim tickets in her carpetbag. When she turned, there was Dr. Beebe galloping towards her.

"Mrs. B, I lost track of the days. I forgot that today was your departure. I'm so sorry."

"It's quite all right, Dr. Beebe. I know you have many things to accomplish before the weather turns."

"Nothing is more important than sending you home with my sincerest appreciation. Your artwork this year was the best. It's certain to please Mr. Grosvenor. It pleases *me*. Else. Mein Freund."

"Oh, Dr. Beebe, you're going to make me cry."

Will enveloped Else with a bear hug. "Your frankness these last few months has made me think, Else. Painful at times, but also cathartic. We've made an excellent team. Whether we'll be able to get people to hear the message, I'm not sure yet…"

"Dr. Beebe, talking with you has cleared some of my own regrets that I did not realize I was still holding on to."

"Really, Else? You seem to be so sure of yourself…"

"No, Dr. Beebe. I realize that I'm hiding behind what appears to be confidence. I'm very angry, angrier than I realized, and I've not been able to express it. I saw it as weak."

"I hope you're not angry with me. I would be deeply disappointed…"

"Of course not. I'm angry with Monroe. I told you that, but I'm angrier with myself for loving the musician, but not the man he was. I failed our marriage, Dr. Beebe. That became aware to me when I was trying to make you see that you haven't forgiven Miss Rice. I am holding Monroe fully responsible for the difficulty we lived through. For his death. I stopped caring for Monroe when his passion for his music faded and new ambitions that confused me came between us. Why? Why did the man who made such beautiful music give up? Why did he give up on life?"

"Those are heavy burdens, Else. You've helped me lift some of mine. I wish I had better insights to share with you."

"I've made progress, Dr. Beebe. You needn't worry. I have you to thank for that. If you hadn't been in my life attracting so many women with your charm and fame – including me – then I may never have thought about my relationship with the man I loved."

Will thought about Else's proclamation. She was attracted to him. He usually knew when an admirer coveted their moments alone. It made him uncomfortable thinking about the hours he and Else spent together.

"I should go, Dr. Beebe," Else said.

"Is it all right if I tell you I don't want you to leave?" Will asked. "I'm not trying to make the moment more difficult for either of us, but I'm afraid to see you go. You've become quite important to me, Else."

"You *are* making it difficult."

Else pulled a handkerchief from her purse and padded the corner of her eyes. She took Dr. Beebe's hand and held it, looking at their hands together. She lifted her eyes to his.

"I miss love, Dr. Beebe. I don't want you to miss it too. It's more than sharing a bed. It's a comfort that is hard to describe and harder to get back once you've lost it. I lost it because I was young and inexperienced."

"I lost it too, Else…"

"…but you have a chance to regain it, Dr. Beebe. You must let the past be in the past. Forgive. I thought I had, but I'm not sure I did it well. Perhaps we both have to keep forgiving over and over, because the pain has been that great."

William Beebe breathed heavily. Still holding Else's hand, Will pulled her closer and hugged her tightly. "You keep giving me more to think about, Else."

They remained embraced when the ship's whistle blast reminded Else she had to board. Will released her reluctantly.

"You have a lot to accomplish, Dr. Beebe," Else told him. "No one can make people understand what's at stake like you can. Your words are so precise. Your passion is so infectious. You've proven with your courage – the courage that frightens me – that your theories were correct. But as you show the world how important our oceans are to our lives, you must have a plan to protect the seas from people. For that reason, we need you to live. Be at peace and live."

"I will, Else. You've helped me understand the limits I've created by holding onto resentment. You are my wrasse and I am your parrotfish. Love, not symbiosis."

"Goodbye, Dr. Beebe. If not now, your discoveries and your passion will surely make a difference in the future."

They kissed each other's cheeks, hugged, and Will watched Else depart.

ABOUT THE PEOPLE

When researching the historical events as I prepared to write *Beebe and Bostelmann*, I discovered dozens of interesting lives. Each had a story of his/her own that is worth noting.

Charles William Beebe, b. 29 July 1877; d. 4 June 1962. After his record dive on Aug. 15, 1934, Beebe continued to lead his Department of Tropical Research efforts in Bermuda, but also expanded his expeditions to the Pacific. He remained active throughout his 84 years writing 24 books and more than 800 articles in addition to publishing a four-volume monograph about pheasants. He gave several critters their official scientific names when identifying their unique species traits. Although he attended Columbia University from around 1896 to 1899, he did not graduate. However, he was granted two honorary doctorates from Tufts and Colgate.

Elswyth Thane (Helen Ricker) Beebe, b. 16 May 1900; d. 31 July 1984. Elswyth Thane wrote more than 30 books and plays in her lifetime. She retired to a farm home in Vermont with Beebe, although he spent much of his time in the Caribbean. Beebe willed half his estate to Thane, the remainder reportedly went to DTR and Jocelyn Crane who cared for him at his death in Trinidad. He is buried there.

Mary **Blair Rice**, b. 15 June 1880; d. 13 April 1959. Blair and Will Beebe were married 6 Aug. 1902 despite Nettie Beebe's objections to the marriage. Blair and Will traveled extensively on expeditions for the New York Zoological Society, both writing articles and collaborating on two books. Blair left Will for their neighbor, a younger man, Robert (Robin) Niles in 1913. Niles was the nephew of a NYZS board member. Blair's divorce and marriage to Niles became front-page news in New York City. Blair Niles published several books and co-founded the Society of Woman Geographers to which Gloria Hollister and Amelia Earhart became members.

Jocelyn Crane, b. 11 June 1909; d. 16 Nov. 1998. Jocelyn continued her zoology research throughout her life recognized for her work in carcinology, which Wikipedia describes as "the study of crustaceans, a group of arthropods that includes lobsters, crayfish, shrimp, krill, copepods, barnacles and crabs. She married Donald Griffin, a fellow zoologist, in 1965 although she spent much of her time with William Beebe up to his death. She became assistant director of Beebe's Department of Tropical Research and was given an honorary master's degree in zoology from Smith College. In retirement, at 82, she earned a doctorate in Art History from New York University.

Gloria Hollister, b.11 June 1900; d. 19 Feb. 1988. Gloria led her own expedition to Guyana (aka British Guiana) in 1936 after securing most of the funding through her lectures and speeches on behalf of DTR and NYZS, today known as Wildlife Conservation Society. She married engineer Anthony Anable in 1941. She joined the American Red Cross at the start of World War II, speaking on its behalf and raising money. She helped fund the first Red Cross

Blood Center in Brooklyn. With Anable, she co-founded the Mianus River Gorge project in Connecticut where the Anables lived. Together, they encouraged the Department of the Interior to recognize the gorge as the first natural history landmark.

I spotted Gloria recently in a 1920 photograph of the American Field Hockey All-Star team that competed internationally. However, I regret that none of the ladies was identified.

Frederick **Otis Barton**, b. 5 June 1899; d. 15 April 1992. Otis completed his film, "Titans of the Deep," about deep-sea diving in 1938. He used Will Beebe's name to promote the movie, which Beebe objected to in New York newspapers. The film was not a box-office hit. So, Otis returned to engineering another submersible that he used in 1949 to eclipse the Beebe/Barton record by diving to 4,500 feet. He also wrote a book about deep-sea adventures and did rain forest exploring about the same time Will Beebe shifted his focus back to the Amazon.

Else (Winkler von Röder) **Bostelmann**, b. 10 Nov. 1882; d. 25 December 1961. Else published additional paintings in National Geographic Magazine for Roy Miner beginning in 1934. In addition, her painting style became popular as book illustrations, especially for children's books. She collaborated on several. She retired to Darien, Connecticut, and for a short time wrote a gardening column for the local newspaper.

Gertraude Hadumodt (Hada) **Bostelmann**, b. 1911; d. Hada converted her art training into becoming an art director for advertising agencies, including J. Walter Thompson. She married Charles Crumpton, but they divorced. They had a son.

Ida (Bostelmann) Cobb, b. 1894; d. 1979. Ida wrote several musical compositions mostly for piano solos although she did write some for piano and cello. She married Edward Cobb in 1932.

Cecilia (Bostelmann) **Fassett, b.** 1885; d. 20 July 1976. Cecilia and her husband, Truman, were among the first to assist Else and Hada when her eldest brother, Monroe, died in 1920. (Cecilia also played the cello) She and Truman helped Else and Hada return to New York and with Else finding employment.

Truman Fassett, 9 May 1885; d. 3 March 1970 in Sarasota, Florida. Truman, a 1909 graduate of Cornell, studied art under various mentors from New York City, Boston, and Paris. The Fassetts moved to Sarasota, Florida, around 1929. His landscapes are what he became most noted for.

John Tee-Van, b. 6 July 1897; d. 5 Nov. 1967. John began work for William Beebe when he was 14 out of necessity. His father, Patrick, also employed at the zoo, died unexpectedly, which put financial responsibilities on John. He met Helen Damrosch at work. They married soon after. John advanced in the New York Zoological Society's hierarchy, becoming general director of the zoo in 1952. After 10 years on the job, he retired and returned to DTR as an ichthyologist.

Helen (Damrosch) **Tee-Van**, b. 1893; d. 1976. Helen contributed many paintings of fish and aquatic life for the New York Zoological Society and Will Beebe's Department of Tropical Research. Later, she used her skills to paint murals and wrote and illustrated several books.

Henry Fairfield Osborn, b. 8 Aug. 1857; d. 6 Nov. 1935. The son of a prominent railroad tycoon, Osborn's science background inspired his leadership with many related organizations. Along with his New York Zoological Society role, he presided over the New York Museum of Natural History for 25 years and was a leading proponent of eugenics. He is the Columbia University professor who recruited Will Beebe to leave school and become assistant curator of birds at the zoo. Will had just turned 21. Osborn's views about evolution were challenged, especially when his theories about the so-called Pliocene era drew criticism when the information about the era turned out to be a hoax.

Madison Grant, b. 19 Nov. 1865; d. 30 May 1937. Grant was a lawyer and zoologist who is most famous for authoring the book, *The Passing of the Great Race* (1916), a diatribe on the superior intelligence of Northern European ancestry, the so-called Nordic race. His attention to conservation proved to be more universally accepted. His book had the distinction of Adolf Hitler referring to it as "my bible." Grant lobbied Congress to pass laws he helped write that called for strong immigration restrictions and anti-miscegenation laws. His care for preserving animal life proved more effective than his goals to dictate human intellectual procreation.

Besides Grant and Osborn's close friendships with presidents Teddy Roosevelt and Herbert Hoover, they were instrumental in the founding of the Boone and Crockett Club, the American Eugenics Society, the Galton Society and the Immigration Restriction League.

Harrison Williams, b. 1873; d. 1953. Starting life modestly building bicycles in Ohio, Williams went to New York to work with carpet sweepers. Then he started American Gas & Electric Company and building his fortune with counsel from his life-long attorney John Foster Dulles. He became wealthy and after the loss of his first wife in 1915, he spent 11 years as a bachelor until wedding Mona Bush, 29, when he was 53.

Mona Williams, b. 5 Feb. 1897; d. 10 July 1983. Mona became widely known for her wardrobe. Besides her beauty, she dressed exquisitely. Williams was her third husband. Their marriage lasted until Williams' death after which she married her secretary Count Edward von Bismarck-Schonhausen. She became Countess Mona von Bismarck and the first American judged "The Best Dressed Woman of the World."

Fannie Hurst, b. 19 Oct. 1885; d. 23 Feb. 1968. Fannie Hurst's novels were popular post-World War I distractions. She covered social issues while writing romance novels that made her the highest paid author of her time.

Prince George (George Edward Alexander Edmund), b. 20 Dec. 1902; d. 25 Aug 1942. George was known to be bisexual when England forbade homosexual contact. His exploits of women and affair with British actor Noel Coward were kept secret from the public but nevertheless troubled King George V. He arranged the prince's marriage to Marina, princess of Greece and Denmark. They were wed in 1934, and George became Duke of Kent. They had three children and George served in the British military during World War II dying mysteriously in a plane crash carrying a briefcase filled with money for an unknown destination. His oldest son, Prince Edward, Duke of Kent, in his late 80s, is a cousin and close advisor to Queen Elizabeth II.

Ford Bond, b. 23 Oct. 1904; d. 15 Aug. 1962. Bond's voice was among the first to be heard across the nation because of the fledgling NBC radio network. He did commercials, announced for soap operas, and did sports play-by-play during the 1930s and '40s. His star is on the Hollywood Walk of Fame, and he holds the record for longest serving voice for one advertiser, Cities Service petroleum company, "almost 30 years," according to his Wikipedia page.

While there are no recordings of early broadcasts, reading about Ford on the *Ready* in Brad Matsen's book, *Descent: The Heroic Discovery of the Abyss,* led me to Princeton University's archives where William Beebe's papers are kept, including the script Ford prepared. So, some of it probably was rehearsed and delivered as written. I borrowed from the script for authenticity but shortened it with paraphrases.

I recommend reading Matsen's book for greater detail about the people and their lives after the bathysphere adventures. His story telling and that of Carol Grant Gould, the Beebe biographer, *The Remarkable Life of William Beebe: Explorer and Naturalist,* are what inspired me to proceed with writing the novel.

My motivation was the Earth.

While we explore space with fanfare, I worry that looking up prevents us from seeing what's in front of us. It appears we're more interested in finding a place to escape than preserving the only known planet in the universe where we're positive life exists. Human life, animal life that Beebe wanted to preserve, and plant life that evolved with us and the rest of the animal kingdom.

Oceans clearly had a role in life's beginning. Oceans have a role in our rescue. Like the canary in the coal mine, the living creatures in our seas are tellers of our future and fortune. Let's not forget to explore the deep while we shoot for the stars. At the present, the budgets are way out of whack.

ACKNOWLEDGMENTS

When I arrived in Florida following my retirement from a government post in Washington, I visited my wife at her new place of work, the Lighthouse ArtCenter Gallery and School of Art in Tequesta. The art displayed was from a show called *Illuminating the Deep: The Fine Art of Exploration.*

Learning more about its origin and the connection between William Beebe, the famed early 20th century explorer, and Else Bostelmann, whose artistic talents Beebe used to illustrate his findings, led me on my own expedition, one of words. I began the story in 2017 while investigating the work of Dr. Edith Widder an oceanographer who displayed amazing photographs of deep-sea creature like what William Beebe claimed was living in the ocean far from human view.

Widder's photos were the other half of *Illuminating the Deep* at Lighthouse ArtCenter. I think of Widder as a Beebe and Bostelmann student who took their work to a higher level. I recommend you watch her "Ted Talks" and read her recently published memoir, *Below the Edge of Darkness.*

For their initial help and inspiration, I thank Janeen Mason, Lighthouse ArtCenter curator, and Shirley Kent who did extensive research about Beebe's Bermuda dives and Bostelmann's personal history as an artist.

Then at the exhibit opening, I met Michael Crumpton and his wife, Marjetta Geerling. From Michael, Else Bostelmann's great-grandson, and Marjetta, I learned more about the human interactions of this amazing collaboration.

My sudden interest put me on a plane to Washington, D.C.'s Library of Congress to meet an inspirational lady, Constance Carter. Retired, but not really, Miss Carter welcomed me into her Jefferson Building office and told me about being a college graduate working for William Beebe and Jocelyn Crane at their Trinidad laboratory off the coast of Venezuela in the late 1950s. I had met a great storyteller who knew William Beebe, knew of his adventures, knew the names of people he called friends, and she gave me a physical link to his past. I thank Miss Carter for the time she spent with me, stories she shared with me, and the honor of meeting a person known extremely well in the halls of the Library of Congress.

When I learned of another art presentation in New York City of photographs and a rebuilt replica of William Beebe's original laboratory office, I headed there next. I met Katherine McLeod, a collaborator on the exhibit, who explained that pictures were found stored at the Bronx Zoo. Many of them were of parties thrown by William Beebe and the Department of Tropical Research while they were in Bermuda. The descriptions of Beebe's tenacity for work and play jumped from the pages of the photos. I knew if I could not find recorded banter from their frivolity, I could make it up from what I saw.

I thank Blaise and Patricia DeAloia for their invitation to spend time with them in Bermuda in late 2017 so I could do first-hand research, including hours at the Bermuda National Archives where kind librarians allowed me to touch and photograph Else's most important paintings for Will Beebe.

I owe special gratitude to Beebe's biographers, Carol Grant Gould (*The Remarkable Life of William Beebe, Explorer and Naturalist*) and Brad Matsen (*Descent: The Heroic Discovery of the Abyss*). Each wrote their books more than 15 years ago and kept alive a legend that I believe may help spark a new movement to preserve our oceans. Gould was thorough in her capture of William Beebe's full life and the people who made him succeed and those who created barriers that also made his efforts more memorable.

Beebe was human, which means he was flawed. But he never let his flaws erase the remarkable accomplishments he put on the record books.

Matsen focused on the event that rose Beebe to a pedestal when the nation and world needed a fearless man to face the unknowns. He did so from a rickety barge in the middle of the Atlantic Ocean as he and Otis Barton descended more than a half mile tethered by a 7/8-inch cable. When they finished, they crawled out of a 14-inch diameter manhole in sweat-soaked khaki clothes as though finishing up a day in coal mines.

Will Beebe was a common man with an uncommon personality. He could strum strings, sing songs, swoon damsels of any age because he looked past every mirror to make sure he kept his eye on his targets. His ambitions were vain, but his person was not. People admired him, including Else Bostelmann.

Else's life was quite different. I found Ida's daughter and granddaughter in California. I thank them for giving me a glimpse of a woman who made an important character in telling Else's story.

The tragic death of Monroe Bostelmann robbed the Bostelmann family of a prodigy son, the oldest son in the family. It is not something easily understood in this age, but a hundred years ago, the eldest son, one loaded with talent, created an enormous void when gone.

I have said before that writing is solitary work. Nevertheless, when writing is done, the challenge of edits and rewrites begins.

I thank my buddy Gene Englehart for being the first to dig through early pages and point out issues that needed attention. My life-long friend, my favorite critic, died before he could read the final chapters and know my appreciation. I miss him.

I thank Christine, my editor, who focused my story. And I thank Danna Mathias for her wonderful graphic designs.

It's always good to have a cousin like Marsha Buck. Her keen eye and love saved me from allowing some embarrassing errors to slip by. Thanks, dear cousin.

I thank many others who read *Beebe and Bostelmann* before publishing and gave opinions that I listened to appreciatively. But most of all I thank Nancy. Just because I want to and because I don't do much of anything enjoyable or productive without her.

Made in the USA
Middletown, DE
22 July 2022